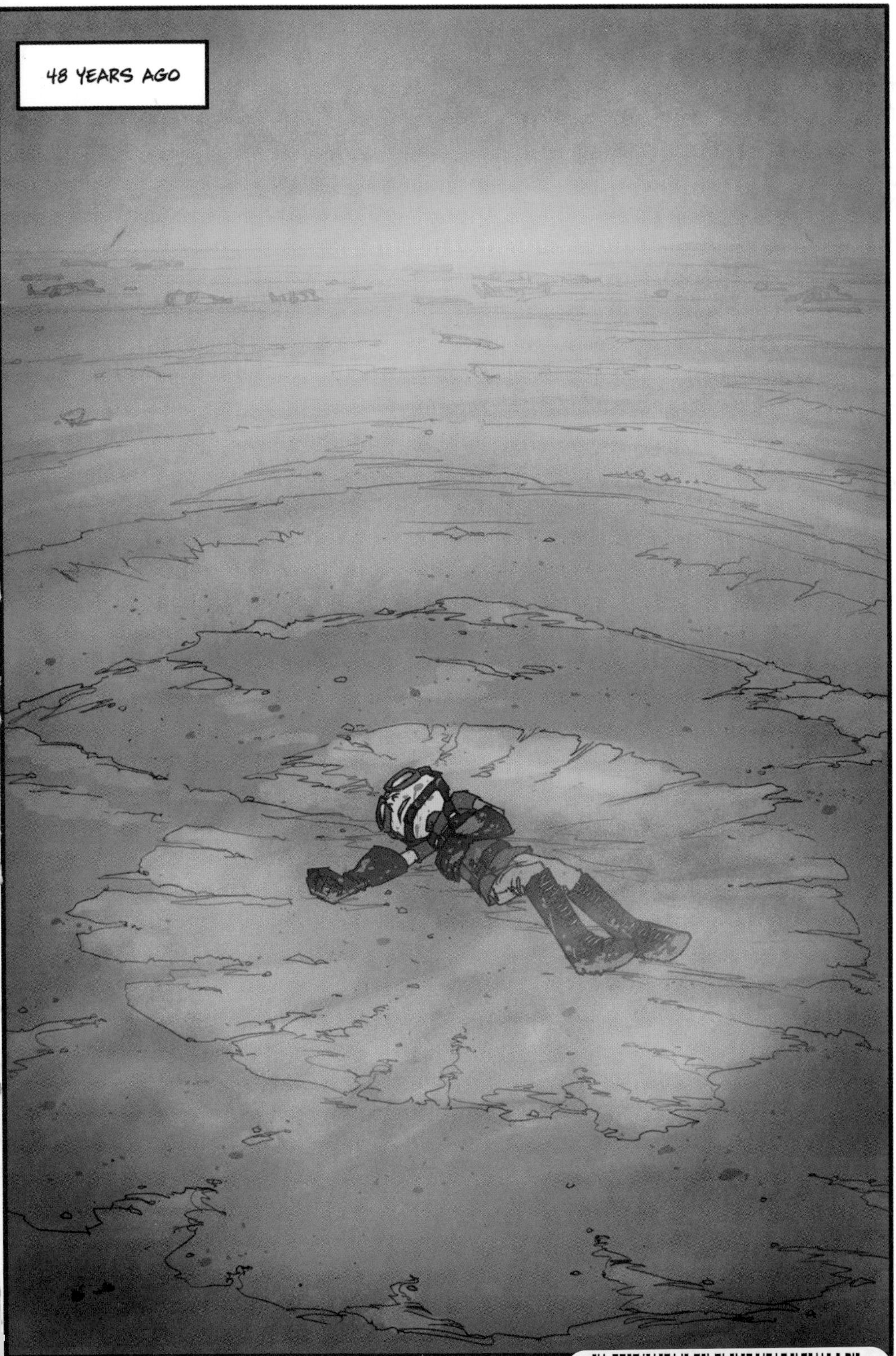
48 YEARS AGO

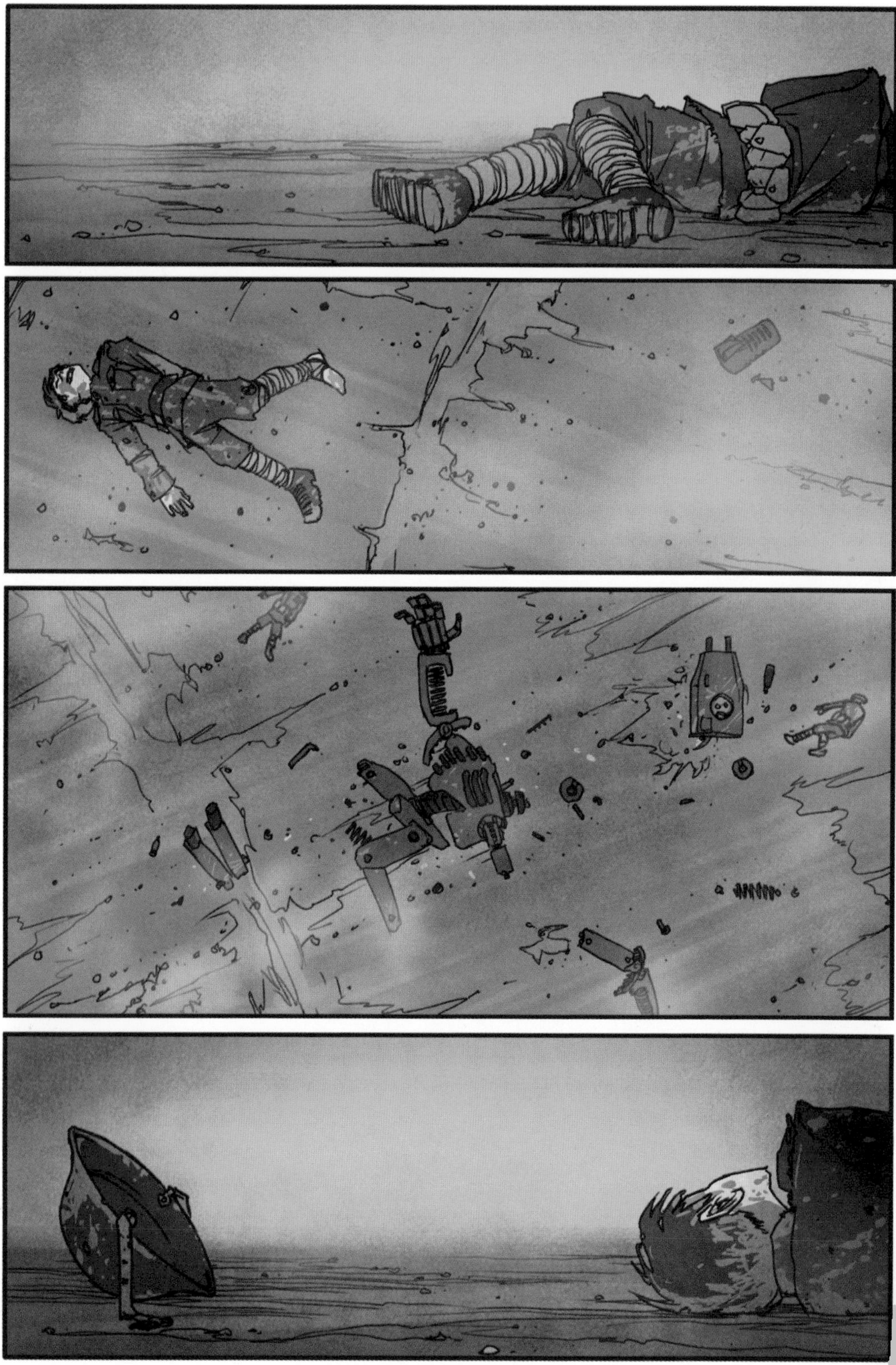

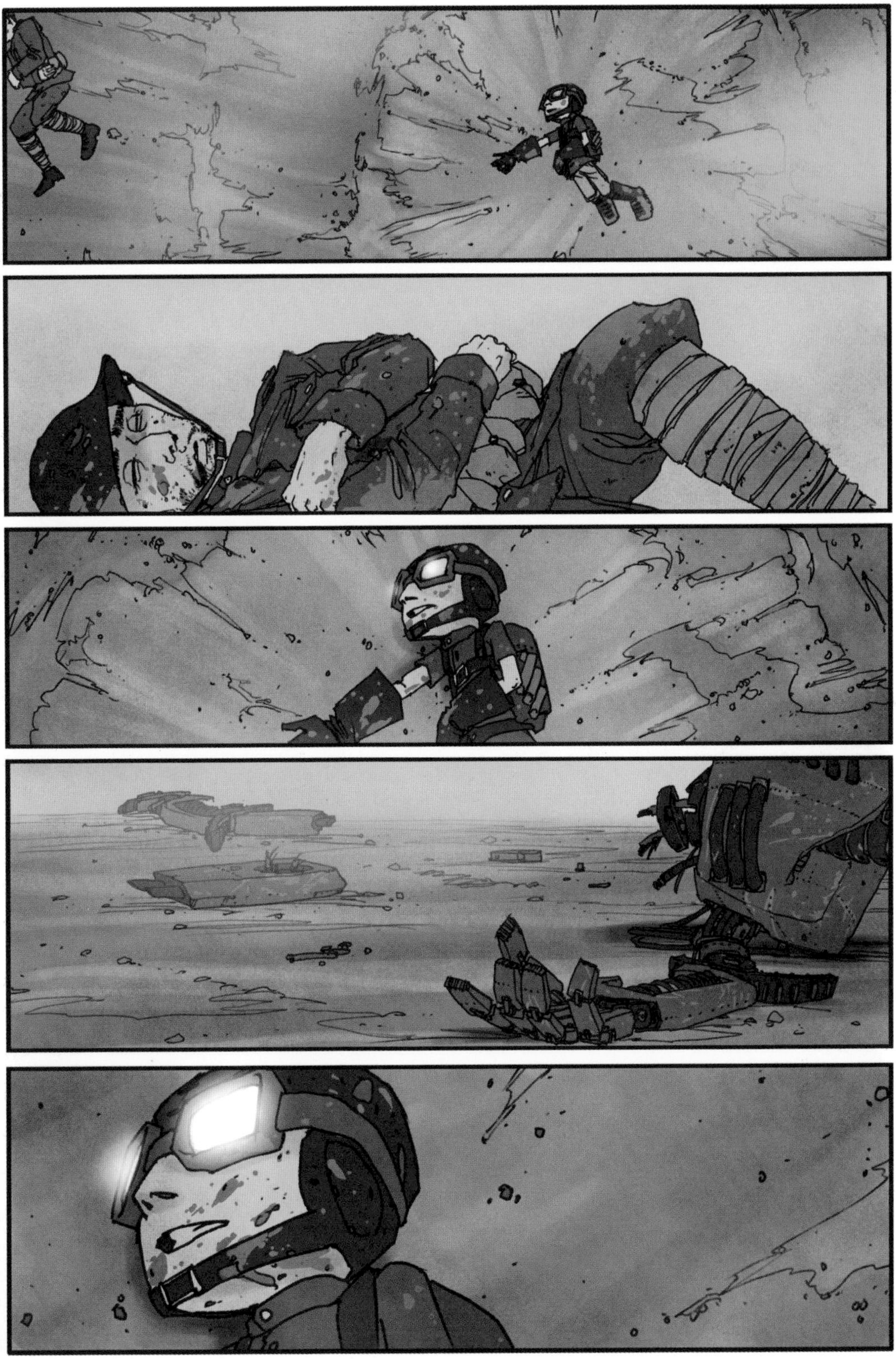

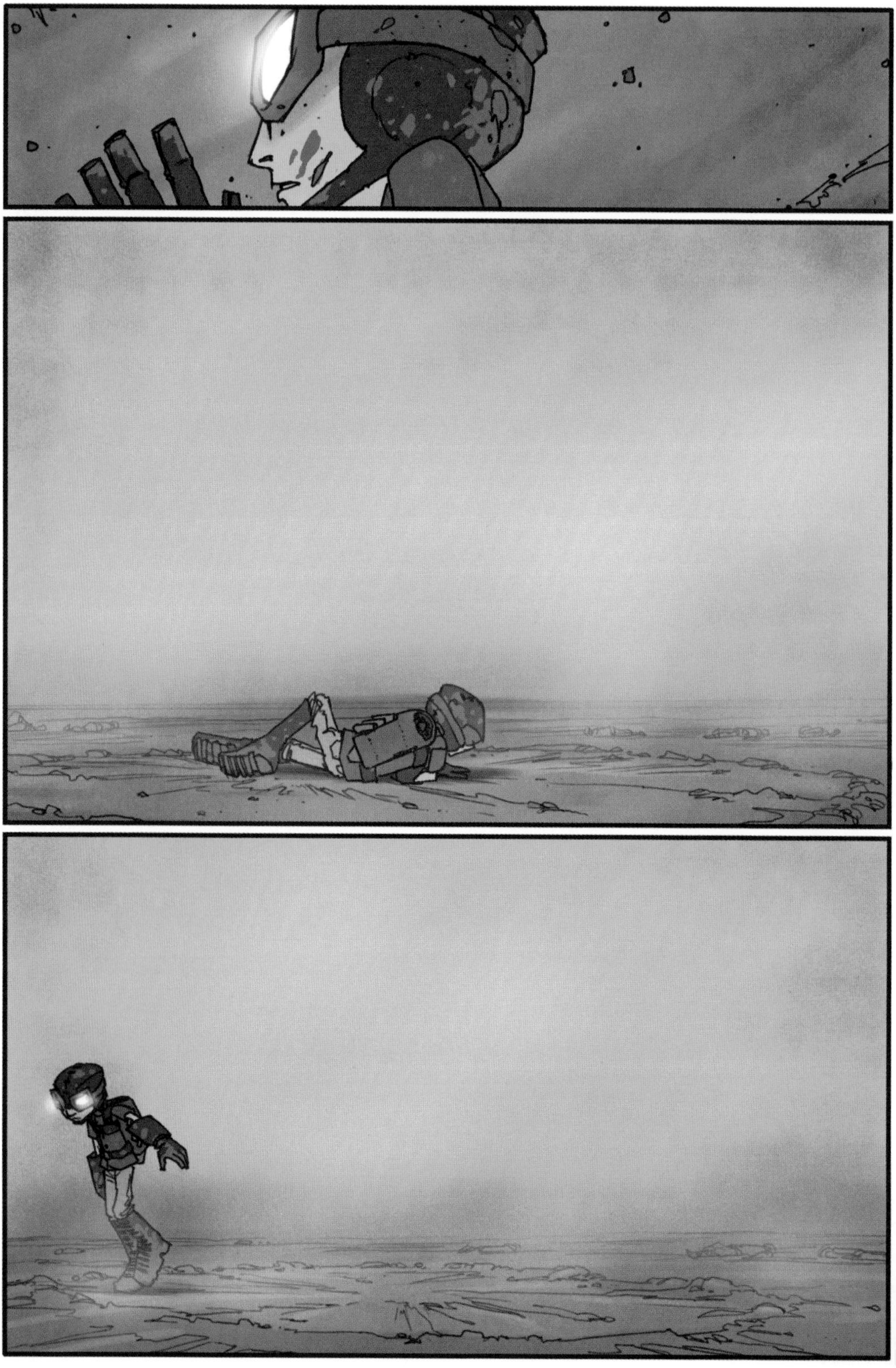

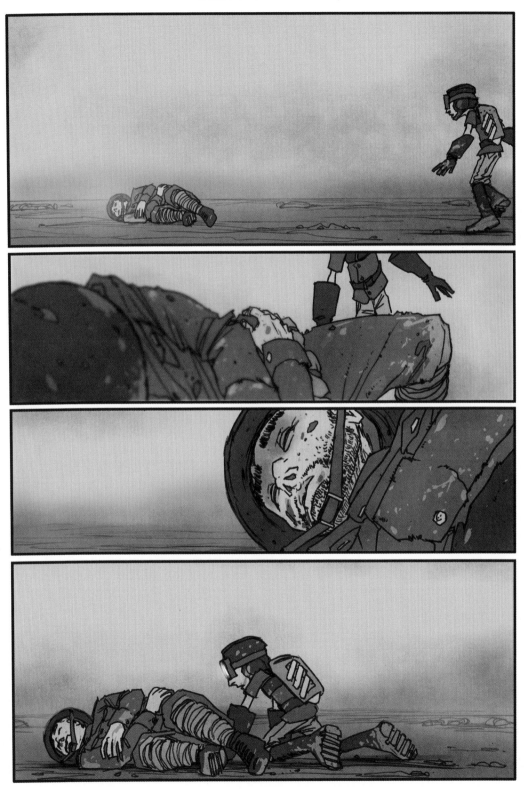

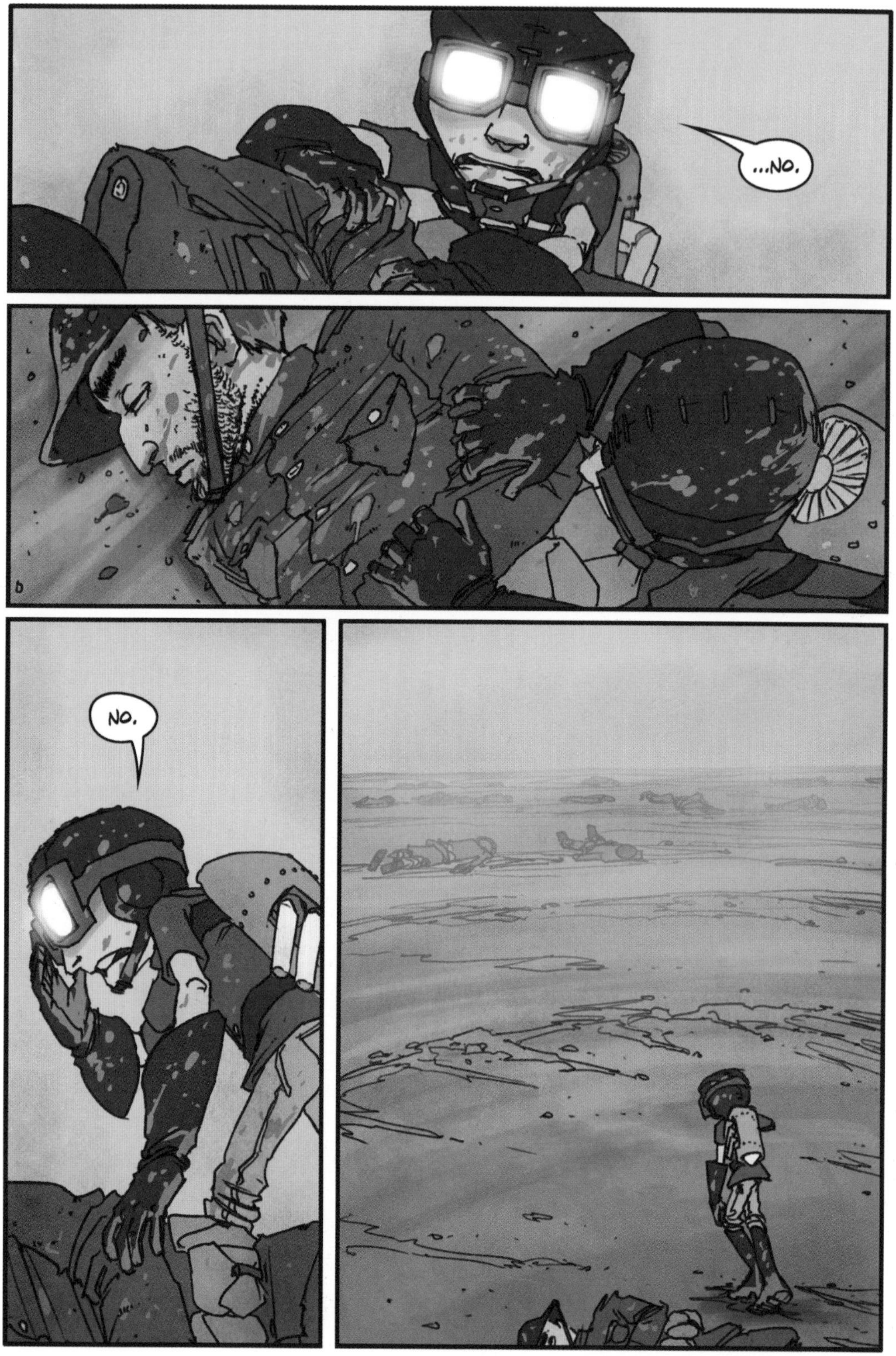
...NO.
NO.

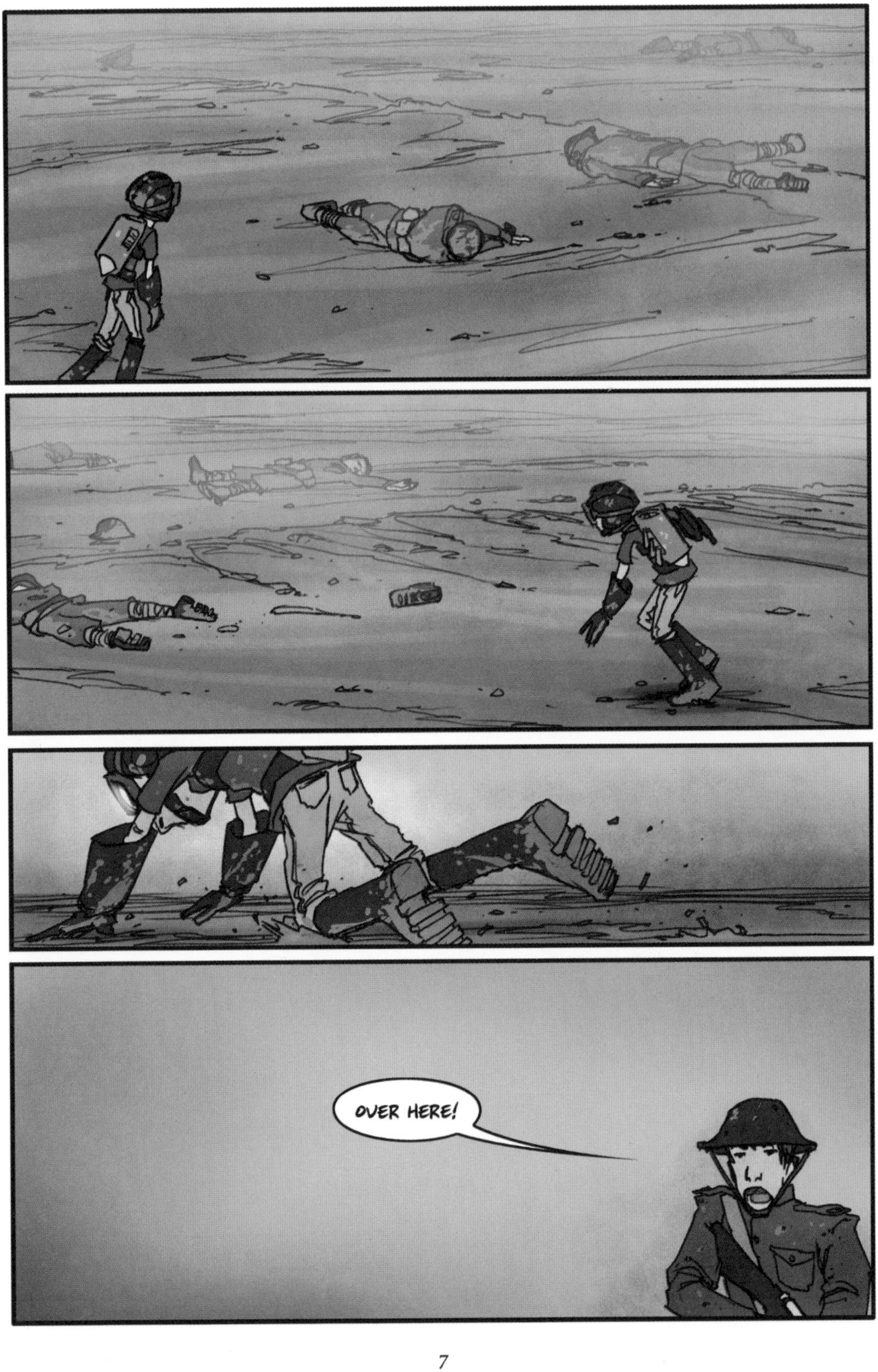
OVER HERE!

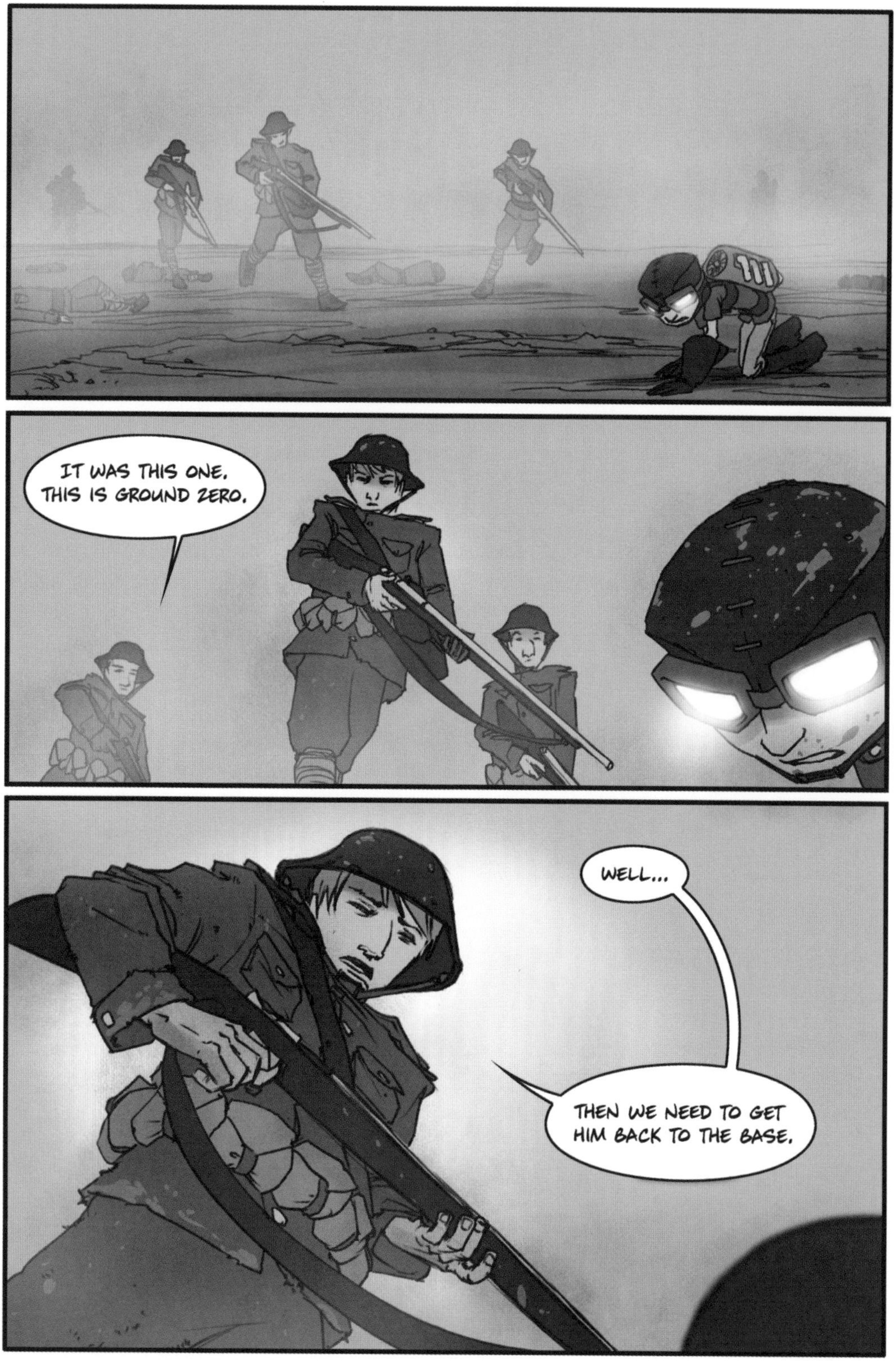
IT WAS THIS ONE.
THIS IS GROUND ZERO.
WELL...
THEN WE NEED TO GET
HIM BACK TO THE BASE.

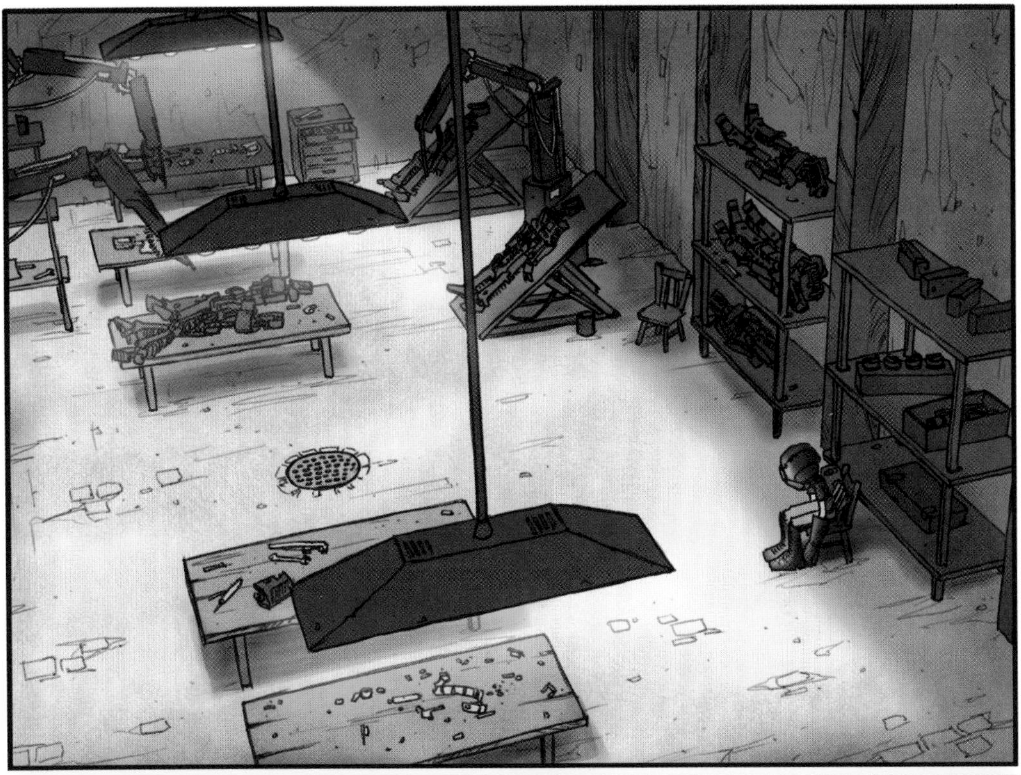

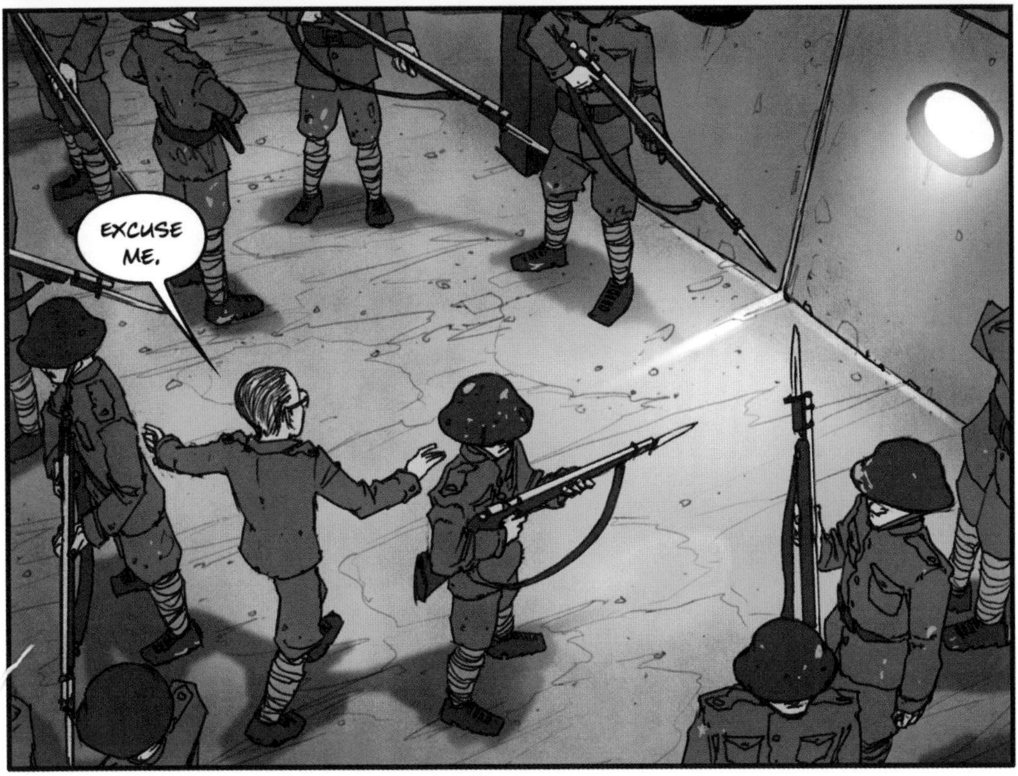
EXCUSE ME.

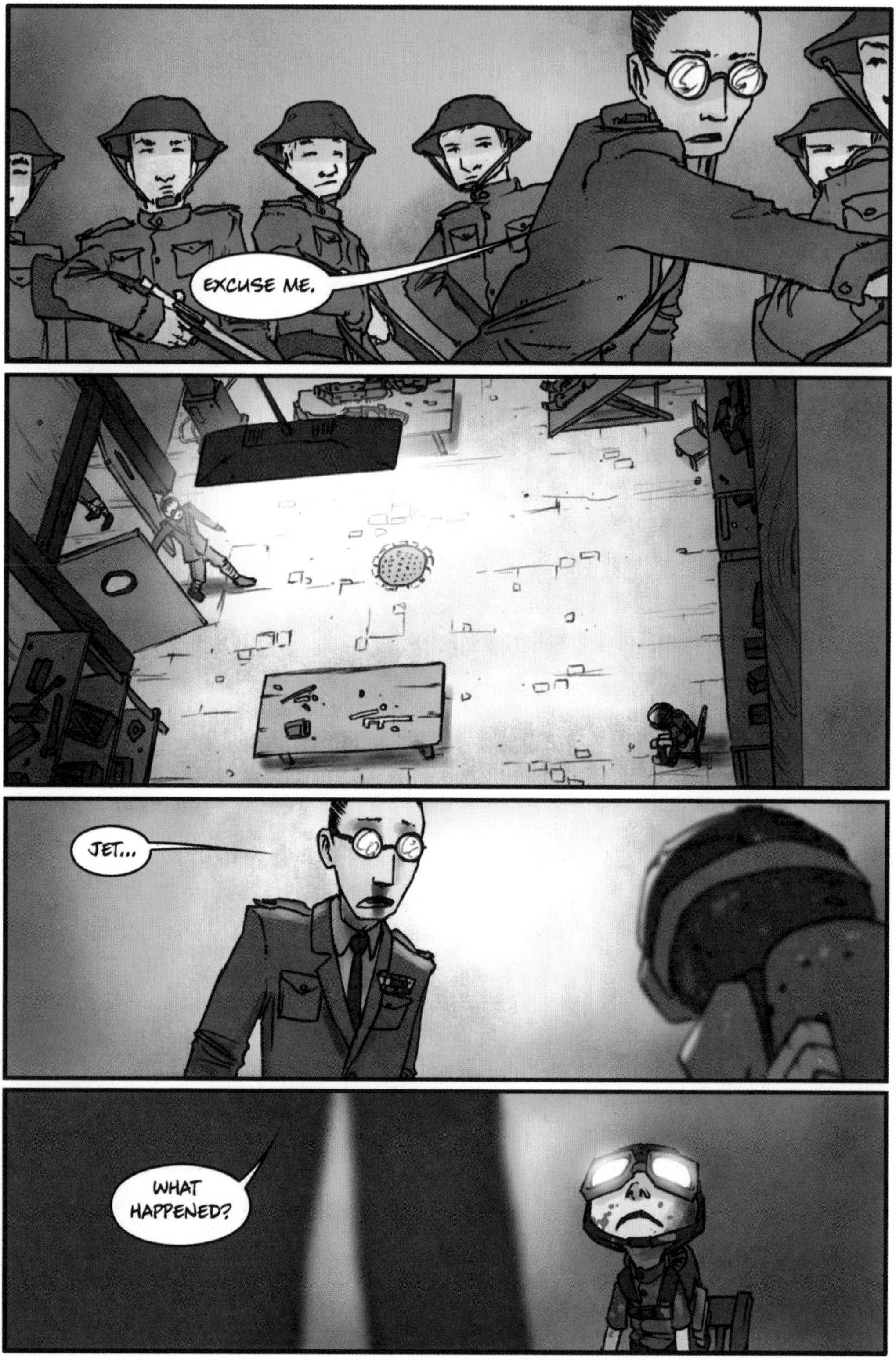
EXCUSE ME.
JET...
WHAT HAPPENED?

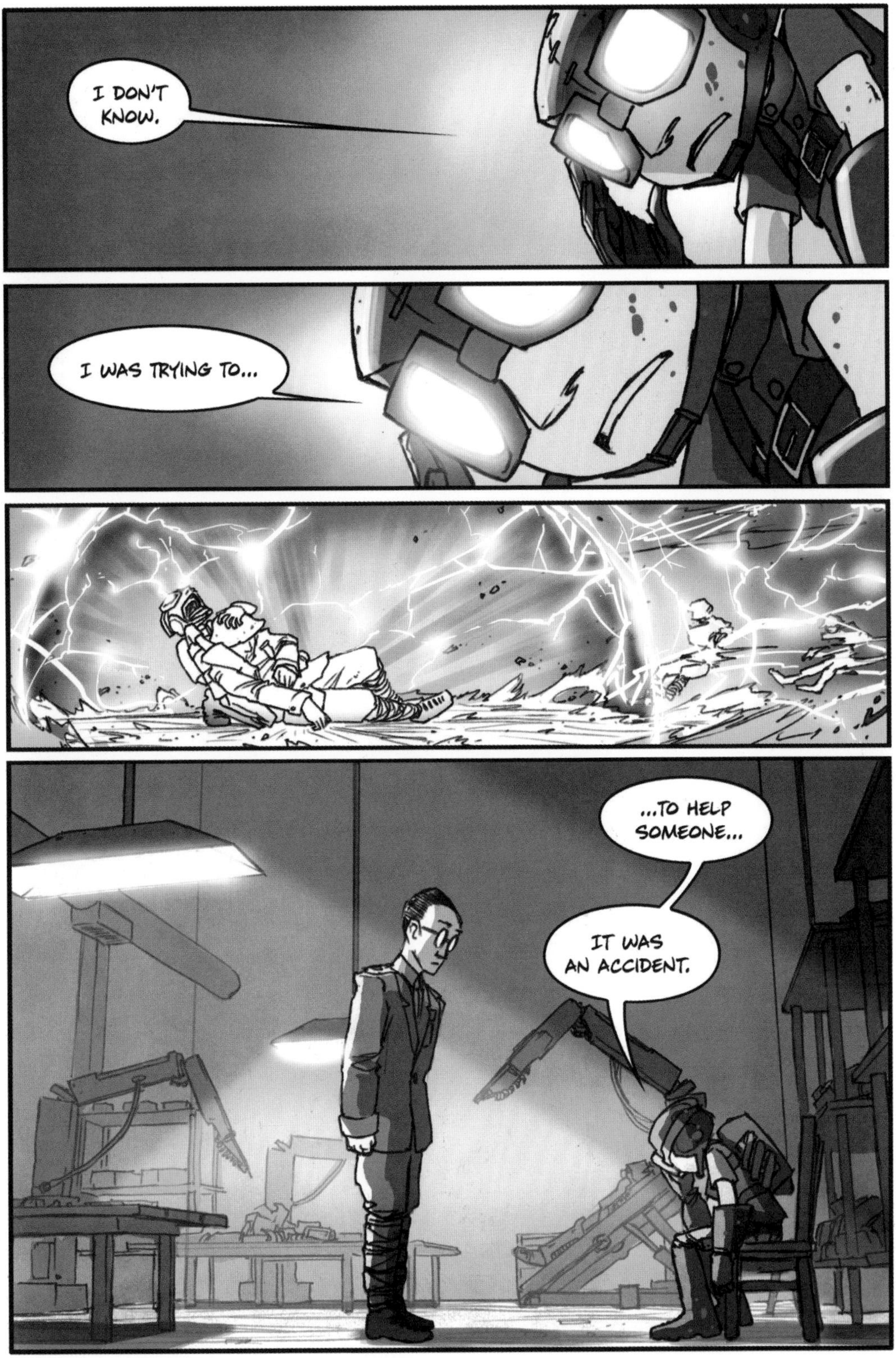
I DON'T KNOW.
I WAS TRYING TO...
...TO HELP SOMEONE...
IT WAS AN ACCIDENT.

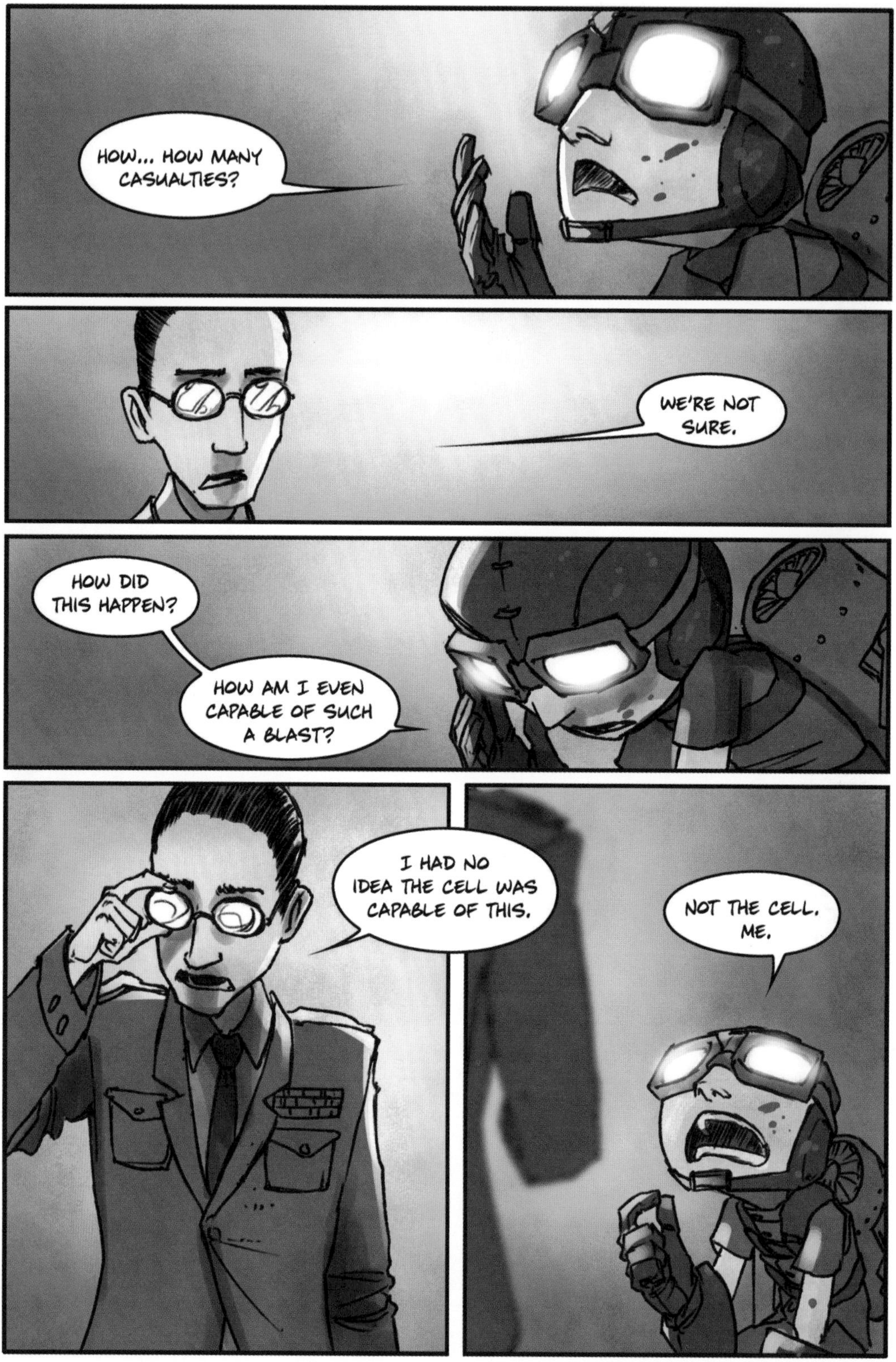
HOW... HOW MANY CASUALTIES?
WE'RE NOT SURE.
HOW DID THIS HAPPEN?
HOW AM I EVEN CAPABLE OF SUCH A BLAST?
I HAD NO IDEA THE CELL WAS CAPABLE OF THIS.
NOT THE CELL. ME.

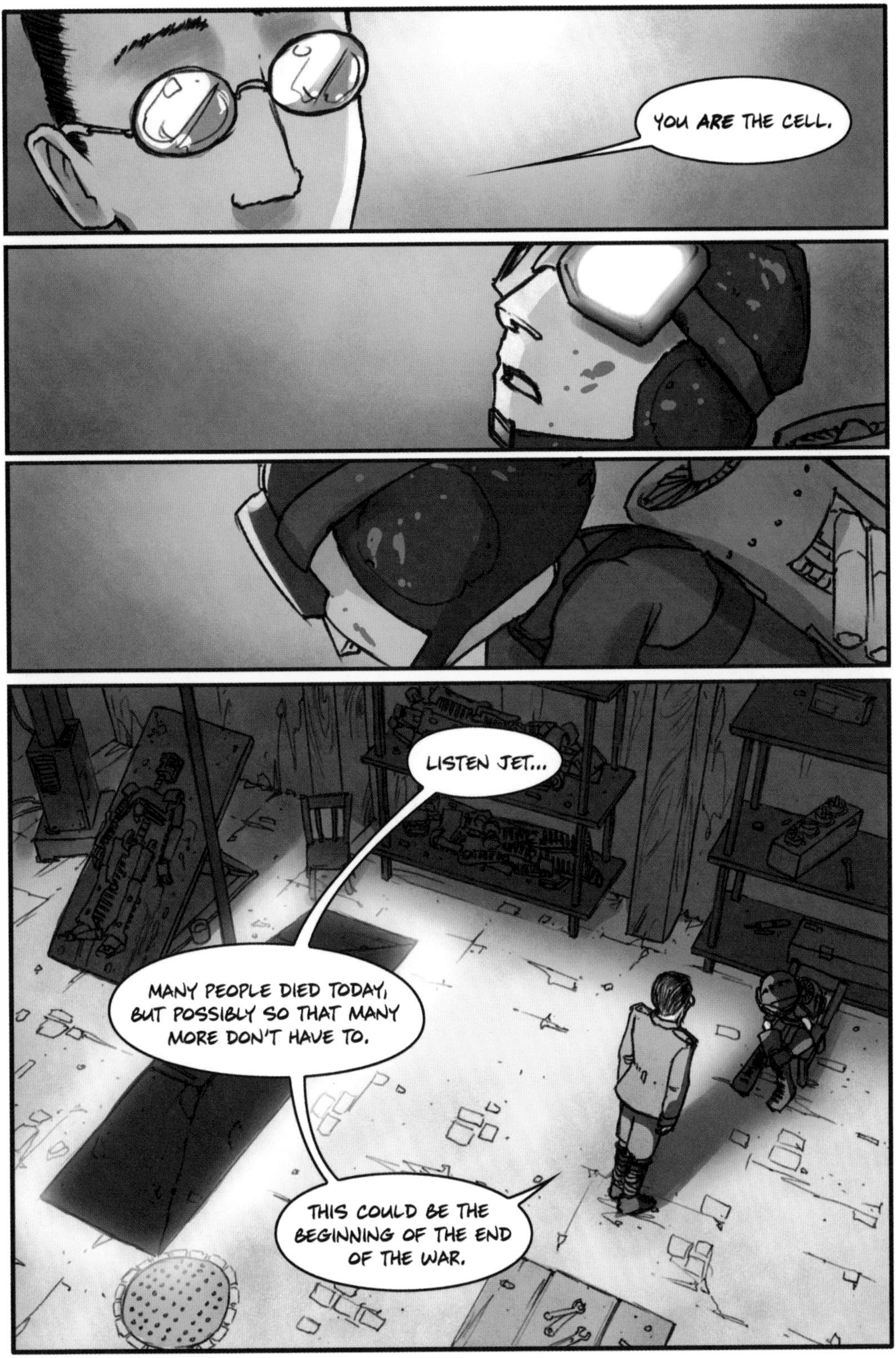
YOU ARE THE CELL.
LISTEN JET...
MANY PEOPLE DIED TODAY, BUT POSSIBLY SO THAT MANY MORE DON'T HAVE TO.
THIS COULD BE THE BEGINNING OF THE END OF THE WAR.

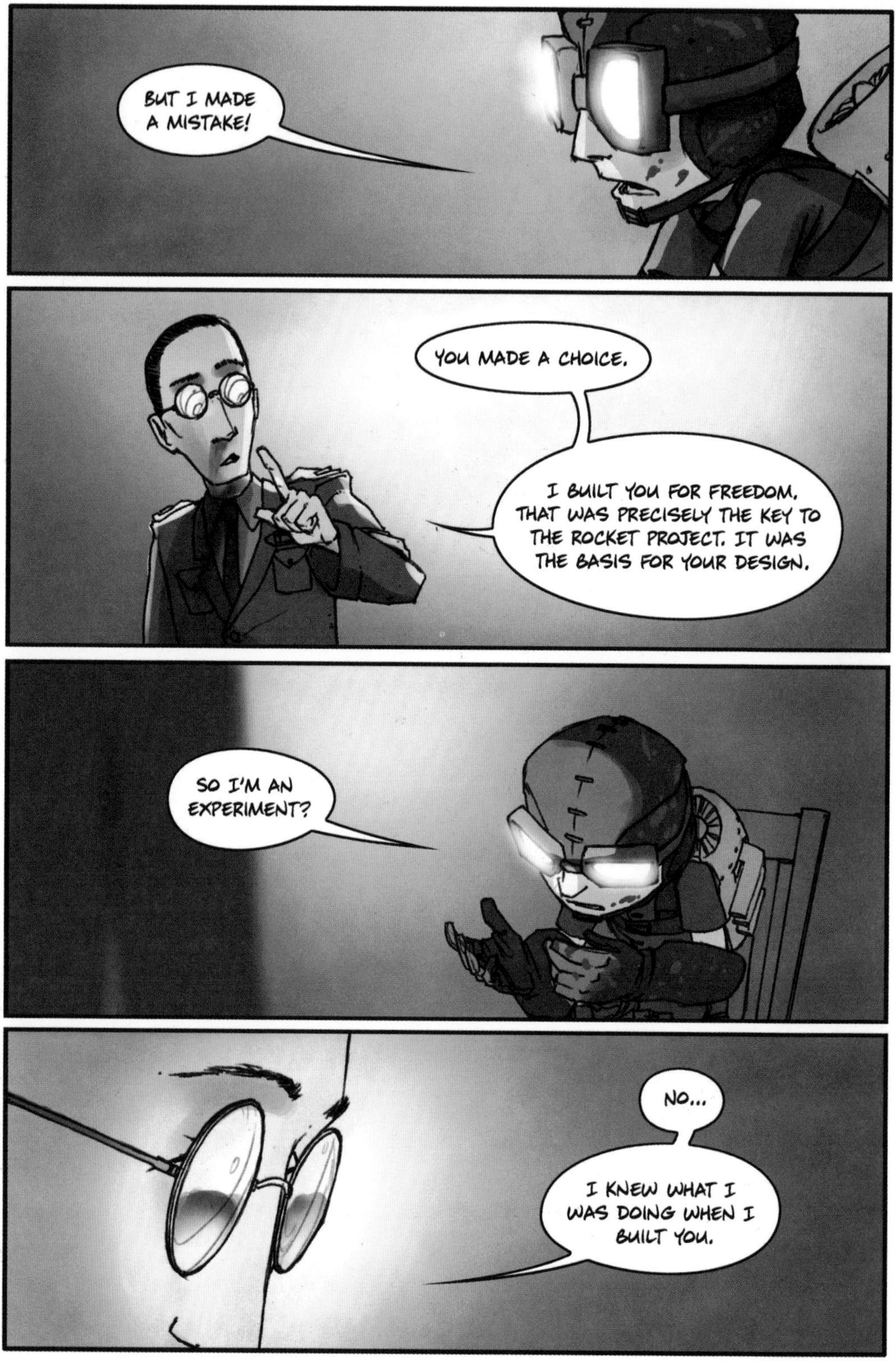
BUT I MADE A MISTAKE!
YOU MADE A CHOICE.
I BUILT YOU FOR FREEDOM. THAT WAS PRECISELY THE KEY TO THE ROCKET PROJECT. IT WAS THE BASIS FOR YOUR DESIGN.
SO I'M AN EXPERIMENT?
NO...
I KNEW WHAT I WAS DOING WHEN I BUILT YOU.

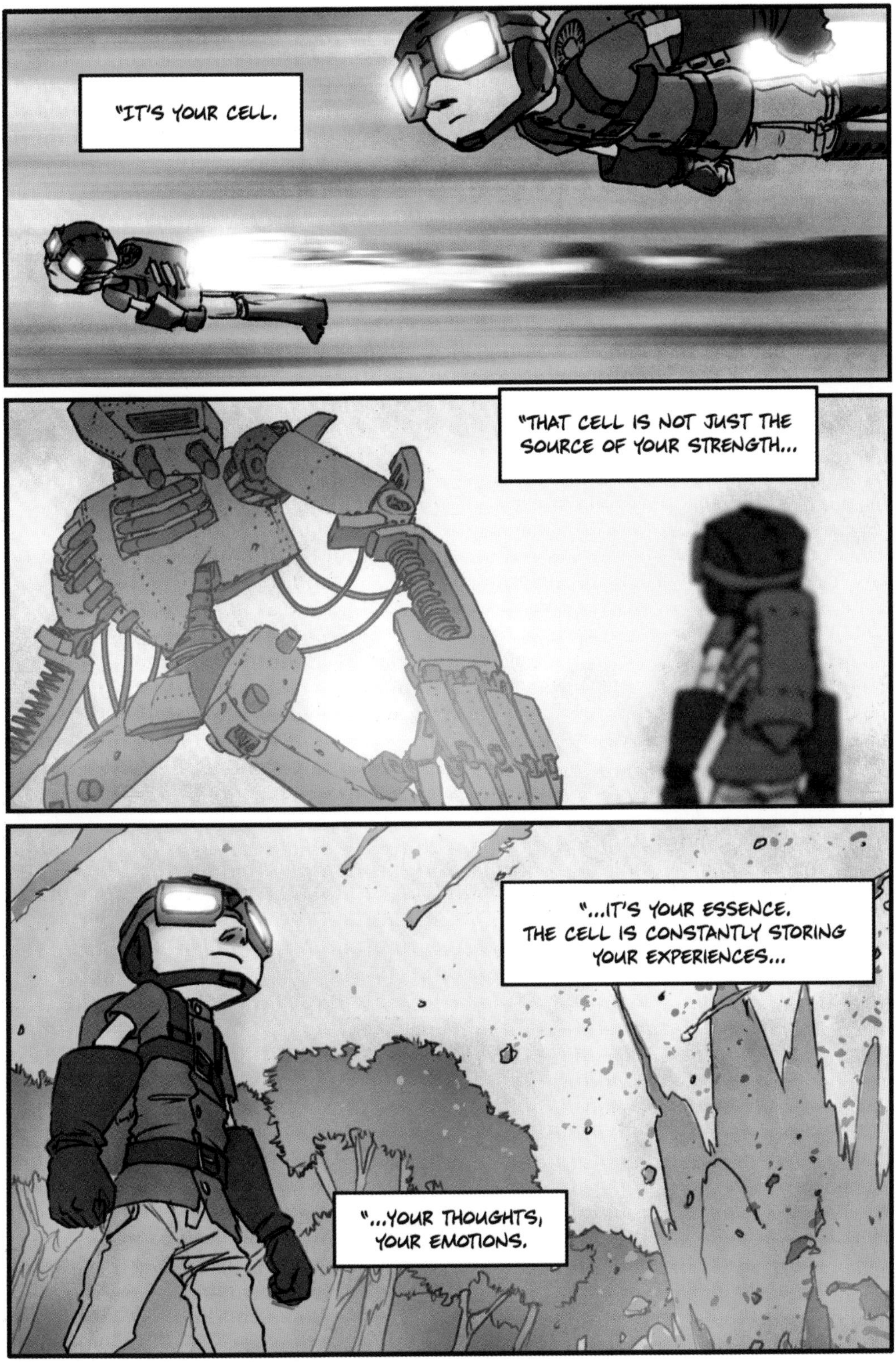
"IT'S YOUR CELL.
"THAT CELL IS NOT JUST THE SOURCE OF YOUR STRENGTH...
"...IT'S YOUR ESSENCE. THE CELL IS CONSTANTLY STORING YOUR EXPERIENCES...
"...YOUR THOUGHTS, YOUR EMOTIONS.

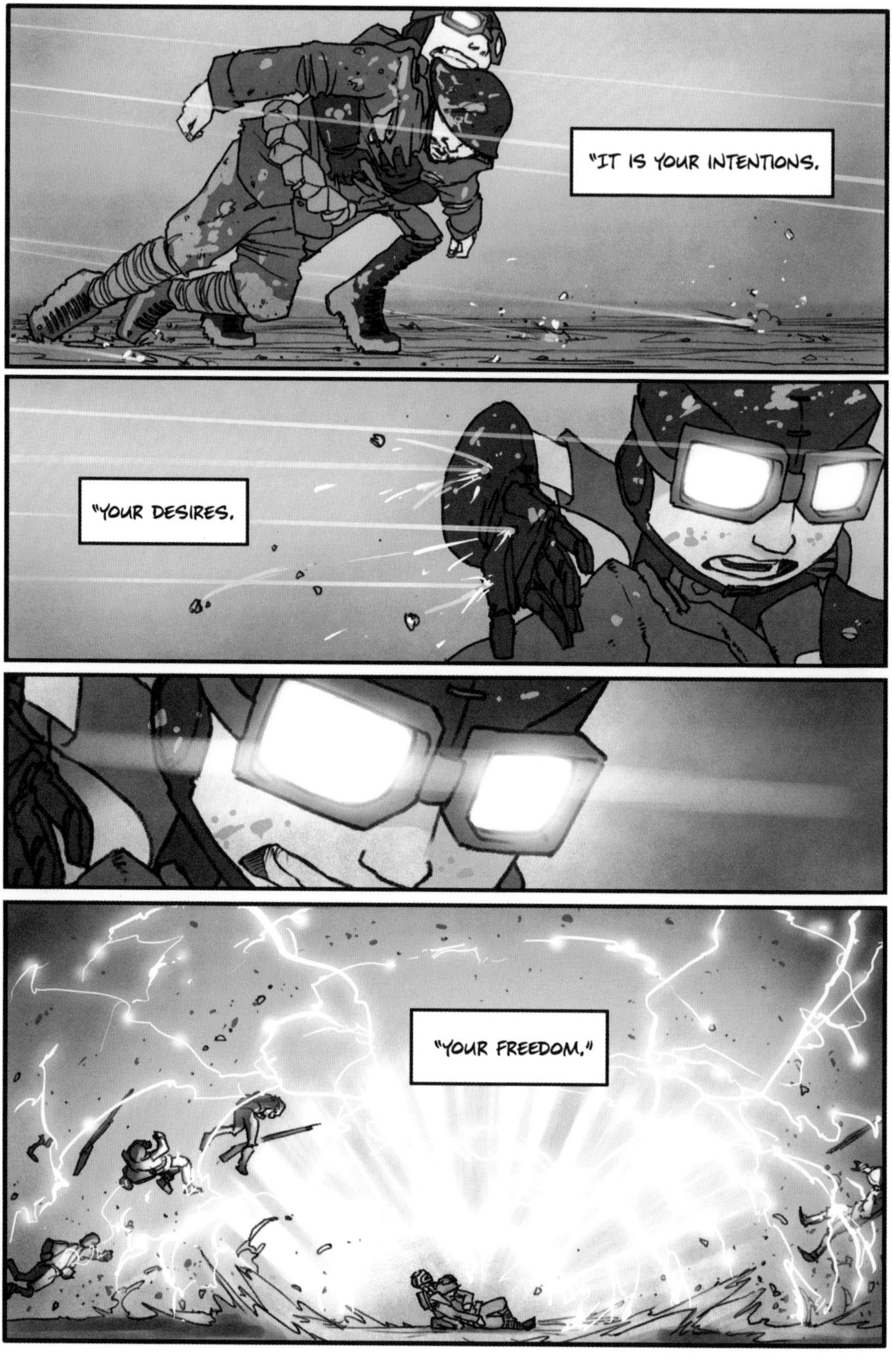
"IT IS YOUR INTENTIONS.
"YOUR DESIRES.
"YOUR FREEDOM."

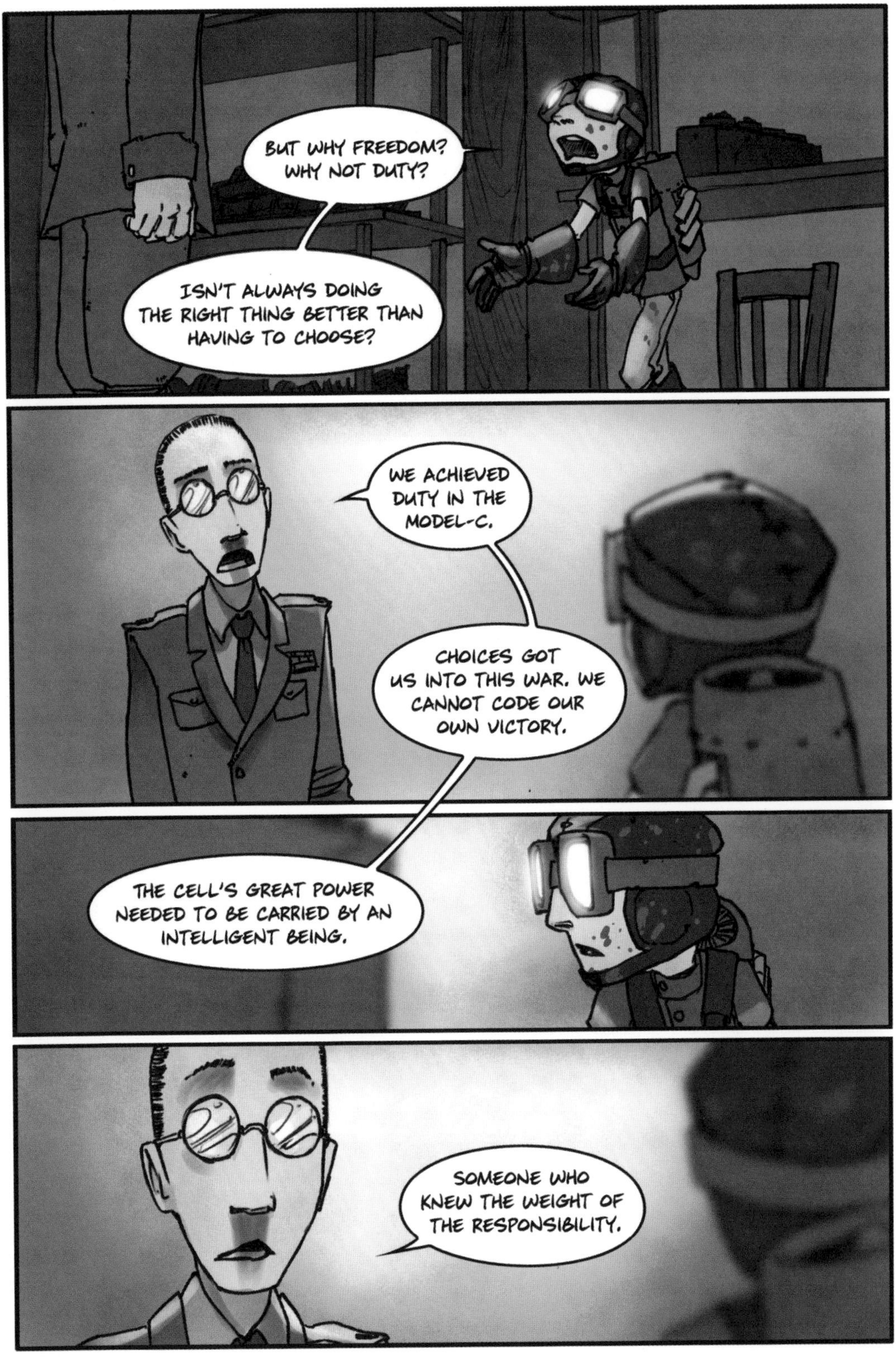
BUT WHY FREEDOM? WHY NOT DUTY?
ISN'T ALWAYS DOING THE RIGHT THING BETTER THAN HAVING TO CHOOSE?
WE ACHIEVED DUTY IN THE MODEL-C.
CHOICES GOT US INTO THIS WAR. WE CANNOT CODE OUR OWN VICTORY.
THE CELL'S GREAT POWER NEEDED TO BE CARRIED BY AN INTELLIGENT BEING.
SOMEONE WHO KNEW THE WEIGHT OF THE RESPONSIBILITY.

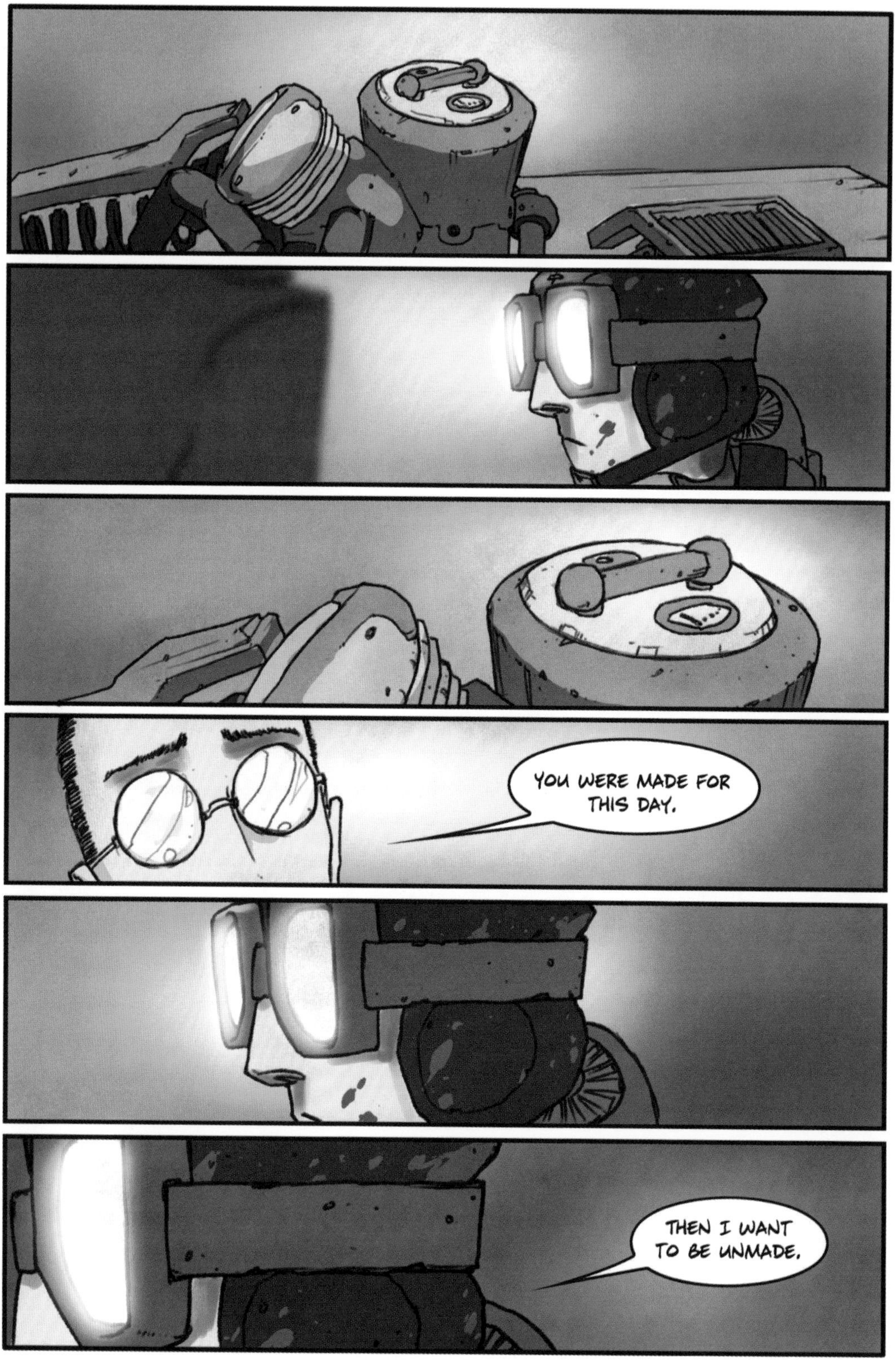
YOU WERE MADE FOR THIS DAY.
THEN I WANT TO BE UNMADE.

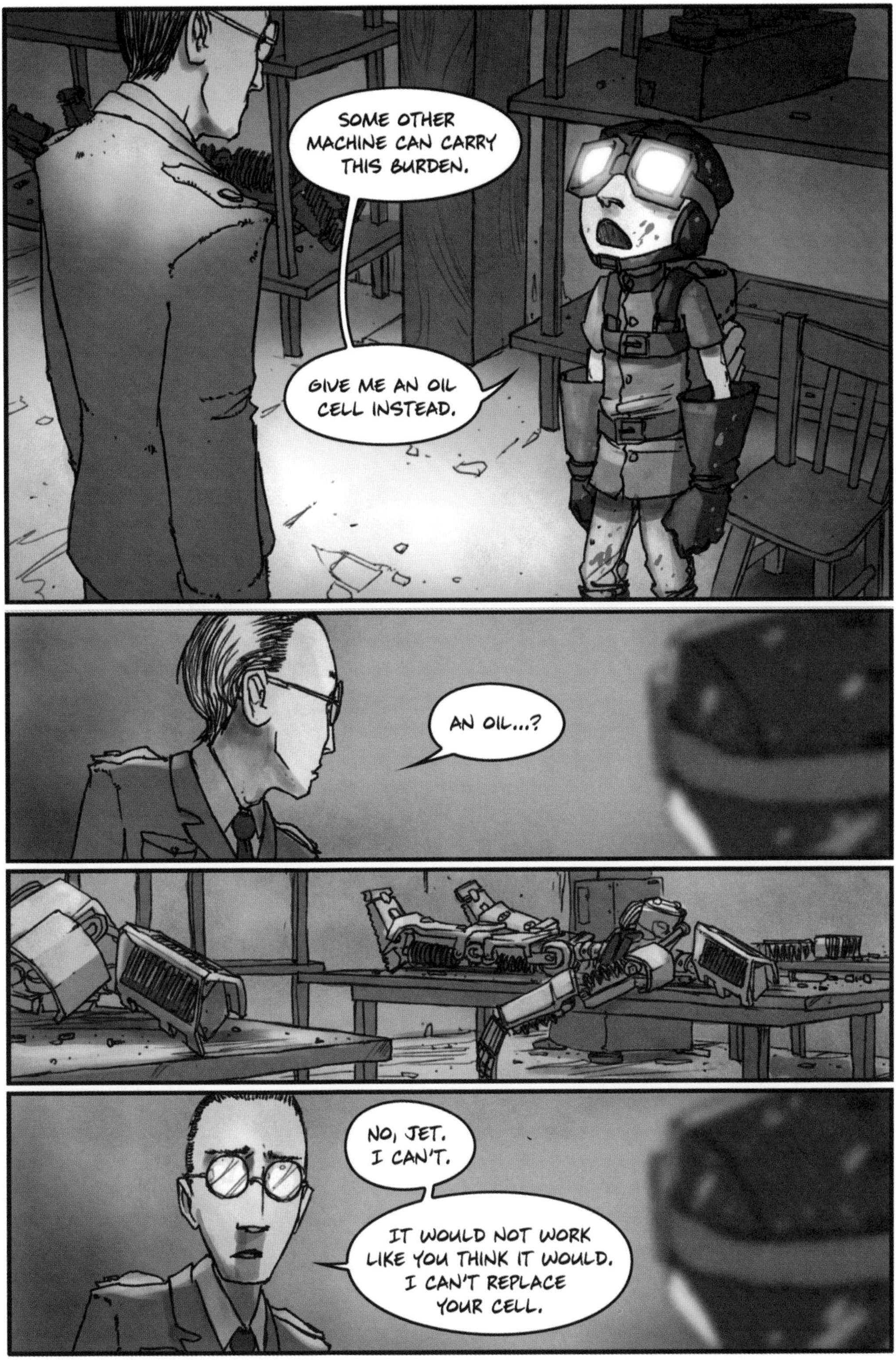
SOME OTHER MACHINE CAN CARRY THIS BURDEN.
GIVE ME AN OIL CELL INSTEAD.
AN OIL...?
NO, JET. I CAN'T.
IT WOULD NOT WORK LIKE YOU THINK IT WOULD. I CAN'T REPLACE YOUR CELL.

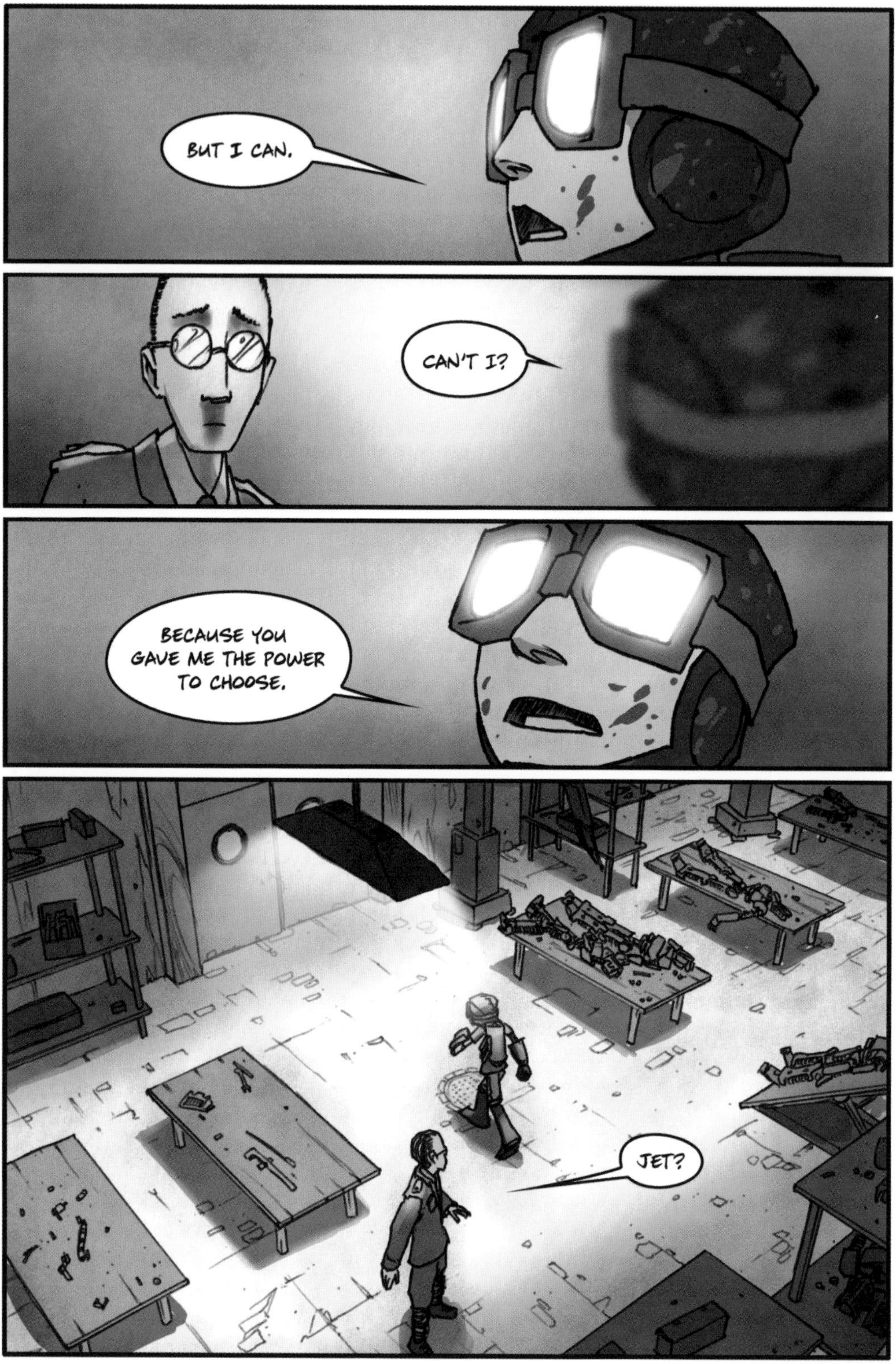
BUT I CAN.
CAN'T I?
BECAUSE YOU GAVE ME THE POWER TO CHOOSE.
JET?

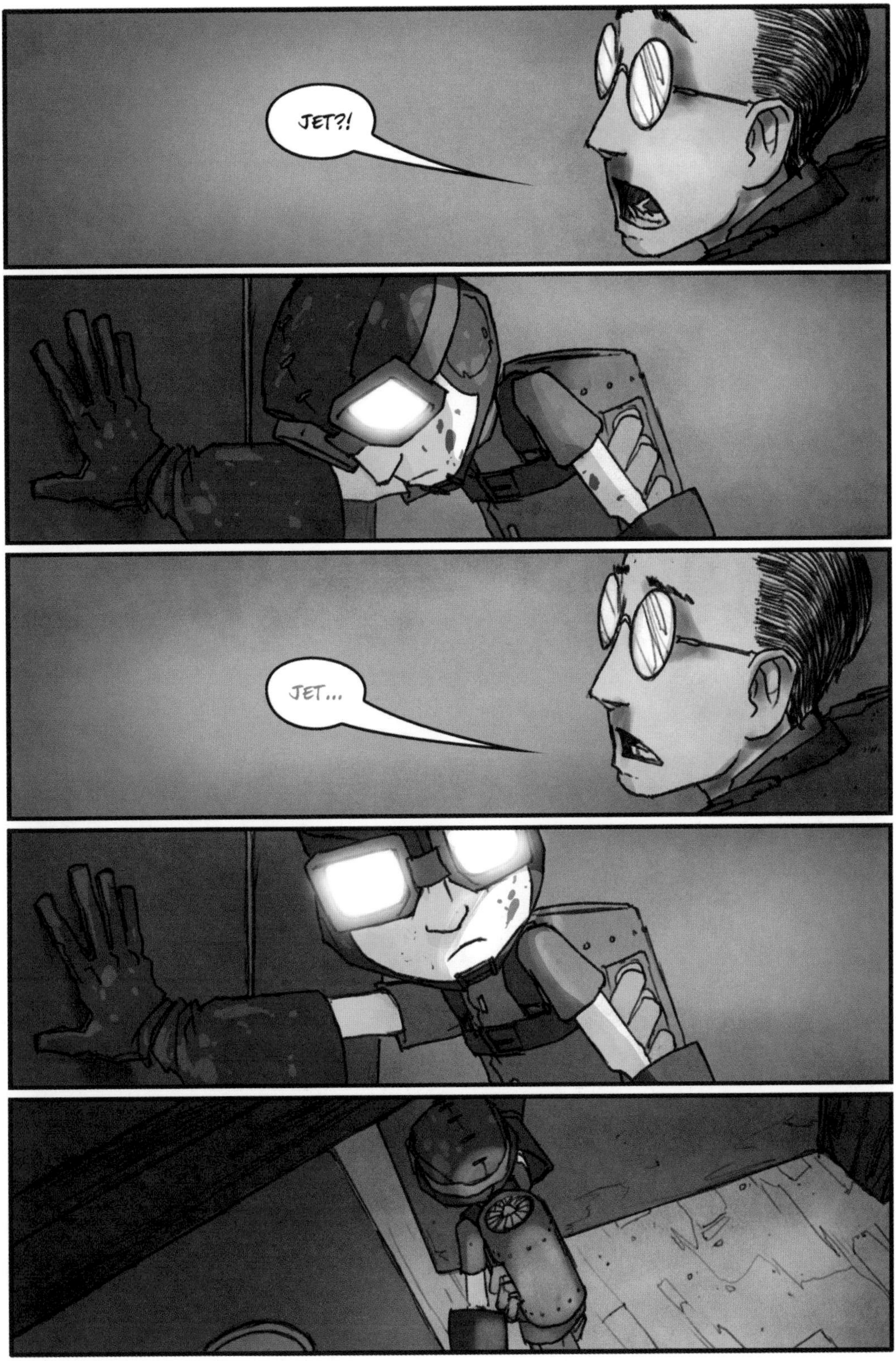
JET?!
JET...

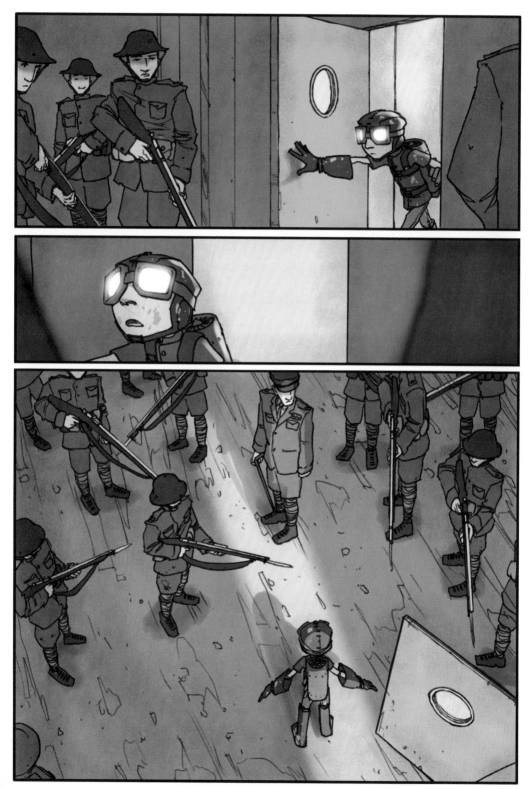

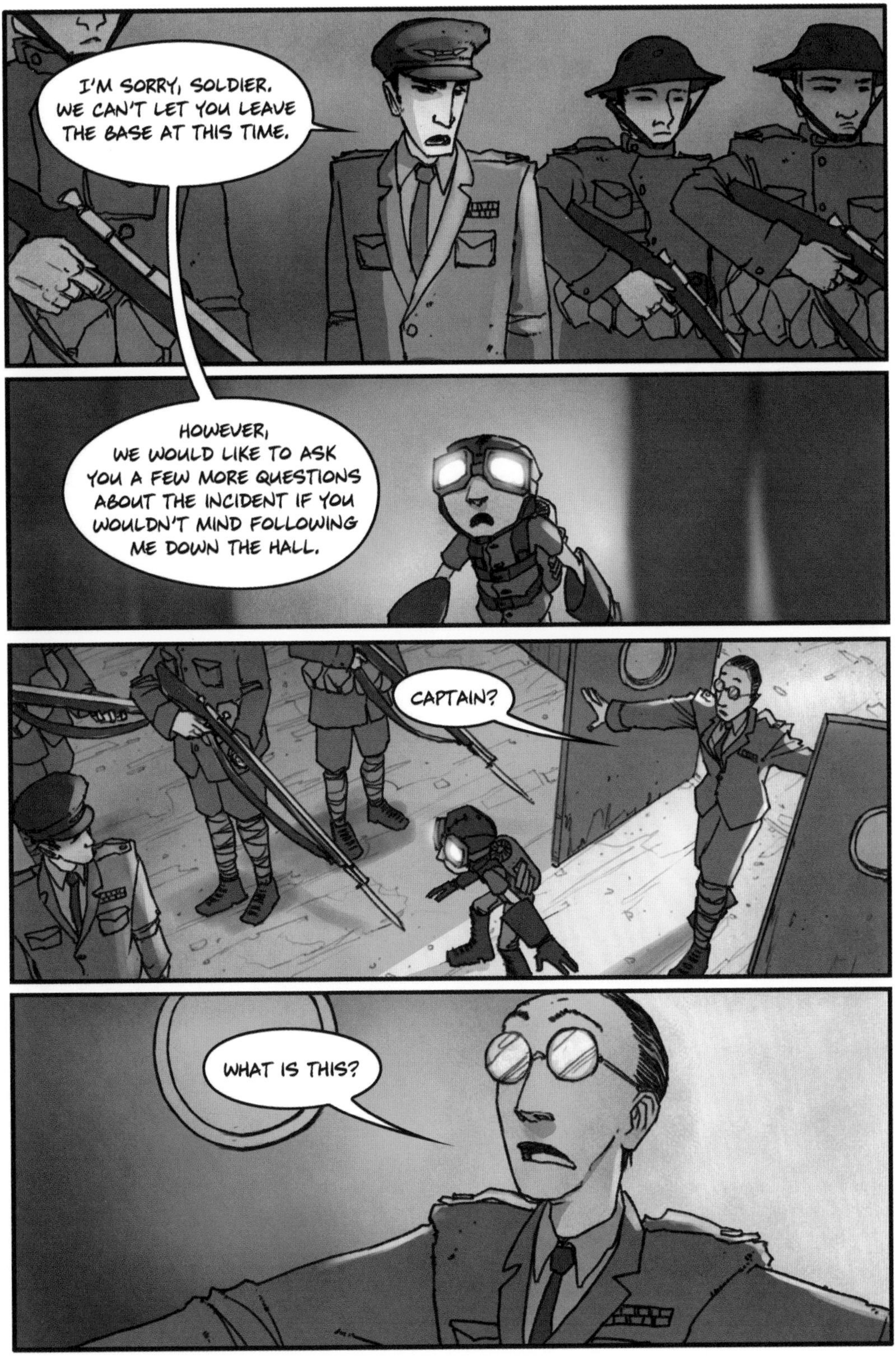
I'M SORRY, SOLDIER. WE CAN'T LET YOU LEAVE THE BASE AT THIS TIME.
HOWEVER, WE WOULD LIKE TO ASK YOU A FEW MORE QUESTIONS ABOUT THE INCIDENT IF YOU WOULDN'T MIND FOLLOWING ME DOWN THE HALL.
CAPTAIN?
WHAT IS THIS?

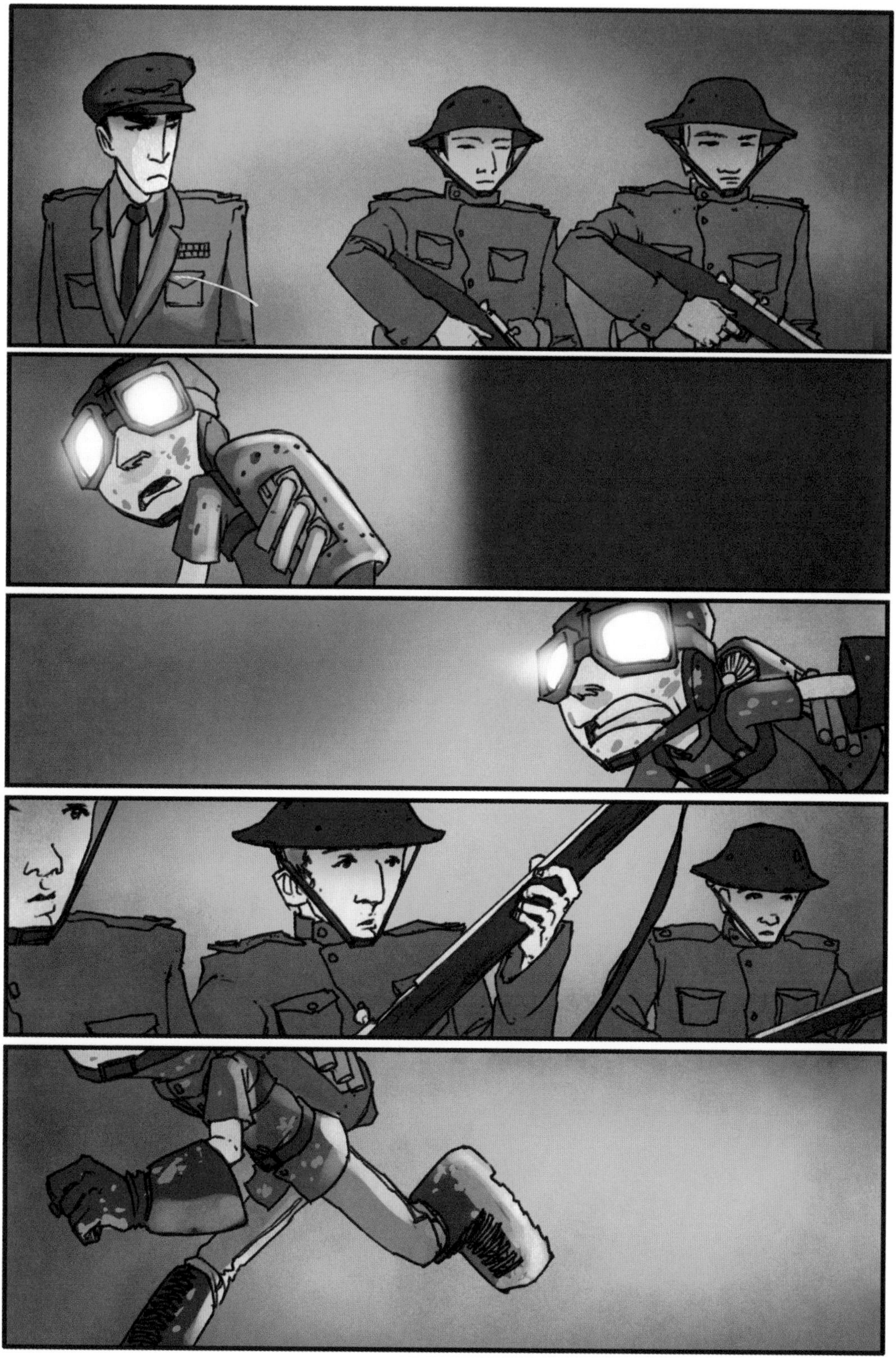

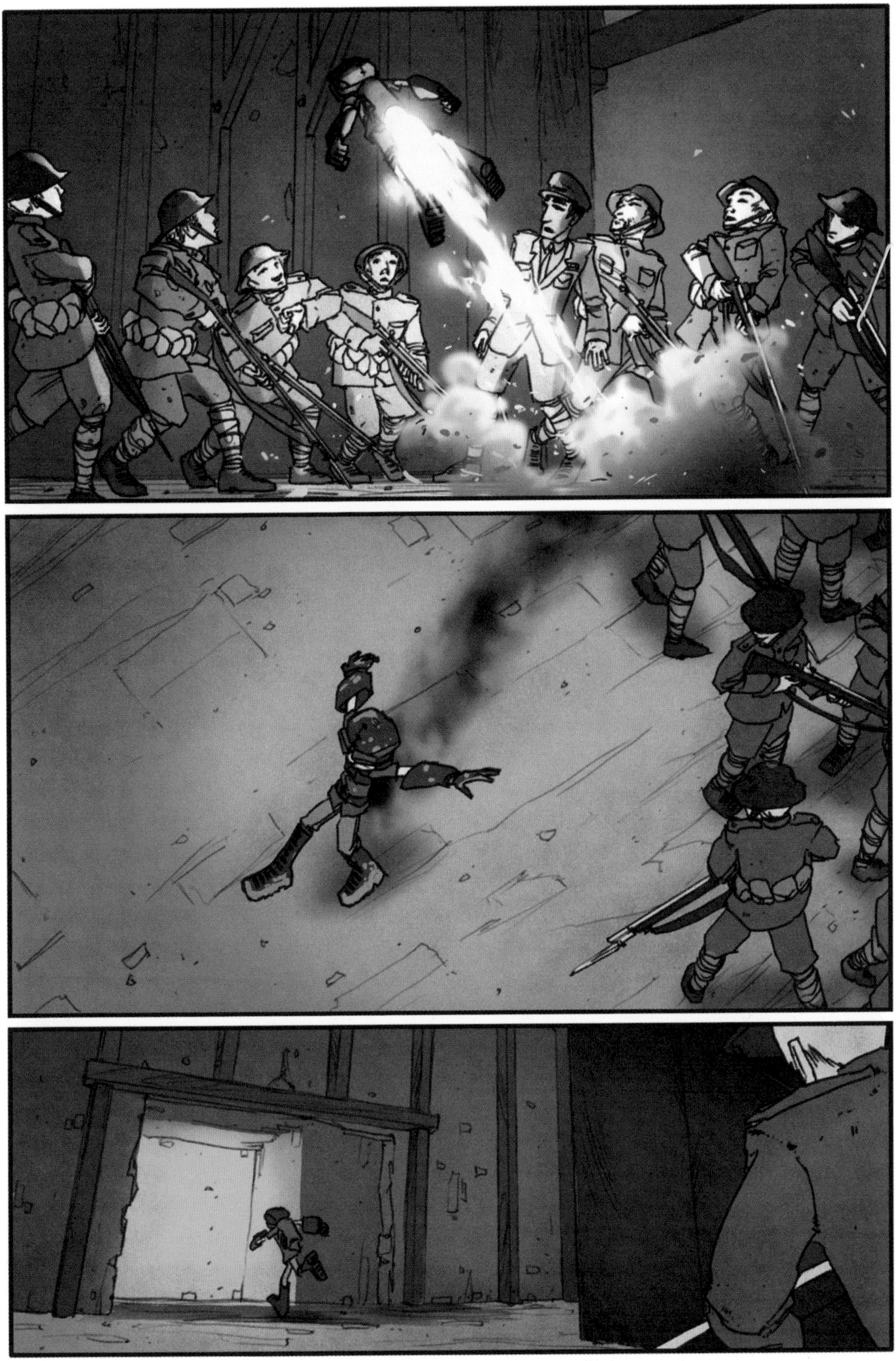

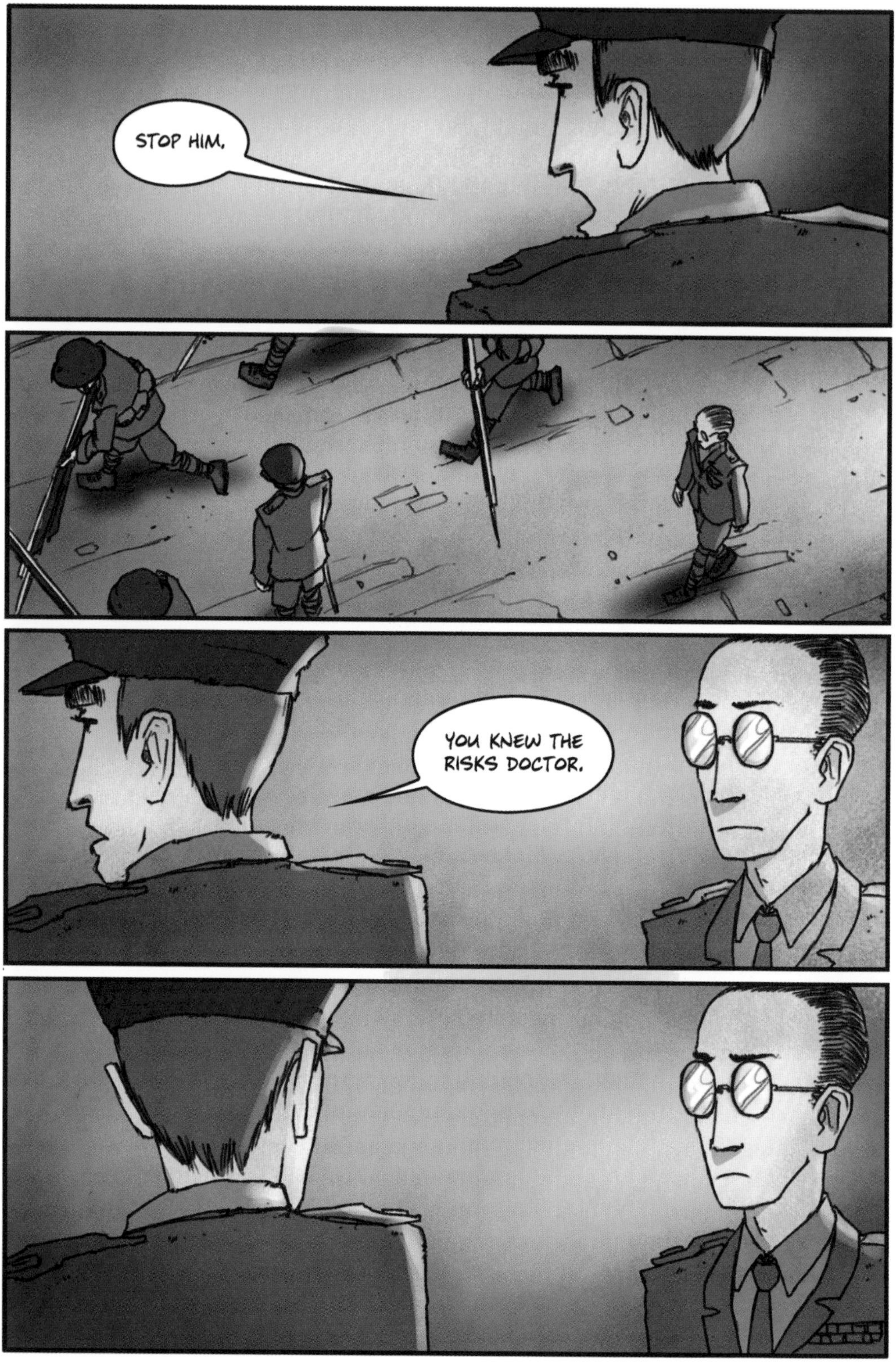
STOP HIM.
YOU KNEW THE RISKS DOCTOR.

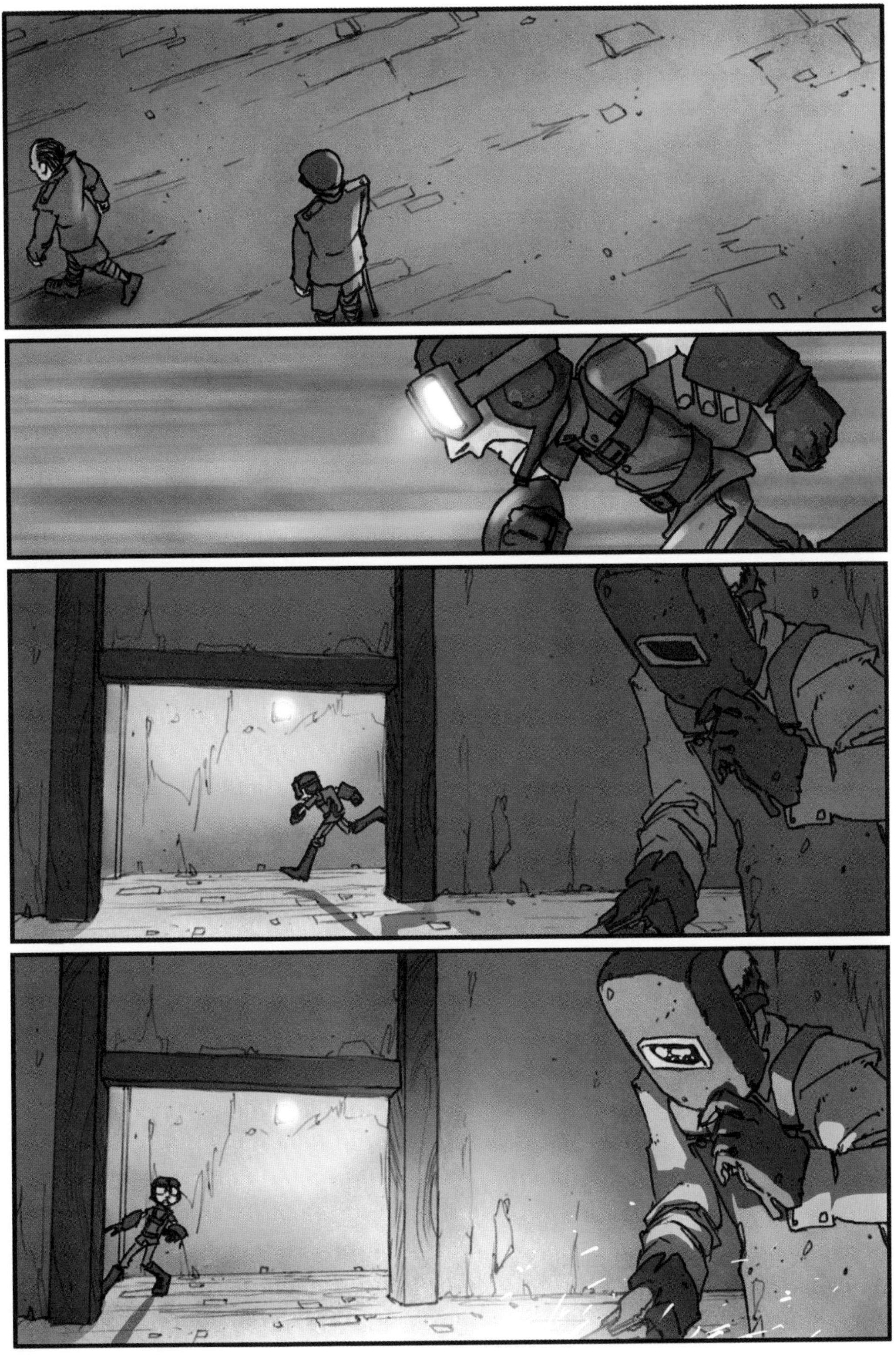

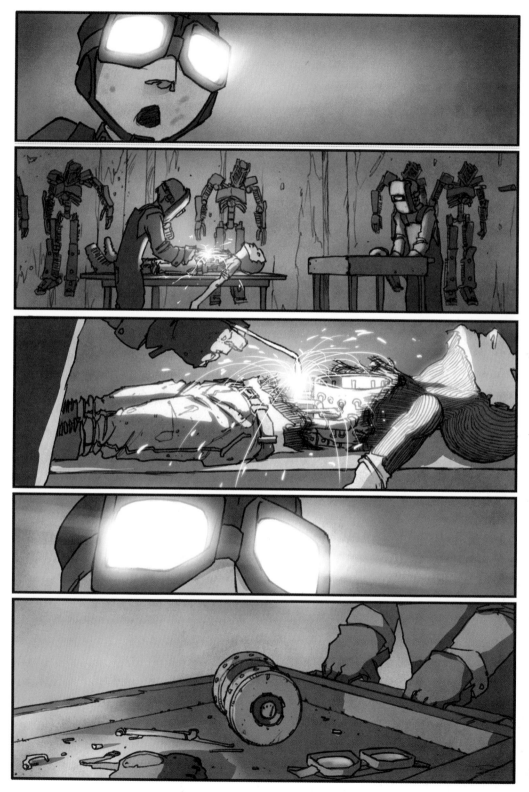

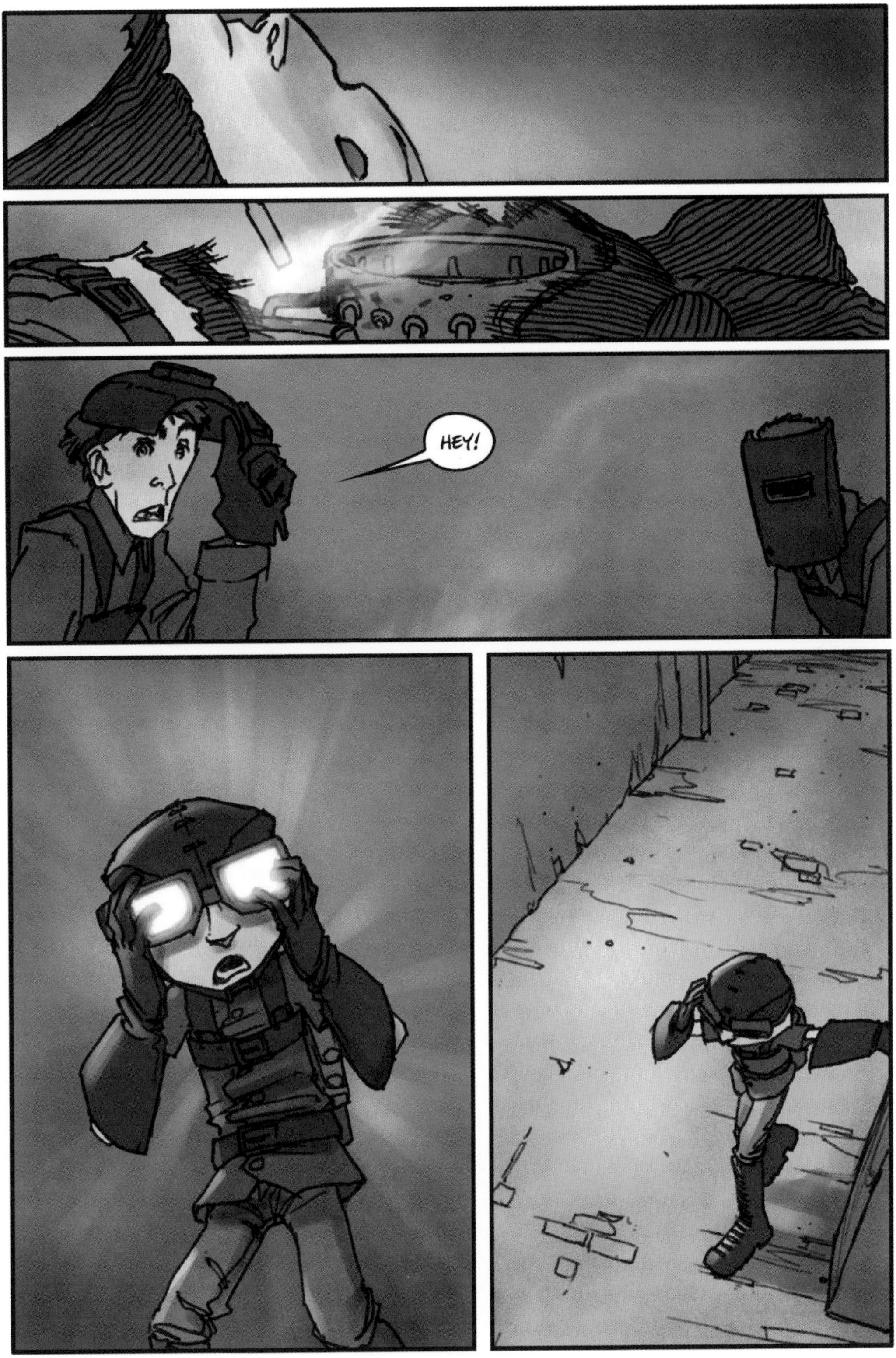
HEY!

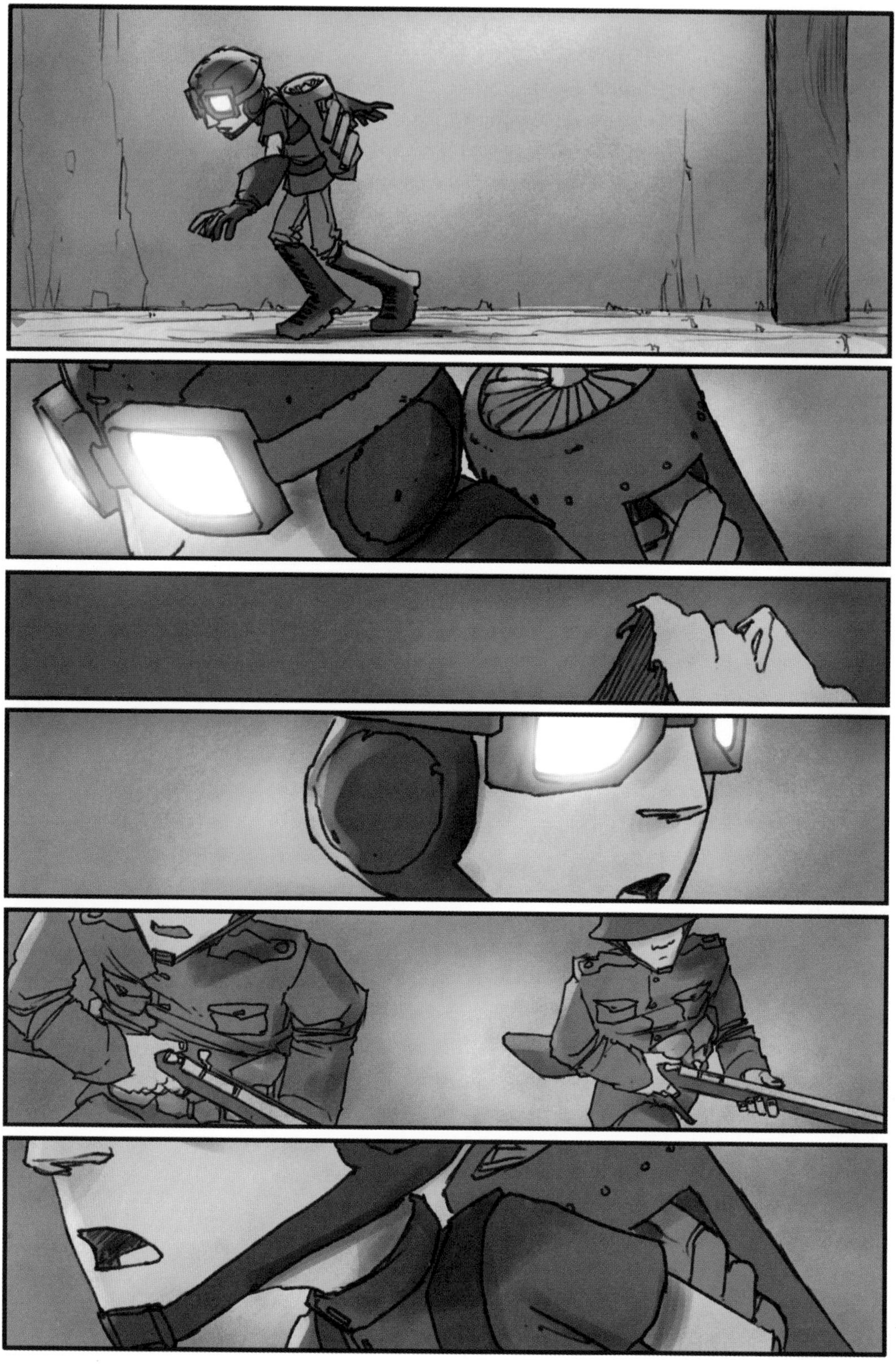

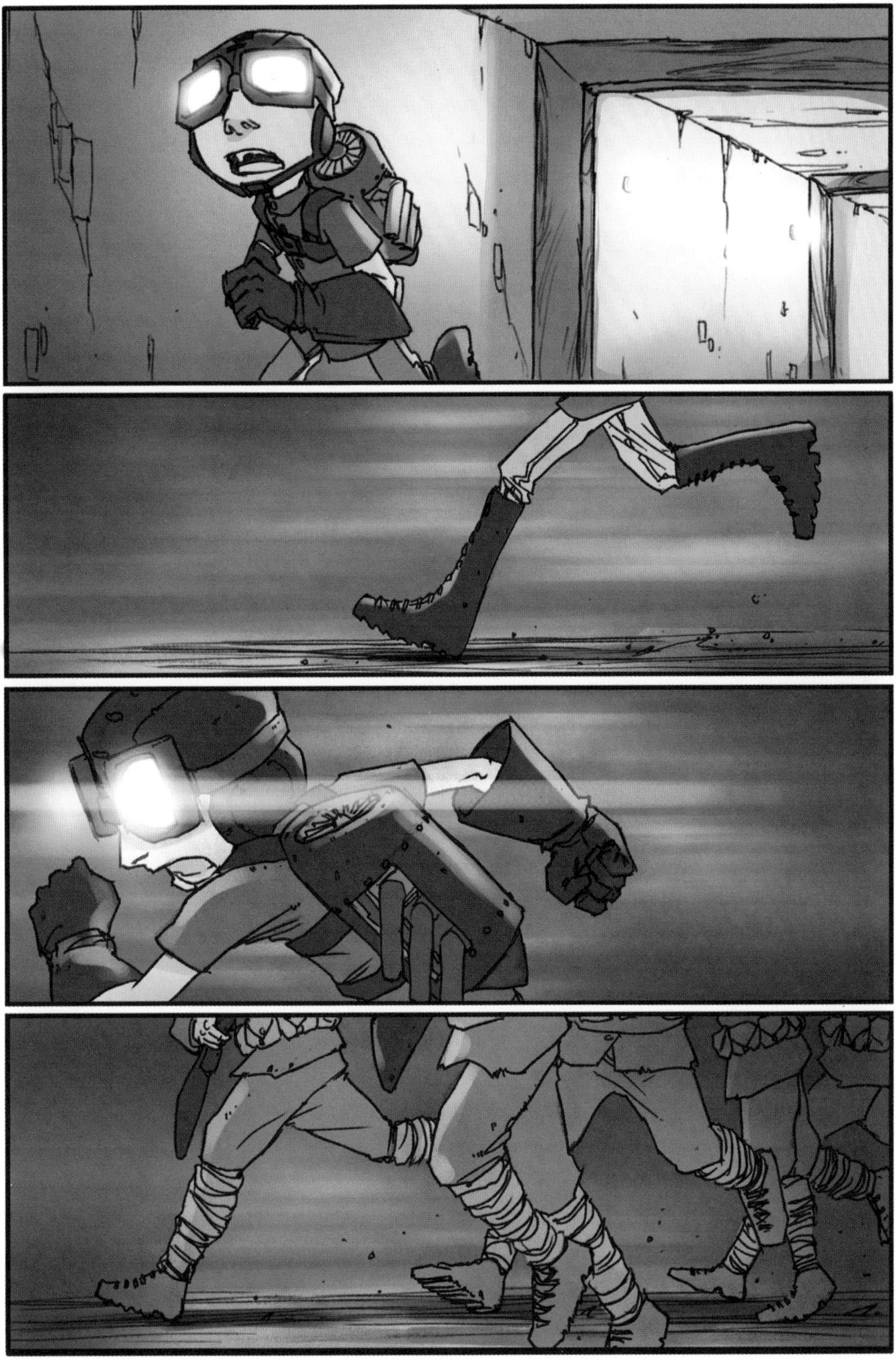

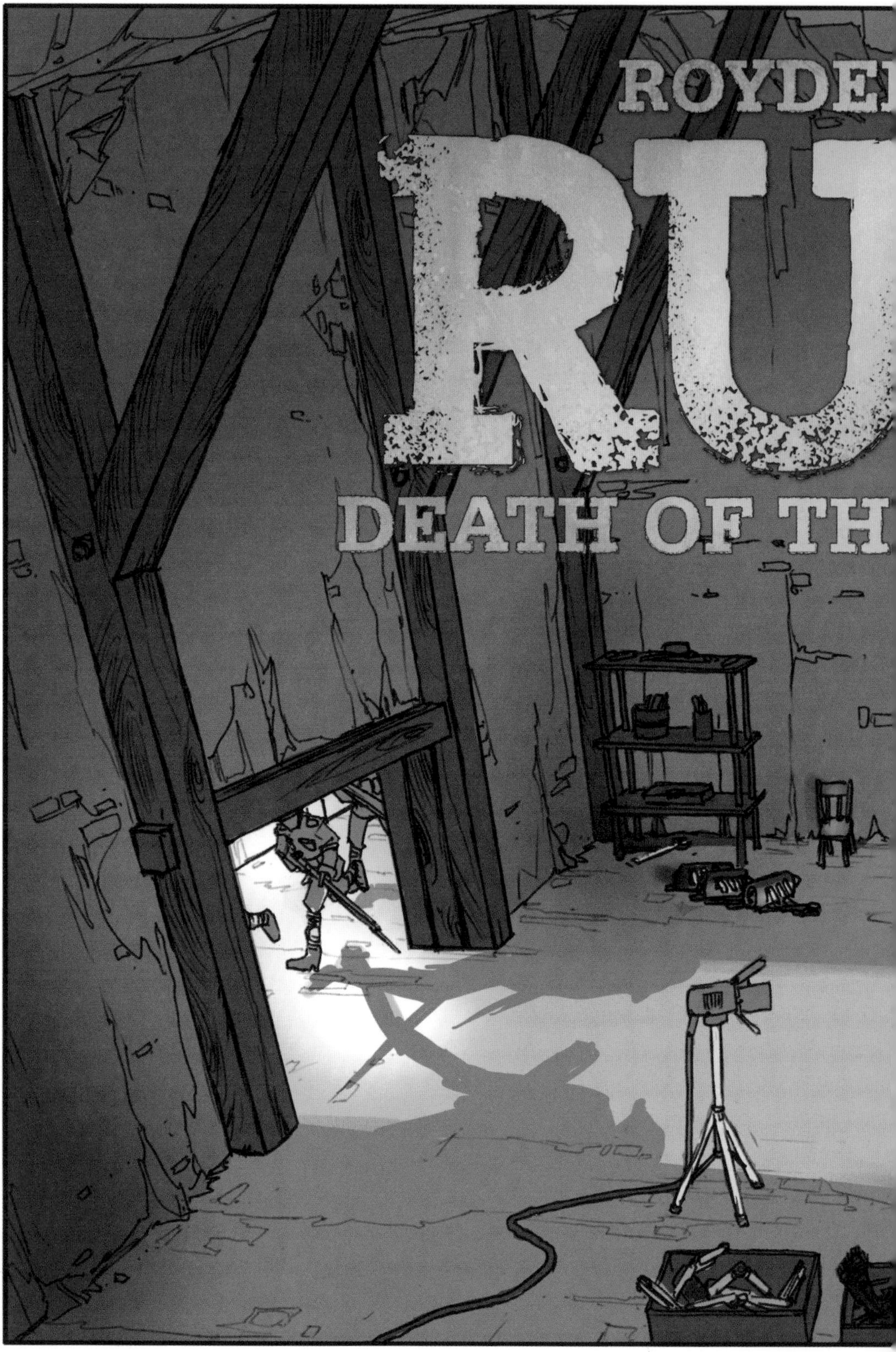
ROYDE
RU
DEATH OF TH

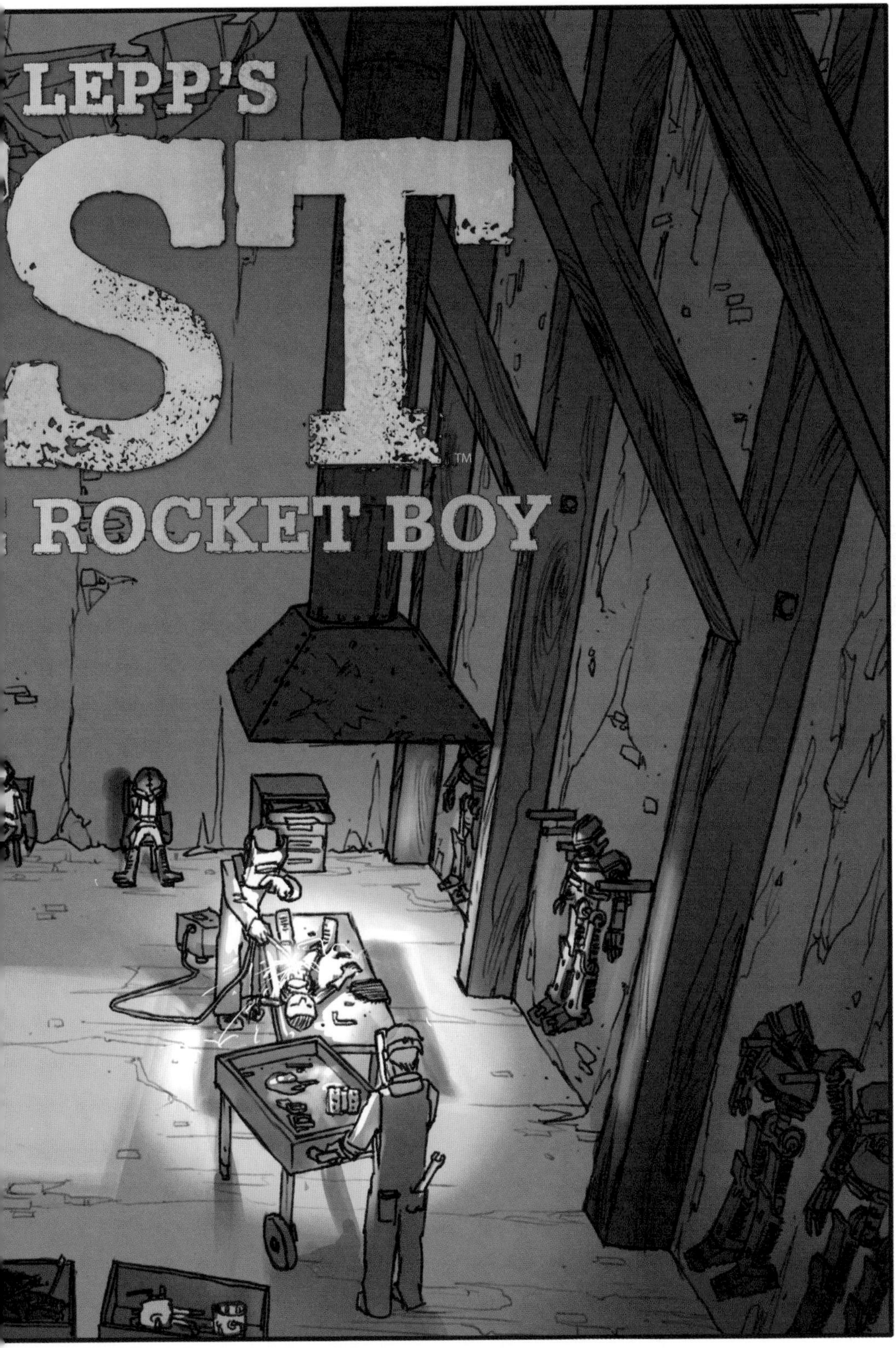
LEPP'S
ST
TM
ROCKET BOY

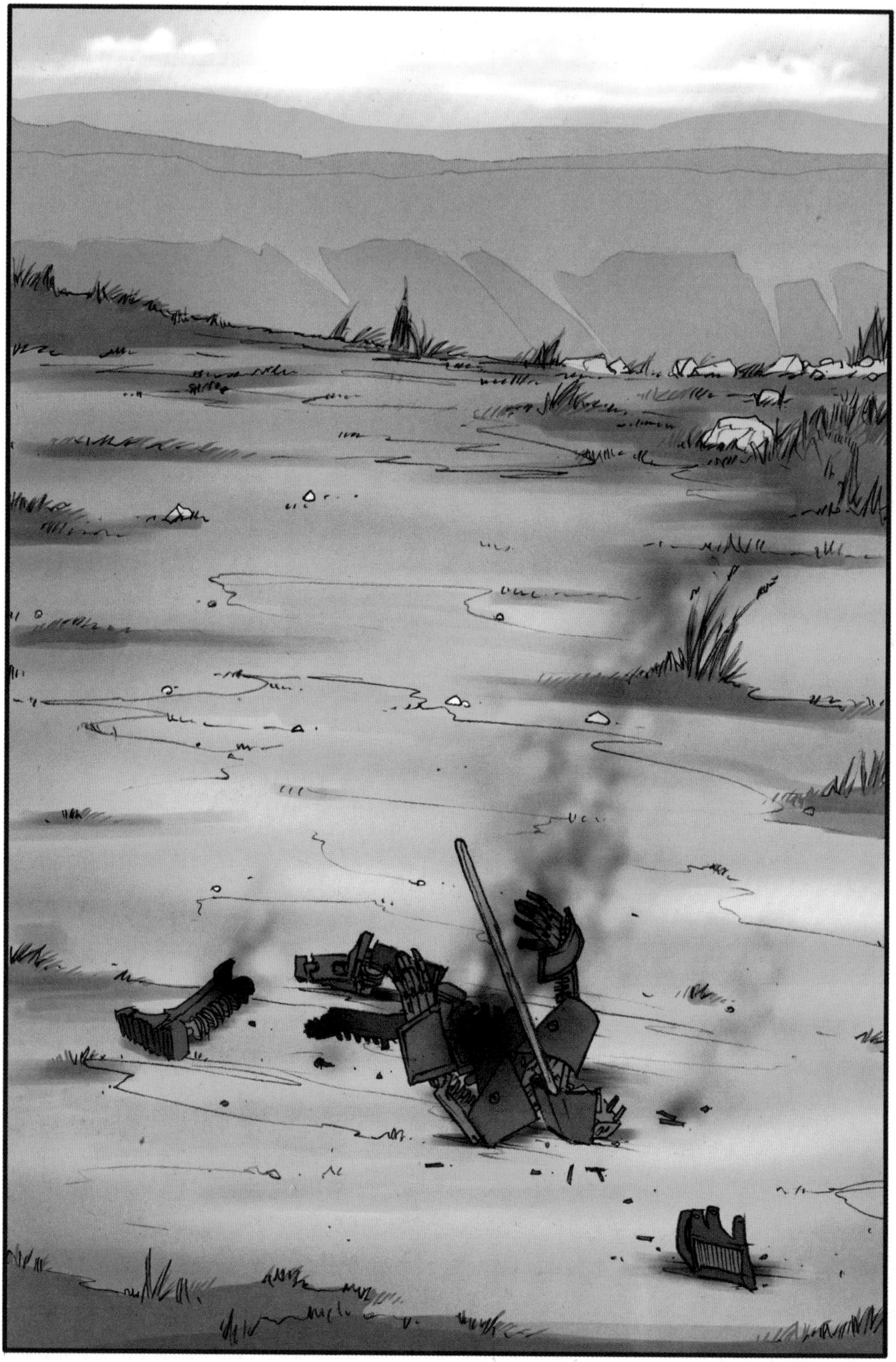

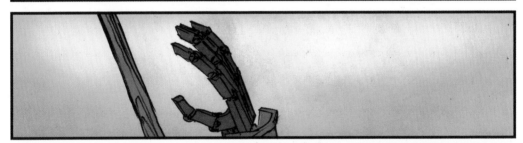

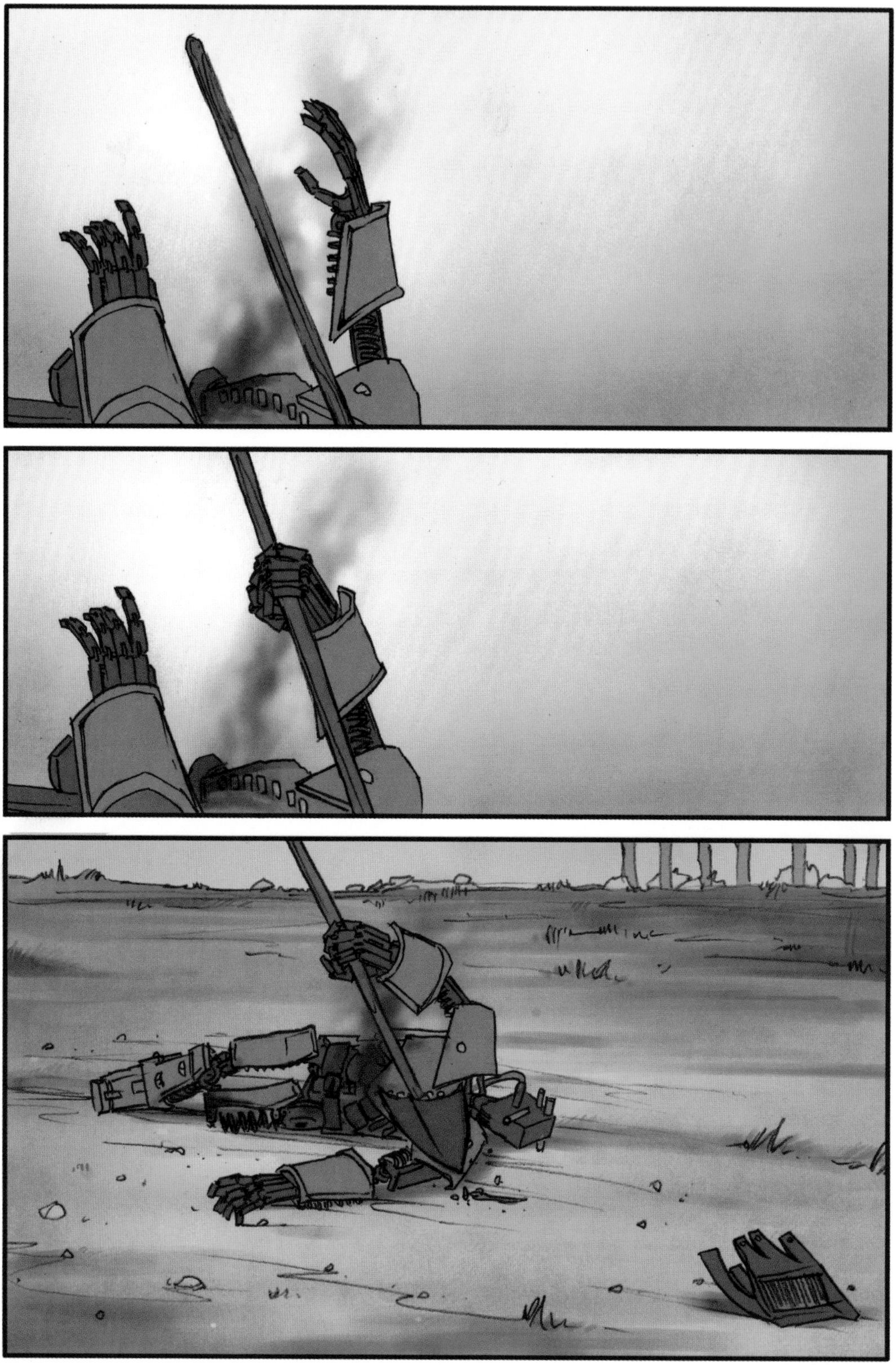

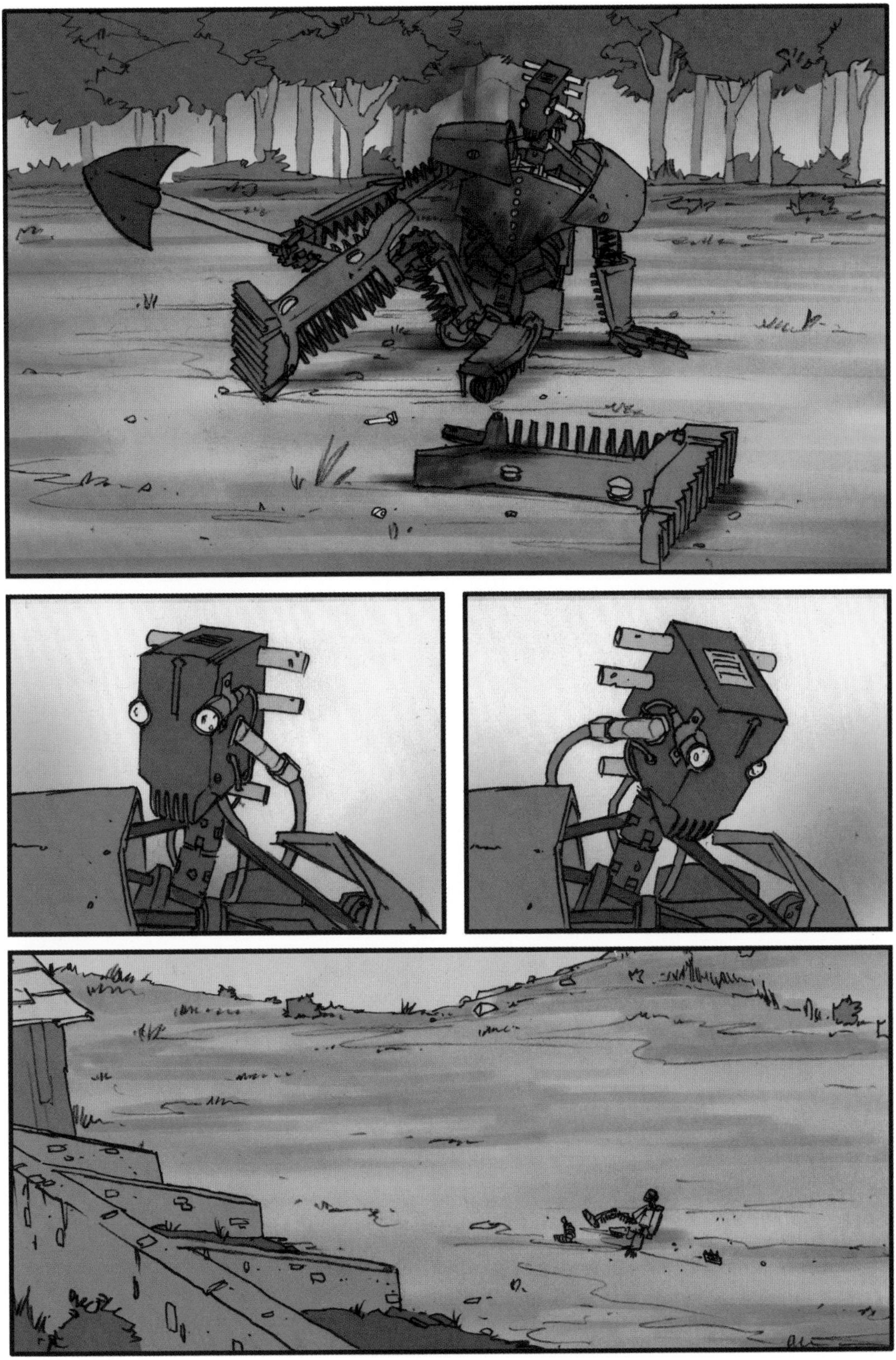

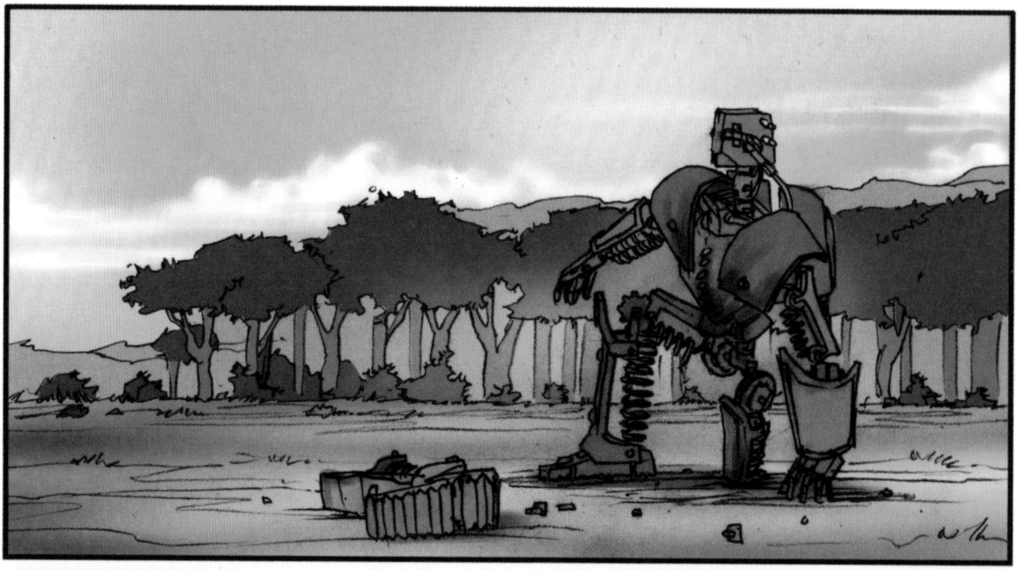

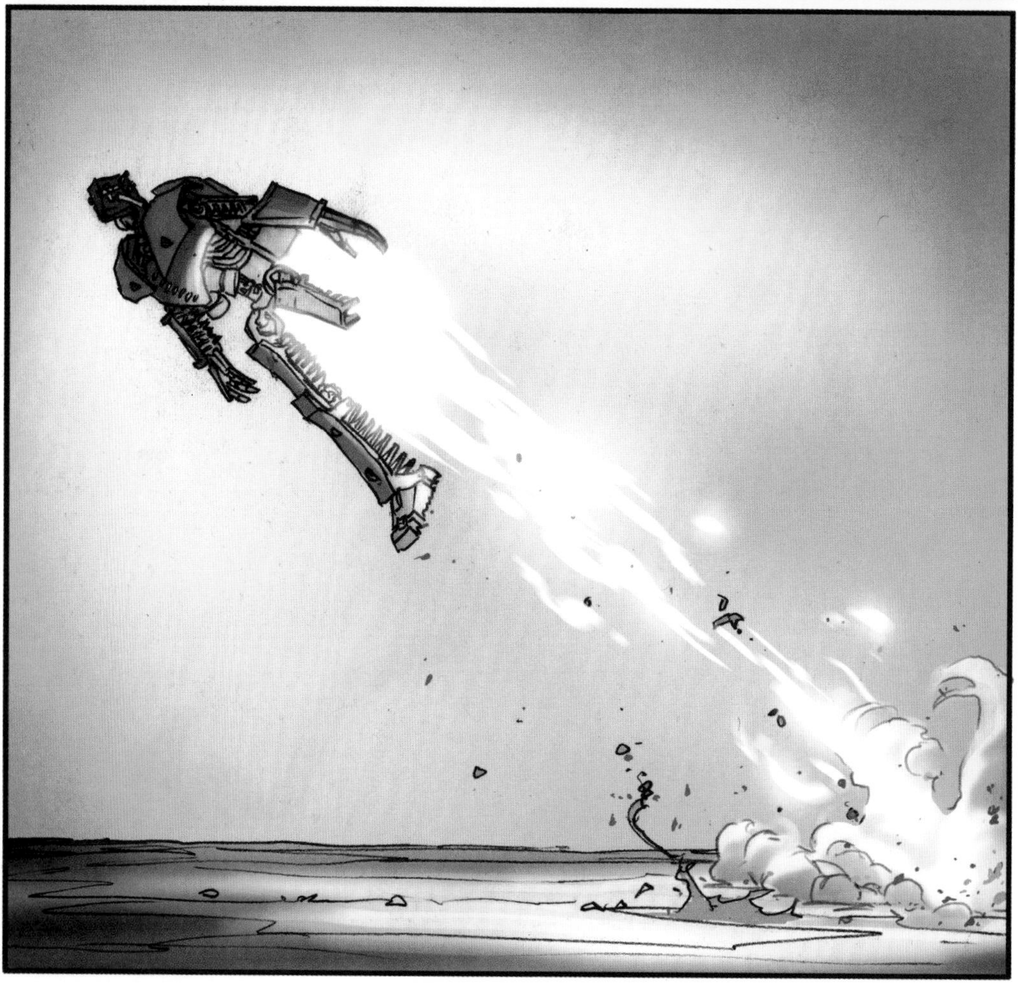

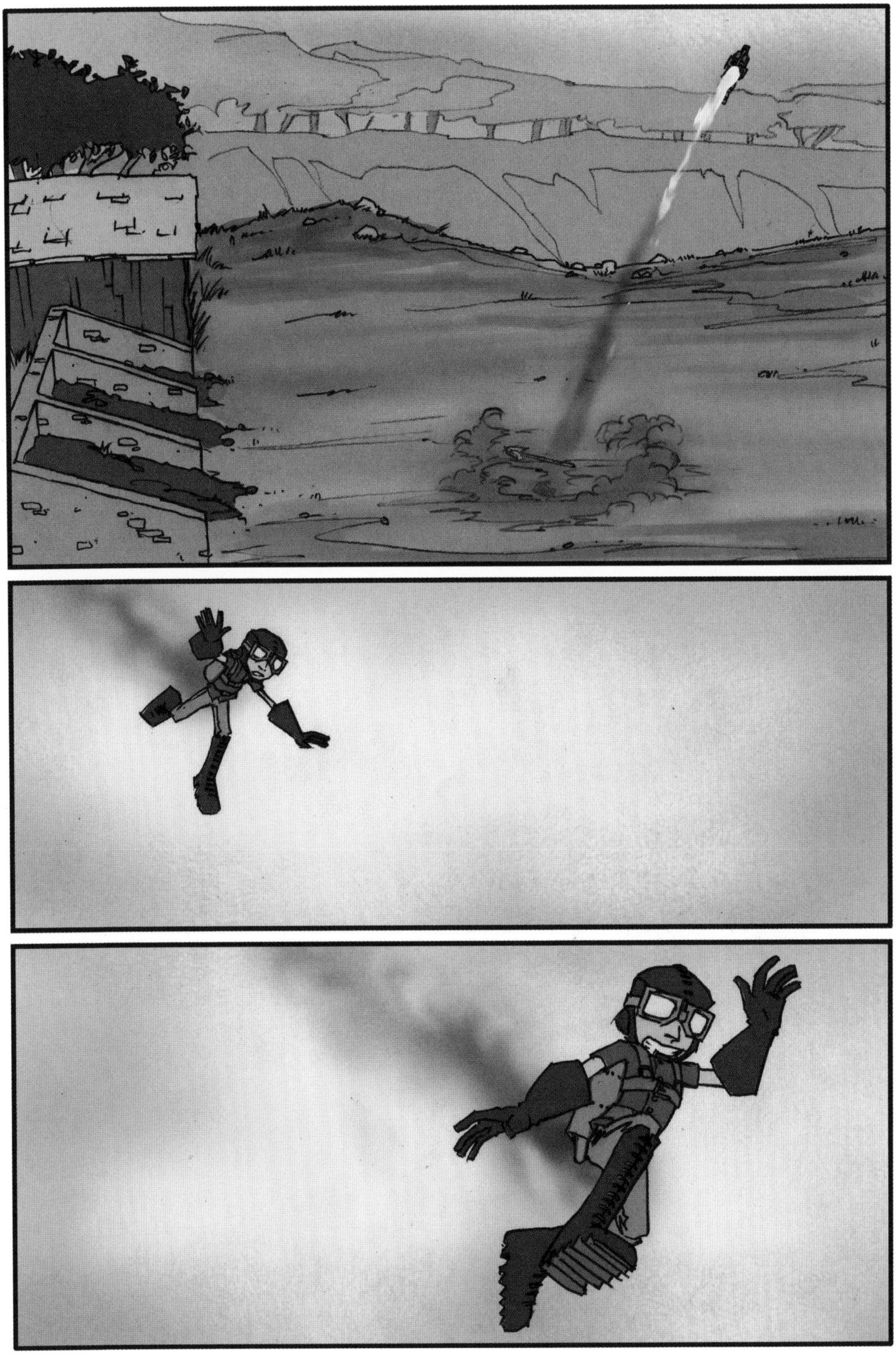

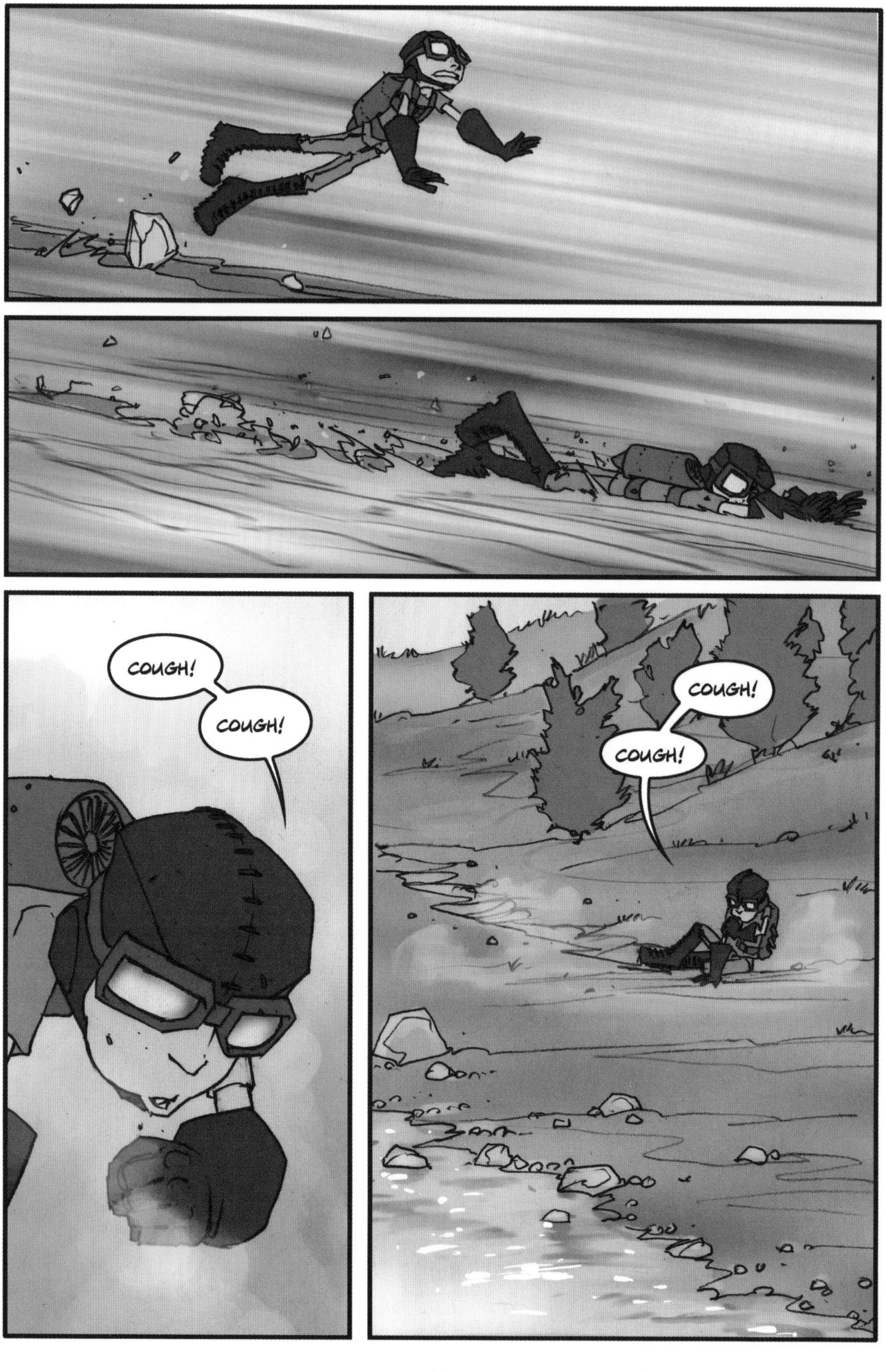
COUGH!
COUGH!
COUGH!
COUGH!

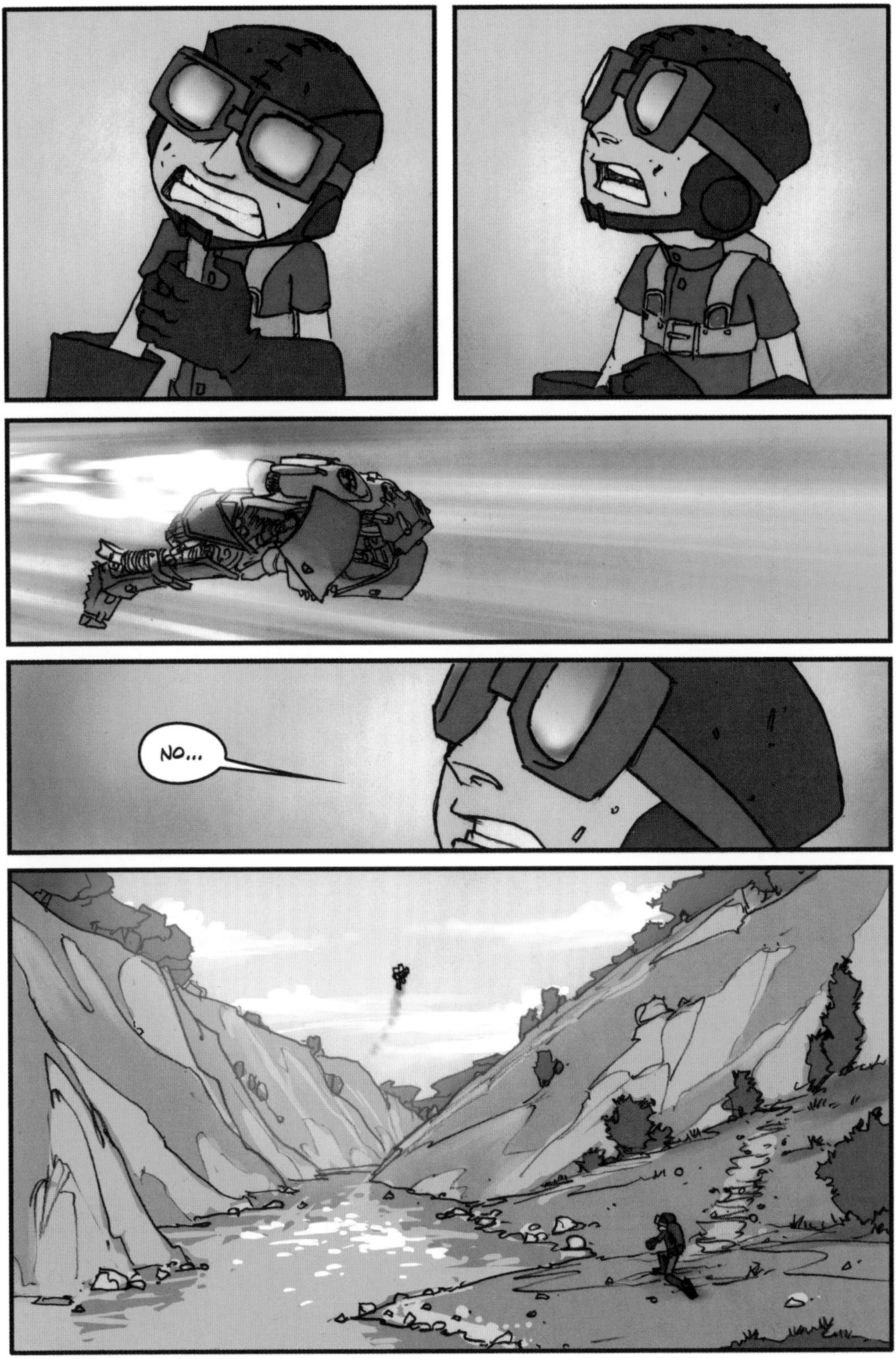
NO...

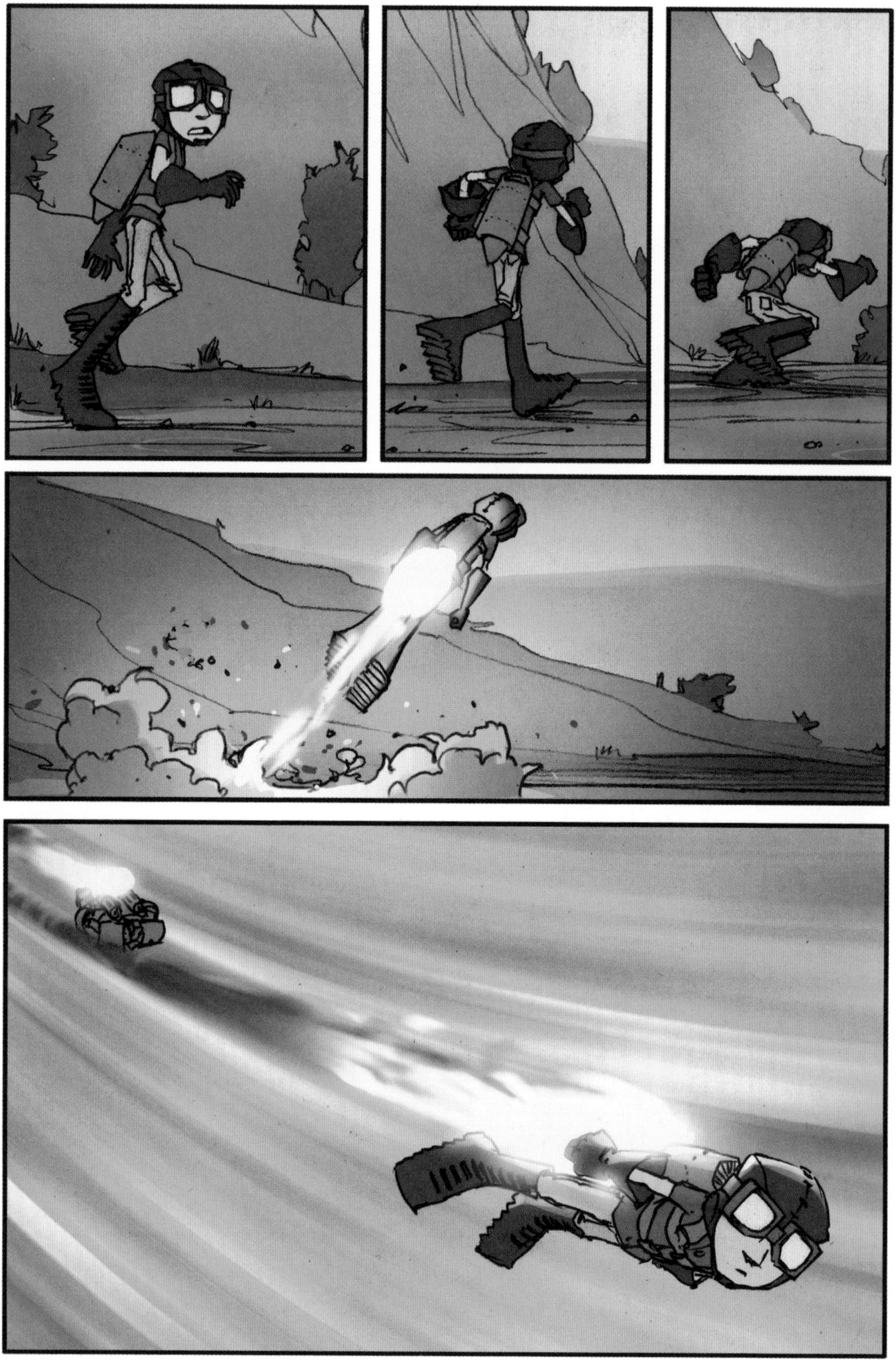

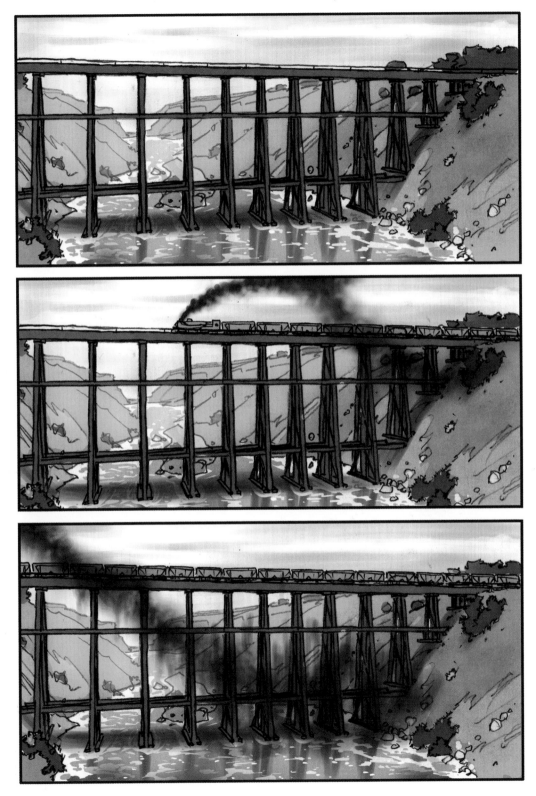

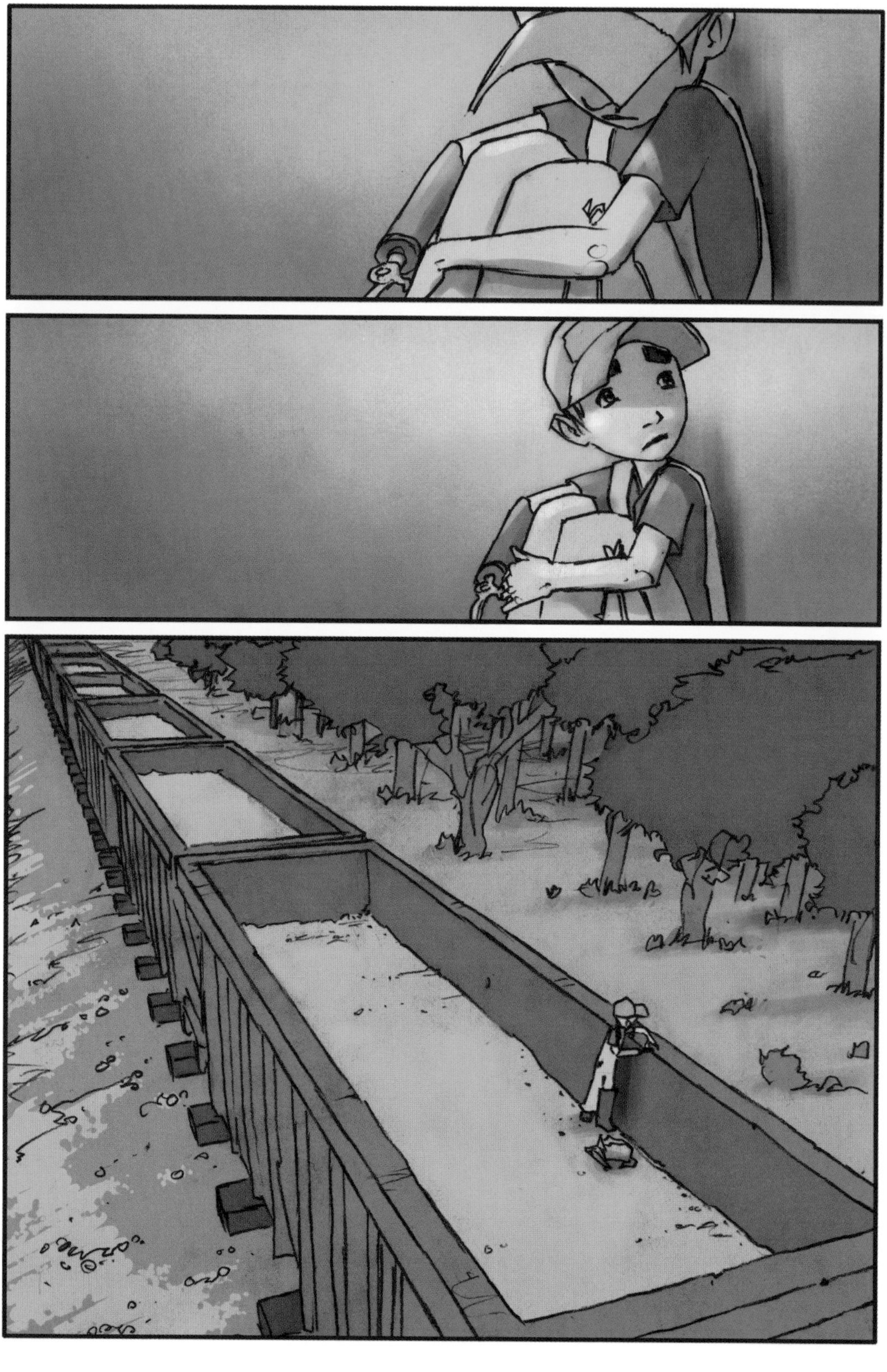

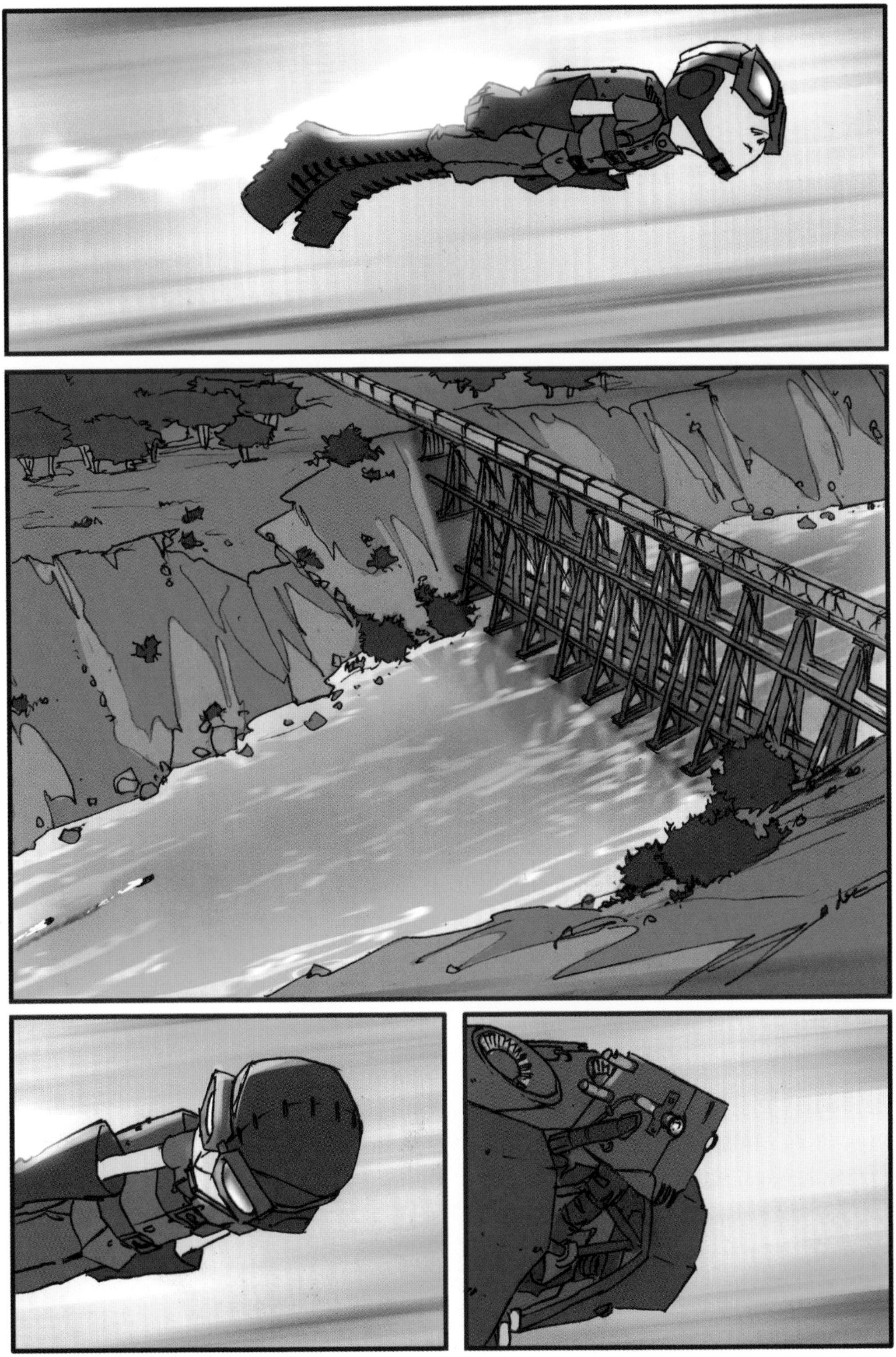

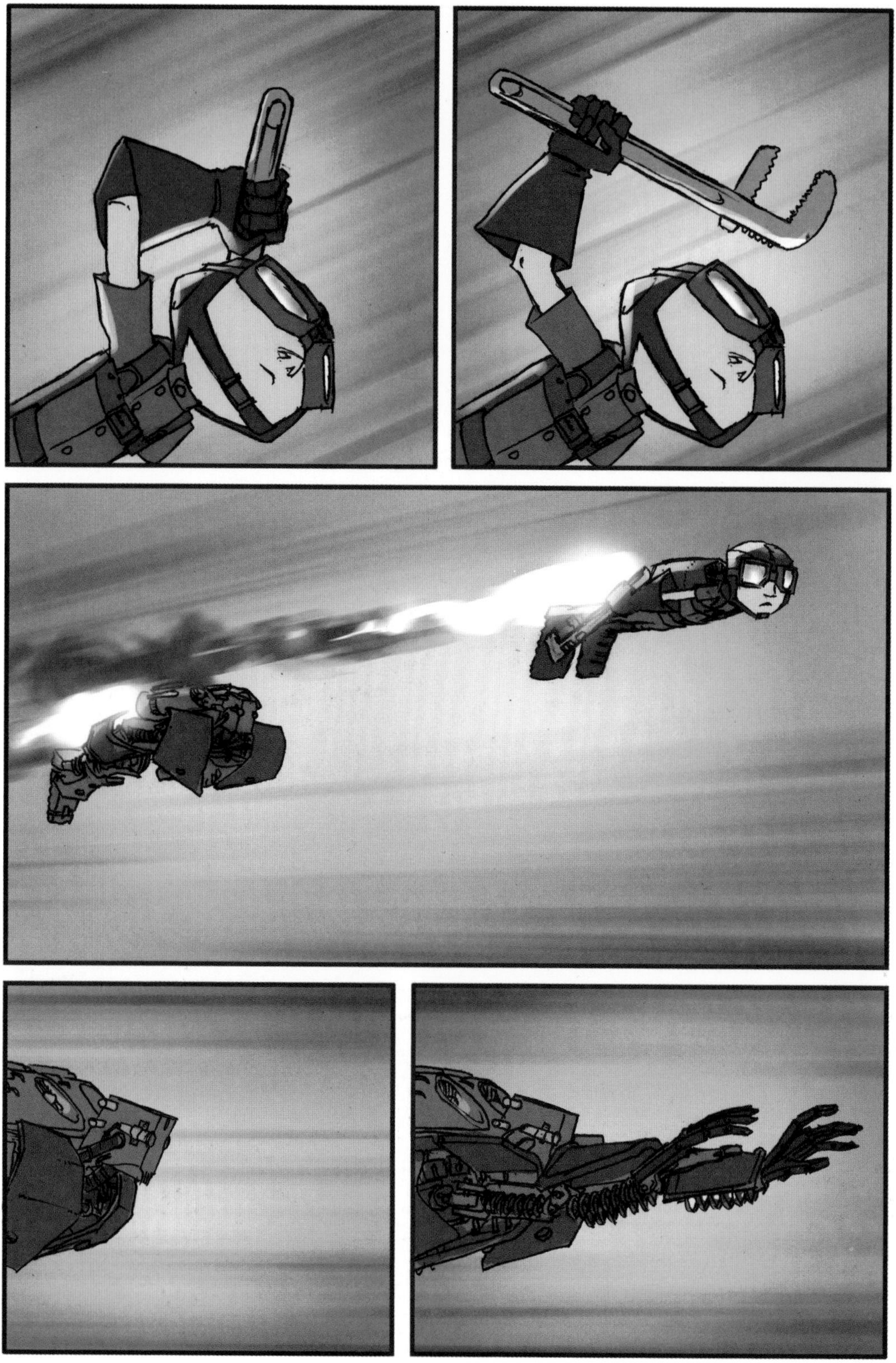

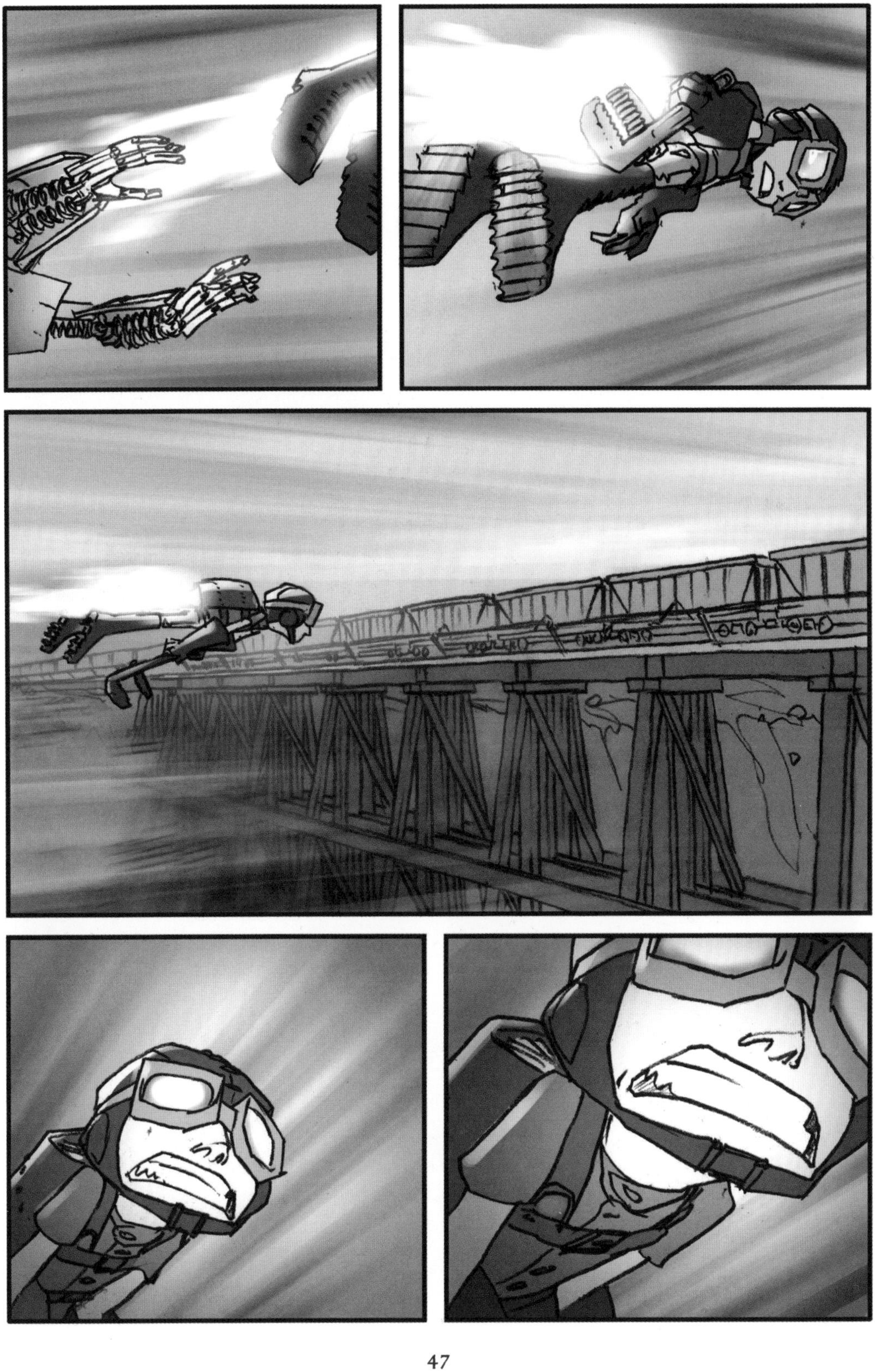

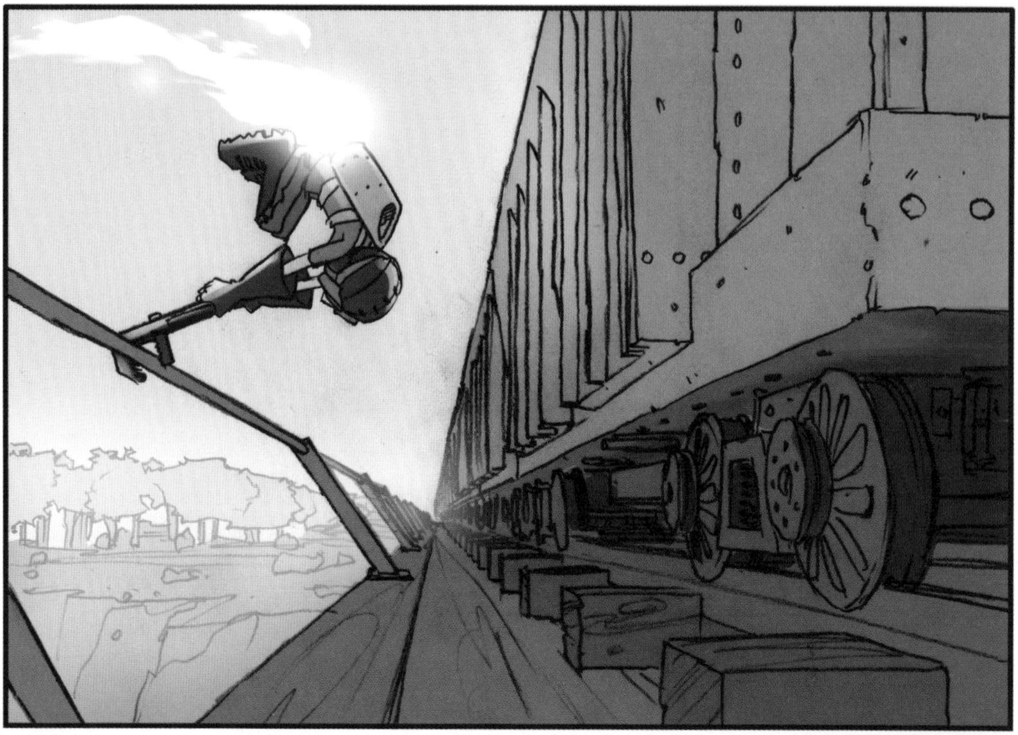

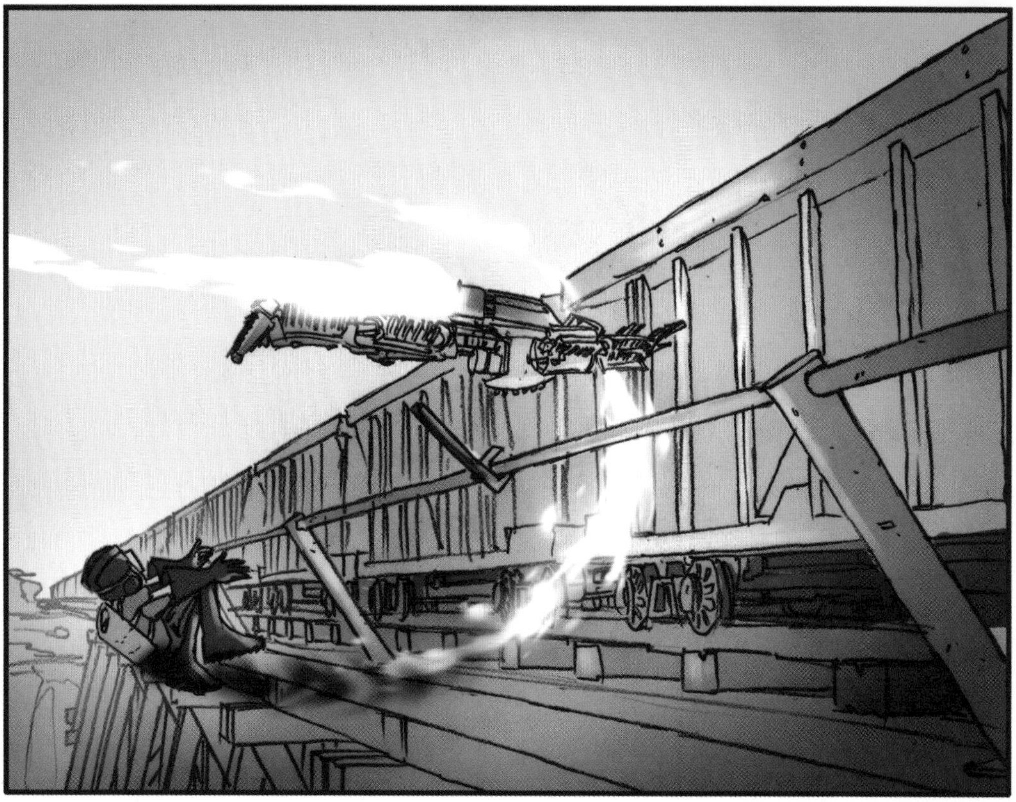

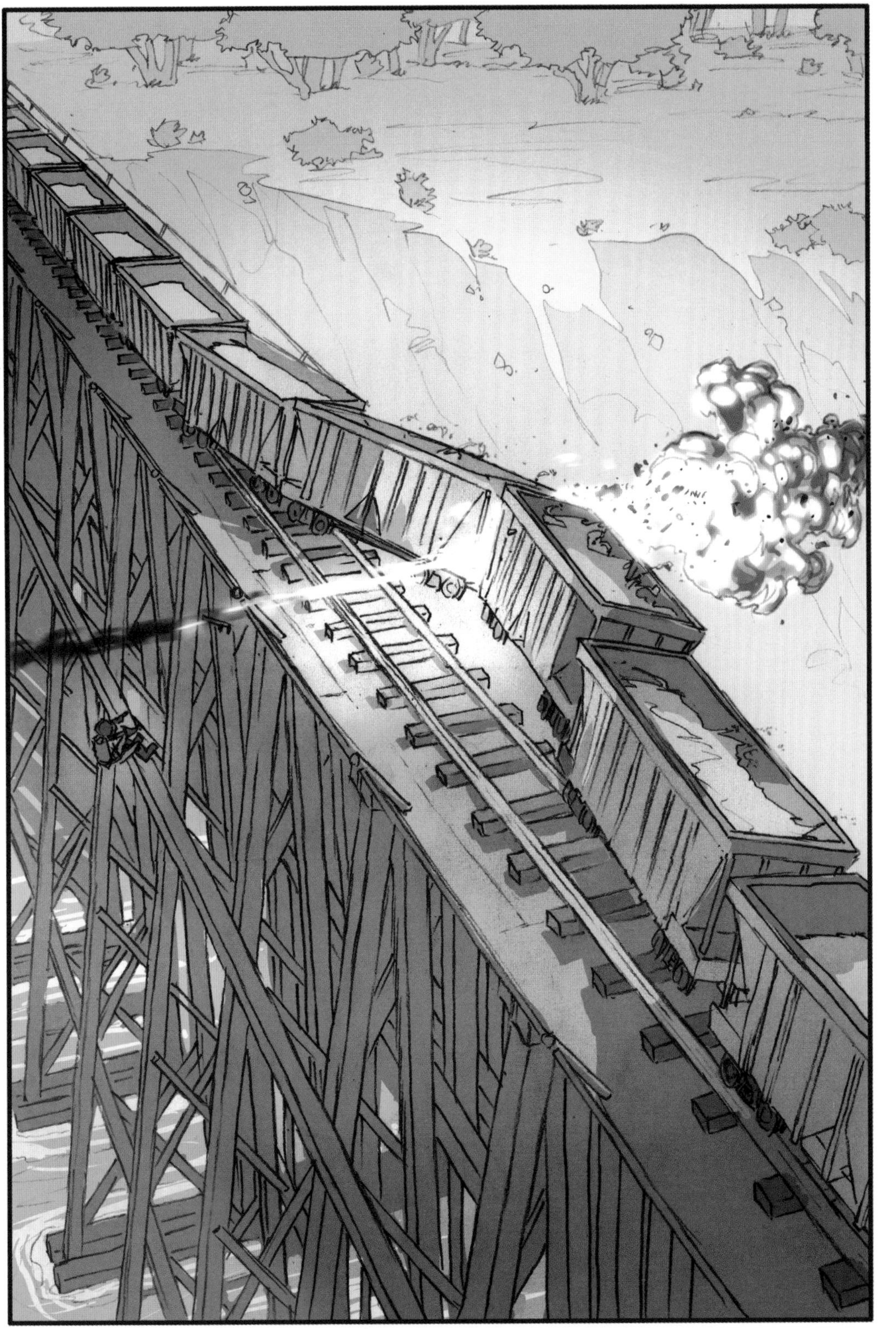

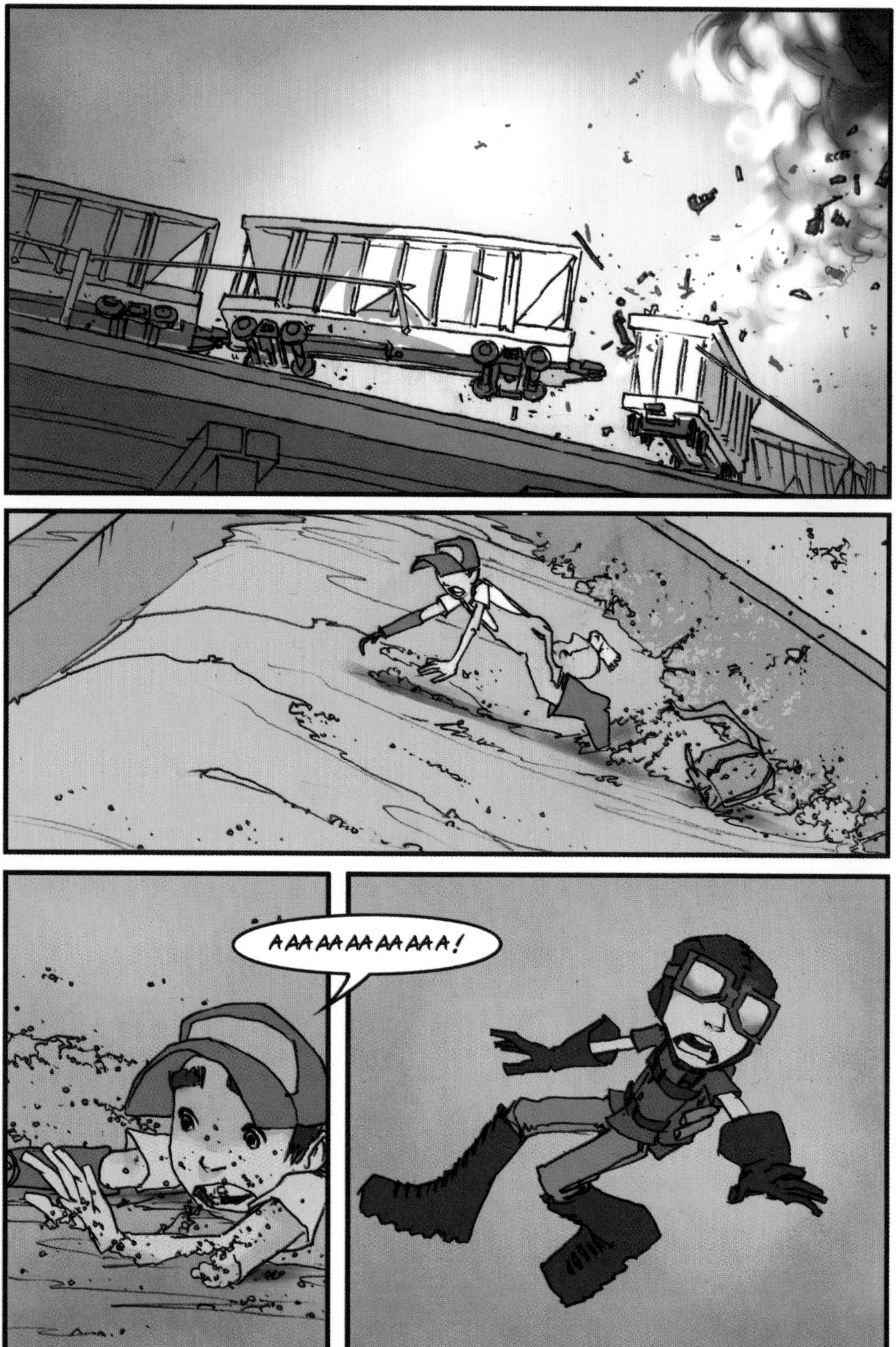
AAAAAAAAAAA!

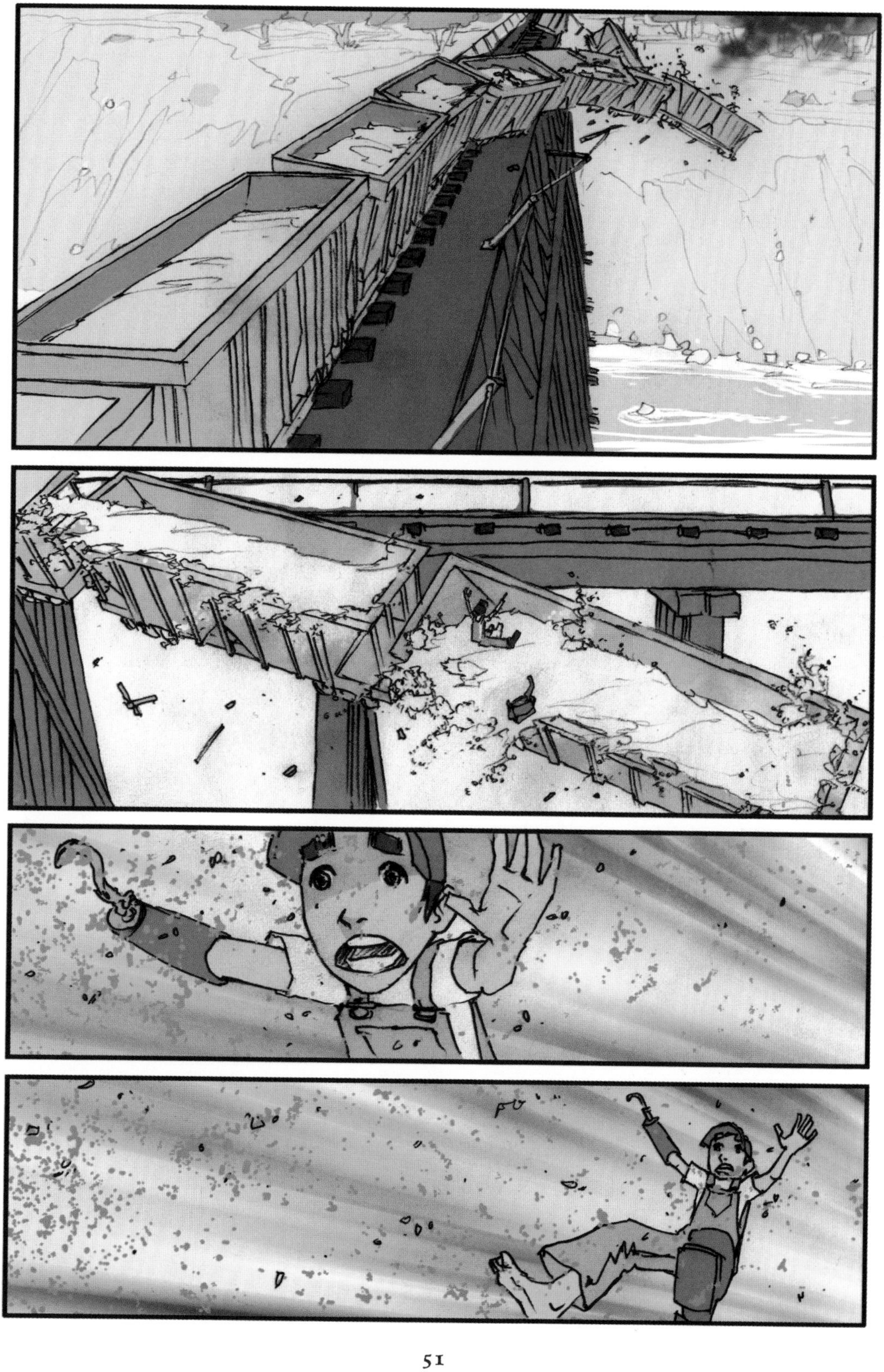

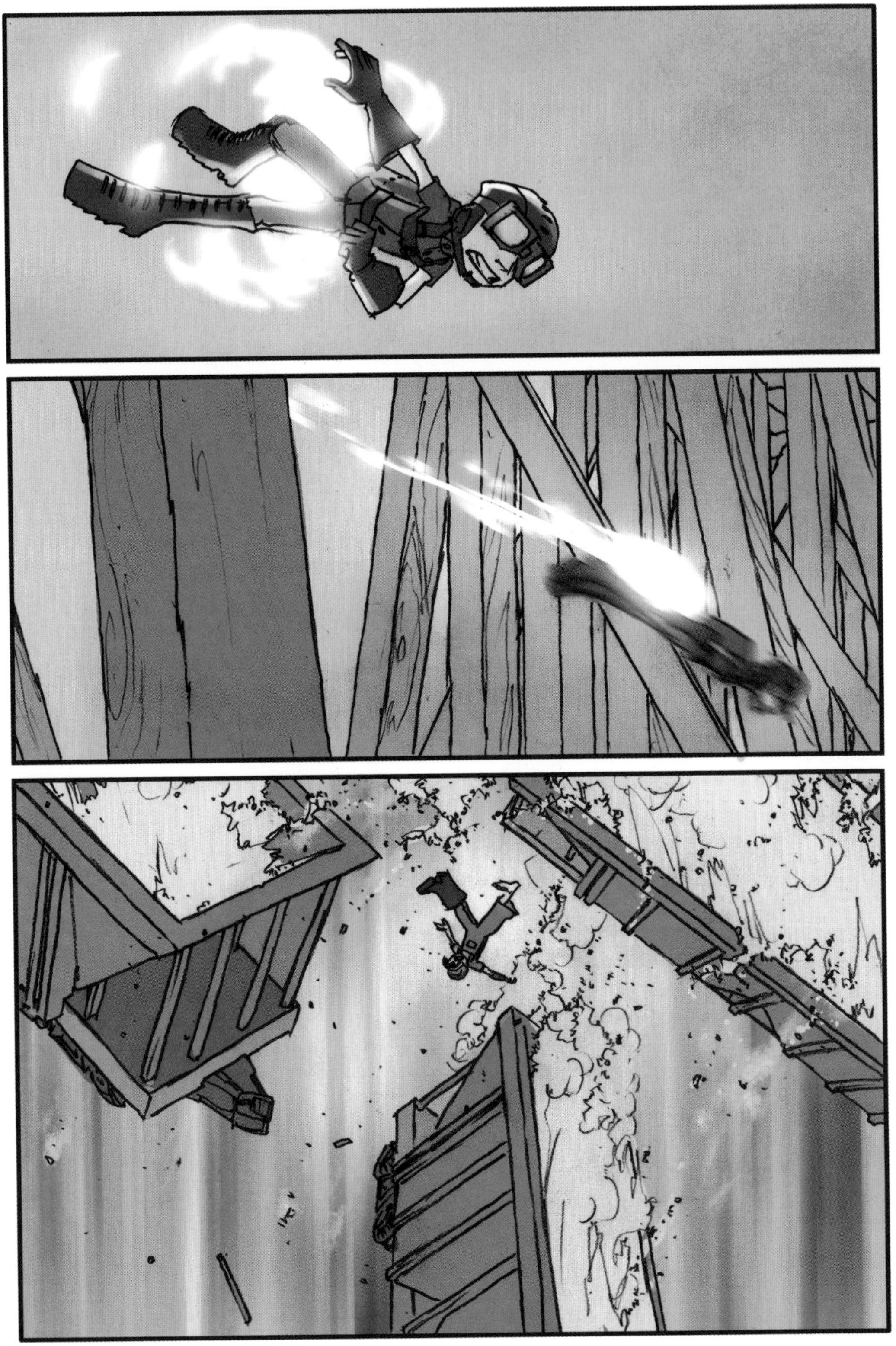

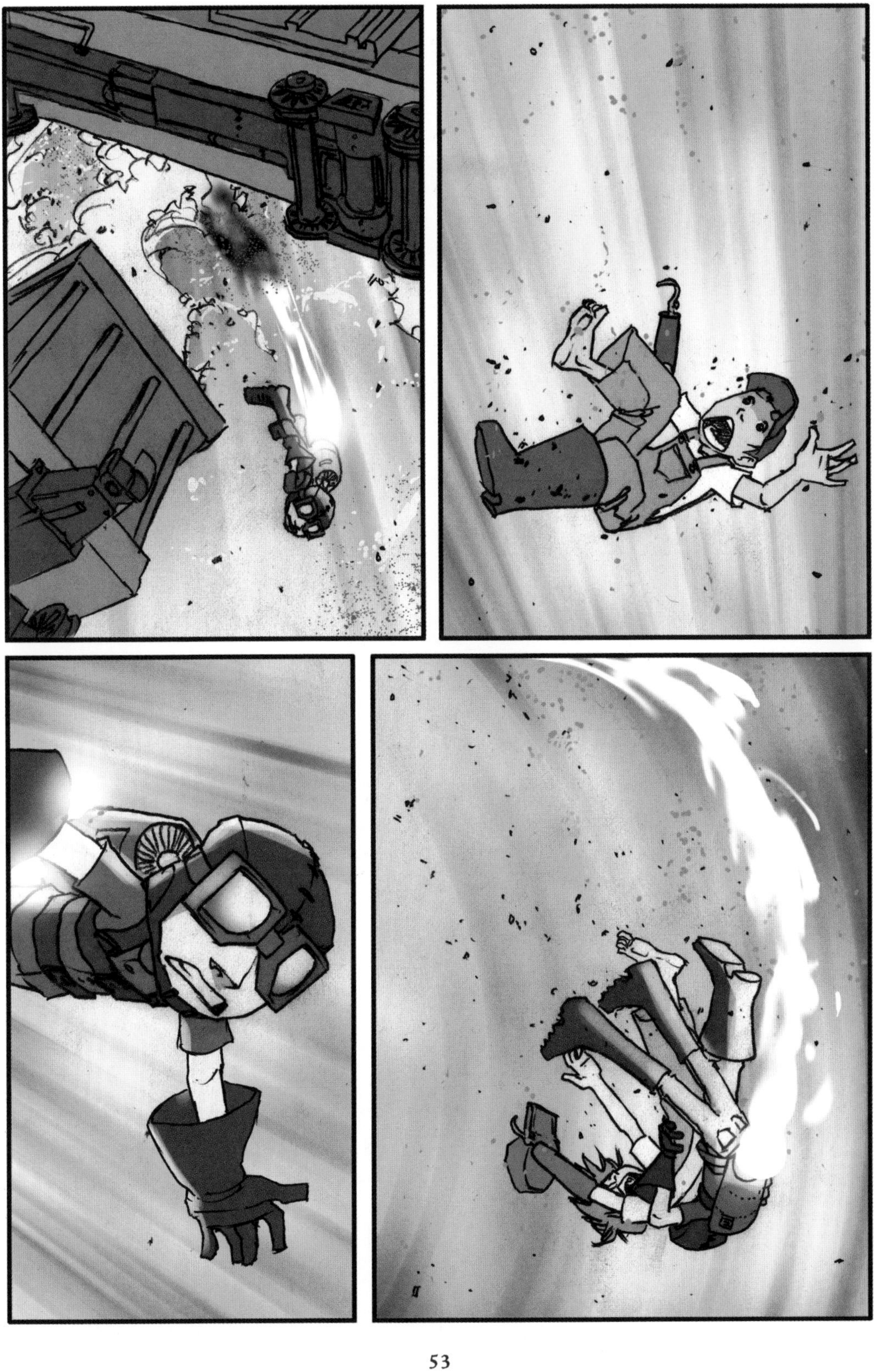

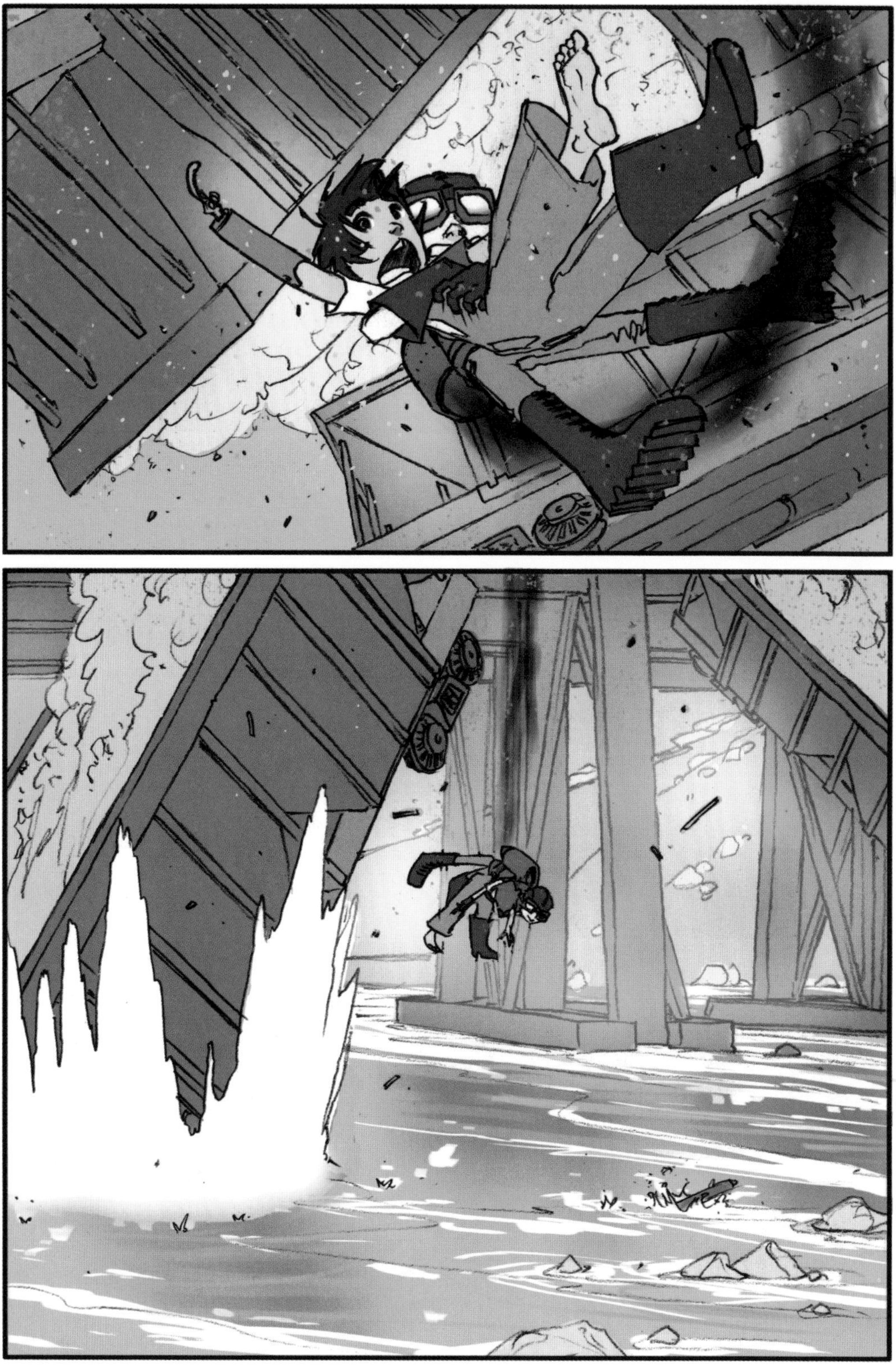

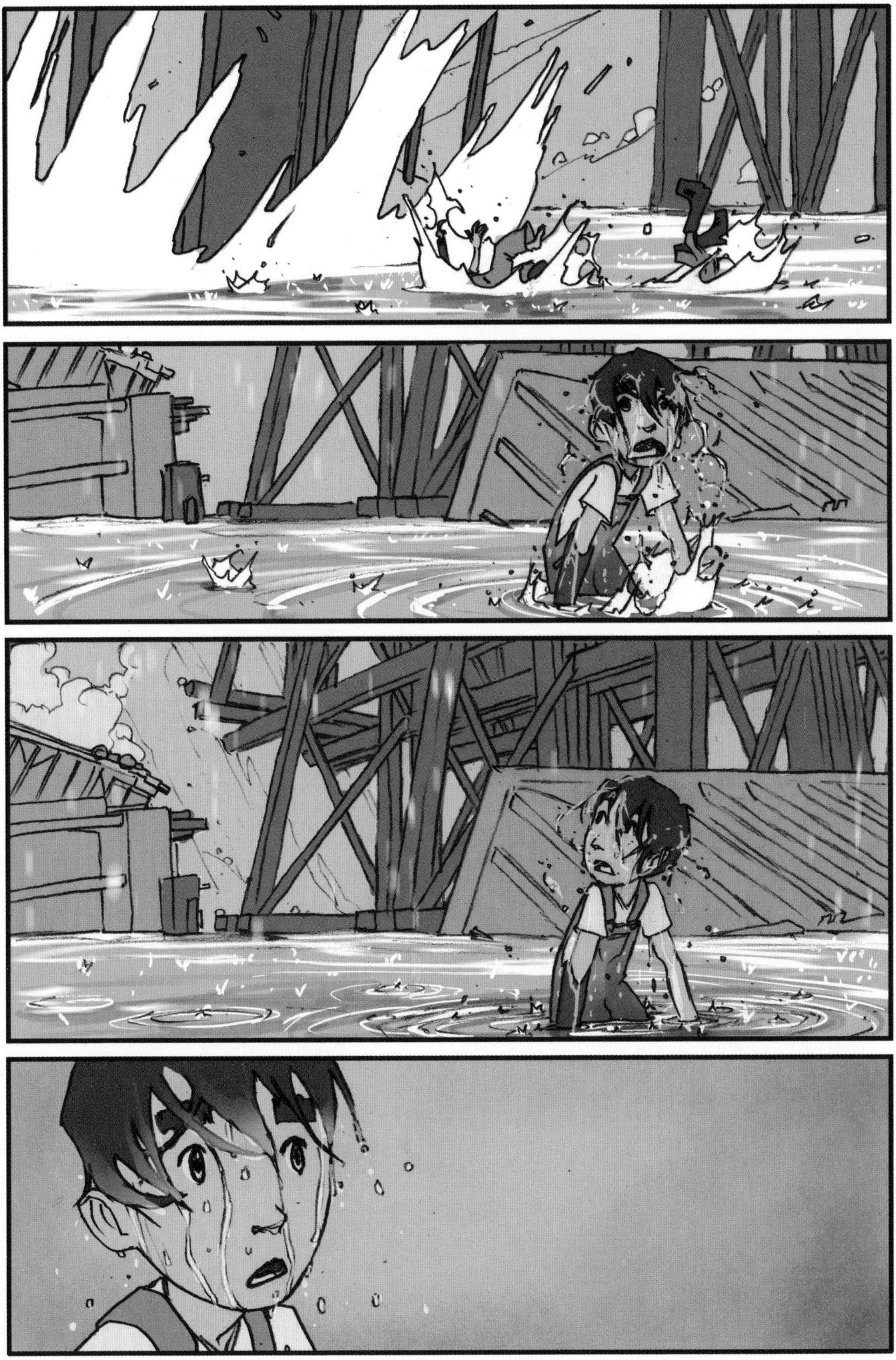

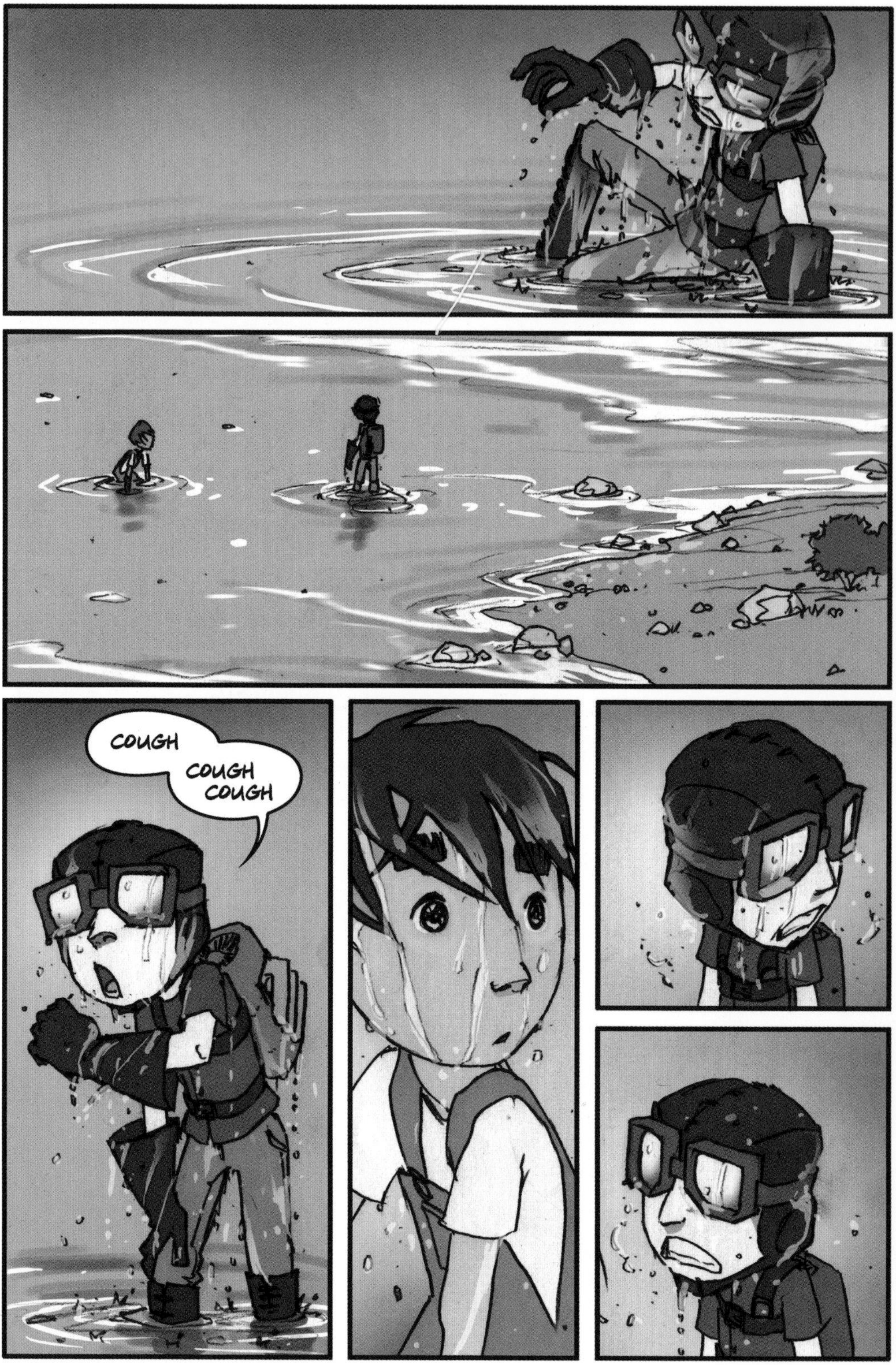
COUGH
COUGH
COUGH

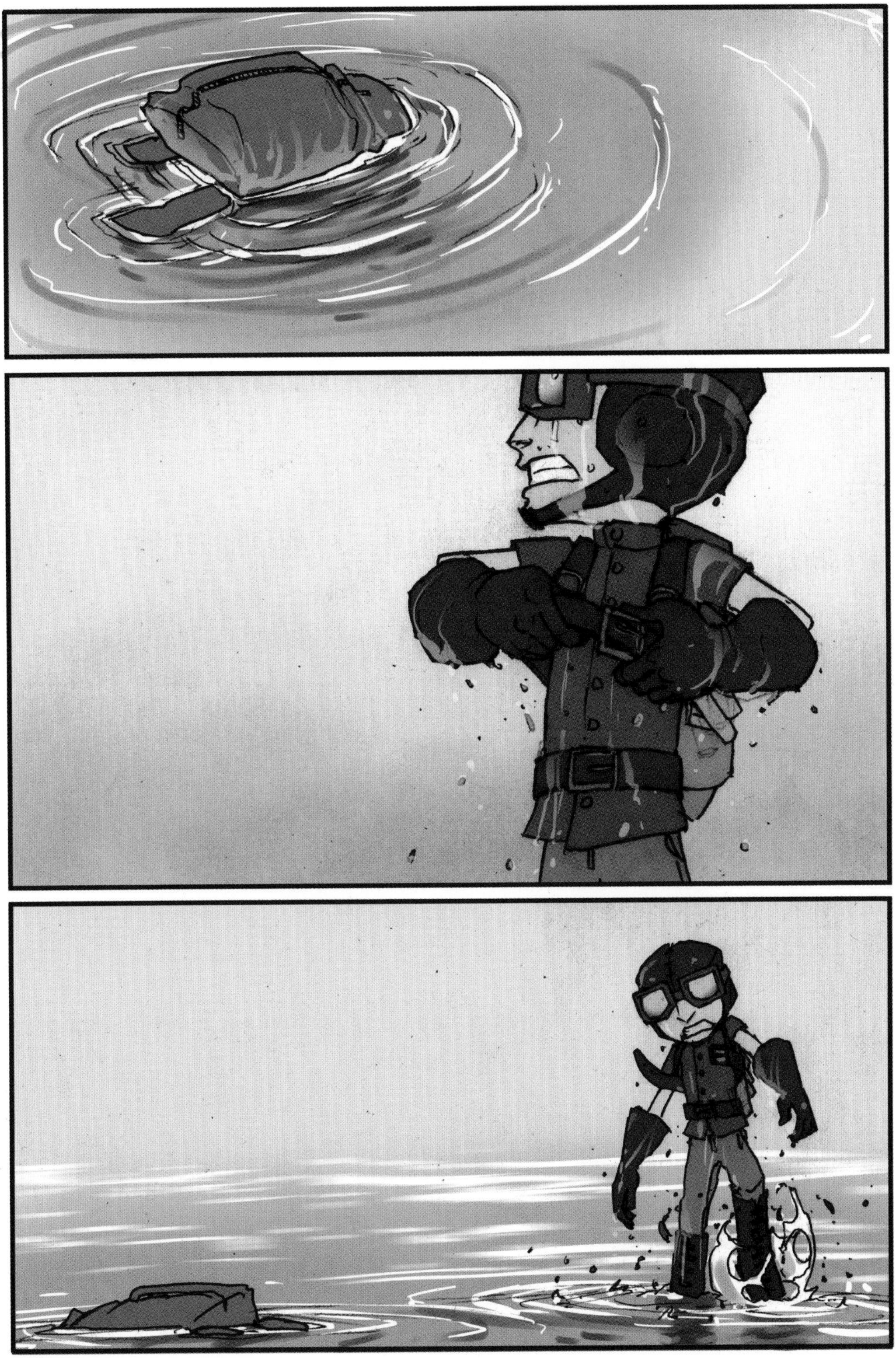

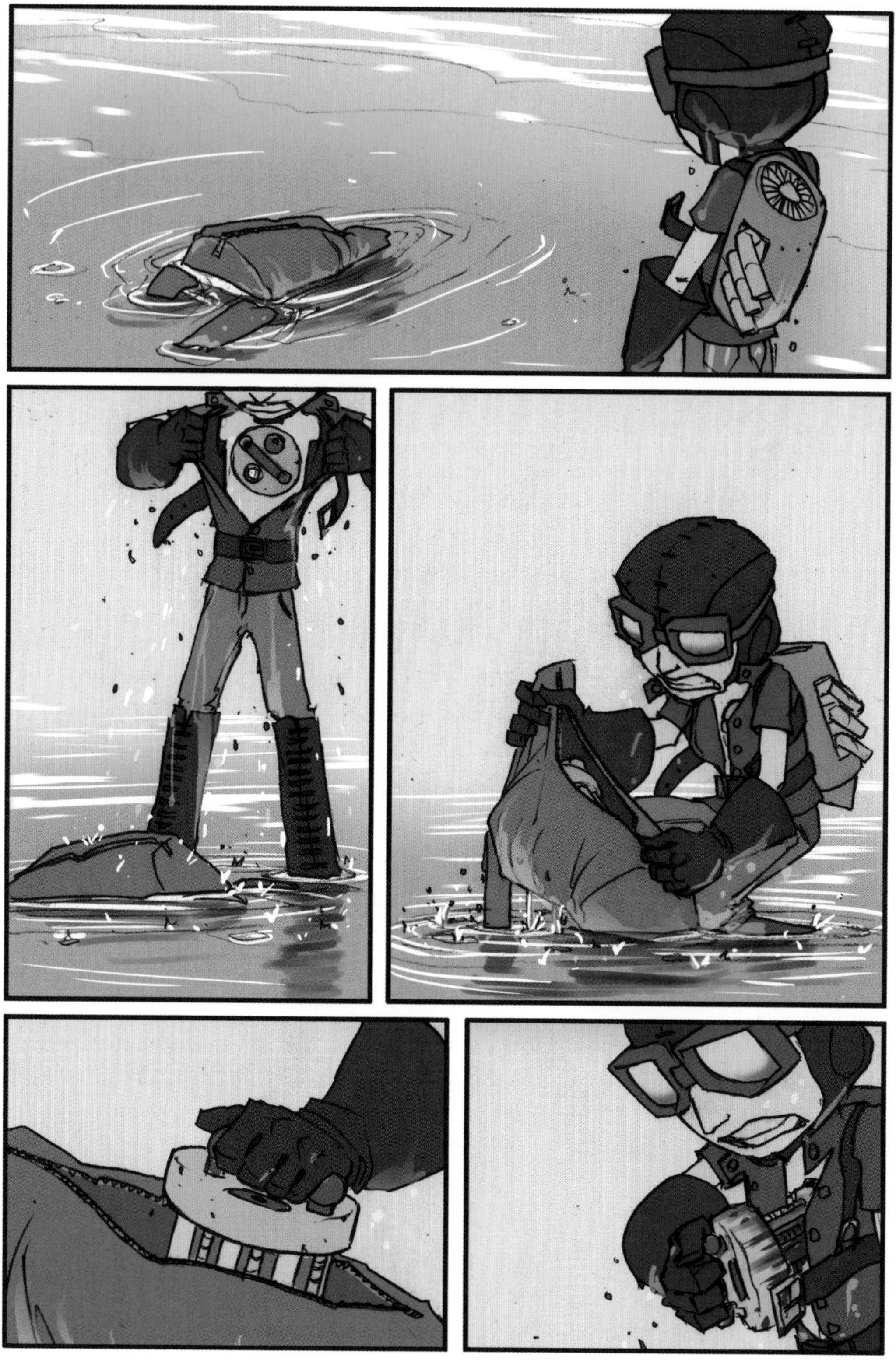

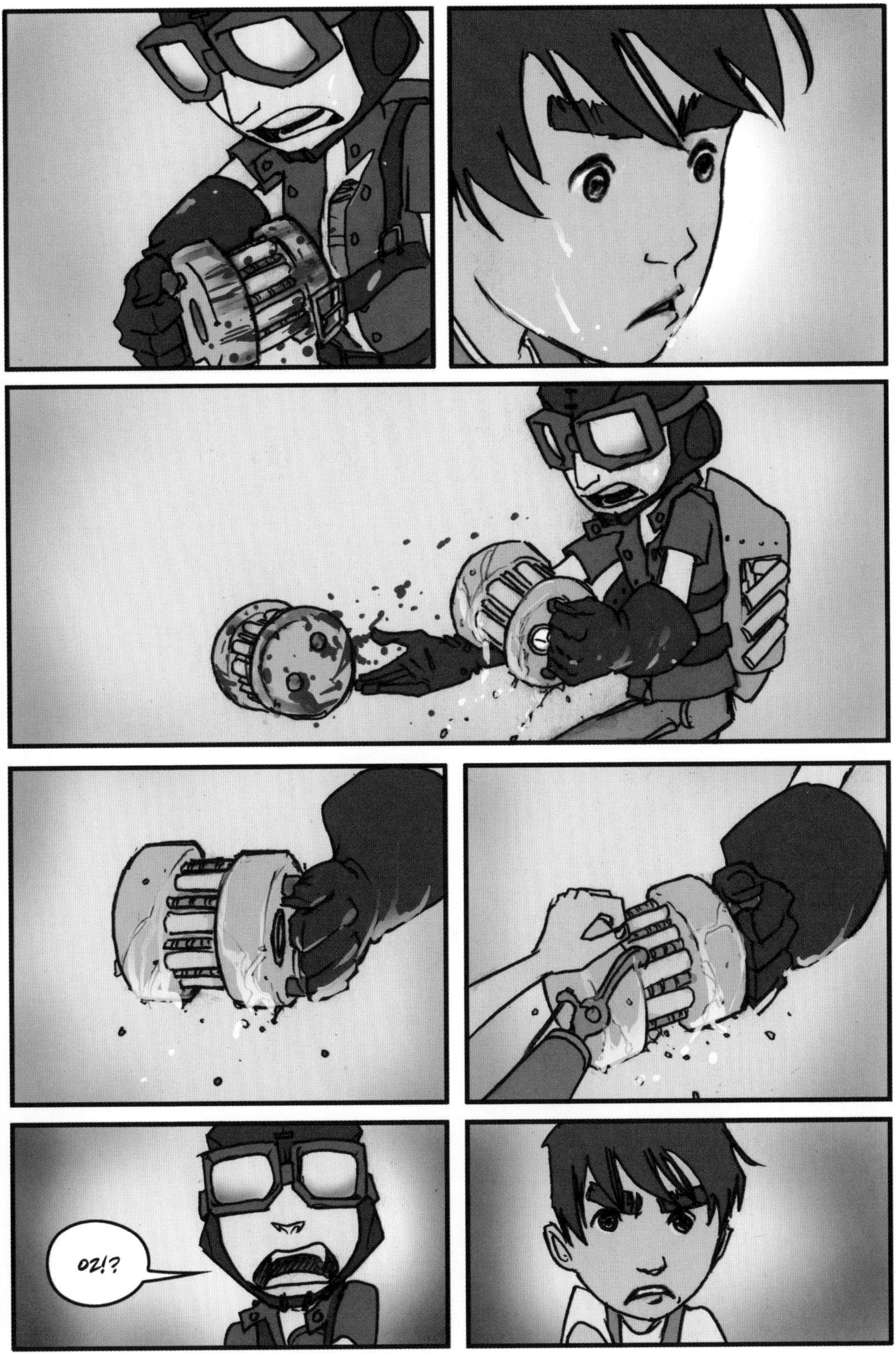
OZ!?

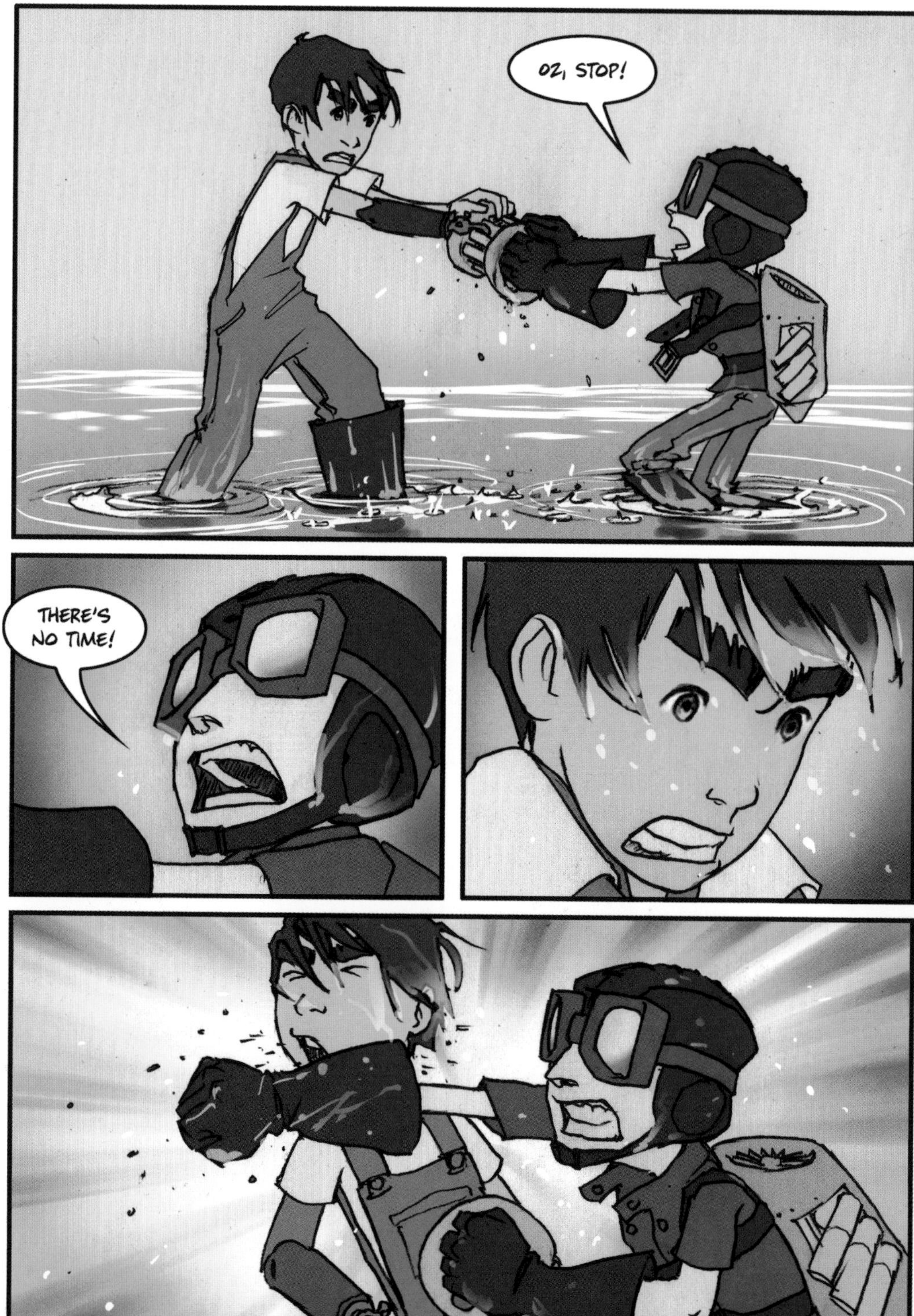
OZ, STOP!
THERE'S NO TIME!

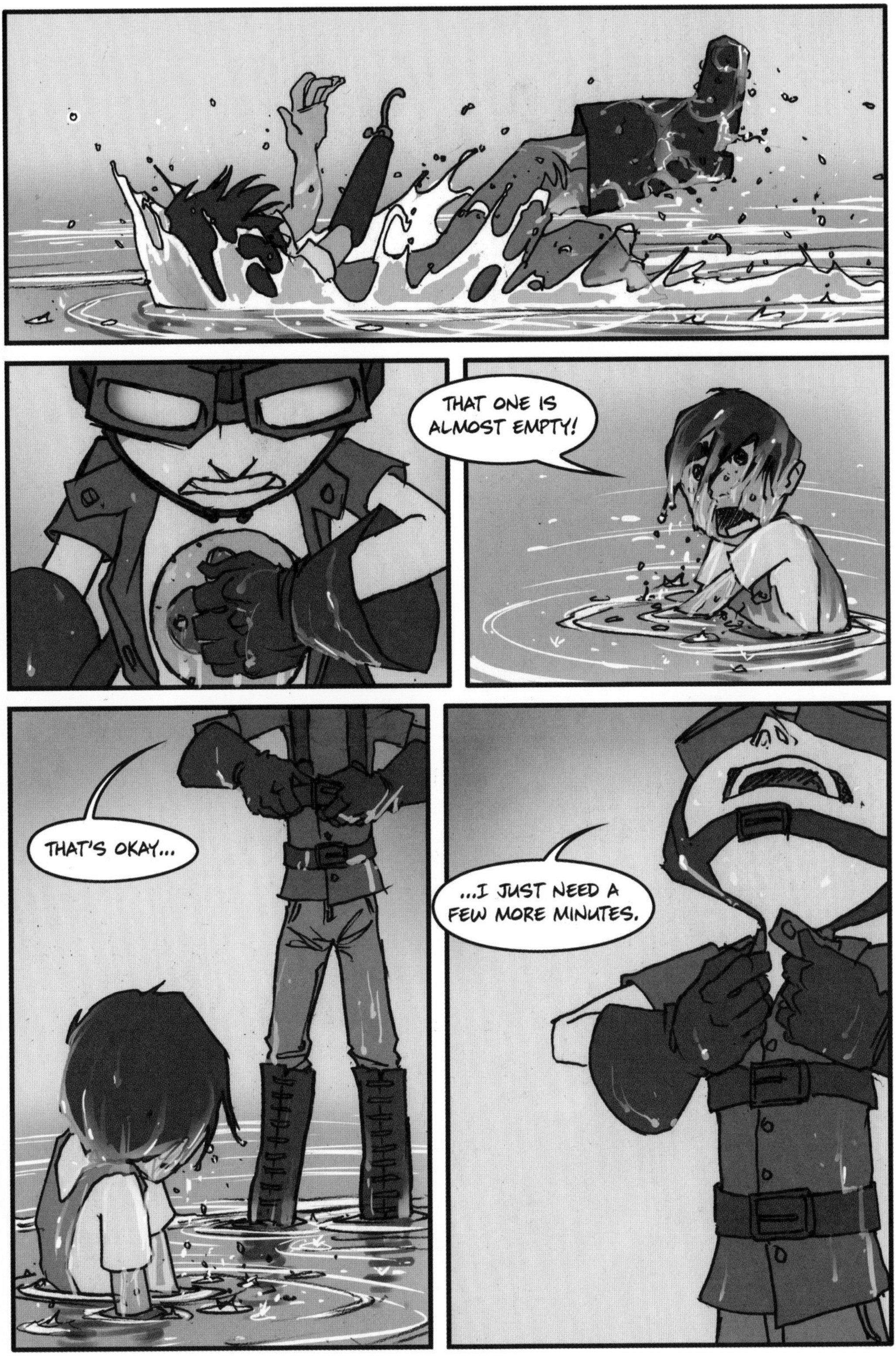
THAT ONE IS ALMOST EMPTY!
THAT'S OKAY...
...I JUST NEED A FEW MORE MINUTES.

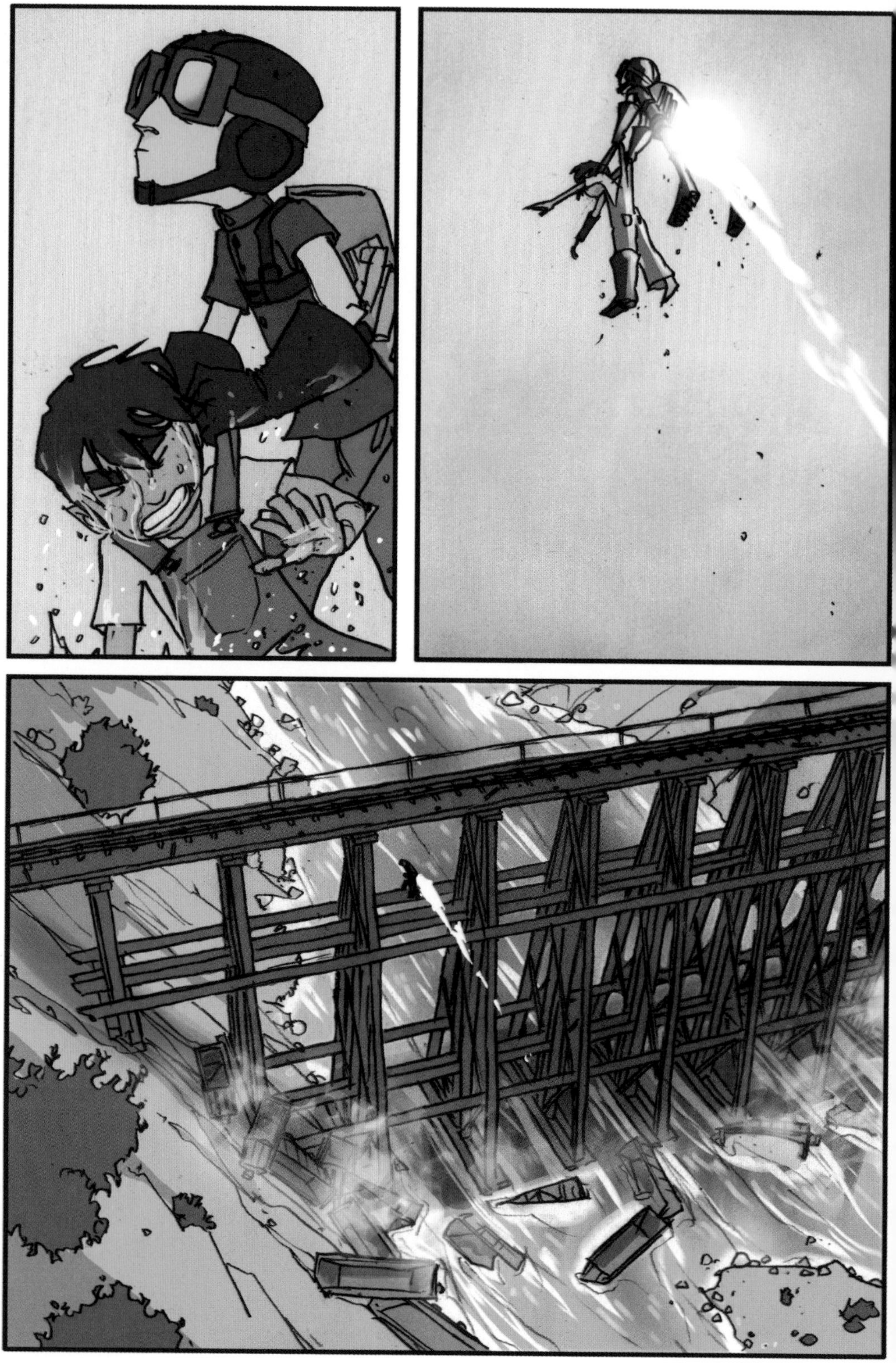

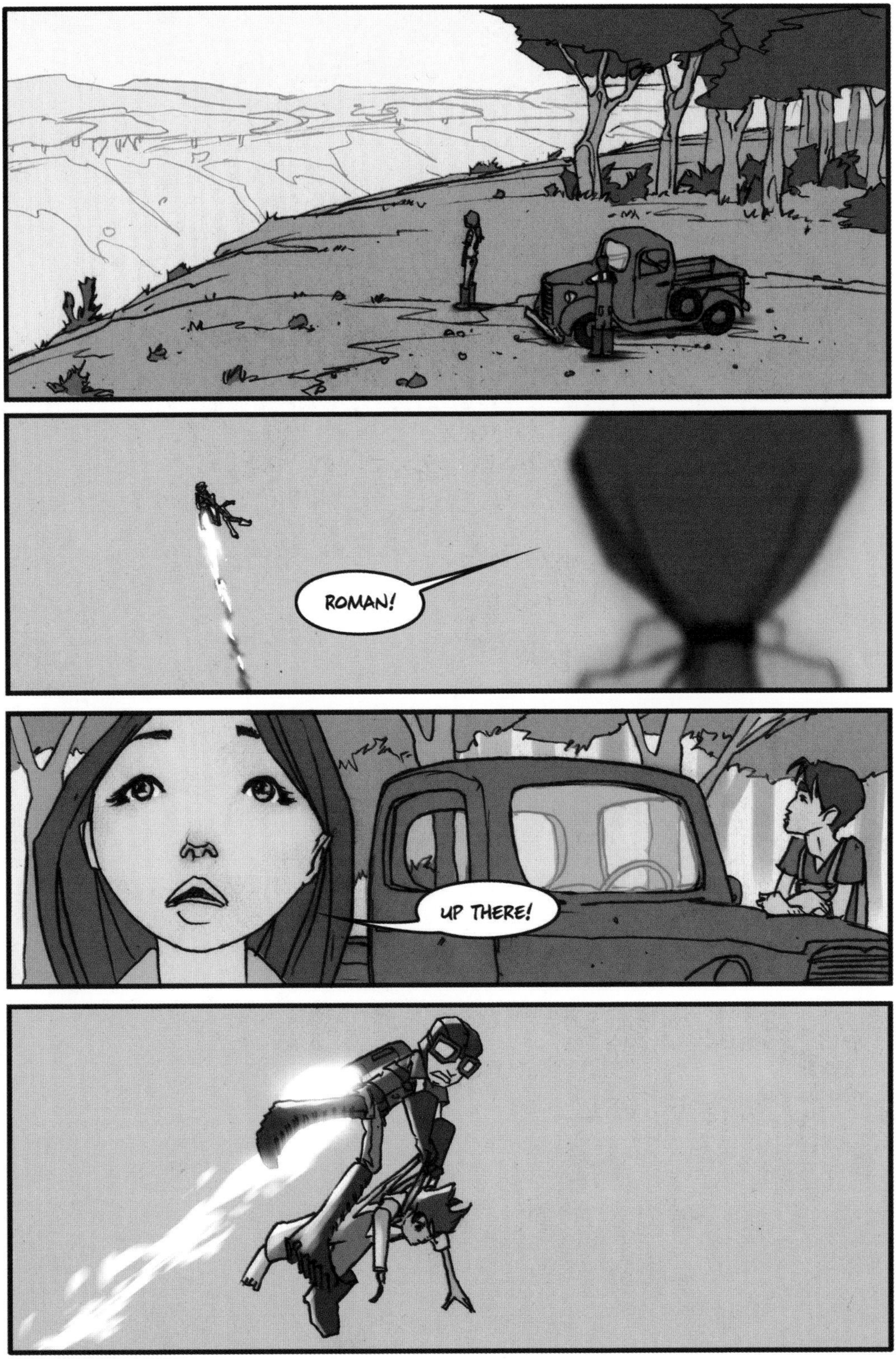
ROMAN!
UP THERE!

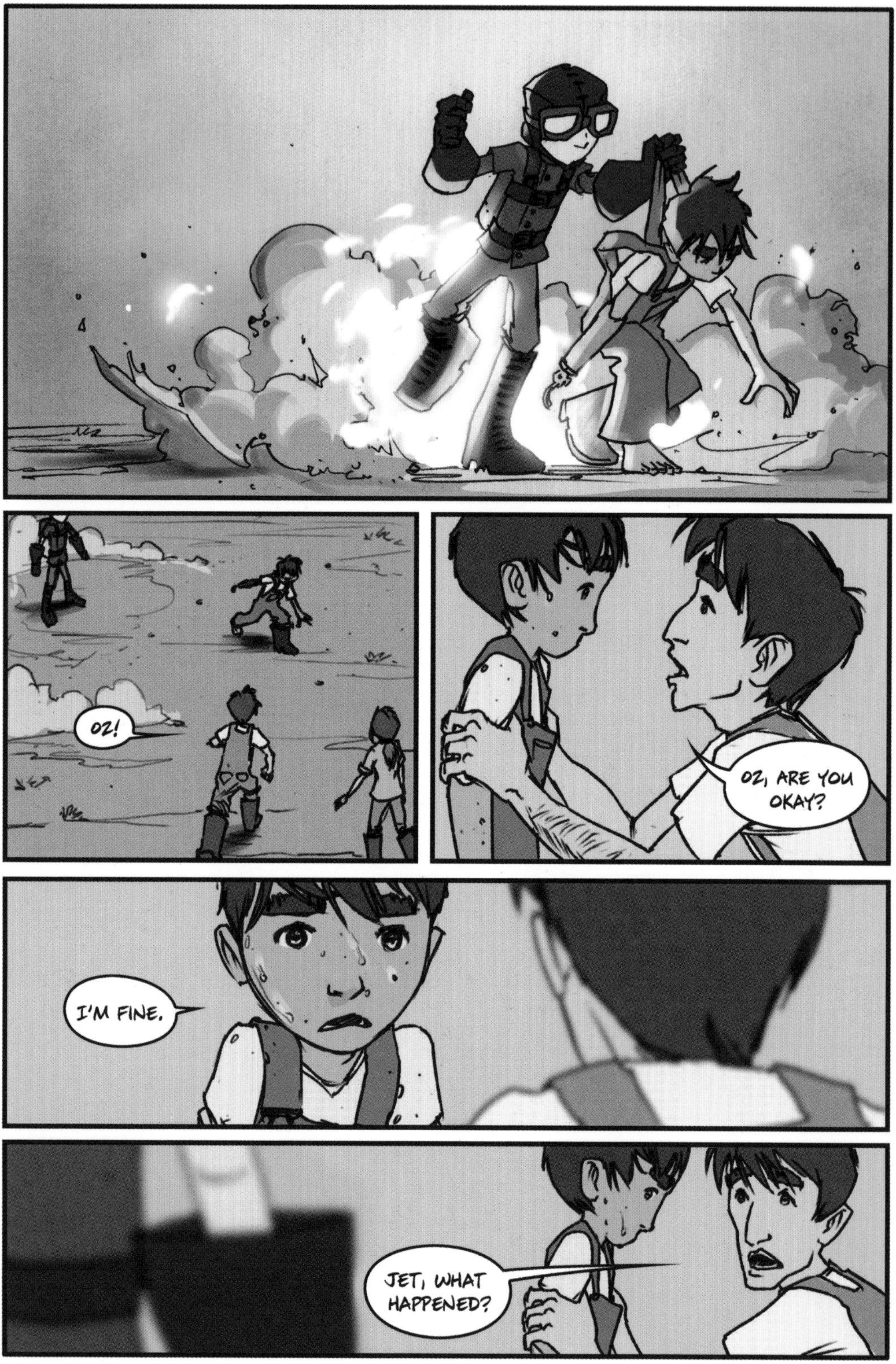
OZ!
OZ, ARE YOU OKAY?
I'M FINE.
JET, WHAT HAPPENED?

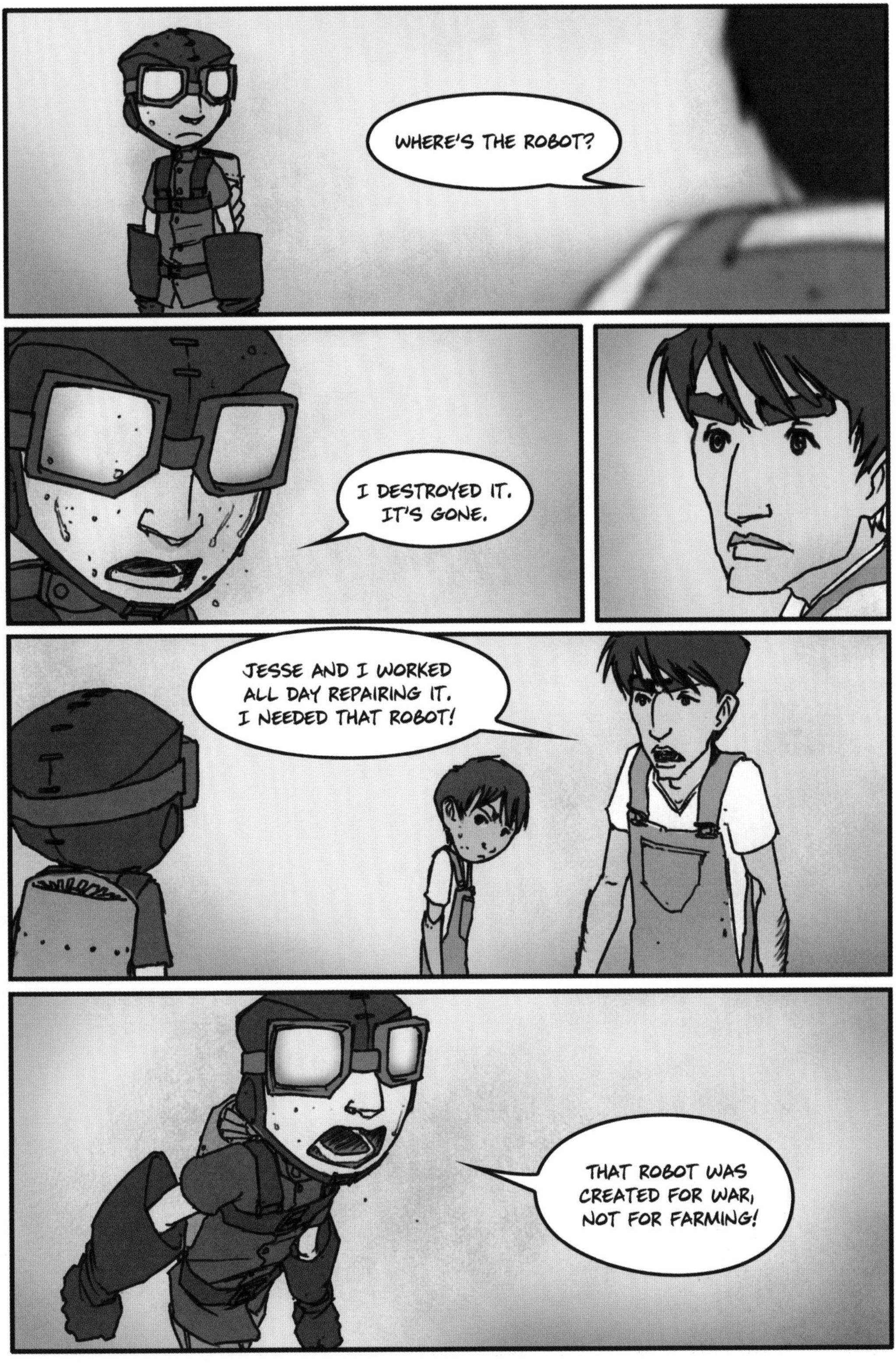
WHERE'S THE ROBOT?
I DESTROYED IT. IT'S GONE.
JESSE AND I WORKED ALL DAY REPAIRING IT. I NEEDED THAT ROBOT!
THAT ROBOT WAS CREATED FOR WAR, NOT FOR FARMING!

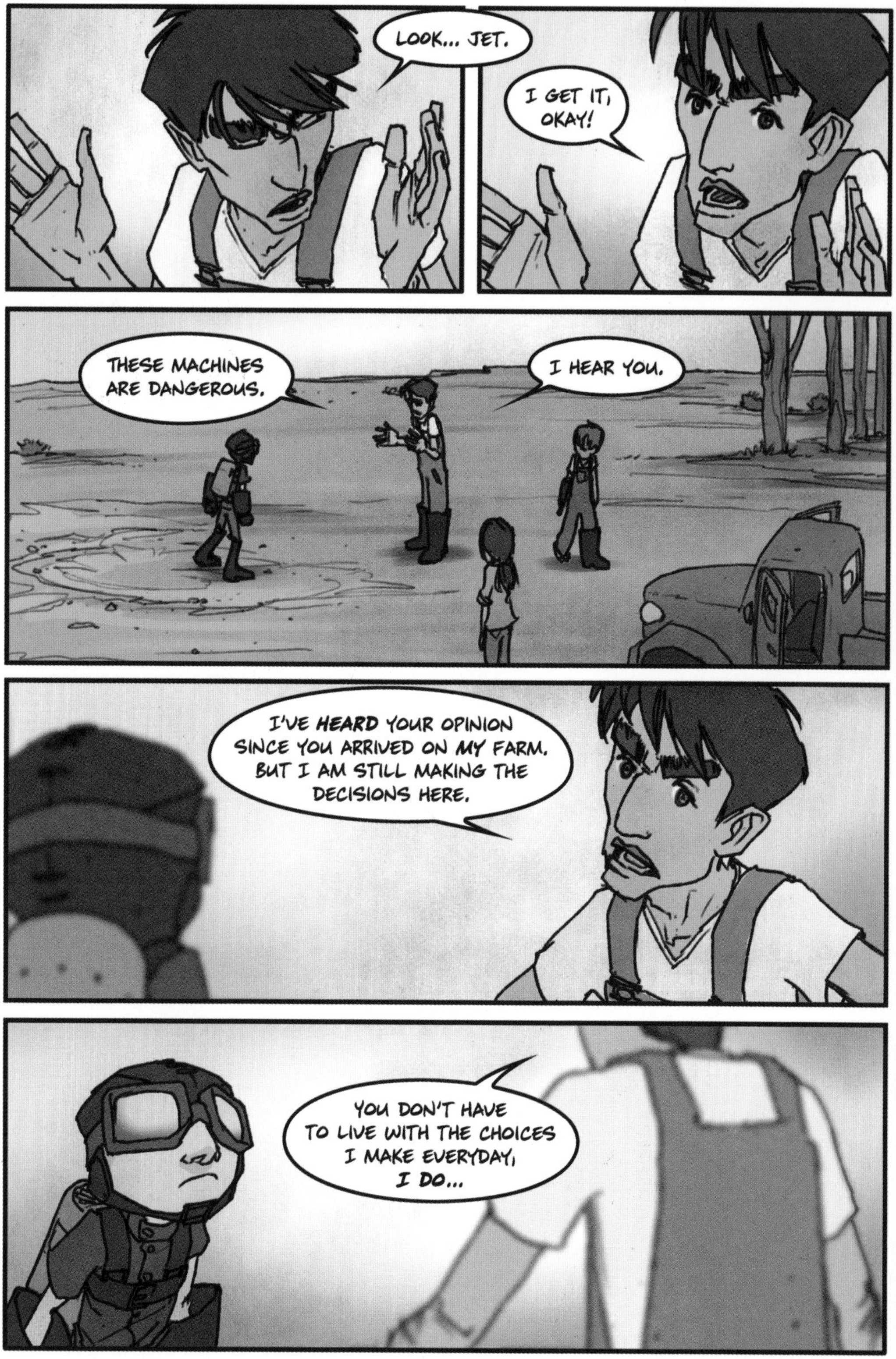
LOOK... JET.
I GET IT, OKAY!
THESE MACHINES ARE DANGEROUS.
I HEAR YOU.
I'VE HEARD YOUR OPINION SINCE YOU ARRIVED ON MY FARM. BUT I AM STILL MAKING THE DECISIONS HERE.
YOU DON'T HAVE TO LIVE WITH THE CHOICES I MAKE EVERYDAY, I DO...

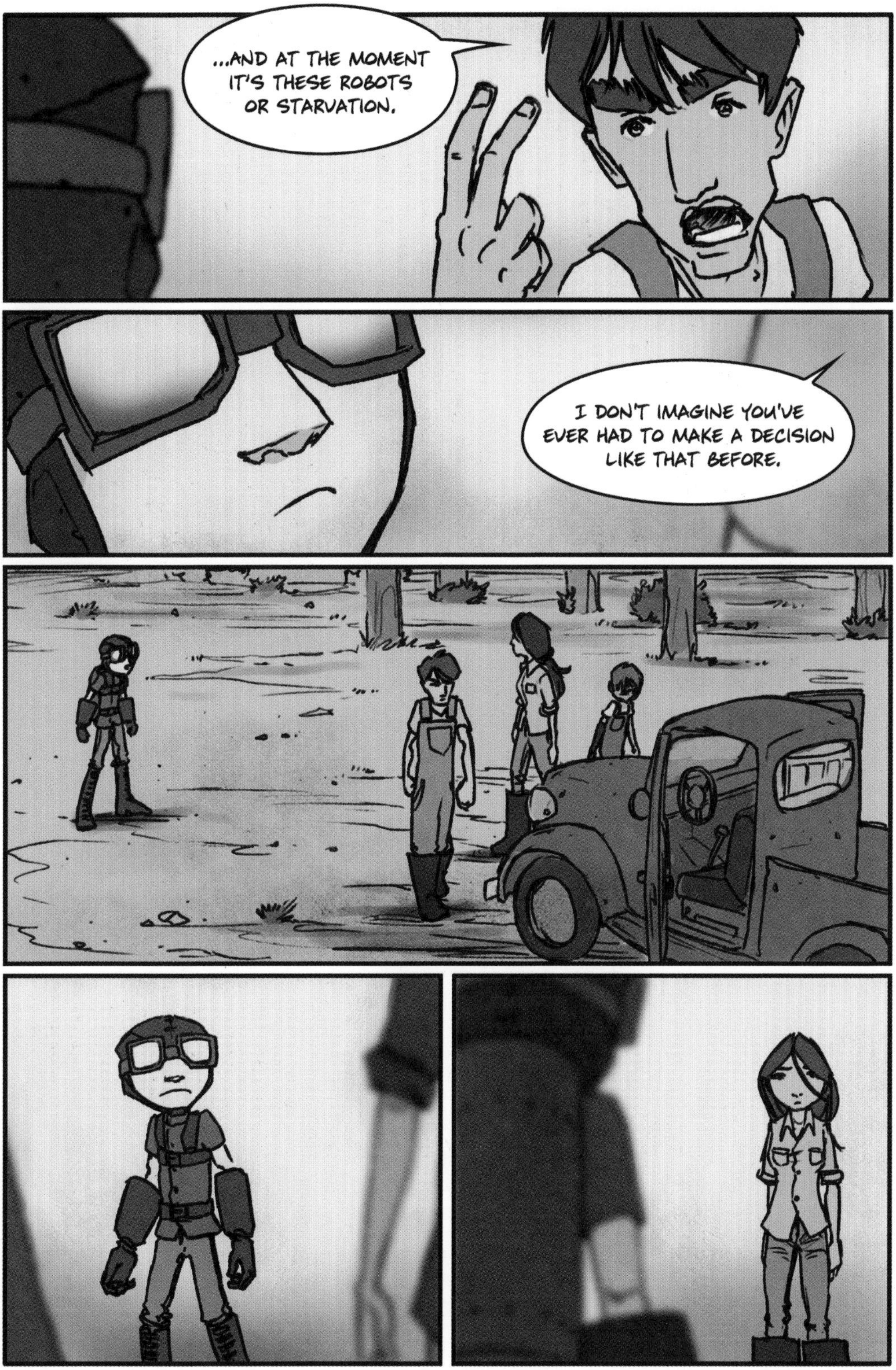
...AND AT THE MOMENT IT'S THESE ROBOTS OR STARVATION.
I DON'T IMAGINE YOU'VE EVER HAD TO MAKE A DECISION LIKE THAT BEFORE.

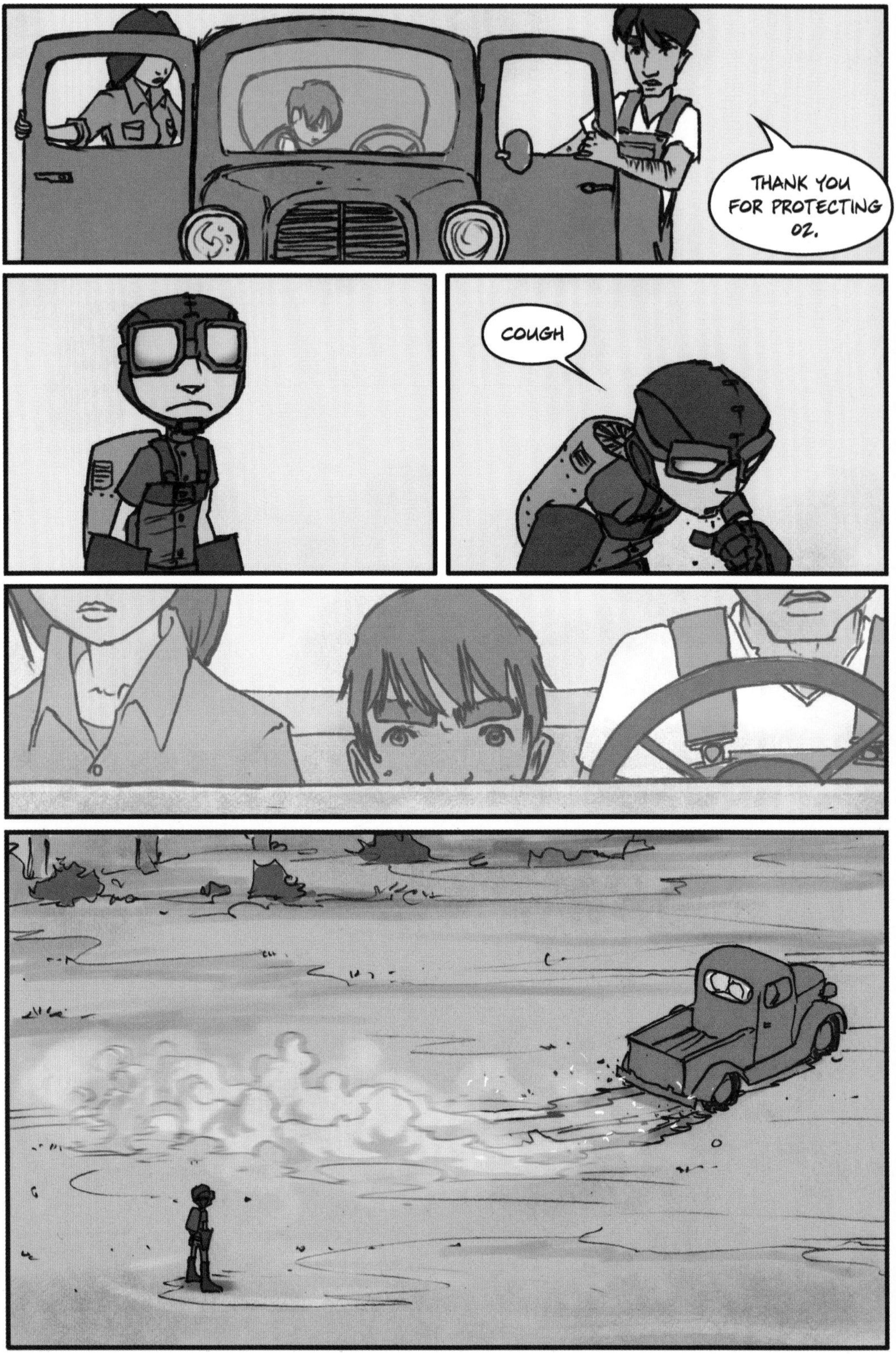
THANK YOU FOR PROTECTING OZ.
COUGH

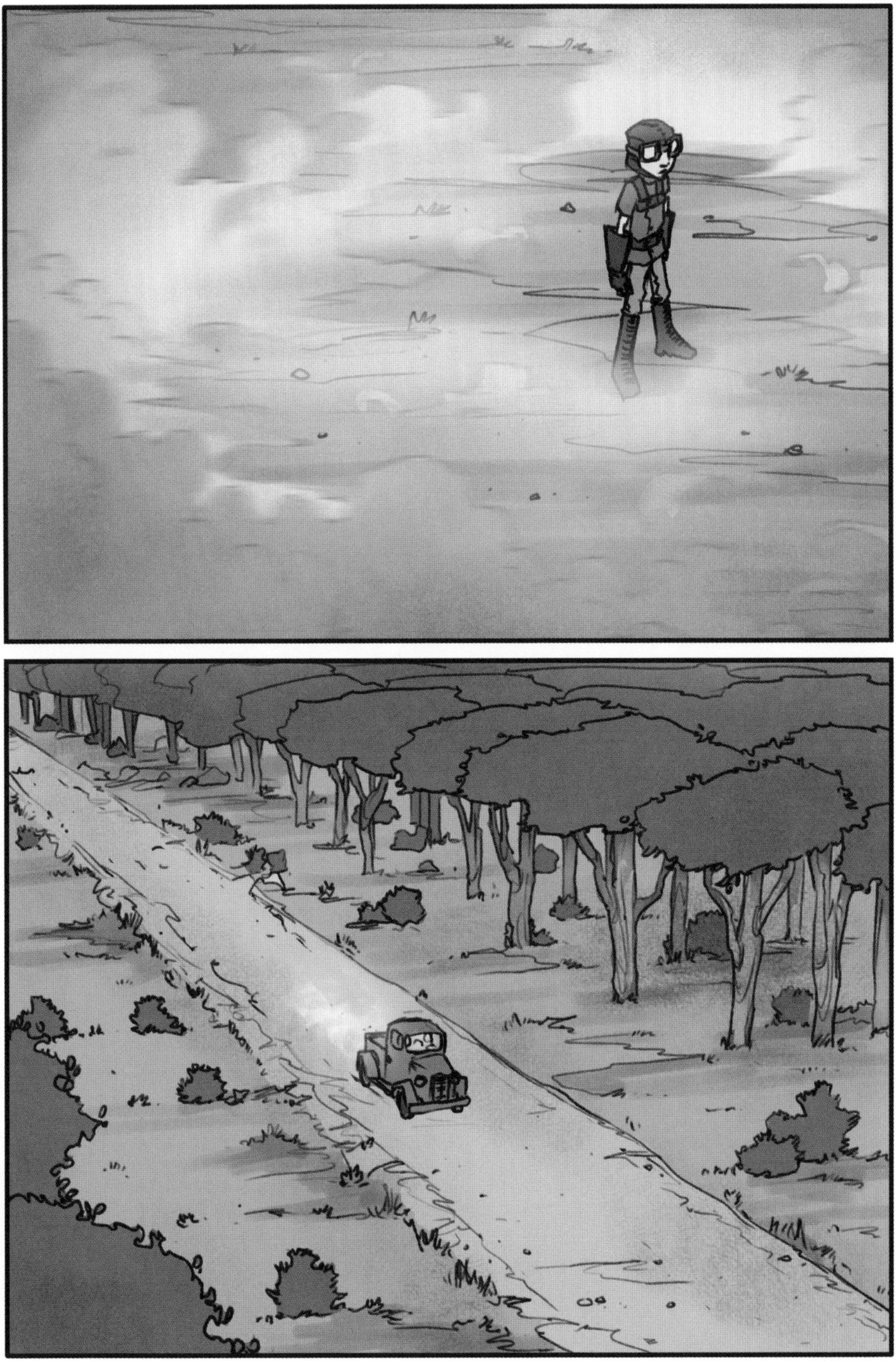

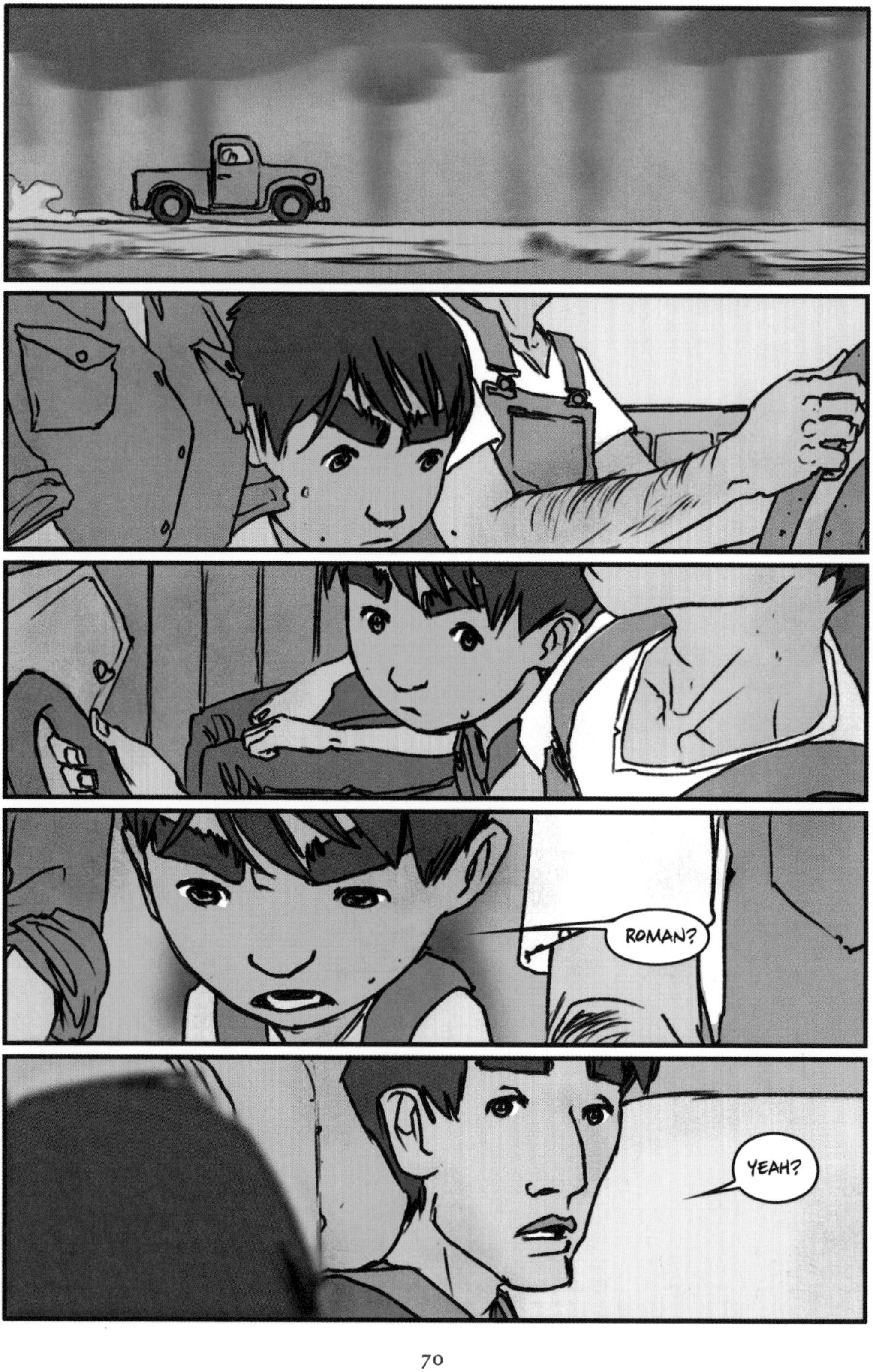
ROMAN?
YEAH?

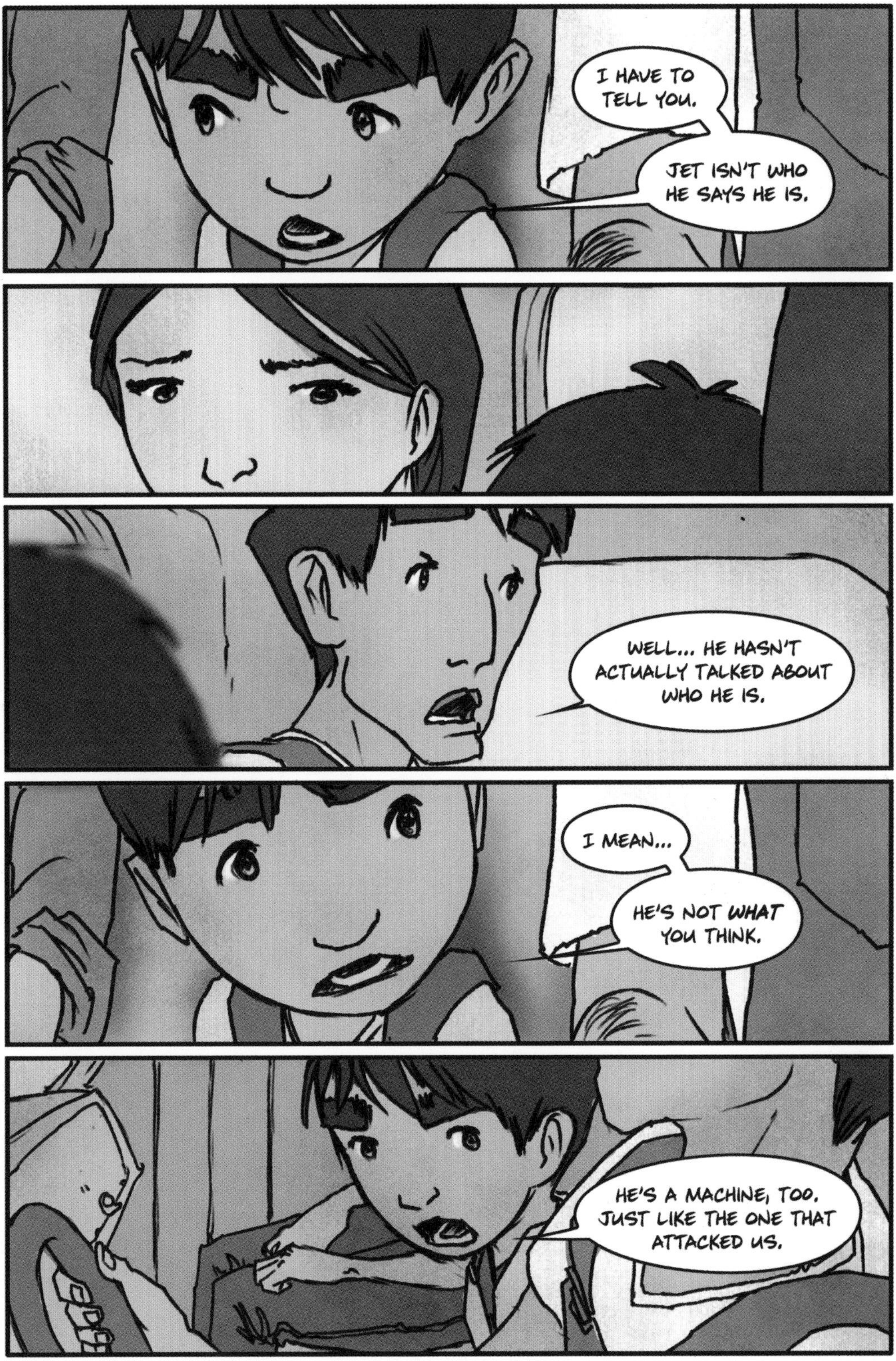
I HAVE TO TELL YOU.
JET ISN'T WHO HE SAYS HE IS.
WELL... HE HASN'T ACTUALLY TALKED ABOUT WHO HE IS.
I MEAN...
HE'S NOT WHAT YOU THINK.
HE'S A MACHINE, TOO. JUST LIKE THE ONE THAT ATTACKED US.

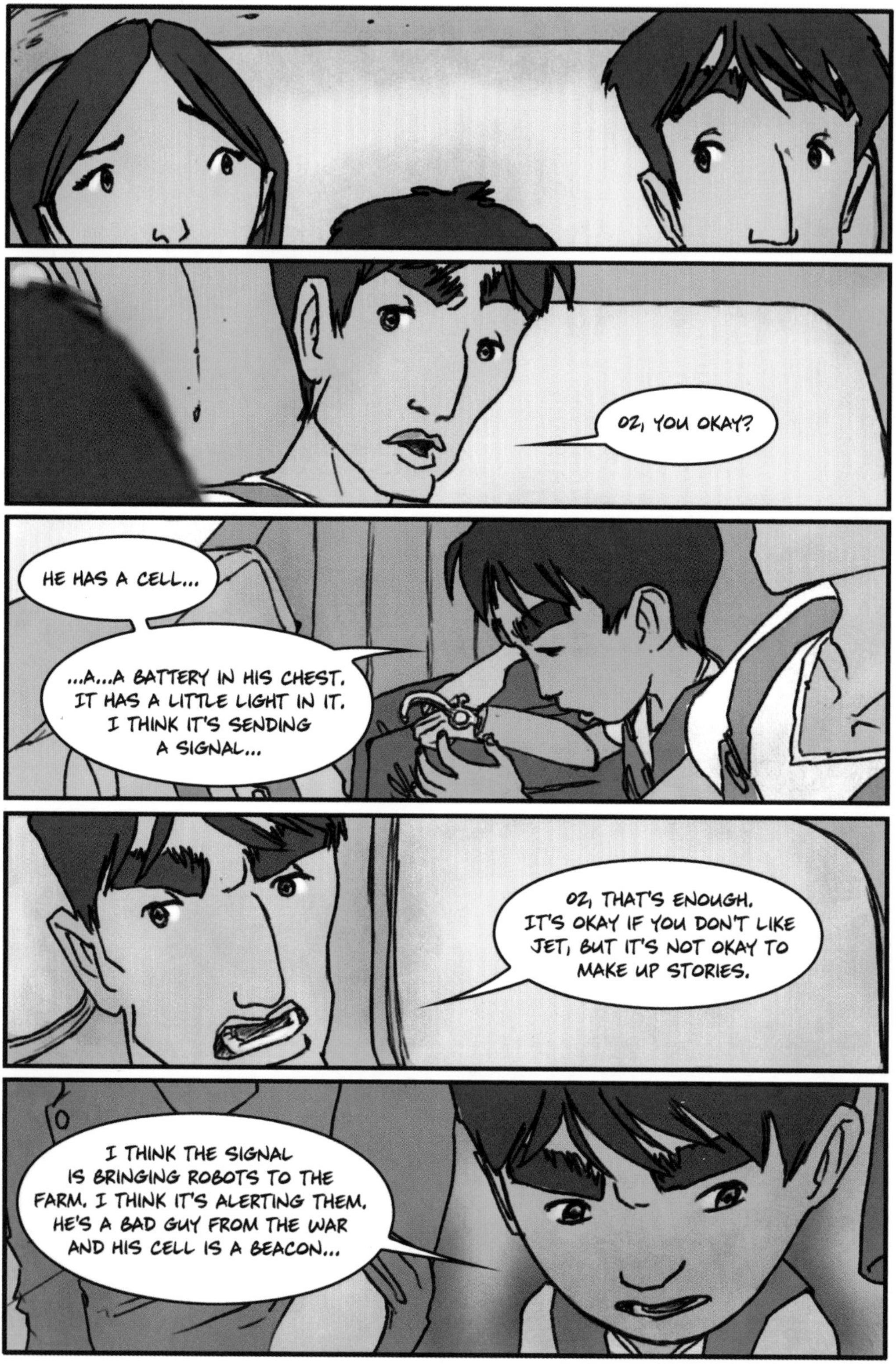
OZ, YOU OKAY?
HE HAS A CELL...
...A...A BATTERY IN HIS CHEST. IT HAS A LITTLE LIGHT IN IT. I THINK IT'S SENDING A SIGNAL...
OZ, THAT'S ENOUGH. IT'S OKAY IF YOU DON'T LIKE JET, BUT IT'S NOT OKAY TO MAKE UP STORIES.
I THINK THE SIGNAL IS BRINGING ROBOTS TO THE FARM. I THINK IT'S ALERTING THEM. HE'S A BAD GUY FROM THE WAR AND HIS CELL IS A BEACON...

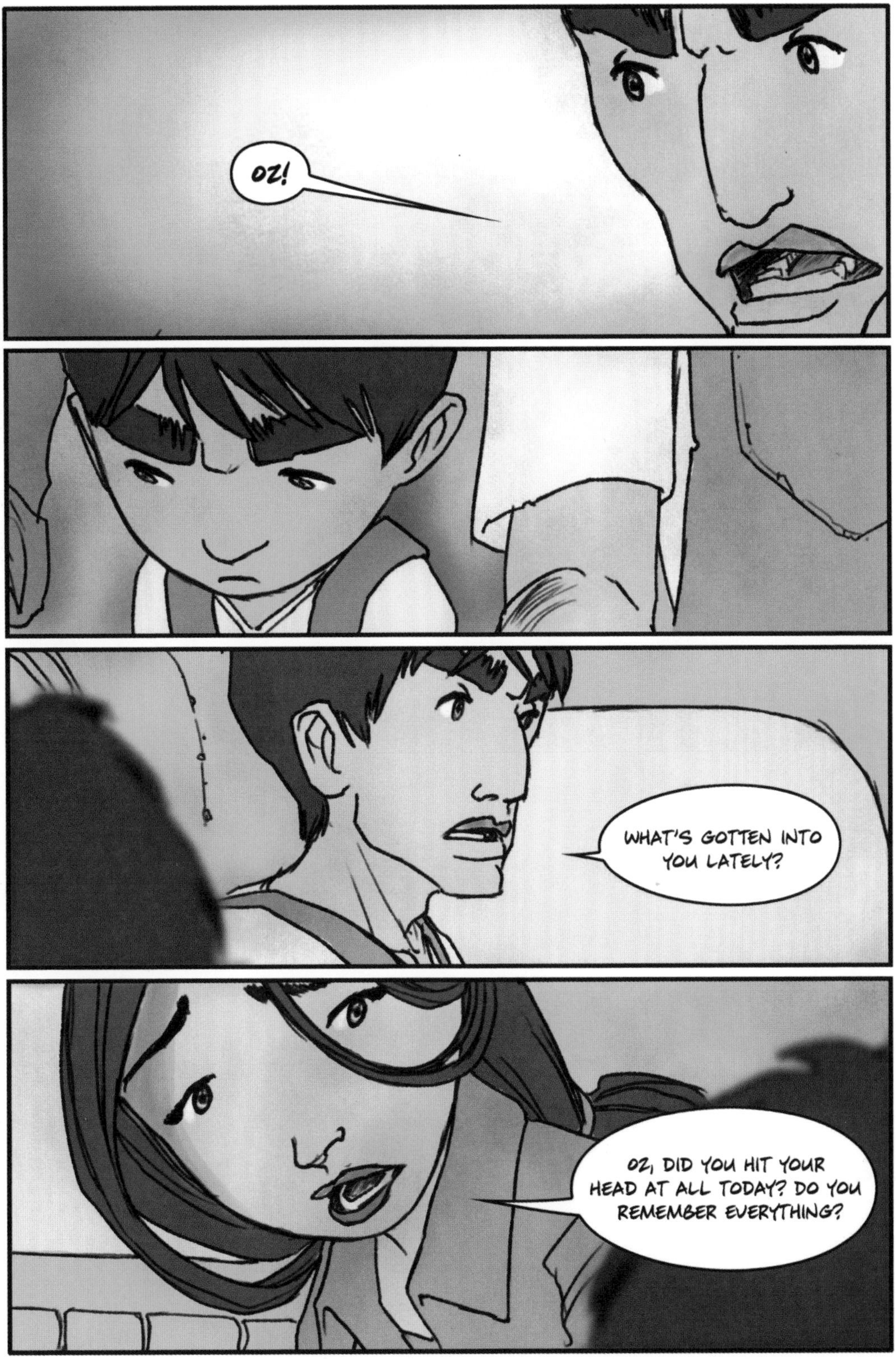
OZ!
WHAT'S GOTTEN INTO YOU LATELY?
OZ, DID YOU HIT YOUR HEAD AT ALL TODAY? DO YOU REMEMBER EVERYTHING?

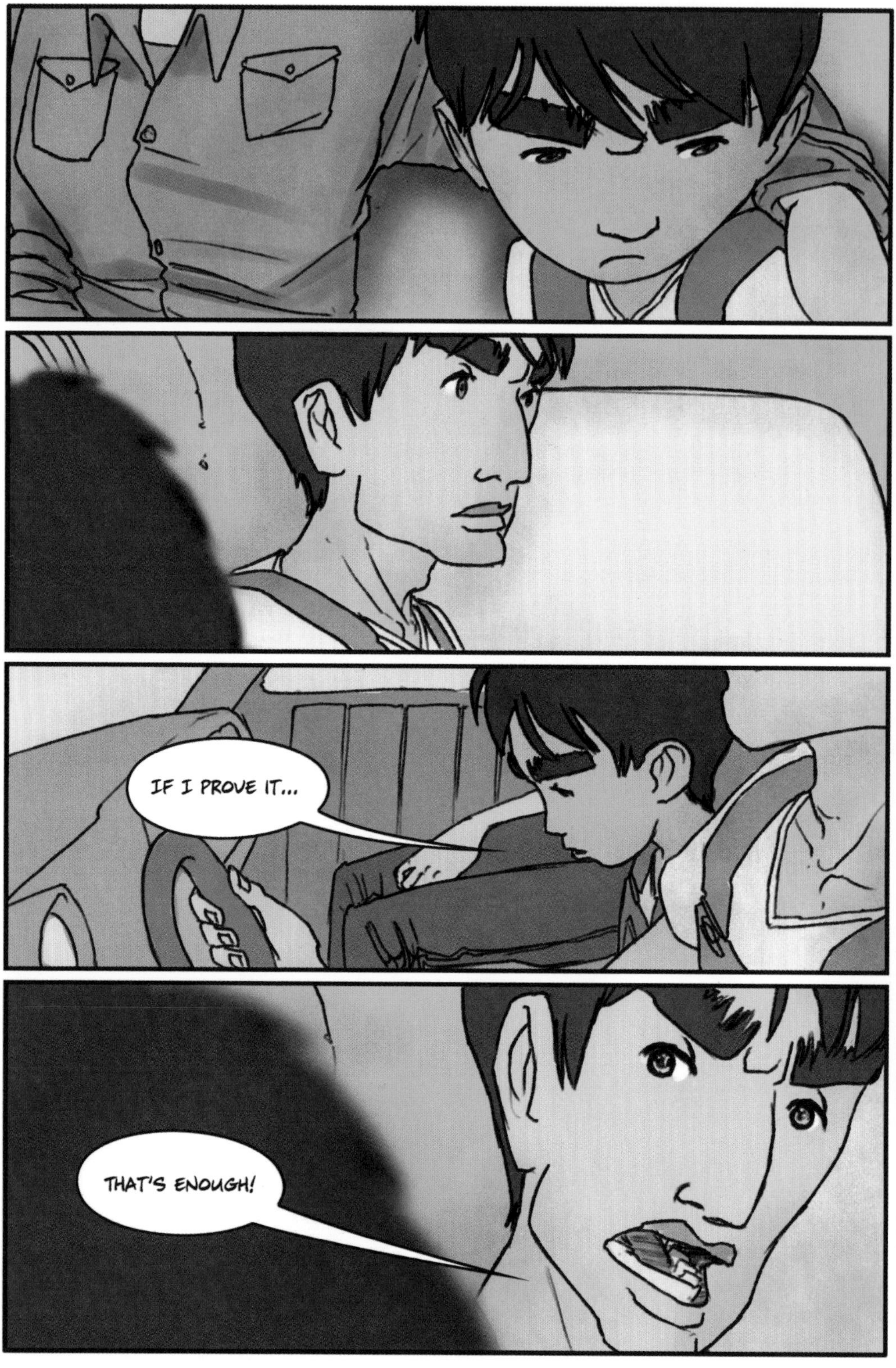
IF I PROVE IT...
THAT'S ENOUGH!

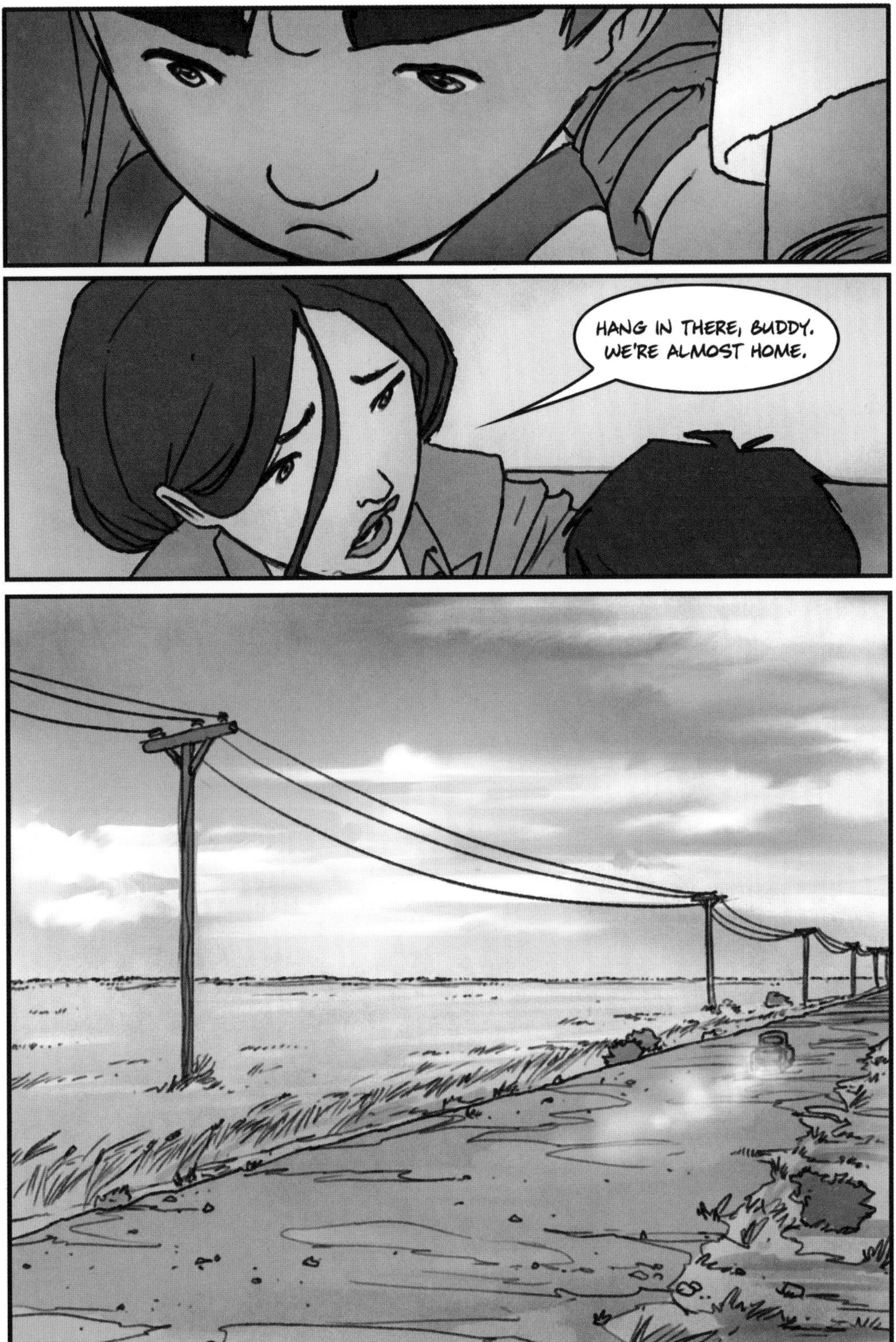
HANG IN THERE, BUDDY. WE'RE ALMOST HOME.

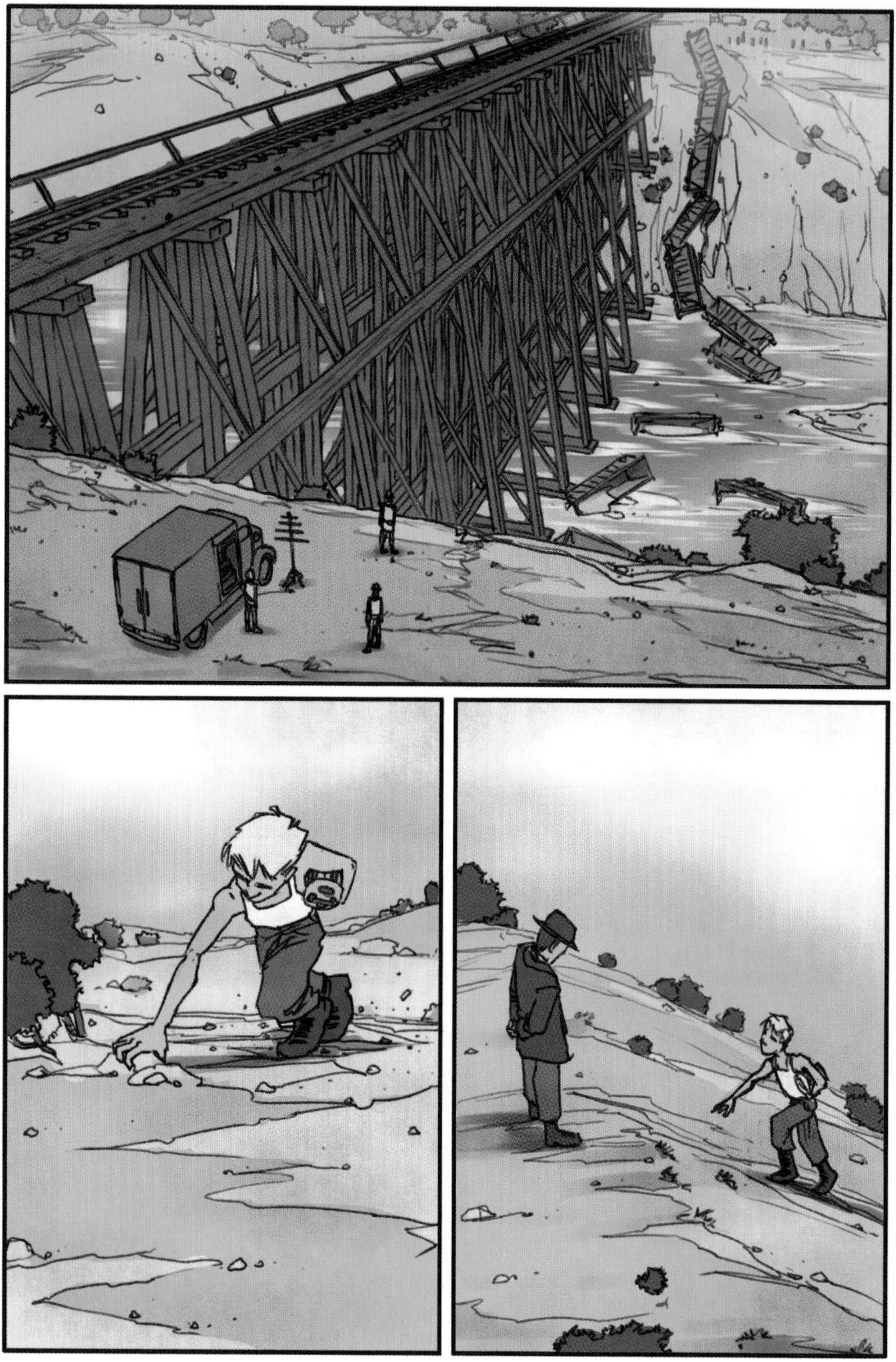

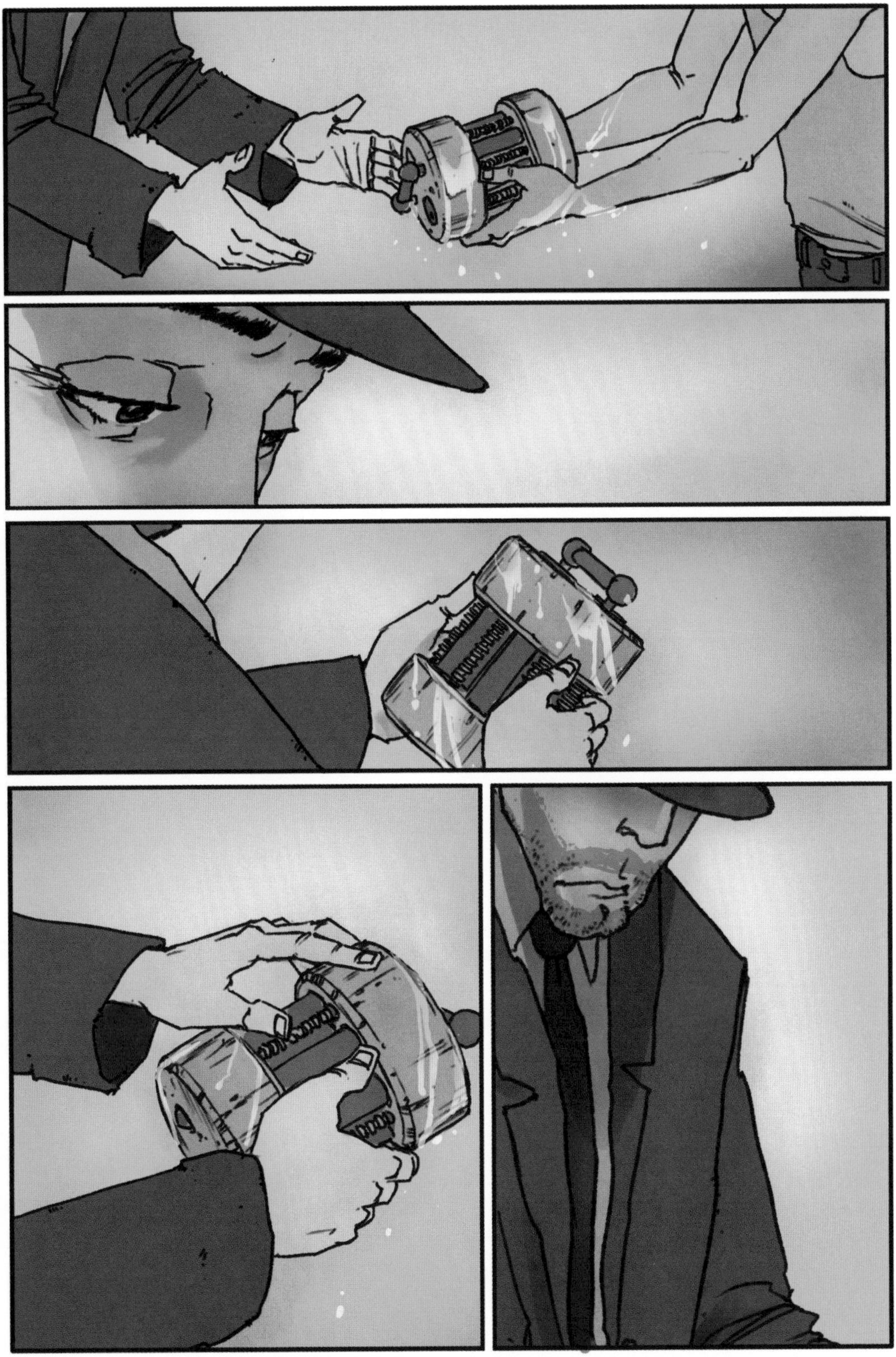

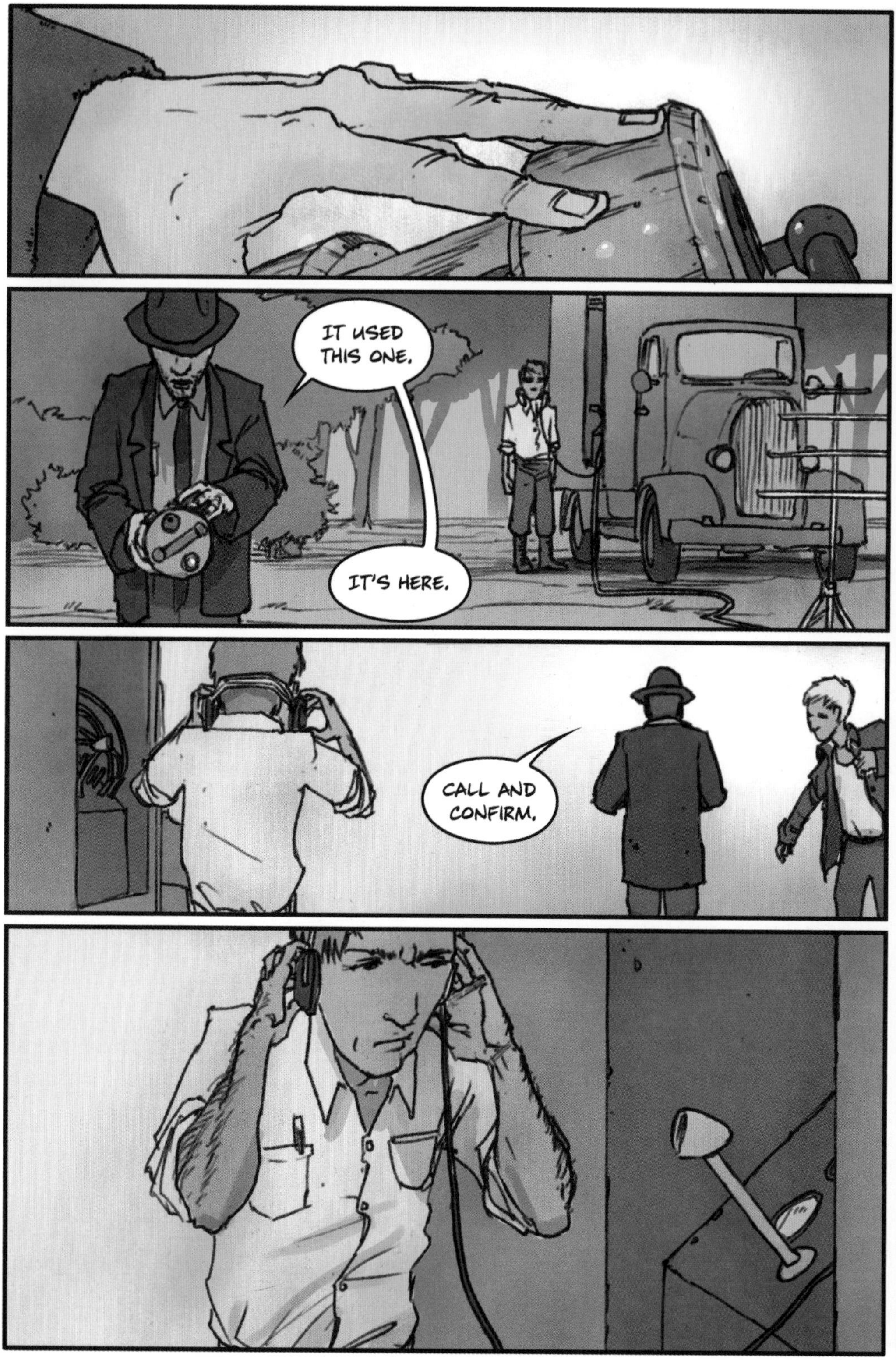
IT USED THIS ONE.
IT'S HERE.
CALL AND CONFIRM.

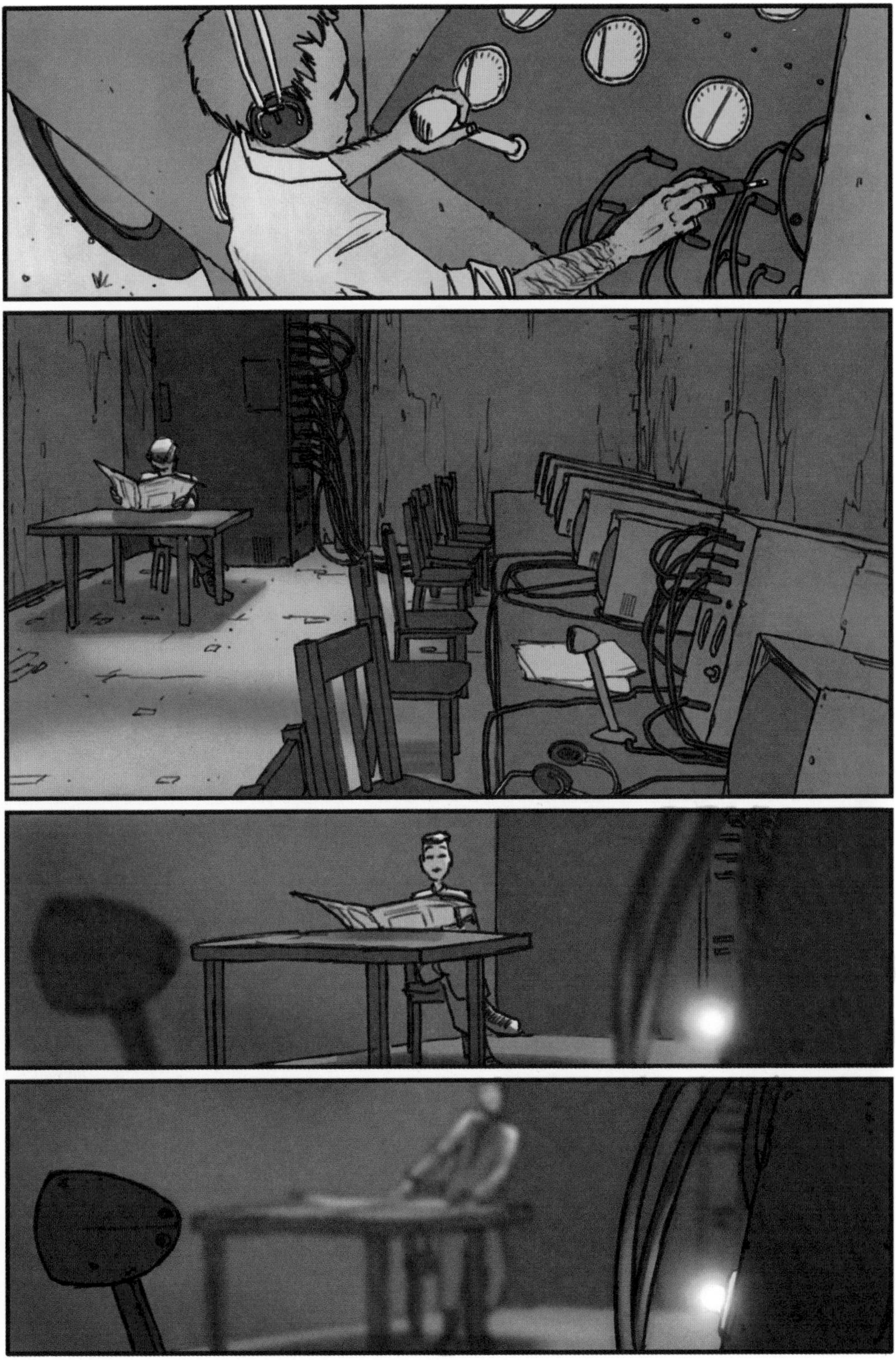

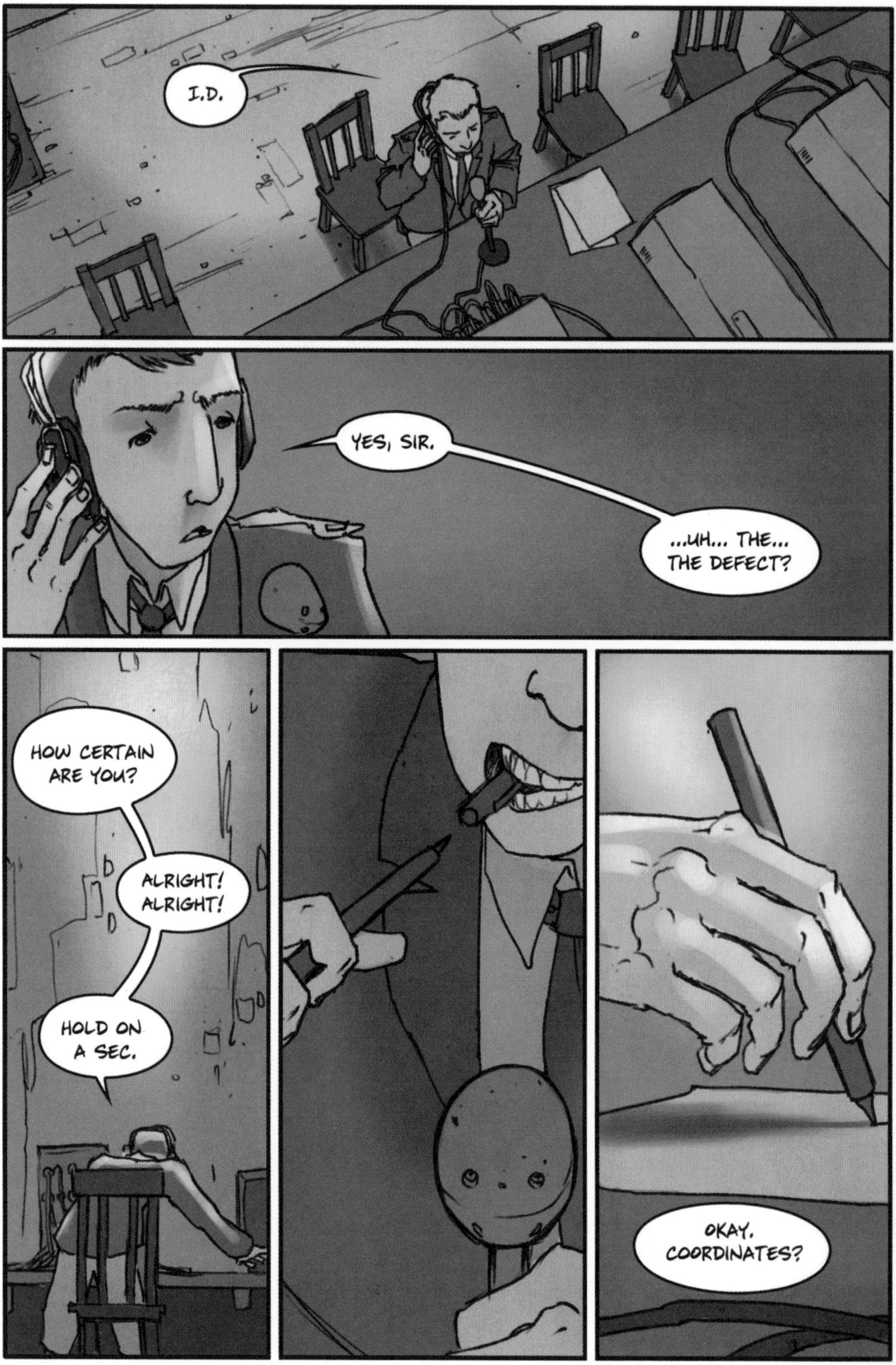
I.D.
YES, SIR.
...UH... THE... THE DEFECT?
HOW CERTAIN ARE YOU?
ALRIGHT! ALRIGHT!
HOLD ON A SEC.
OKAY. COORDINATES?

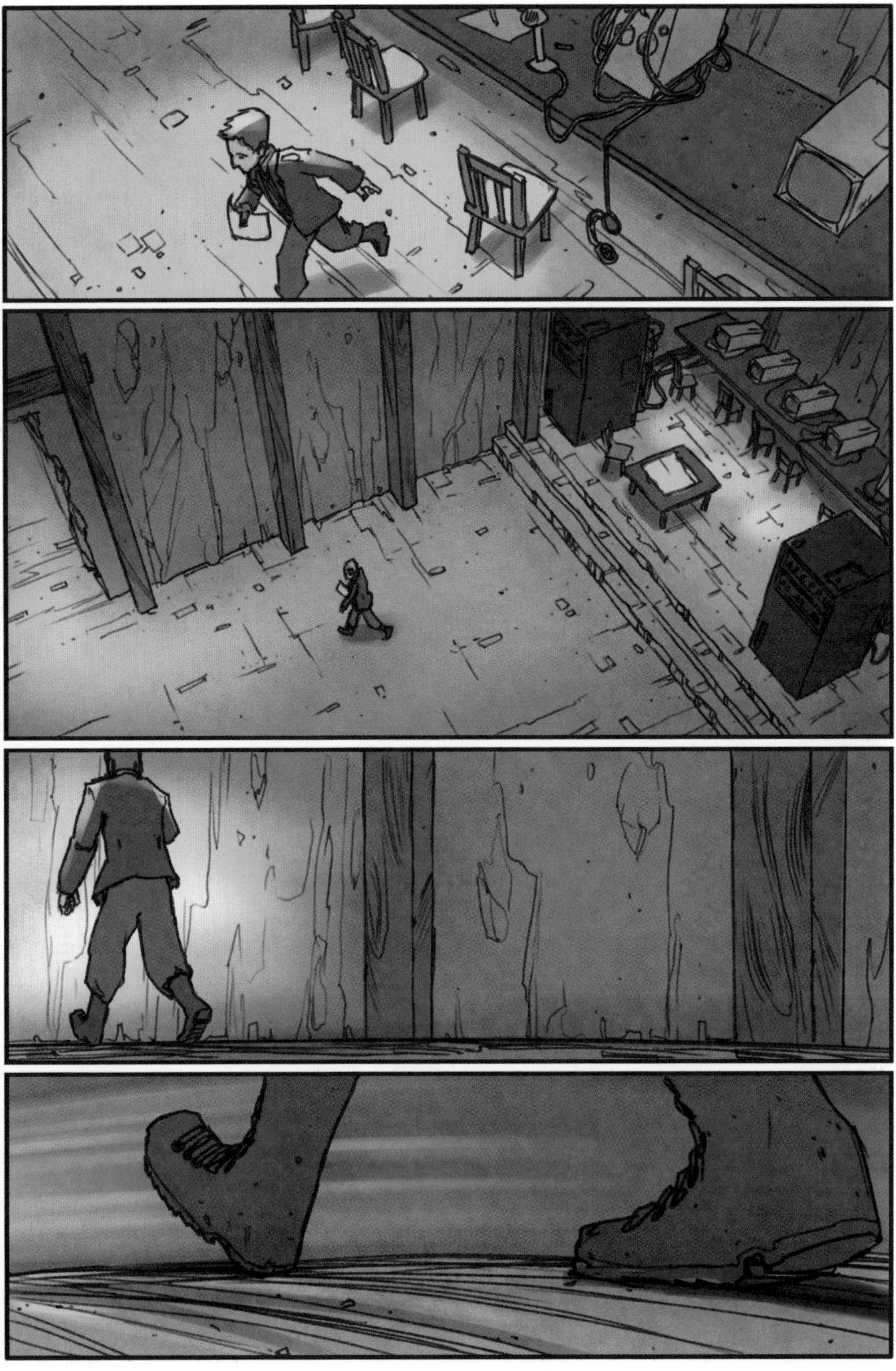

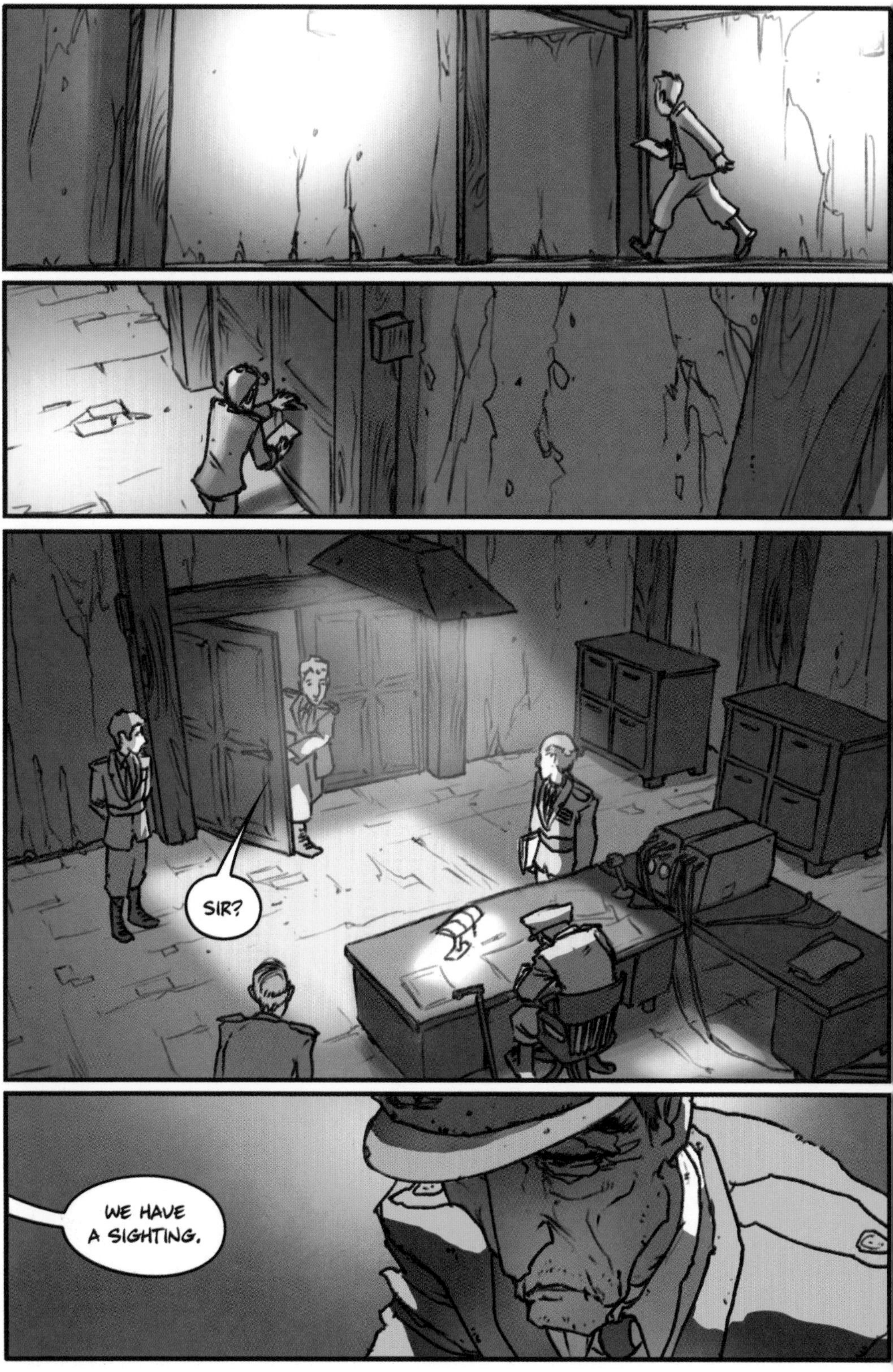
SIR?
WE HAVE A SIGHTING.

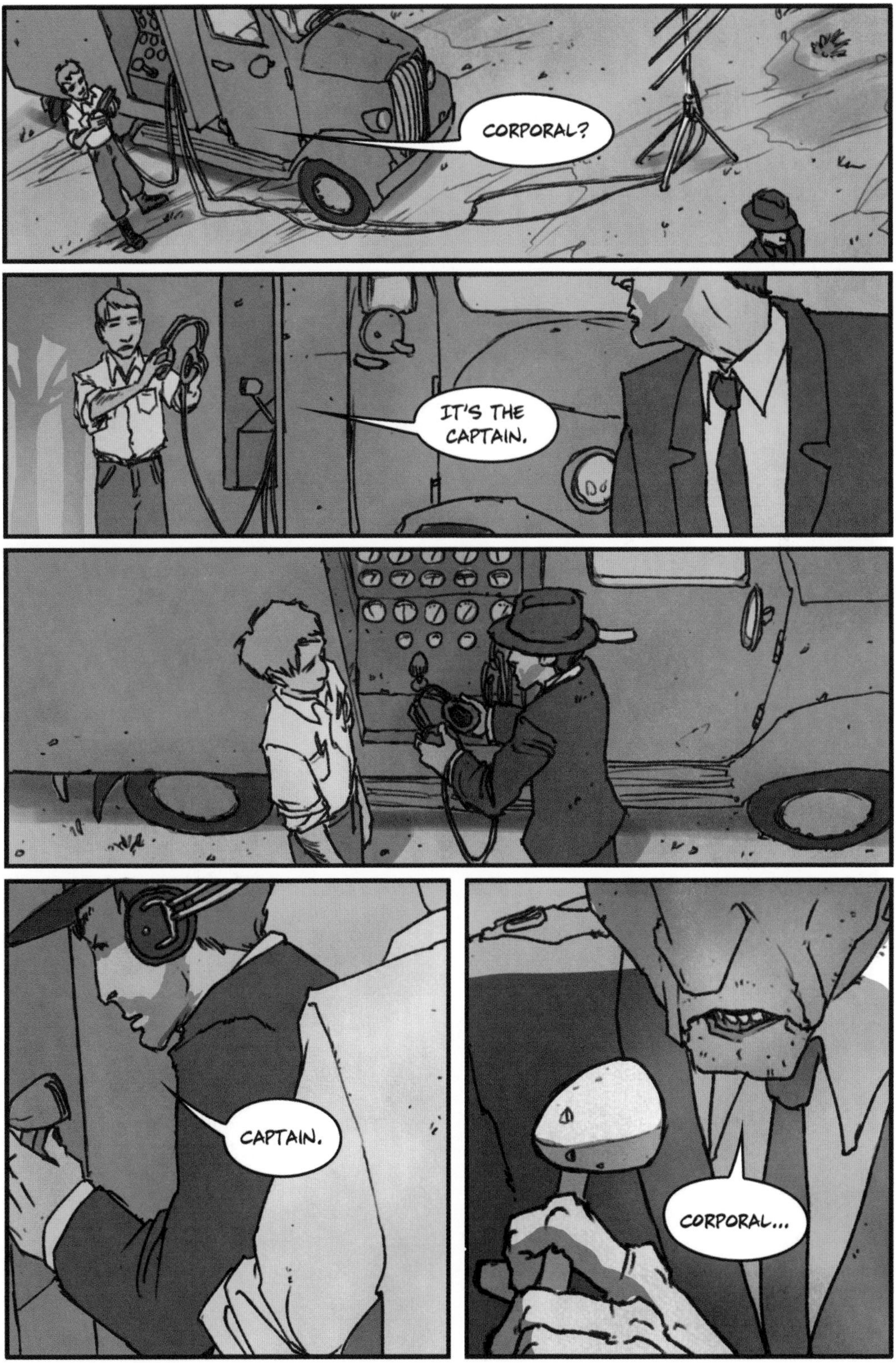
CORPORAL?
IT'S THE CAPTAIN.
CAPTAIN.
CORPORAL...

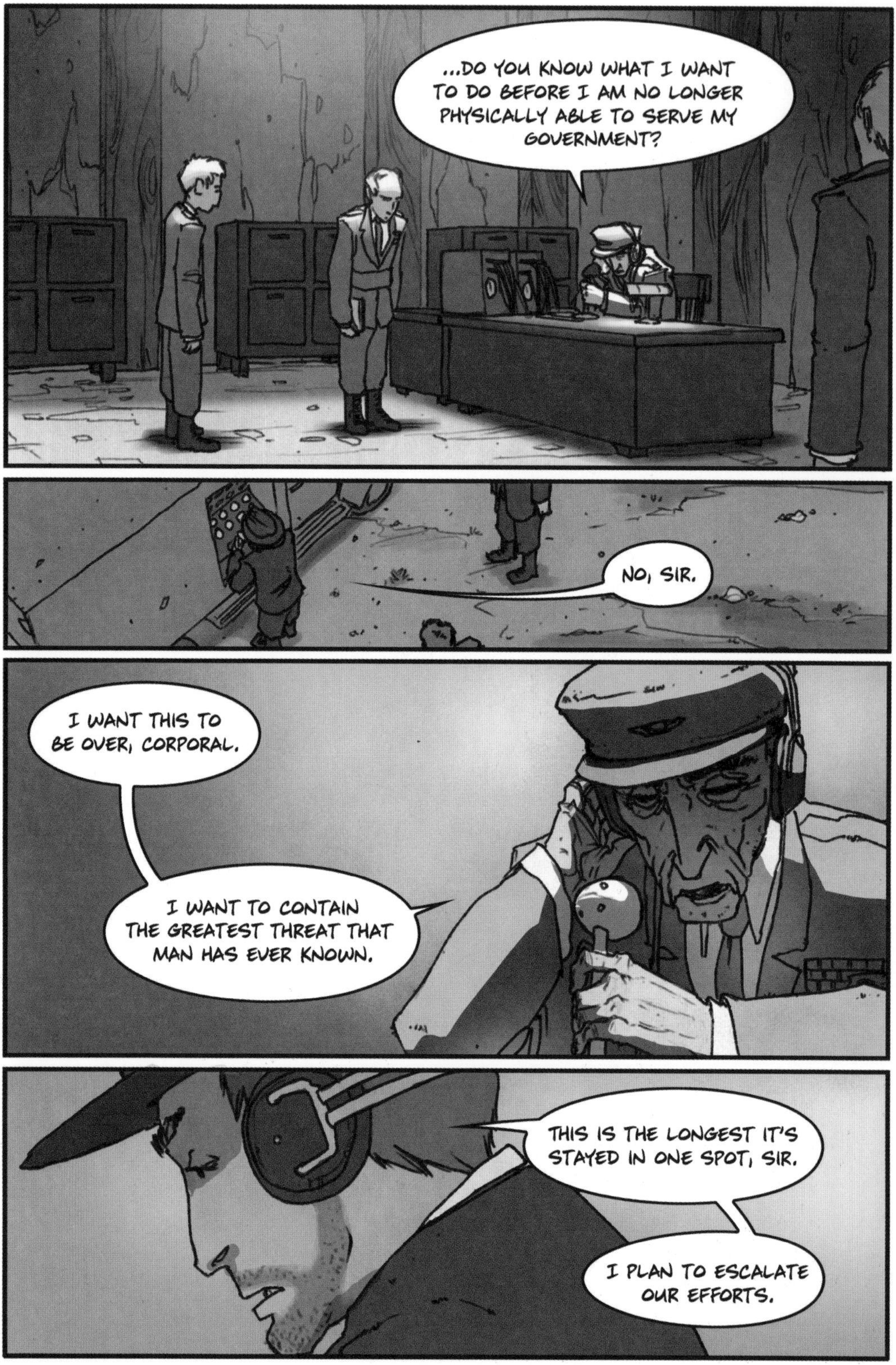
...DO YOU KNOW WHAT I WANT TO DO BEFORE I AM NO LONGER PHYSICALLY ABLE TO SERVE MY GOVERNMENT?
NO, SIR.
I WANT THIS TO BE OVER, CORPORAL.
I WANT TO CONTAIN THE GREATEST THREAT THAT MAN HAS EVER KNOWN.
THIS IS THE LONGEST IT'S STAYED IN ONE SPOT, SIR.
I PLAN TO ESCALATE OUR EFFORTS.

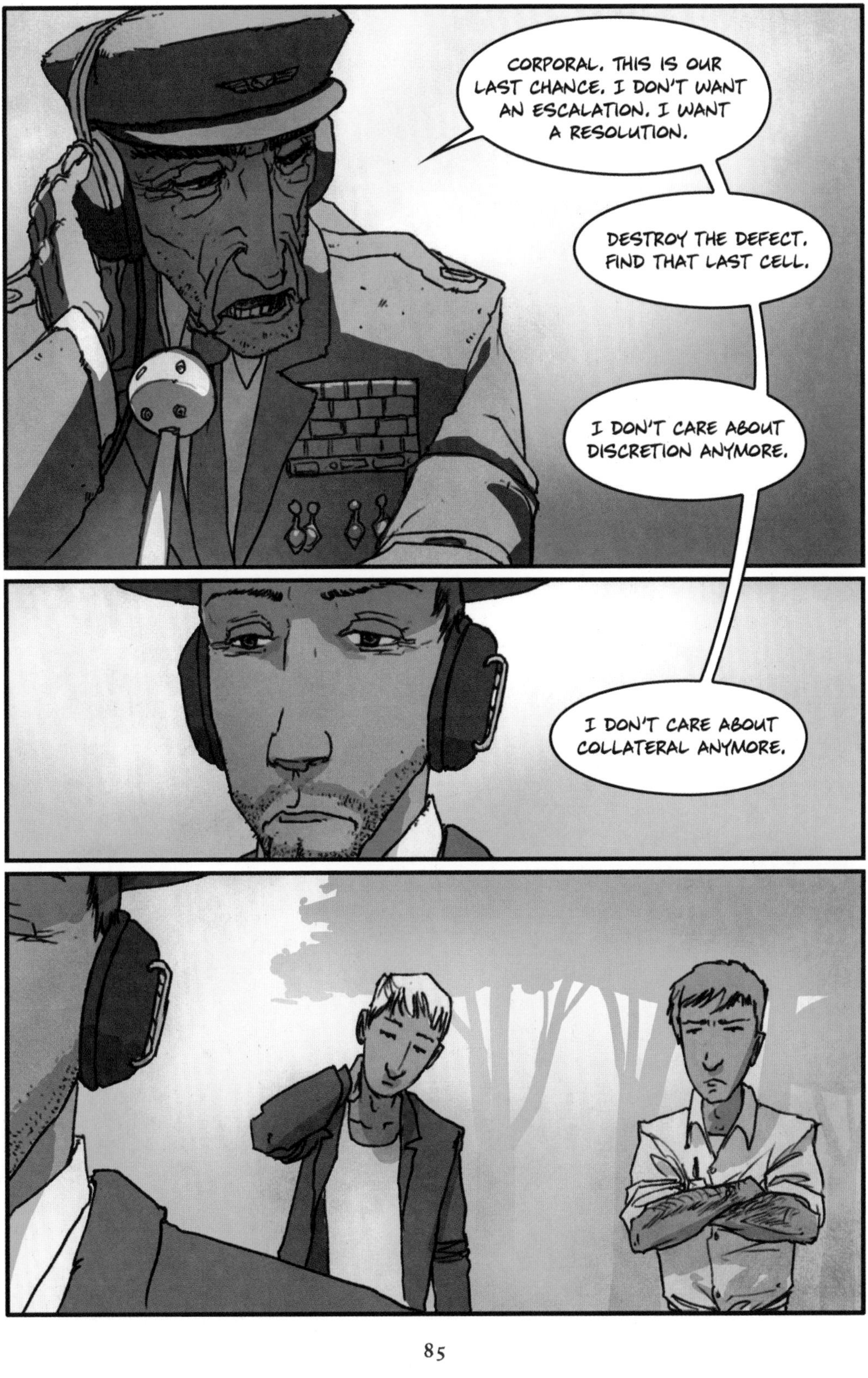
CORPORAL. THIS IS OUR LAST CHANCE. I DON'T WANT AN ESCALATION. I WANT A RESOLUTION.
DESTROY THE DEFECT. FIND THAT LAST CELL.
I DON'T CARE ABOUT DISCRETION ANYMORE.
I DON'T CARE ABOUT COLLATERAL ANYMORE.

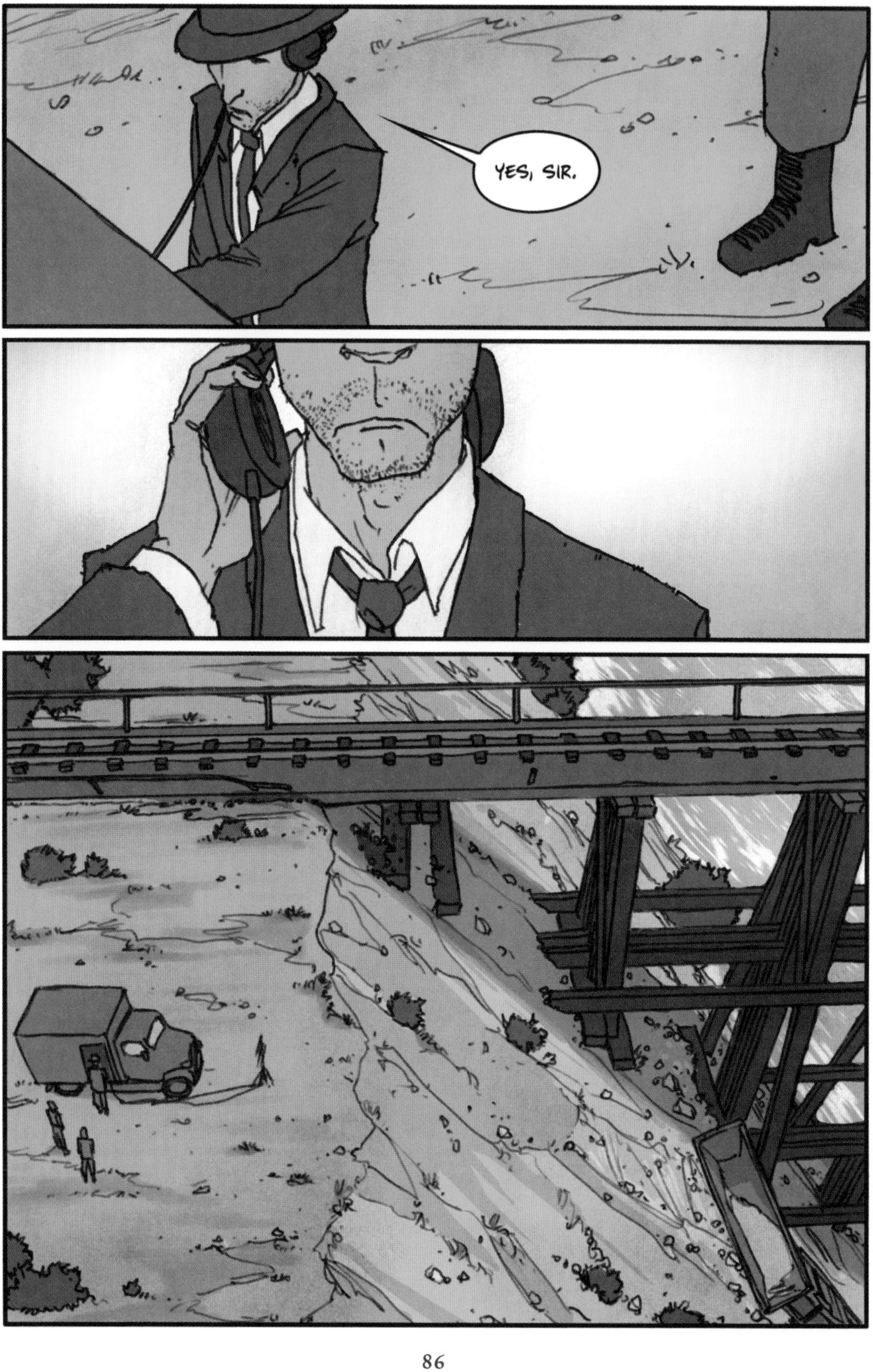
YES, SIR.

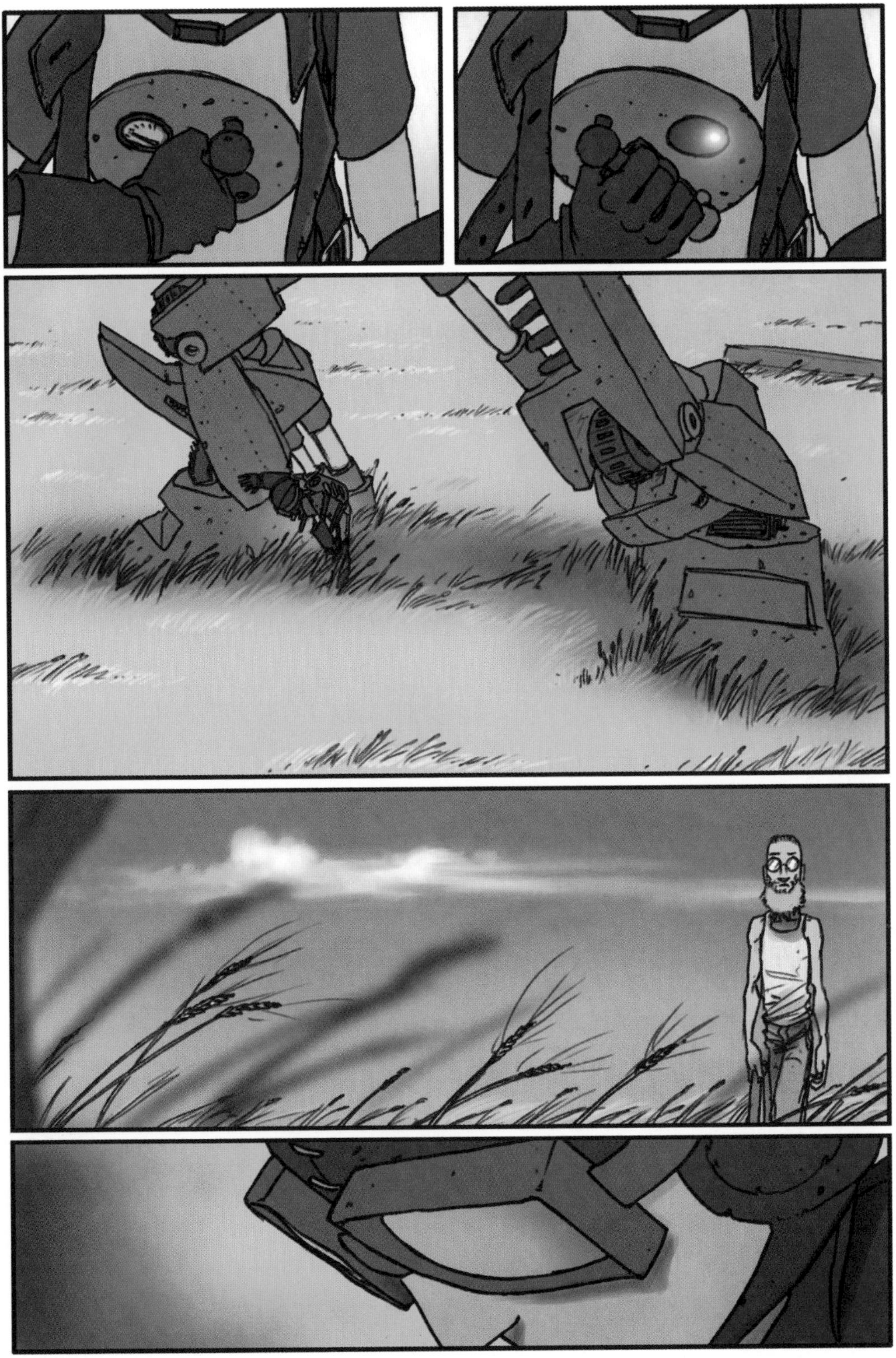

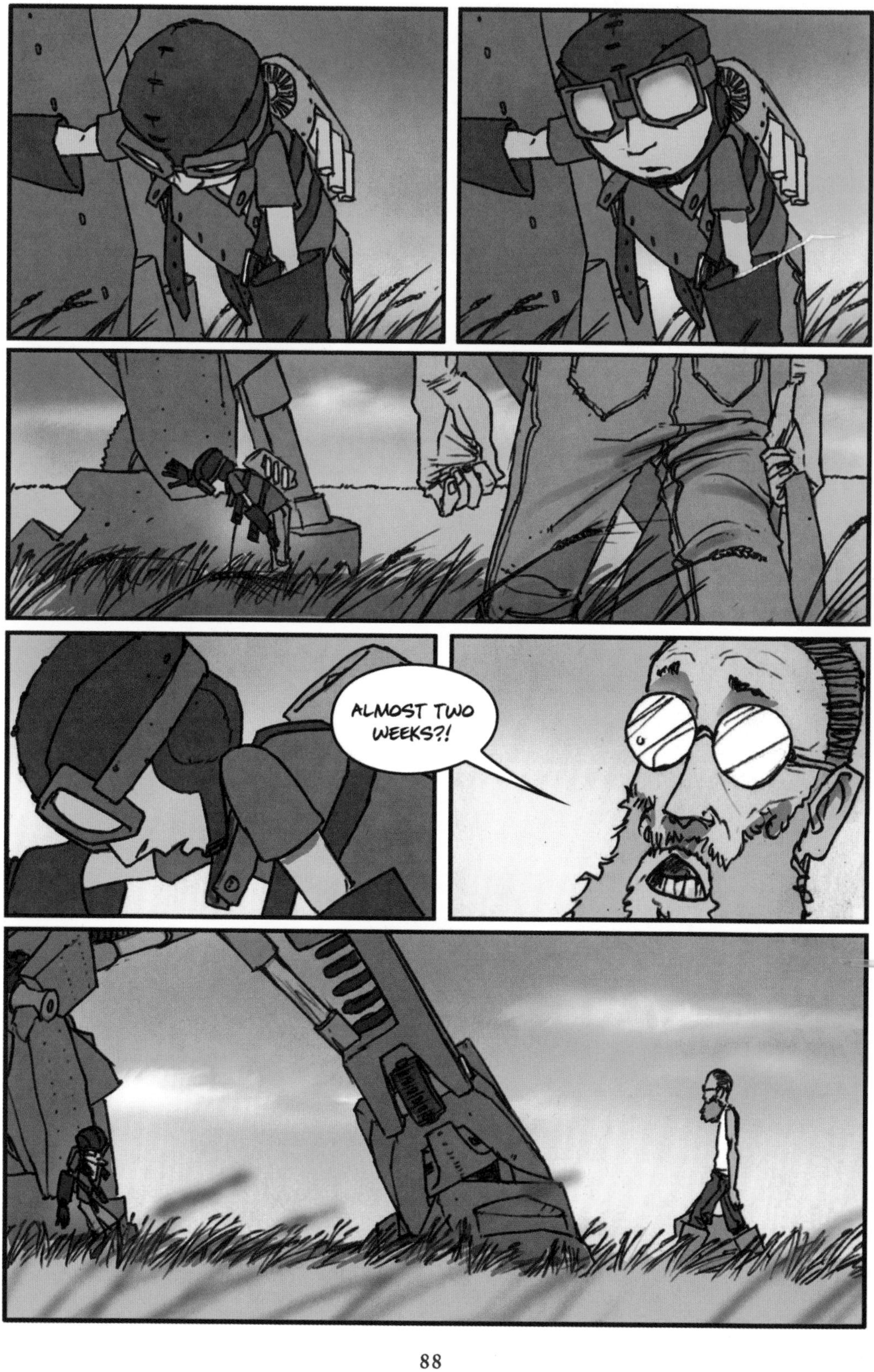
ALMOST TWO WEEKS?!

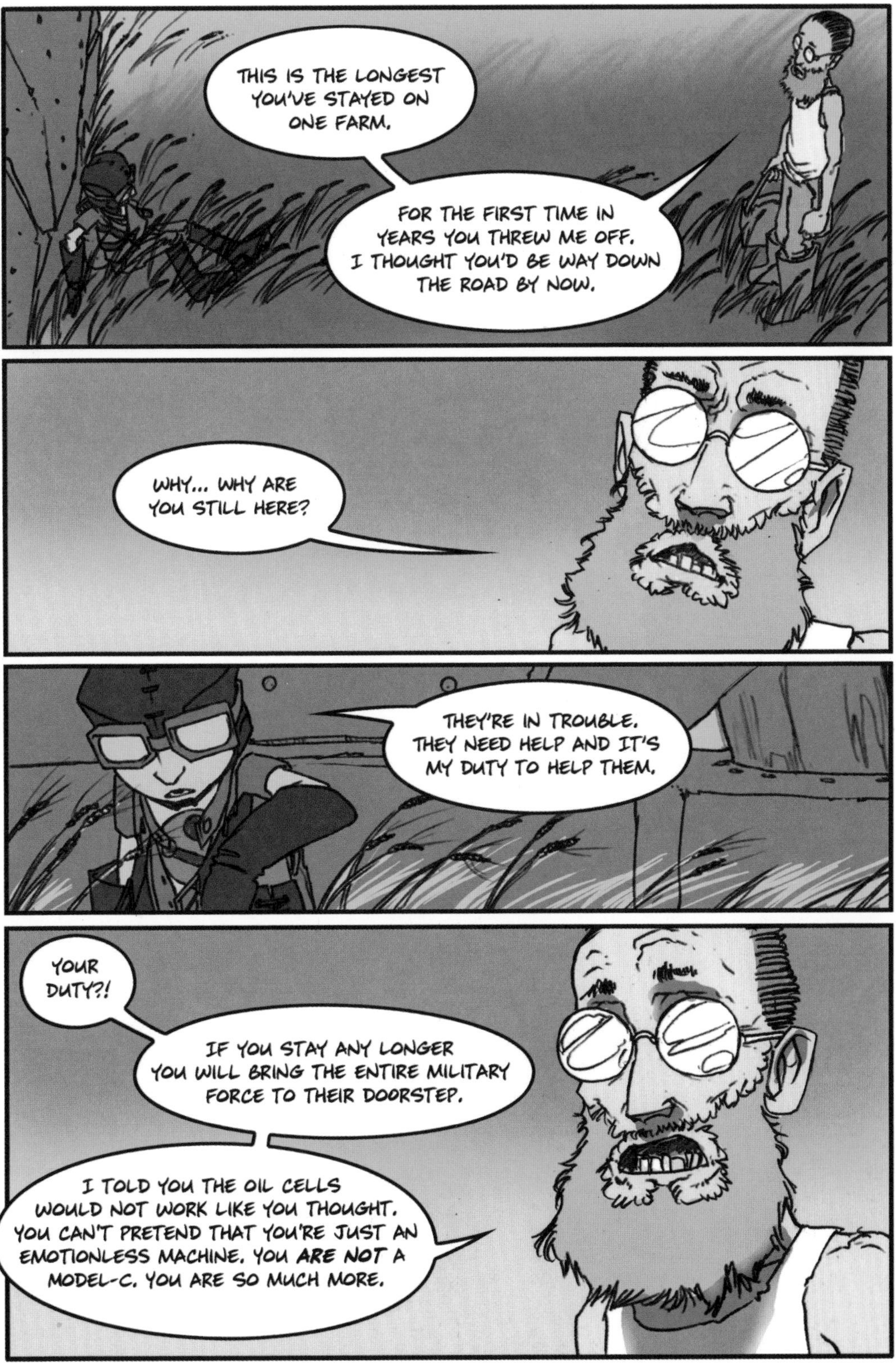
THIS IS THE LONGEST YOU'VE STAYED ON ONE FARM.
FOR THE FIRST TIME IN YEARS YOU THREW ME OFF. I THOUGHT YOU'D BE WAY DOWN THE ROAD BY NOW.
WHY... WHY ARE YOU STILL HERE?
THEY'RE IN TROUBLE. THEY NEED HELP AND IT'S MY DUTY TO HELP THEM.
YOUR DUTY?!
IF YOU STAY ANY LONGER YOU WILL BRING THE ENTIRE MILITARY FORCE TO THEIR DOORSTEP.
I TOLD YOU THE OIL CELLS WOULD NOT WORK LIKE YOU THOUGHT. YOU CAN'T PRETEND THAT YOU'RE JUST AN EMOTIONLESS MACHINE. YOU **ARE NOT** A MODEL-C. YOU ARE SO MUCH MORE.

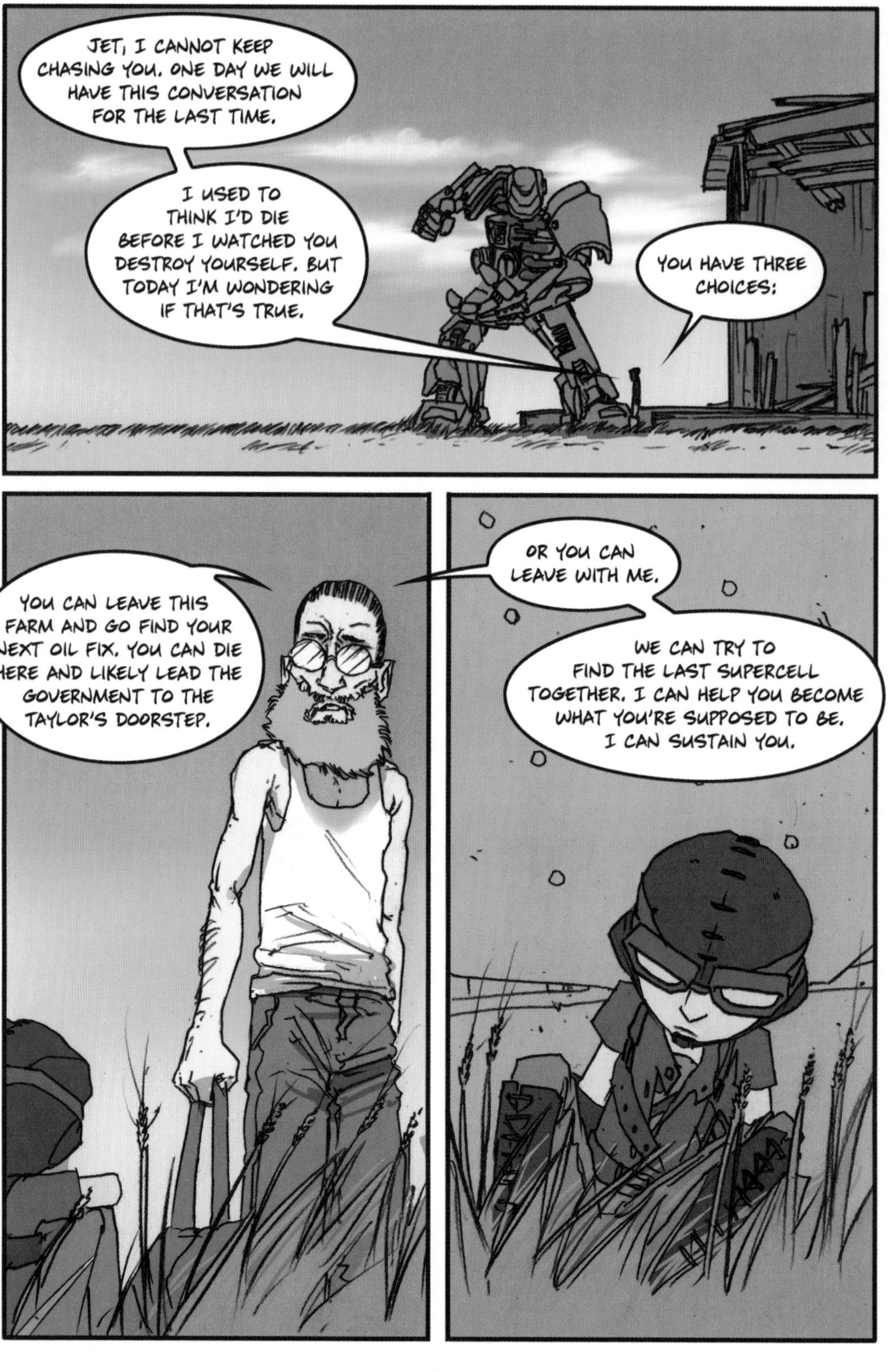
JET, I CANNOT KEEP CHASING YOU. ONE DAY WE WILL HAVE THIS CONVERSATION FOR THE LAST TIME.
I USED TO THINK I'D DIE BEFORE I WATCHED YOU DESTROY YOURSELF. BUT TODAY I'M WONDERING IF THAT'S TRUE.
YOU HAVE THREE CHOICES:
YOU CAN LEAVE THIS FARM AND GO FIND YOUR NEXT OIL FIX. YOU CAN DIE HERE AND LIKELY LEAD THE GOVERNMENT TO THE TAYLOR'S DOORSTEP.
OR YOU CAN LEAVE WITH ME.
WE CAN TRY TO FIND THE LAST SUPERCELL TOGETHER. I CAN HELP YOU BECOME WHAT YOU'RE SUPPOSED TO BE. I CAN SUSTAIN YOU.

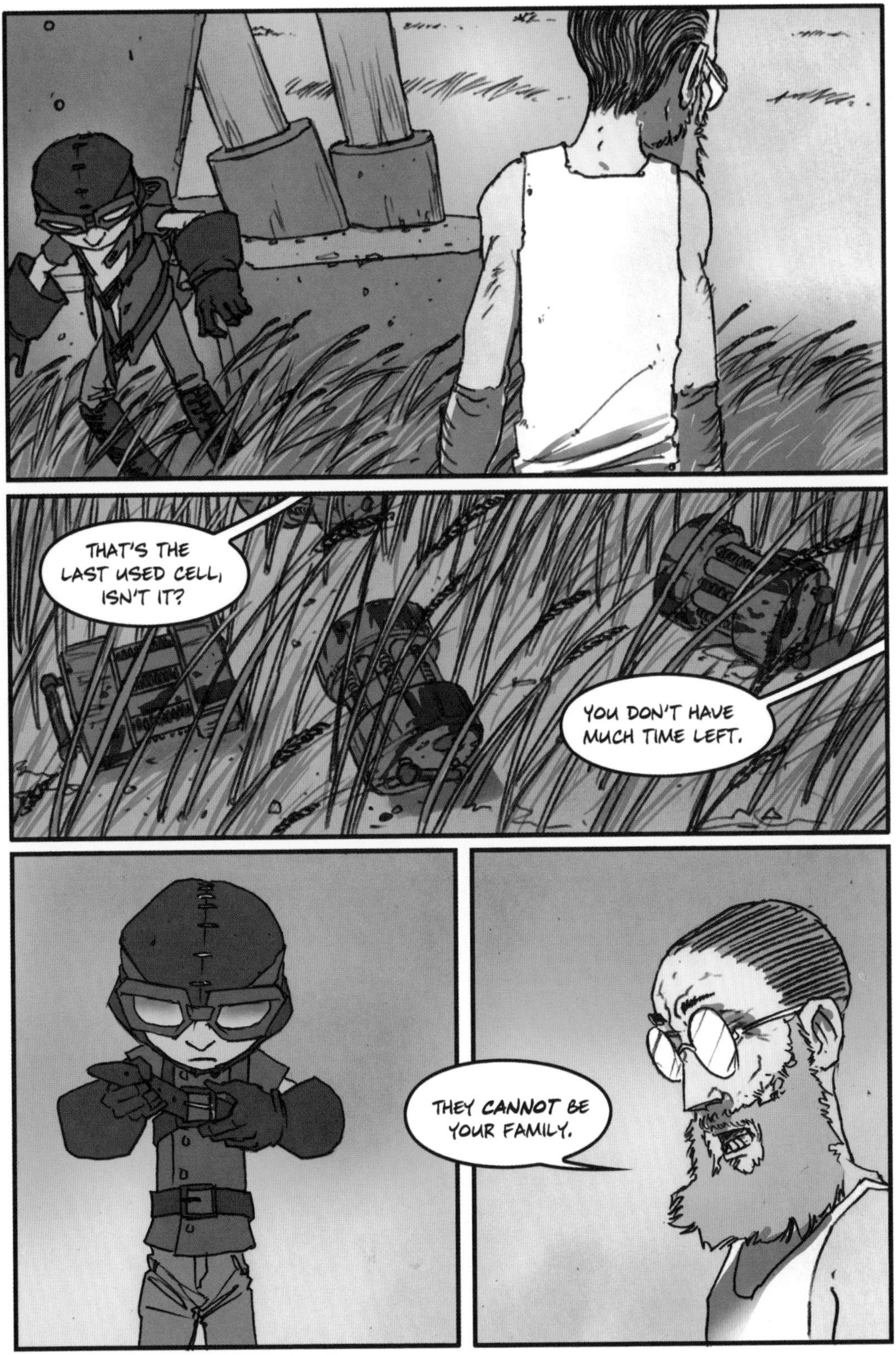
THAT'S THE LAST USED CELL, ISN'T IT?
YOU DON'T HAVE MUCH TIME LEFT.
THEY *CANNOT* BE YOUR FAMILY.

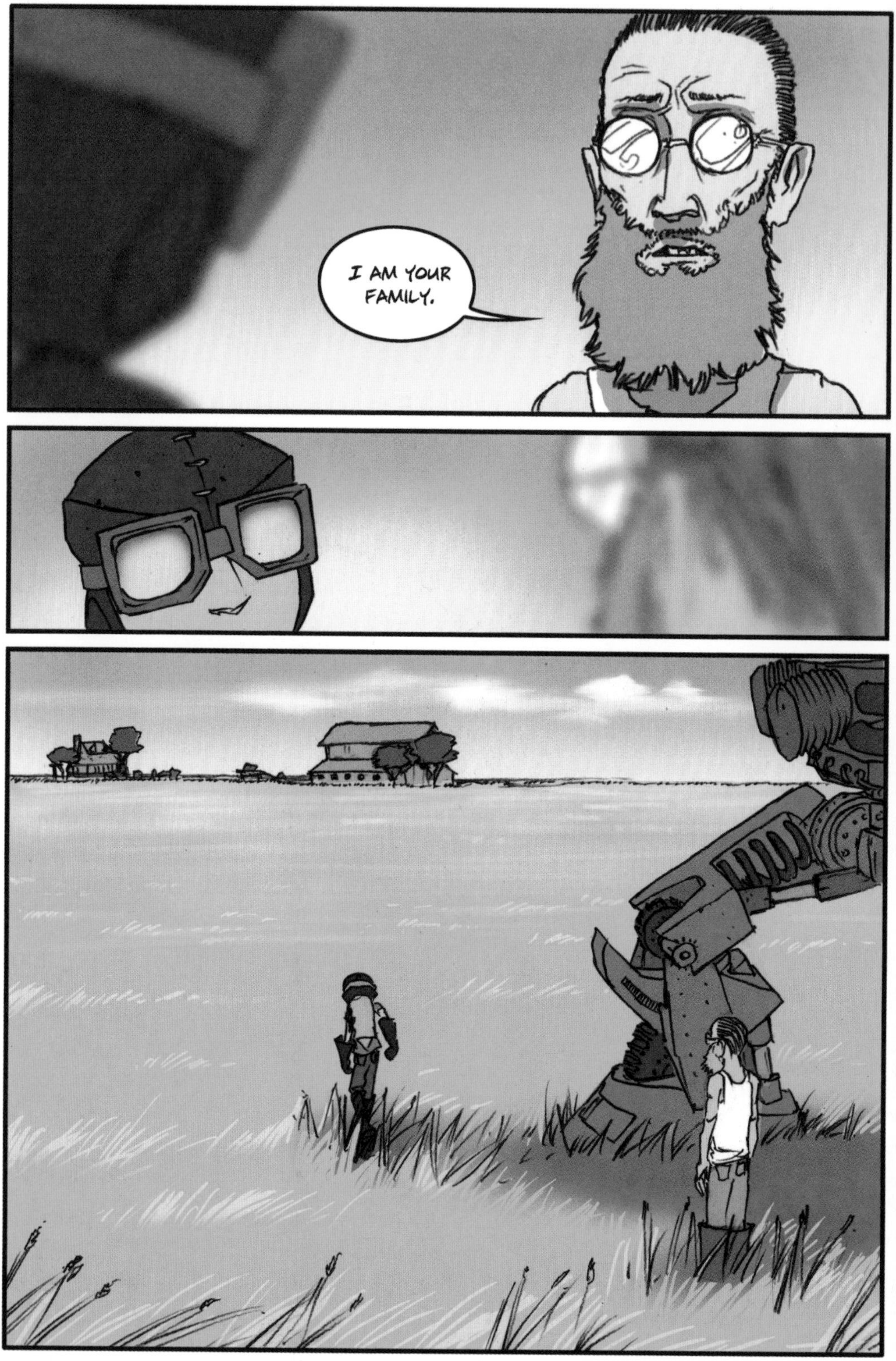
I AM YOUR FAMILY.

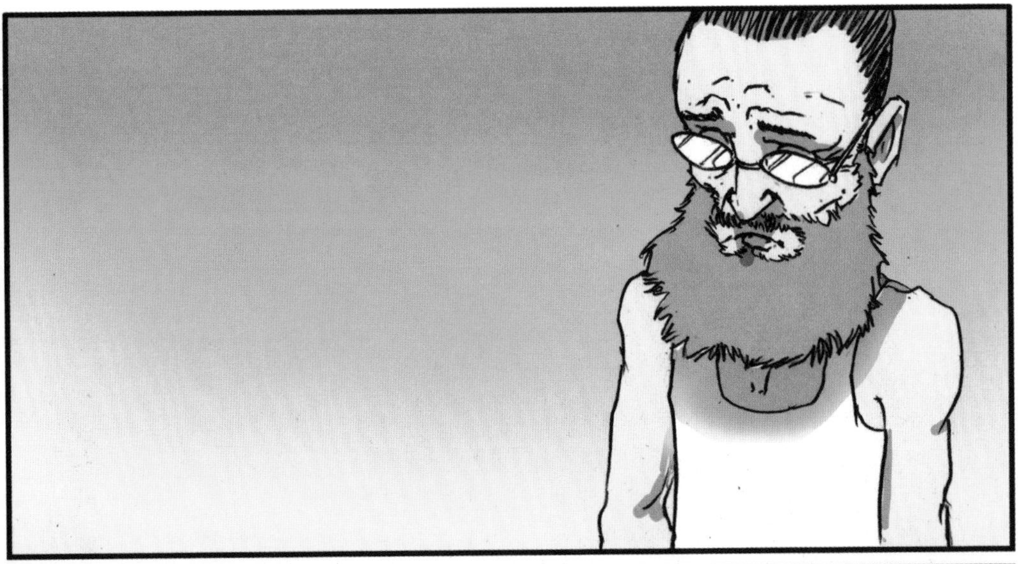

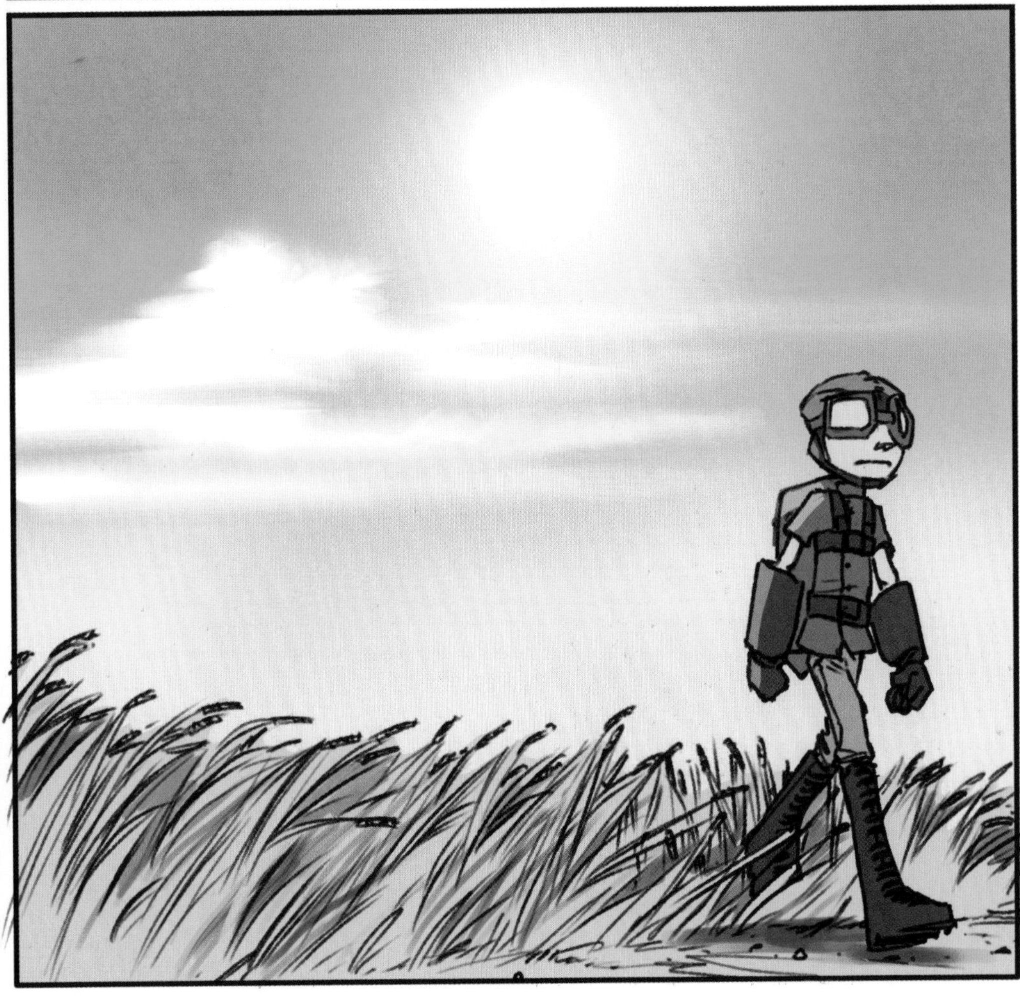

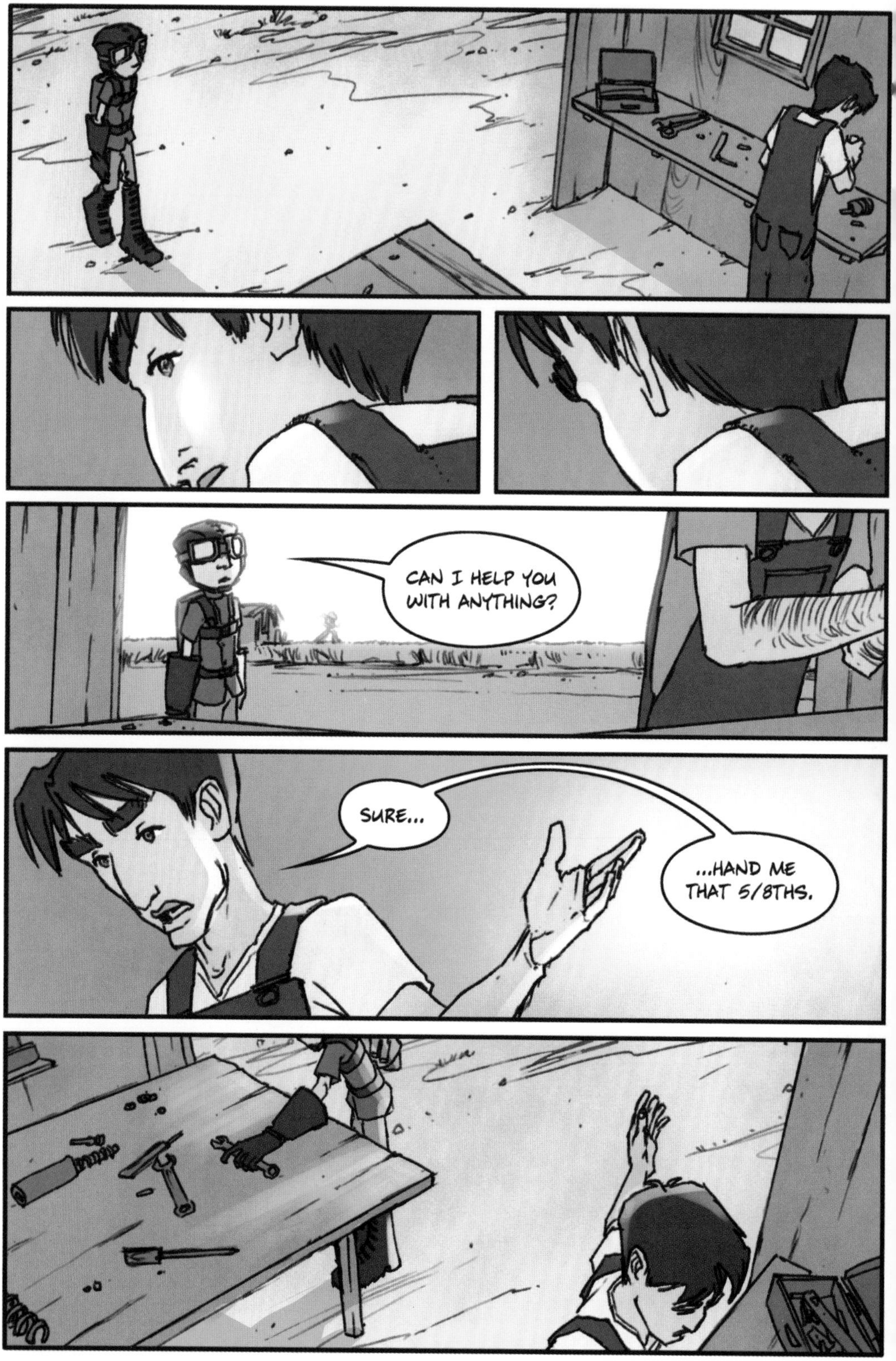
CAN I HELP YOU WITH ANYTHING?
SURE...
...HAND ME THAT 5/8THS.

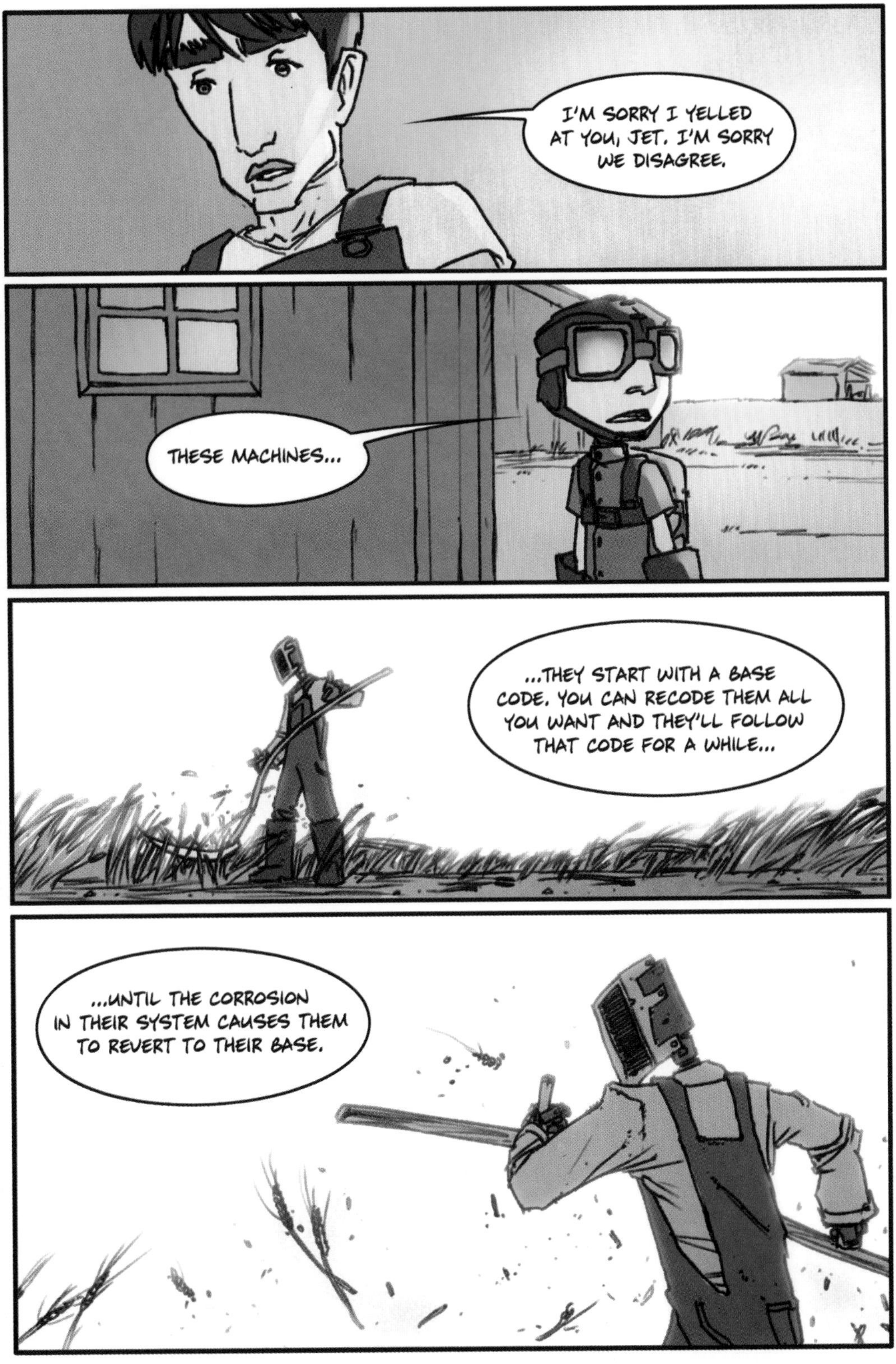
I'M SORRY I YELLED AT YOU, JET. I'M SORRY WE DISAGREE.
THESE MACHINES...
...THEY START WITH A BASE CODE. YOU CAN RECODE THEM ALL YOU WANT AND THEY'LL FOLLOW THAT CODE FOR A WHILE...
...UNTIL THE CORROSION IN THEIR SYSTEM CAUSES THEM TO REVERT TO THEIR BASE.

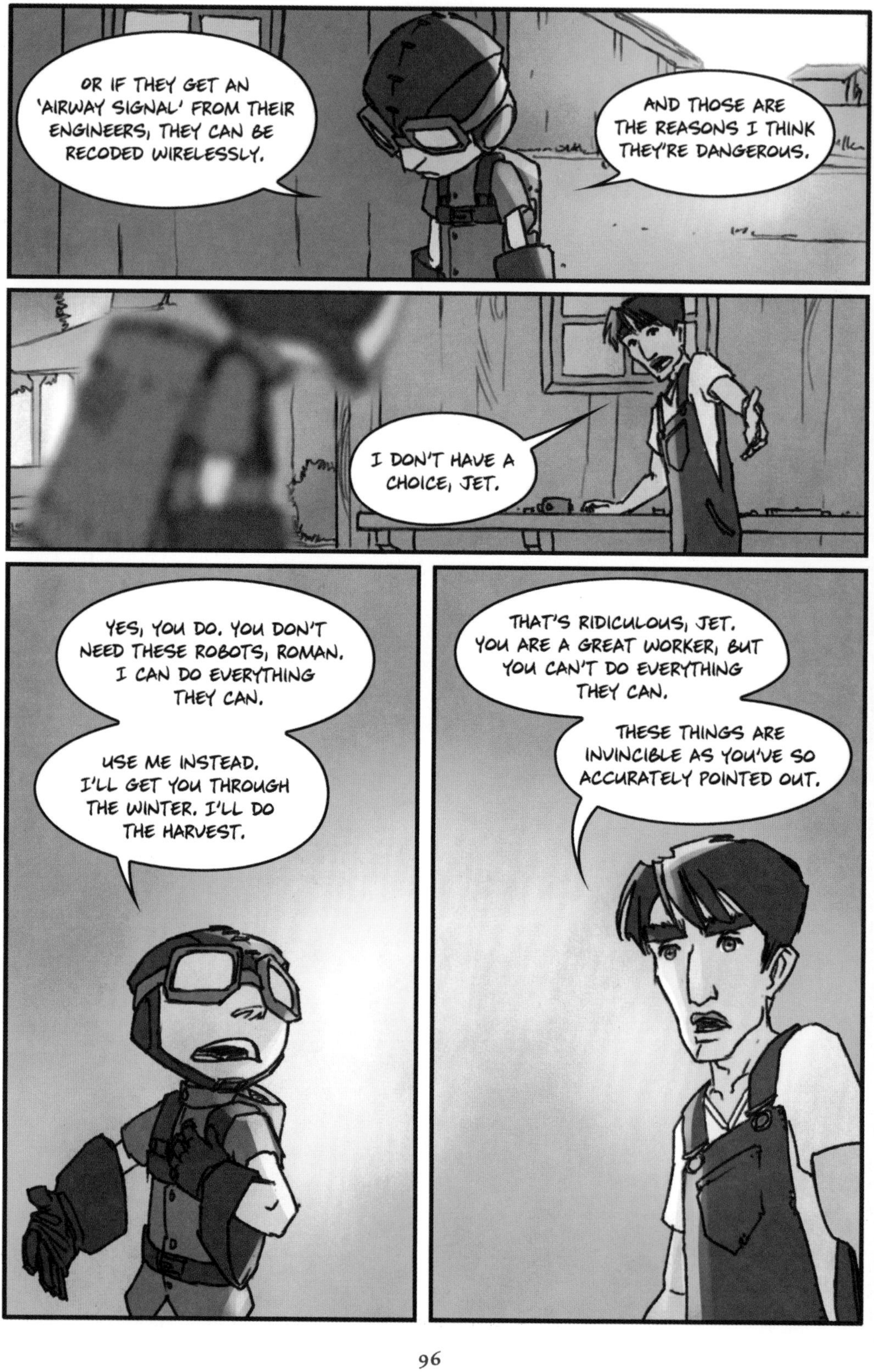
OR IF THEY GET AN 'AIRWAY SIGNAL' FROM THEIR ENGINEERS, THEY CAN BE RECODED WIRELESSLY.
AND THOSE ARE THE REASONS I THINK THEY'RE DANGEROUS.
I DON'T HAVE A CHOICE, JET.
YES, YOU DO. YOU DON'T NEED THESE ROBOTS, ROMAN. I CAN DO EVERYTHING THEY CAN.
USE ME INSTEAD. I'LL GET YOU THROUGH THE WINTER. I'LL DO THE HARVEST.
THAT'S RIDICULOUS, JET. YOU ARE A GREAT WORKER, BUT YOU CAN'T DO EVERYTHING THEY CAN.
THESE THINGS ARE INVINCIBLE AS YOU'VE SO ACCURATELY POINTED OUT.

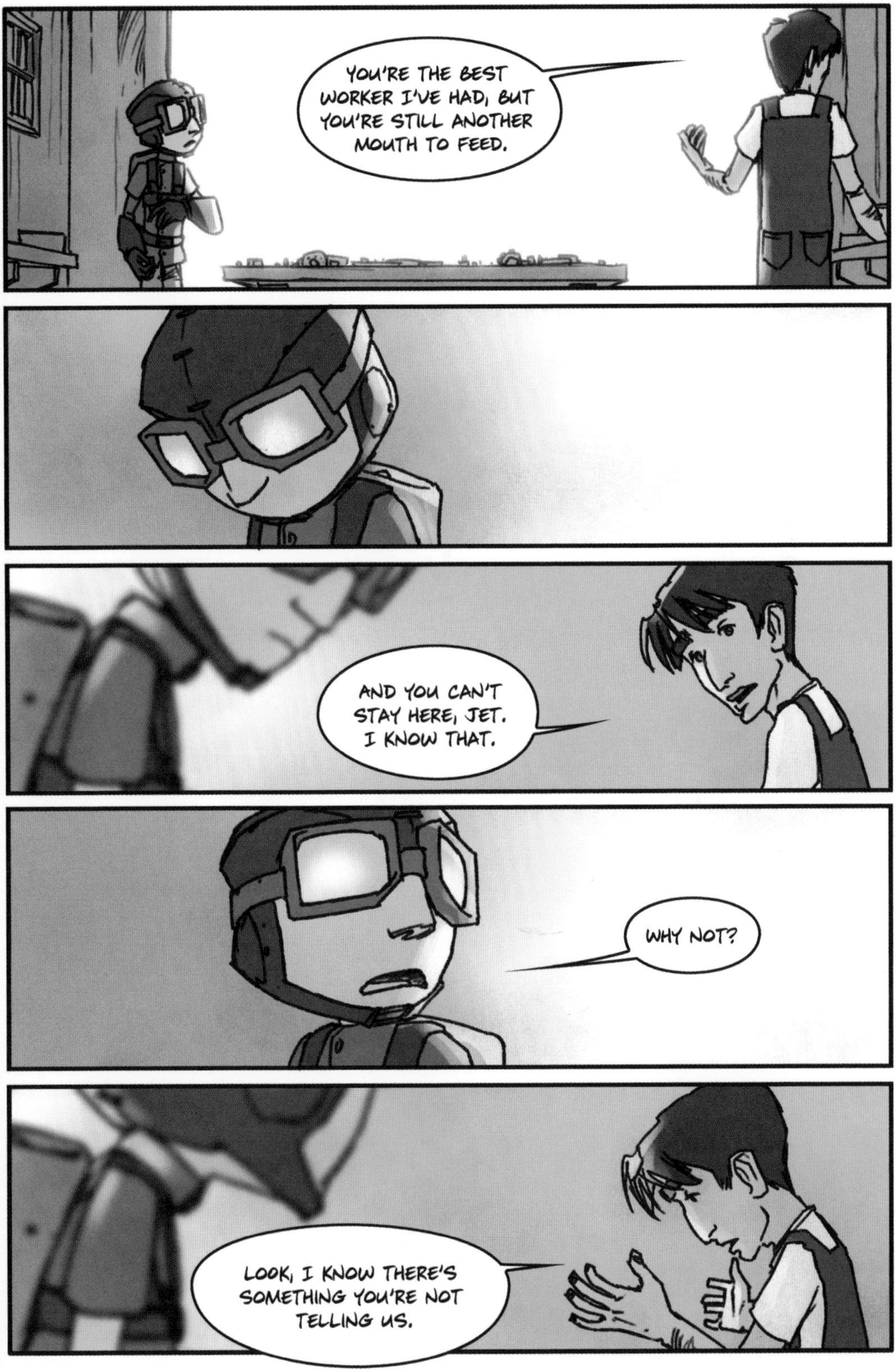
YOU'RE THE BEST WORKER I'VE HAD, BUT YOU'RE STILL ANOTHER MOUTH TO FEED.
AND YOU CAN'T STAY HERE, JET. I KNOW THAT.
WHY NOT?
LOOK, I KNOW THERE'S SOMETHING YOU'RE NOT TELLING US.

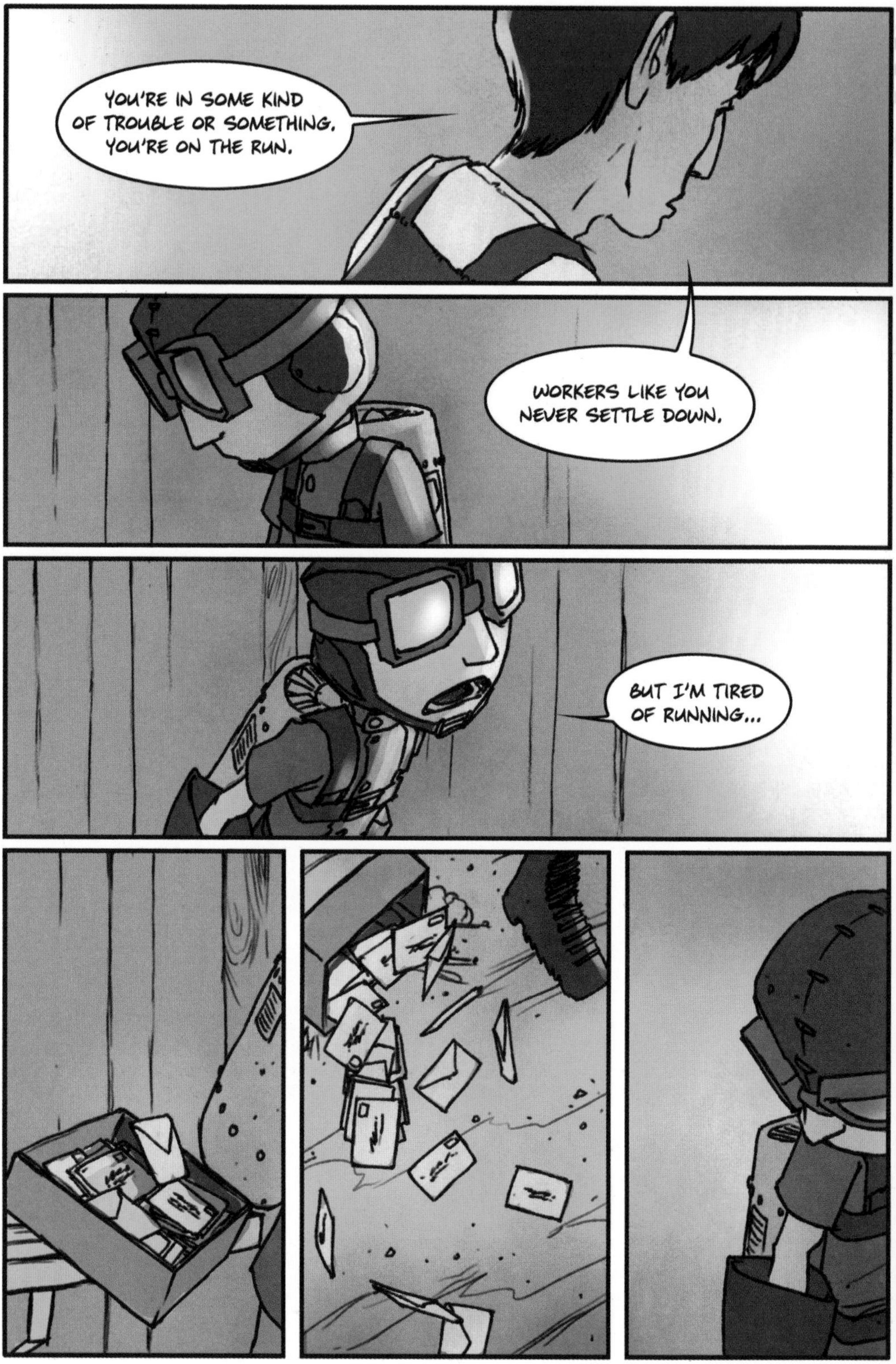
YOU'RE IN SOME KIND OF TROUBLE OR SOMETHING. YOU'RE ON THE RUN.
WORKERS LIKE YOU NEVER SETTLE DOWN.
BUT I'M TIRED OF RUNNING...

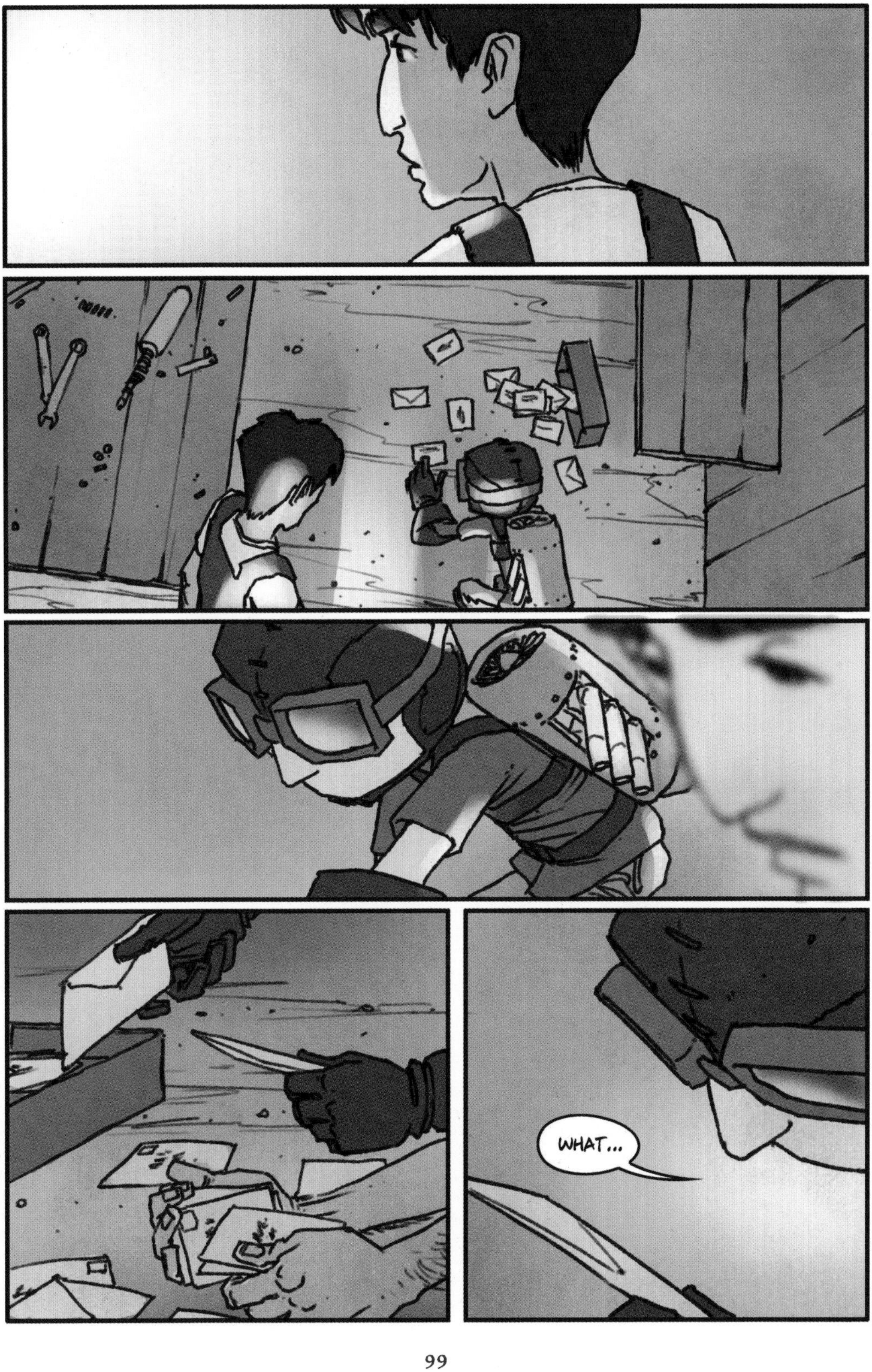
WHAT...

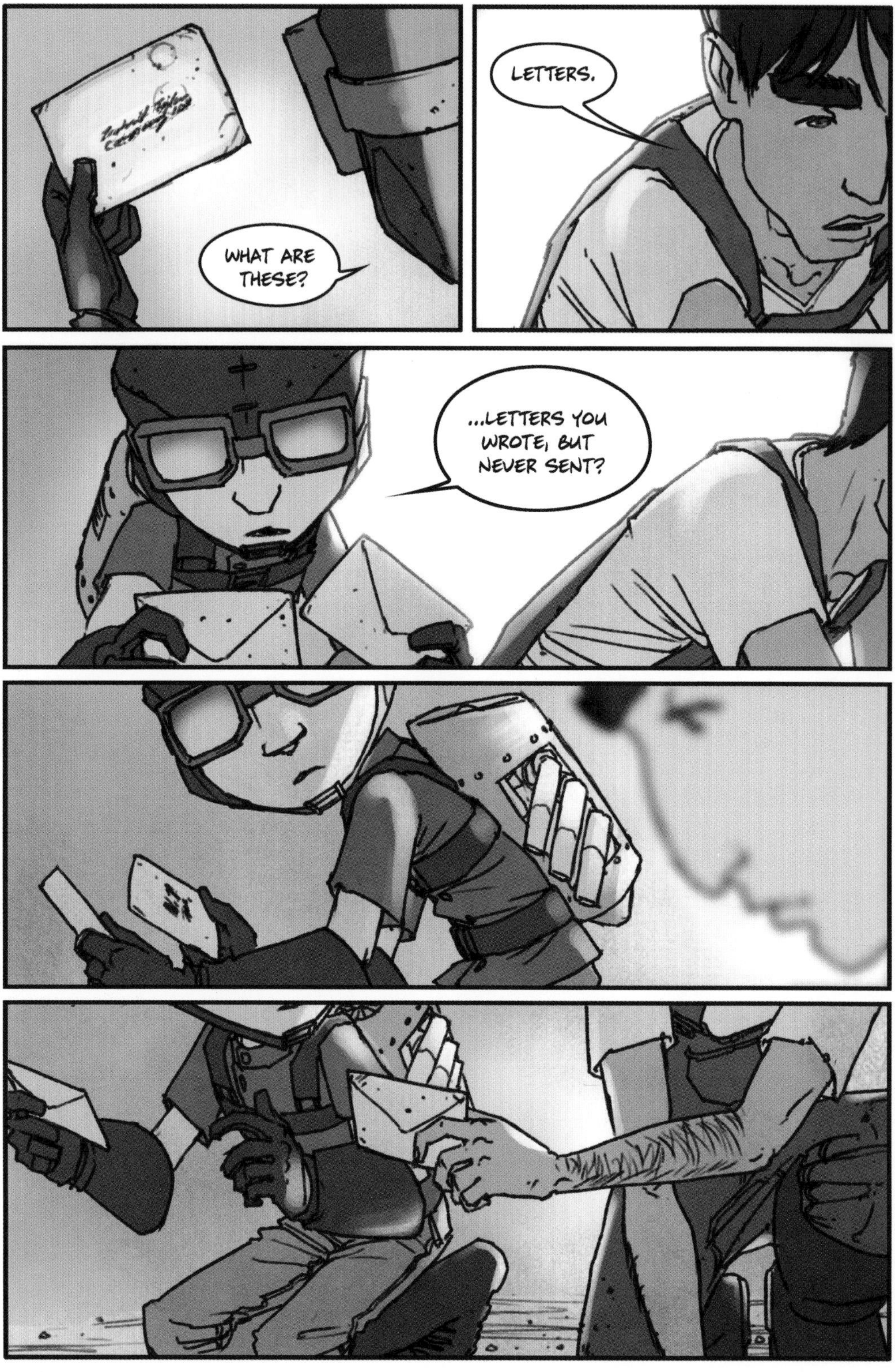
WHAT ARE THESE?
LETTERS.
...LETTERS YOU WROTE, BUT NEVER SENT?

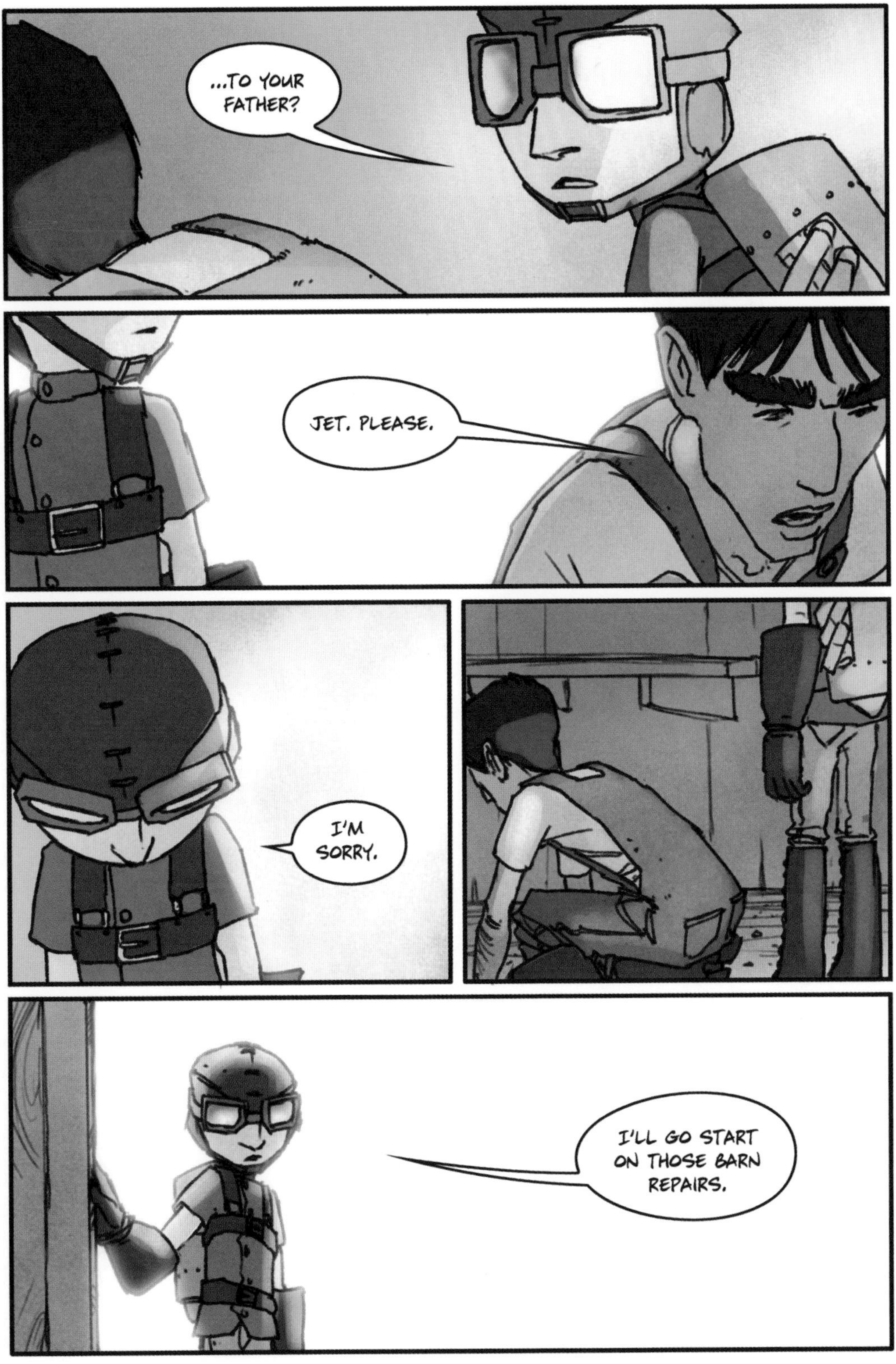
...TO YOUR FATHER?
JET. PLEASE.
I'M SORRY.
I'LL GO START ON THOSE BARN REPAIRS.

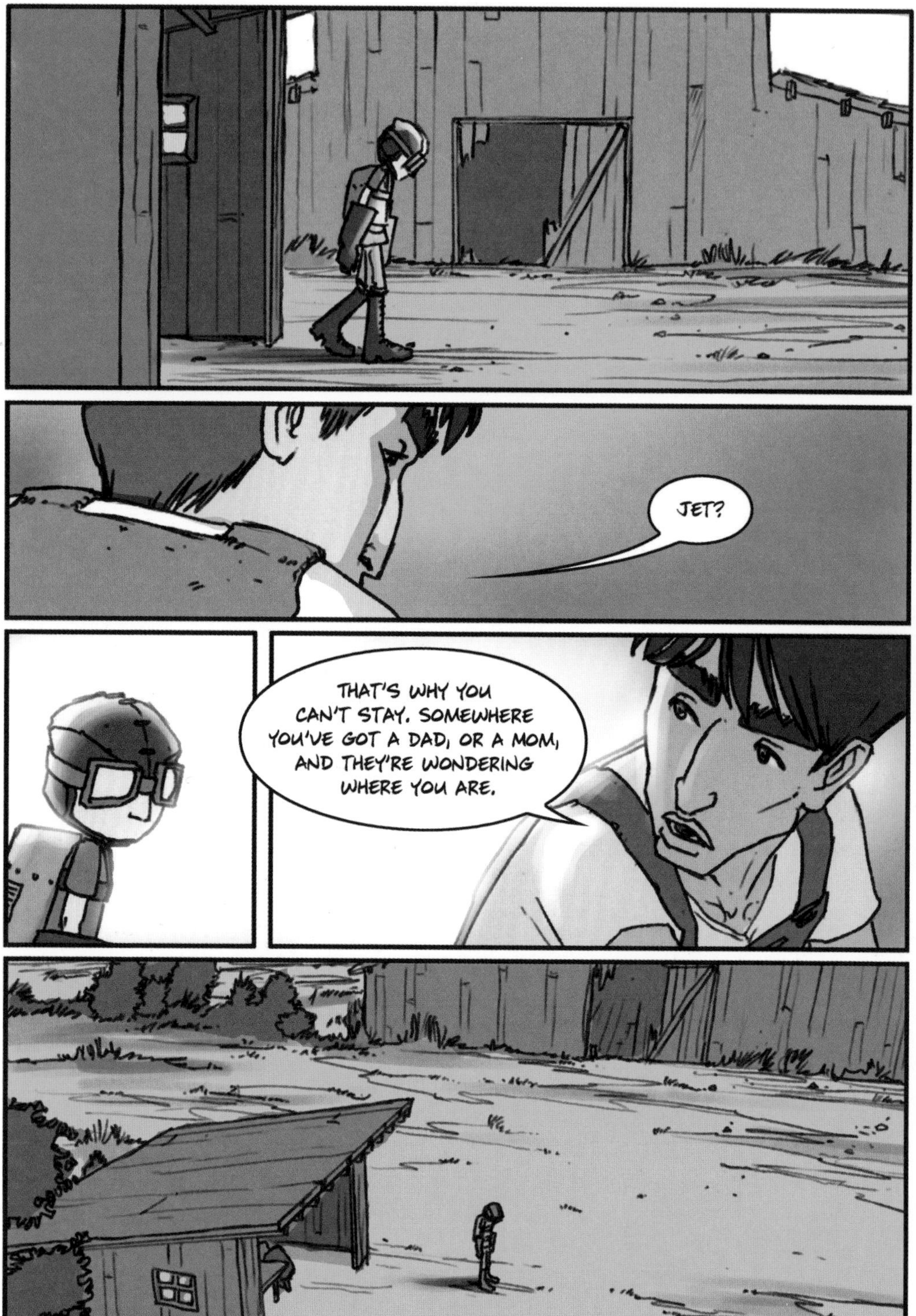
JET?
THAT'S WHY YOU CAN'T STAY. SOMEWHERE YOU'VE GOT A DAD, OR A MOM, AND THEY'RE WONDERING WHERE YOU ARE.

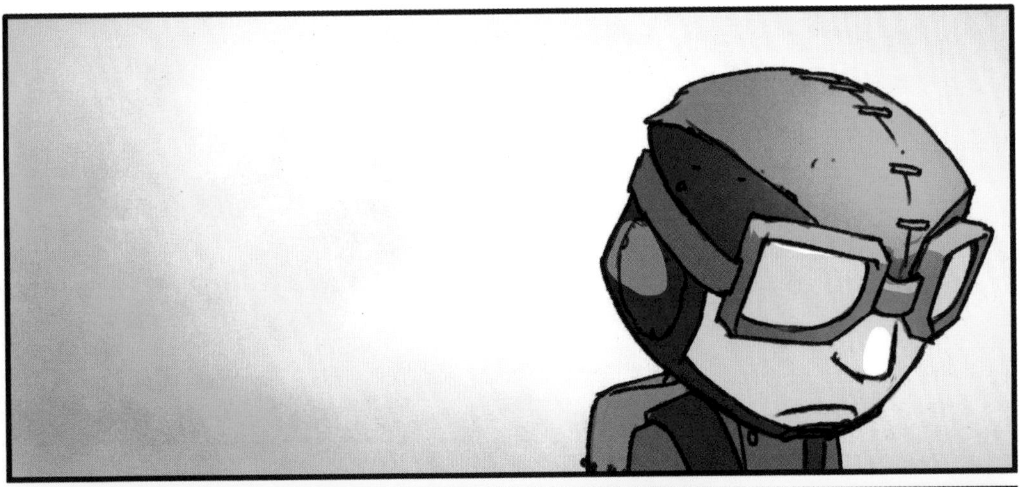

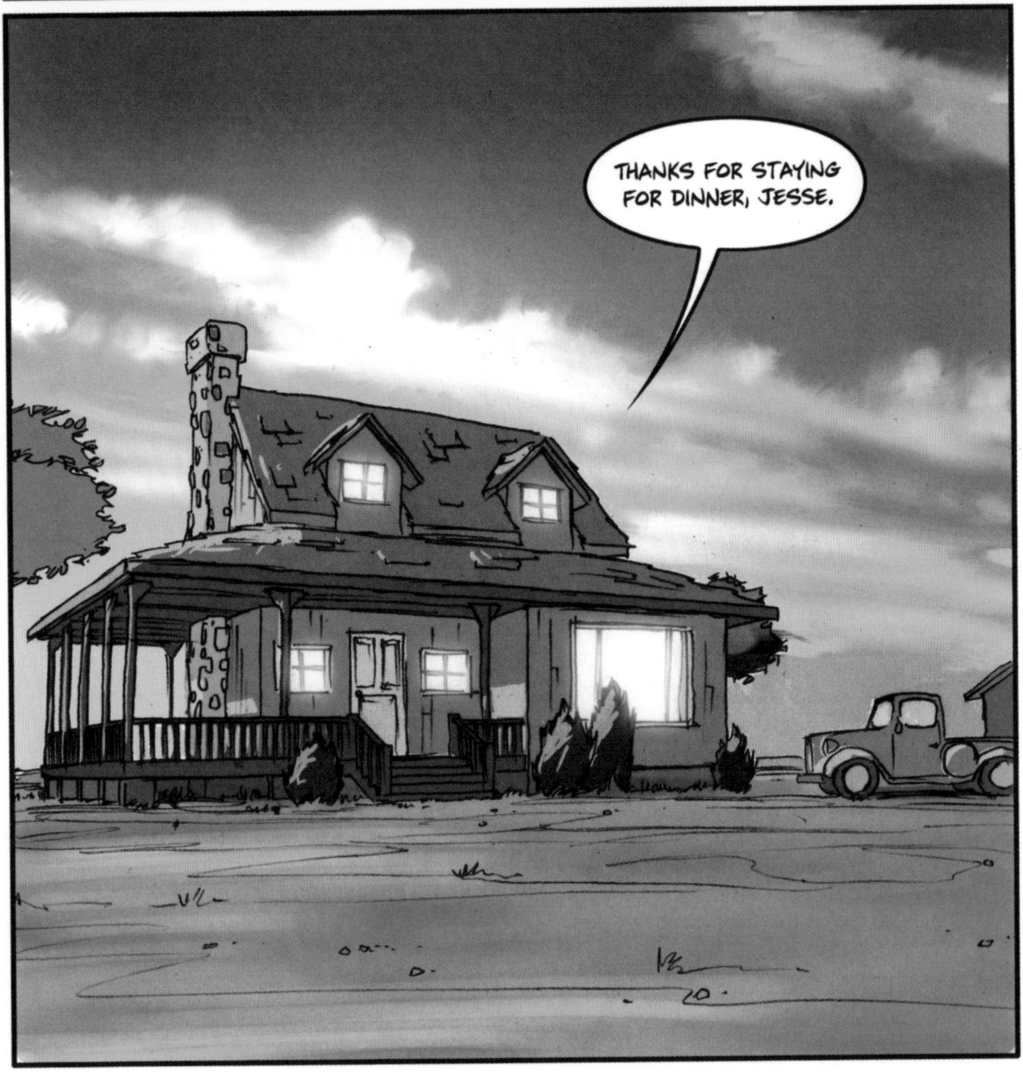
THANKS FOR STAYING FOR DINNER, JESSE.

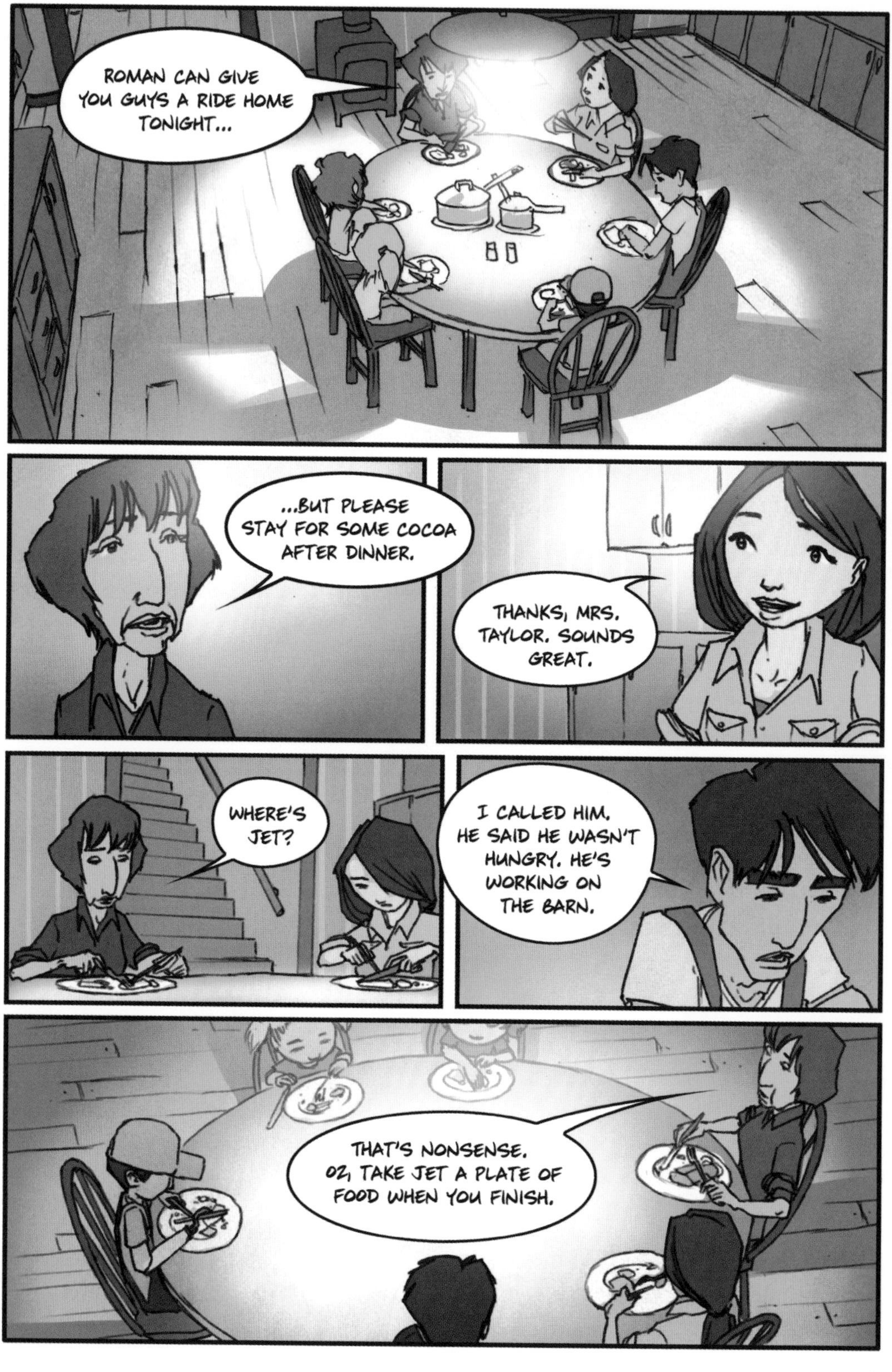
ROMAN CAN GIVE YOU GUYS A RIDE HOME TONIGHT...
...BUT PLEASE STAY FOR SOME COCOA AFTER DINNER.
THANKS, MRS. TAYLOR. SOUNDS GREAT.
WHERE'S JET?
I CALLED HIM. HE SAID HE WASN'T HUNGRY. HE'S WORKING ON THE BARN.
THAT'S NONSENSE. OZ, TAKE JET A PLATE OF FOOD WHEN YOU FINISH.

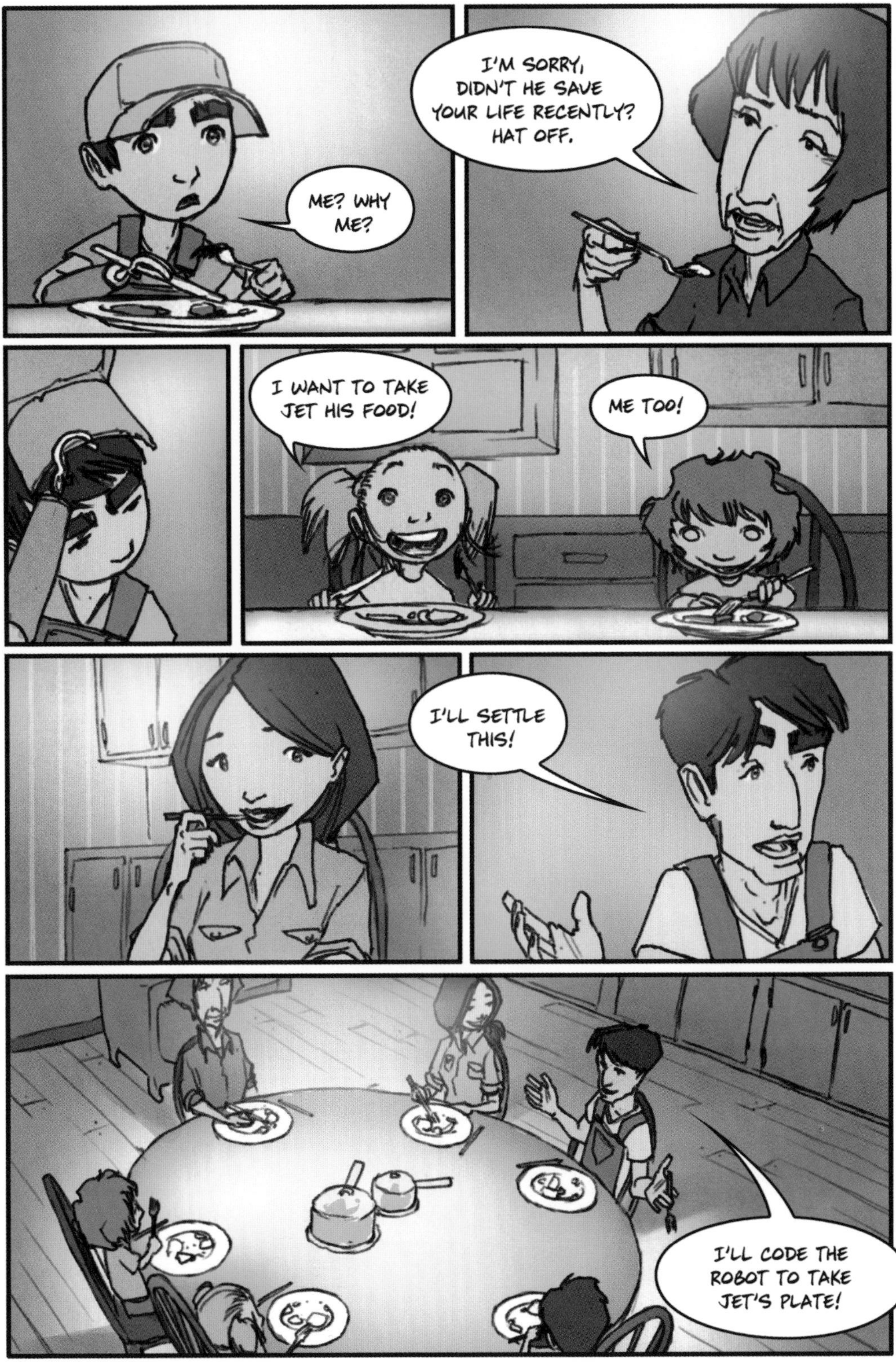
ME? WHY ME?
I'M SORRY, DIDN'T HE SAVE YOUR LIFE RECENTLY? HAT OFF.
I WANT TO TAKE JET HIS FOOD!
ME TOO!
I'LL SETTLE THIS!
I'LL CODE THE ROBOT TO TAKE JET'S PLATE!

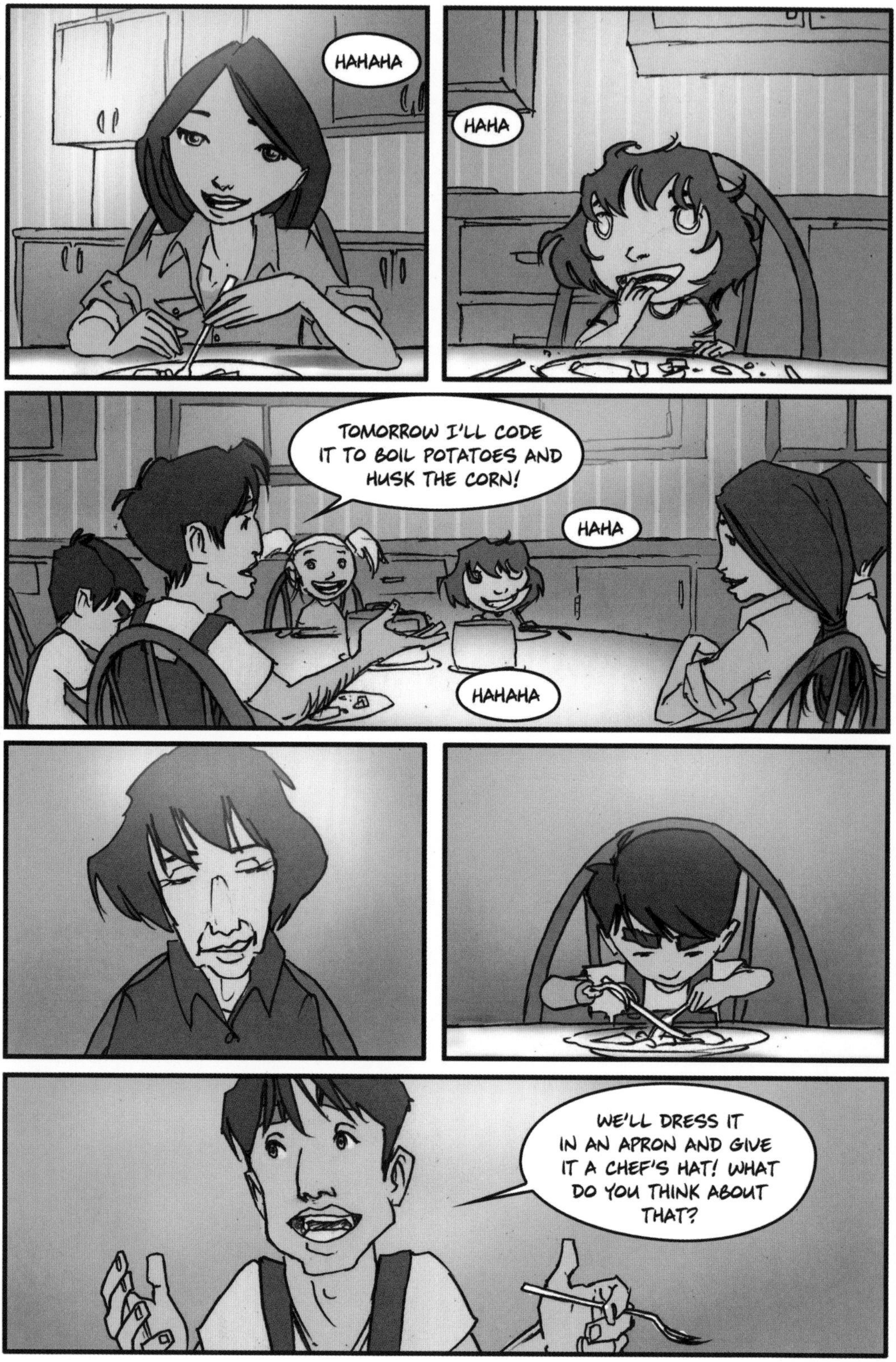
HAHAHA
HAHA
TOMORROW I'LL CODE IT TO BOIL POTATOES AND HUSK THE CORN!
HAHA
HAHAHA
WE'LL DRESS IT IN AN APRON AND GIVE IT A CHEF'S HAT! WHAT DO YOU THINK ABOUT THAT?

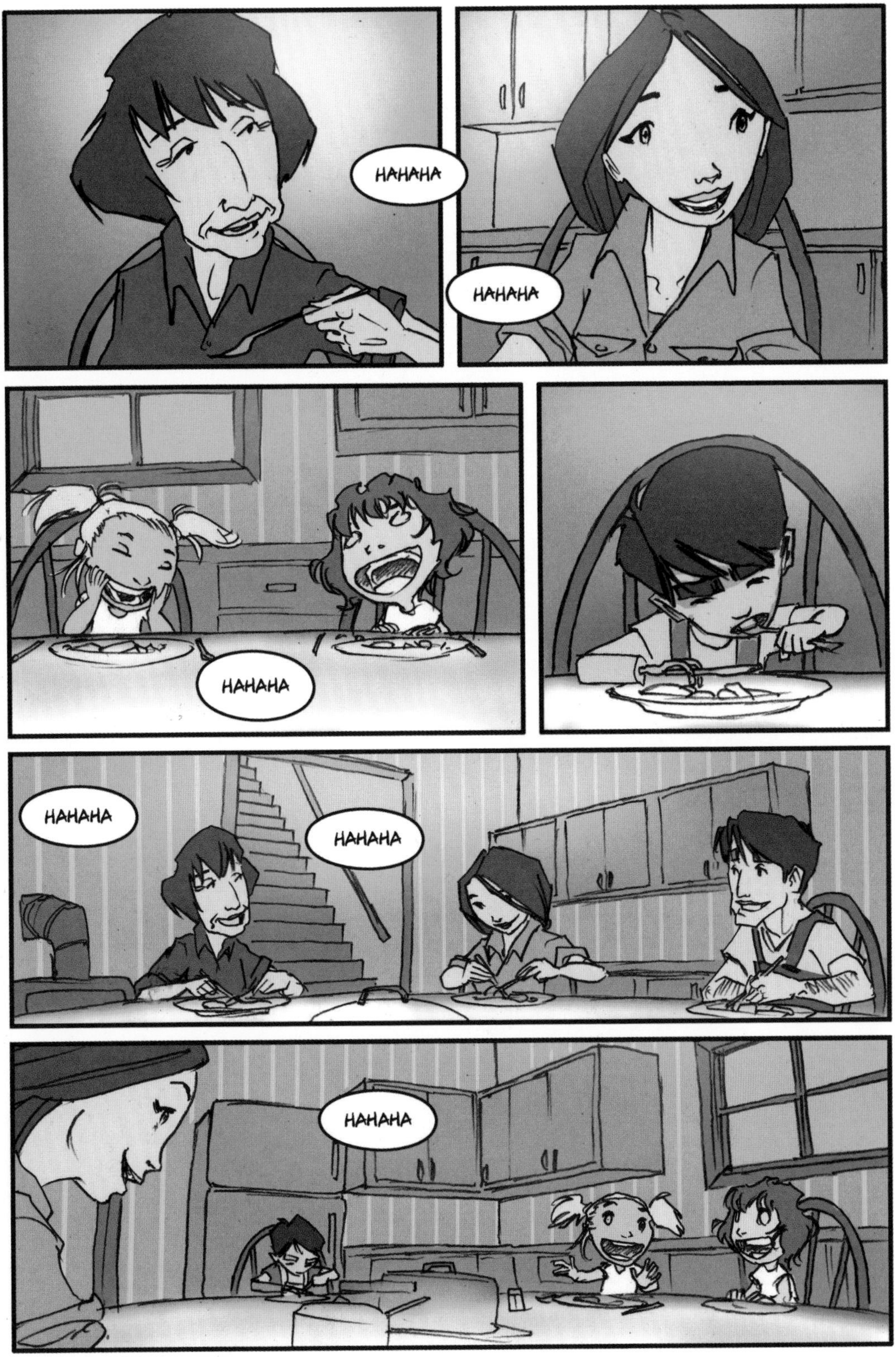
HAHAHA
HAHAHA
HAHAHA
HAHAHA
HAHAHA
HAHAHA

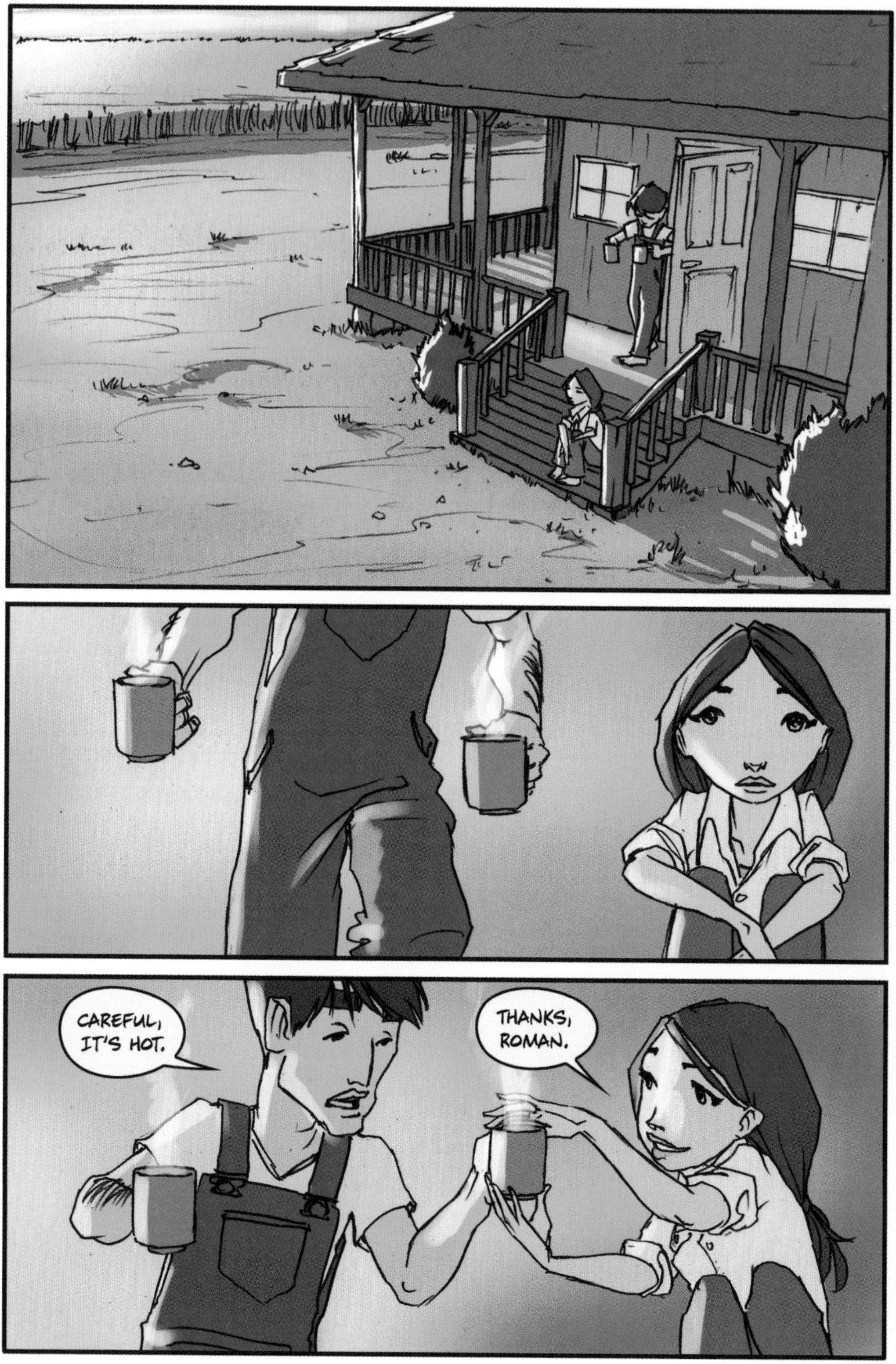
CAREFUL, IT'S HOT.
THANKS, ROMAN.

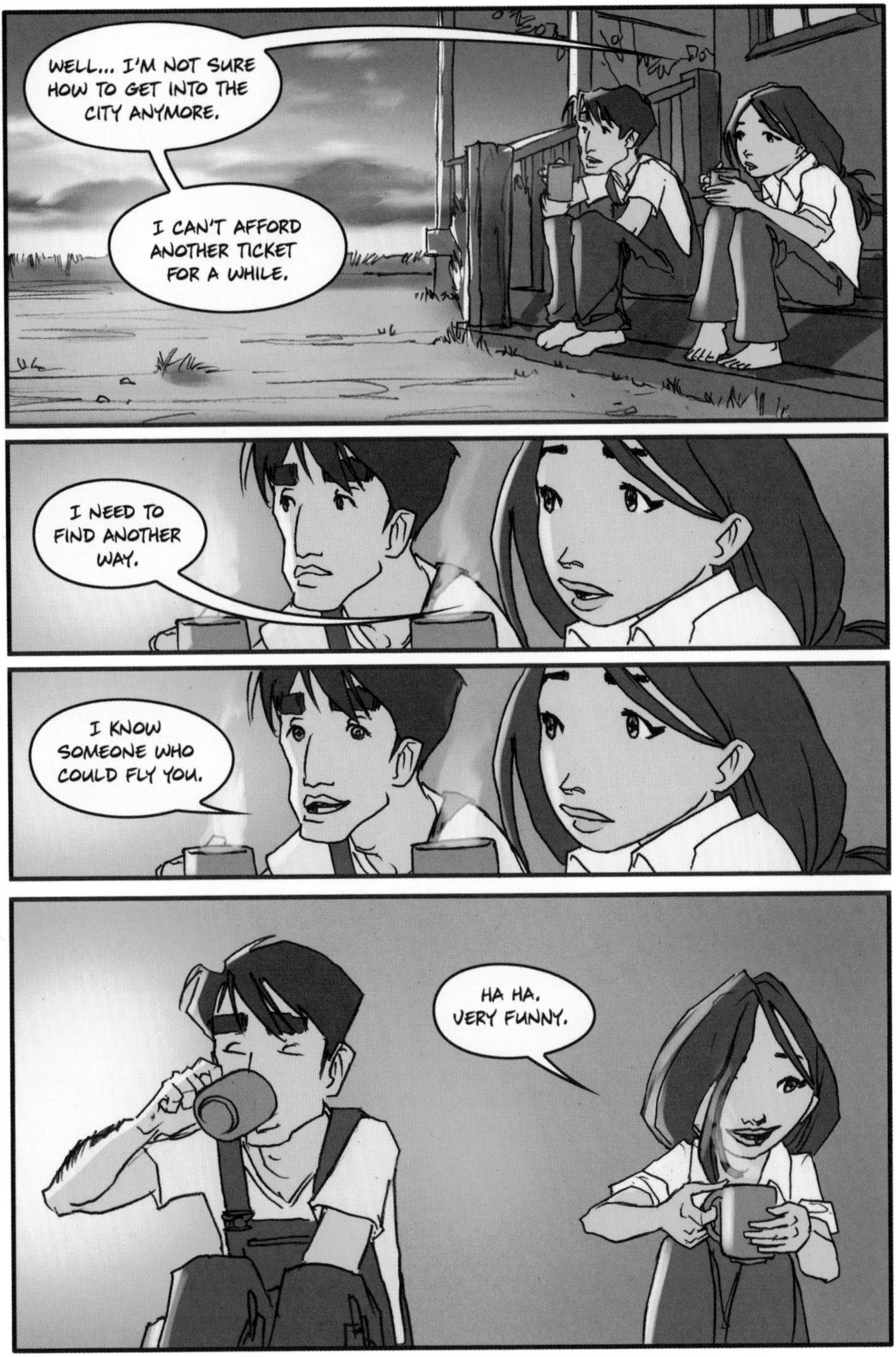
WELL... I'M NOT SURE HOW TO GET INTO THE CITY ANYMORE.
I CAN'T AFFORD ANOTHER TICKET FOR A WHILE.
I NEED TO FIND ANOTHER WAY.
I KNOW SOMEONE WHO COULD FLY YOU.
HA HA. VERY FUNNY.

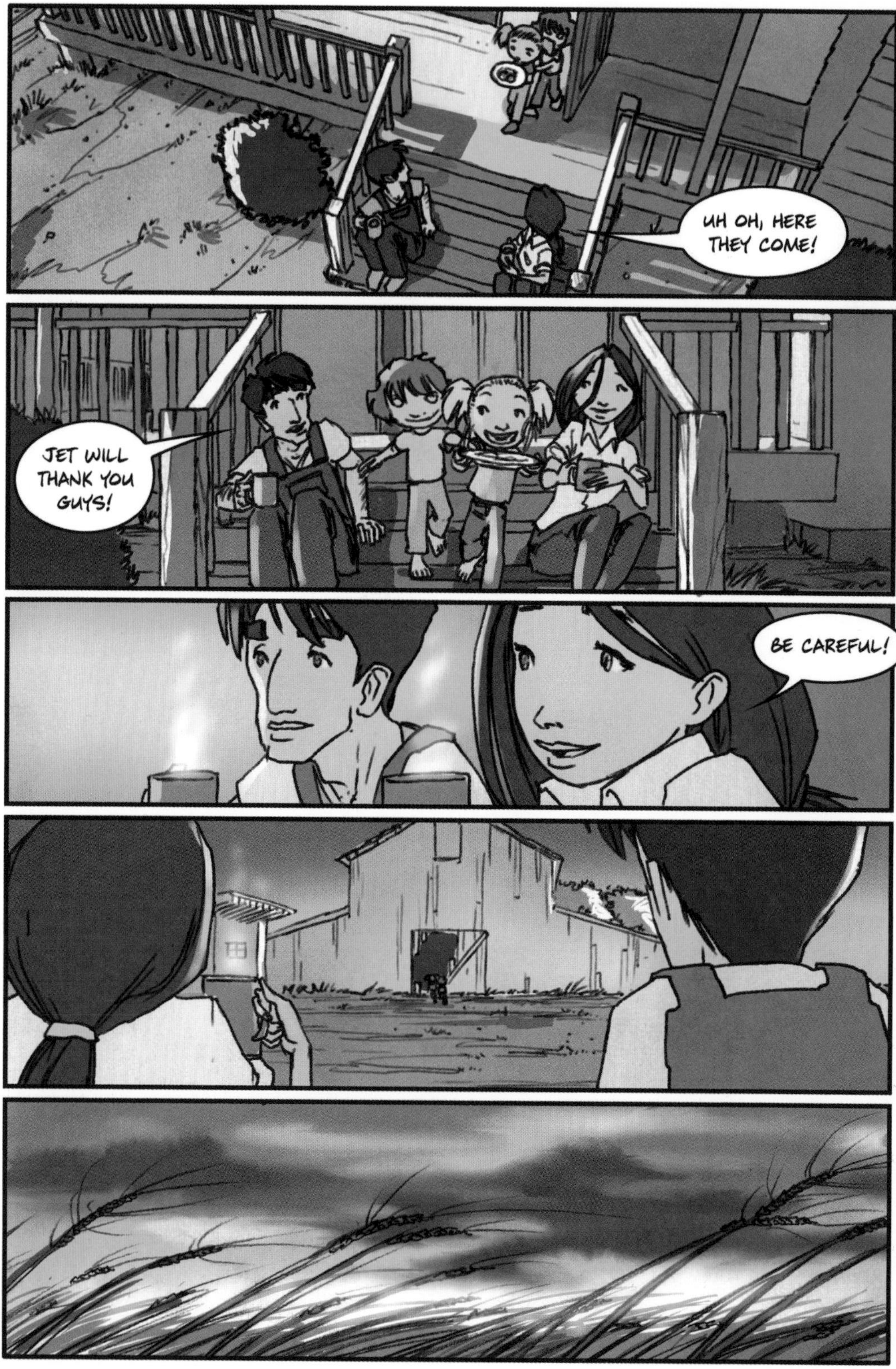
UH OH, HERE THEY COME!
JET WILL THANK YOU GUYS!
BE CAREFUL!

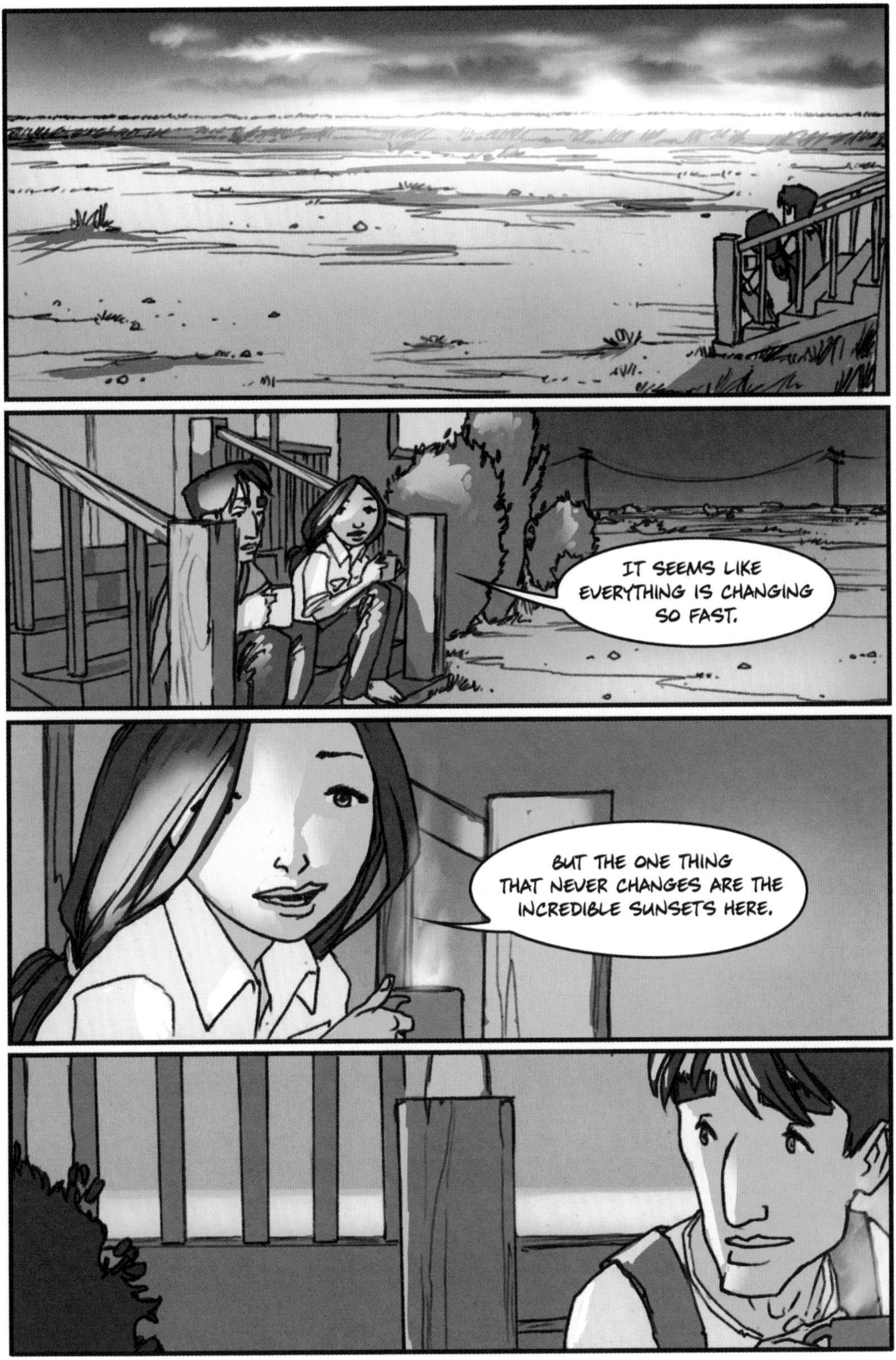
IT SEEMS LIKE EVERYTHING IS CHANGING SO FAST.
BUT THE ONE THING THAT NEVER CHANGES ARE THE INCREDIBLE SUNSETS HERE.

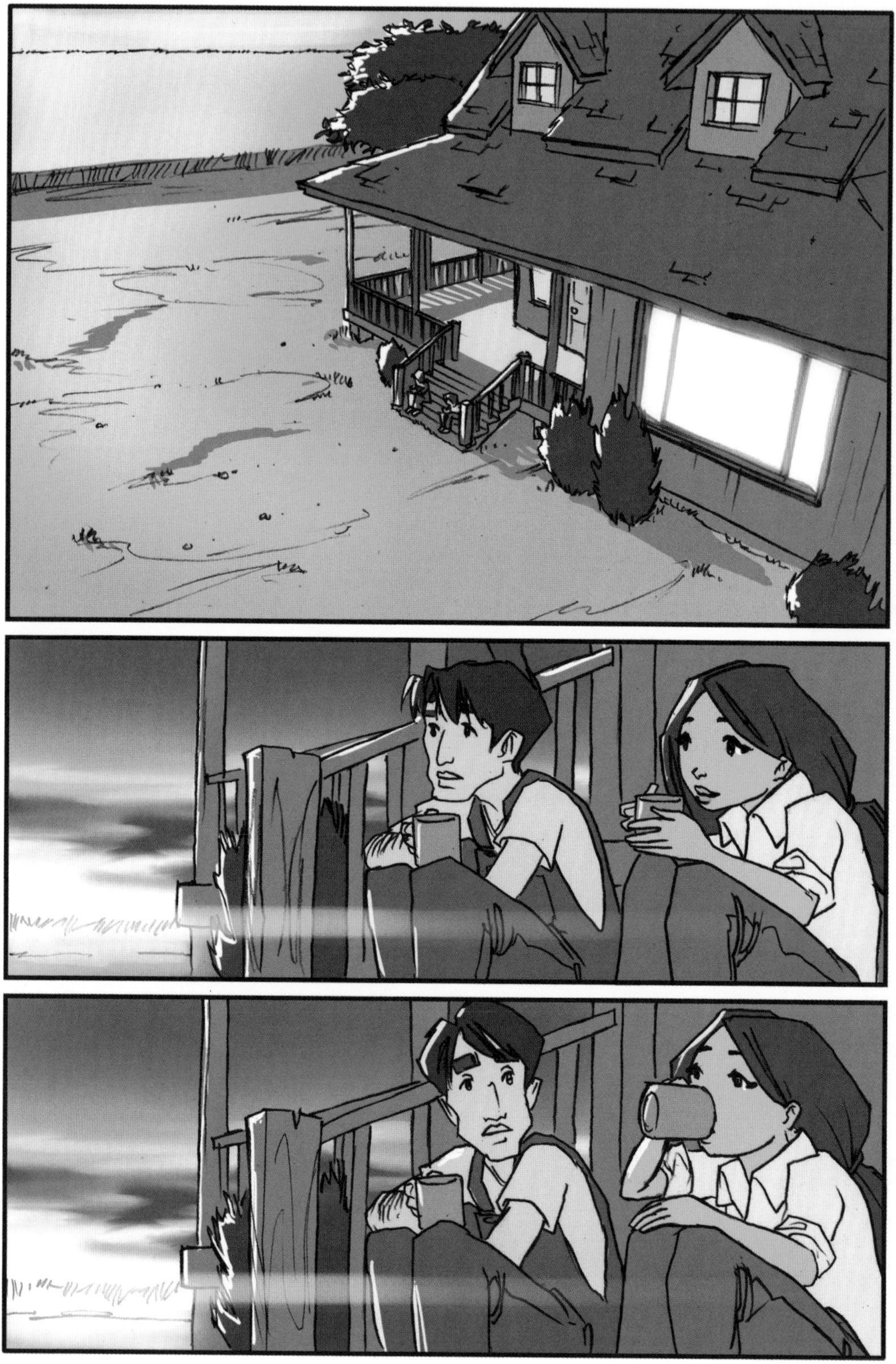

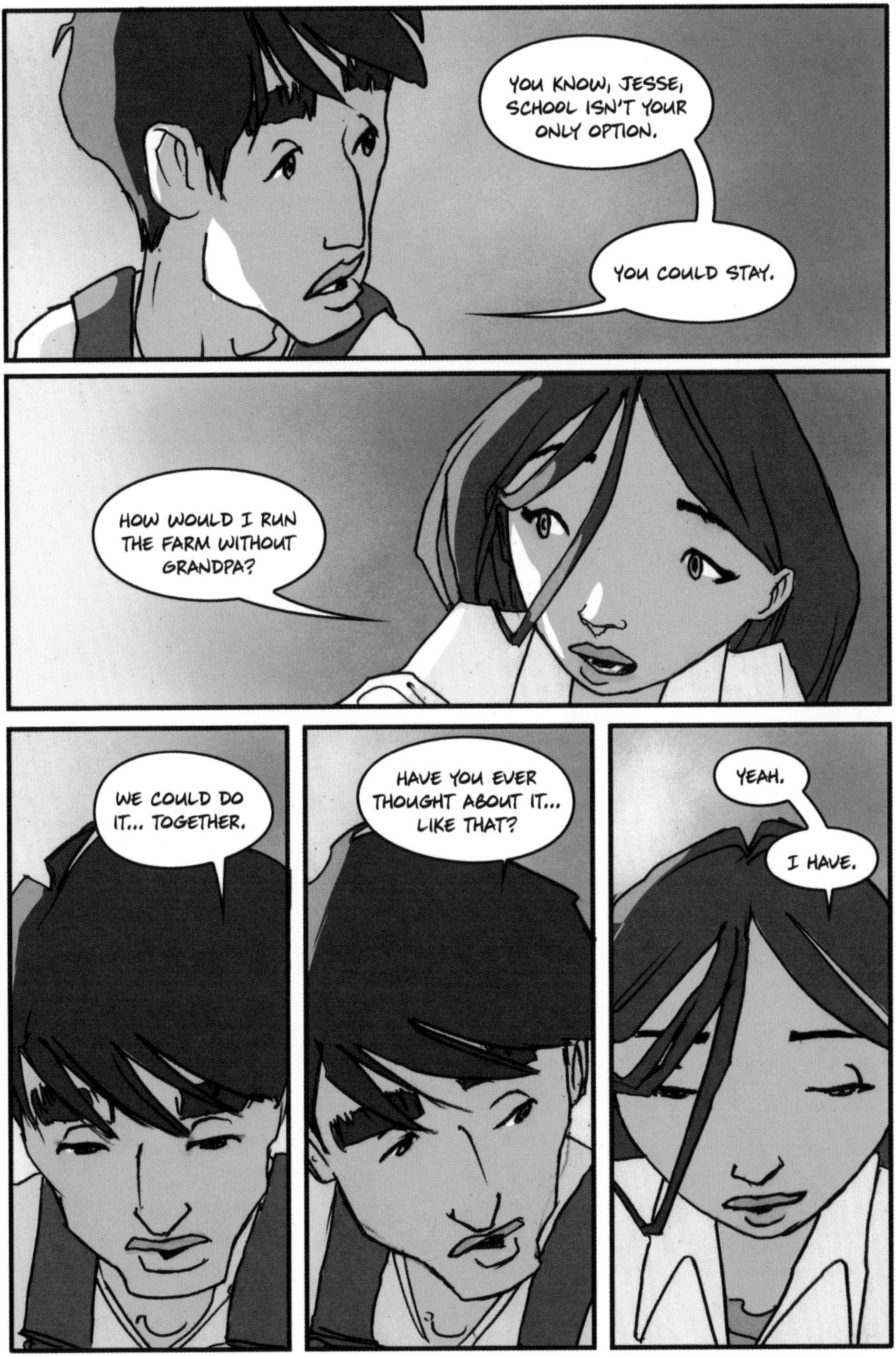
YOU KNOW, JESSE, SCHOOL ISN'T YOUR ONLY OPTION.
YOU COULD STAY.
HOW WOULD I RUN THE FARM WITHOUT GRANDPA?
WE COULD DO IT... TOGETHER.
HAVE YOU EVER THOUGHT ABOUT IT... LIKE THAT?
YEAH.
I HAVE.

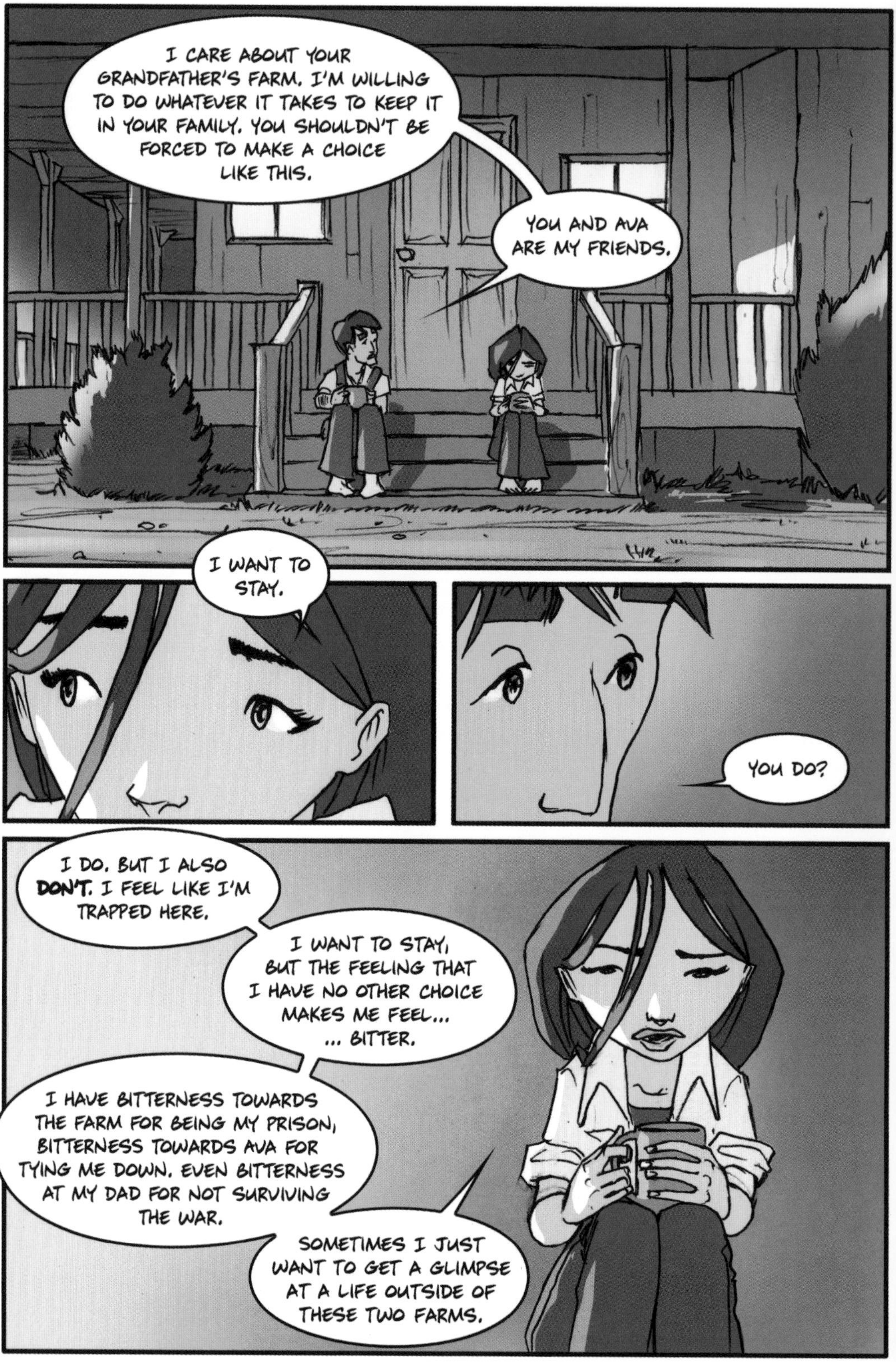
I CARE ABOUT YOUR GRANDFATHER'S FARM. I'M WILLING TO DO WHATEVER IT TAKES TO KEEP IT IN YOUR FAMILY. YOU SHOULDN'T BE FORCED TO MAKE A CHOICE LIKE THIS.
YOU AND AVA ARE MY FRIENDS.
I WANT TO STAY.
YOU DO?
I DO. BUT I ALSO **DON'T**. I FEEL LIKE I'M TRAPPED HERE.
I WANT TO STAY, BUT THE FEELING THAT I HAVE NO OTHER CHOICE MAKES ME FEEL... ... BITTER.
I HAVE BITTERNESS TOWARDS THE FARM FOR BEING MY PRISON, BITTERNESS TOWARDS AVA FOR TYING ME DOWN. EVEN BITTERNESS AT MY DAD FOR NOT SURVIVING THE WAR.
SOMETIMES I JUST WANT TO GET A GLIMPSE AT A LIFE OUTSIDE OF THESE TWO FARMS.

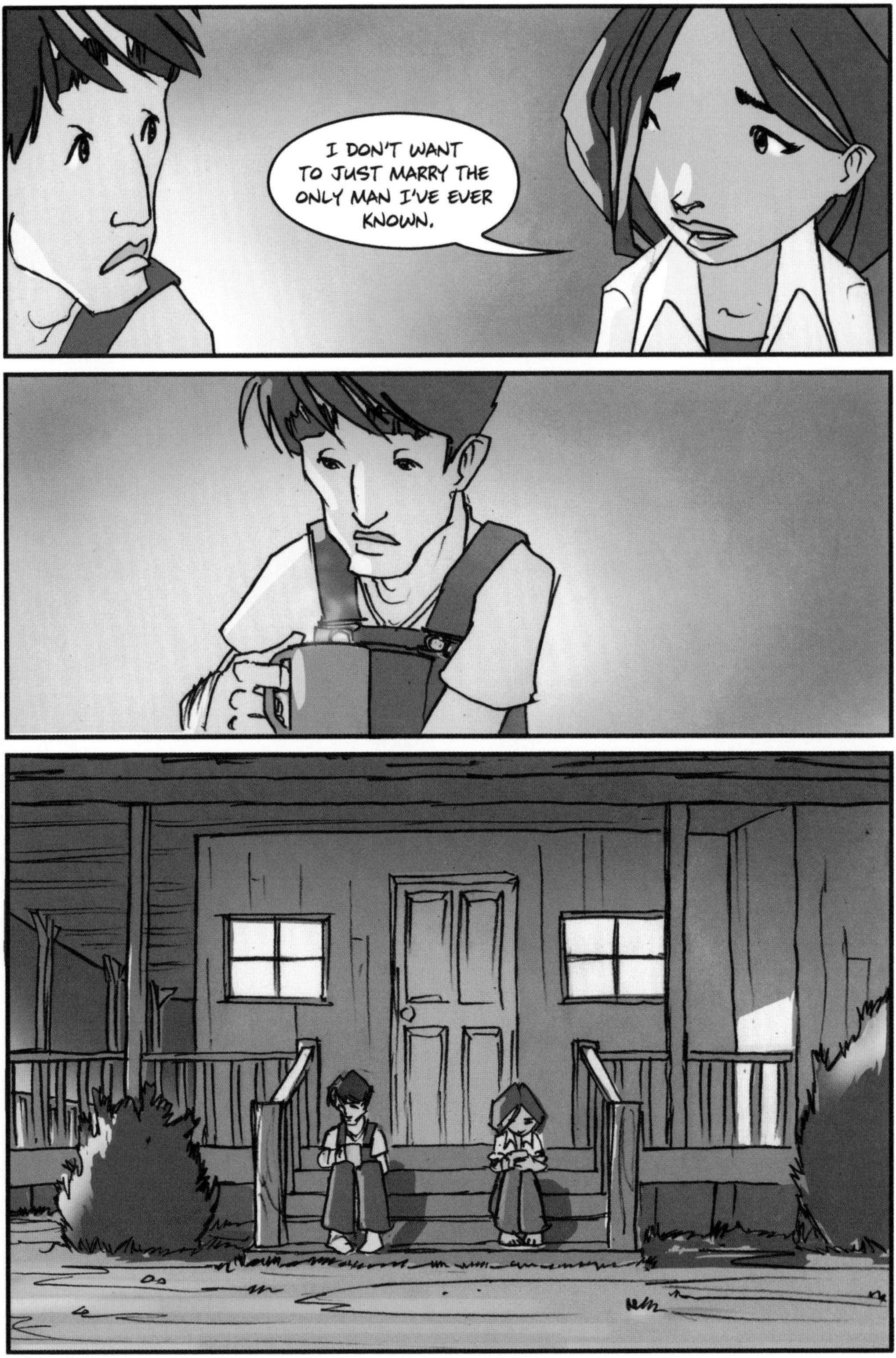
I DON'T WANT TO JUST MARRY THE ONLY MAN I'VE EVER KNOWN.

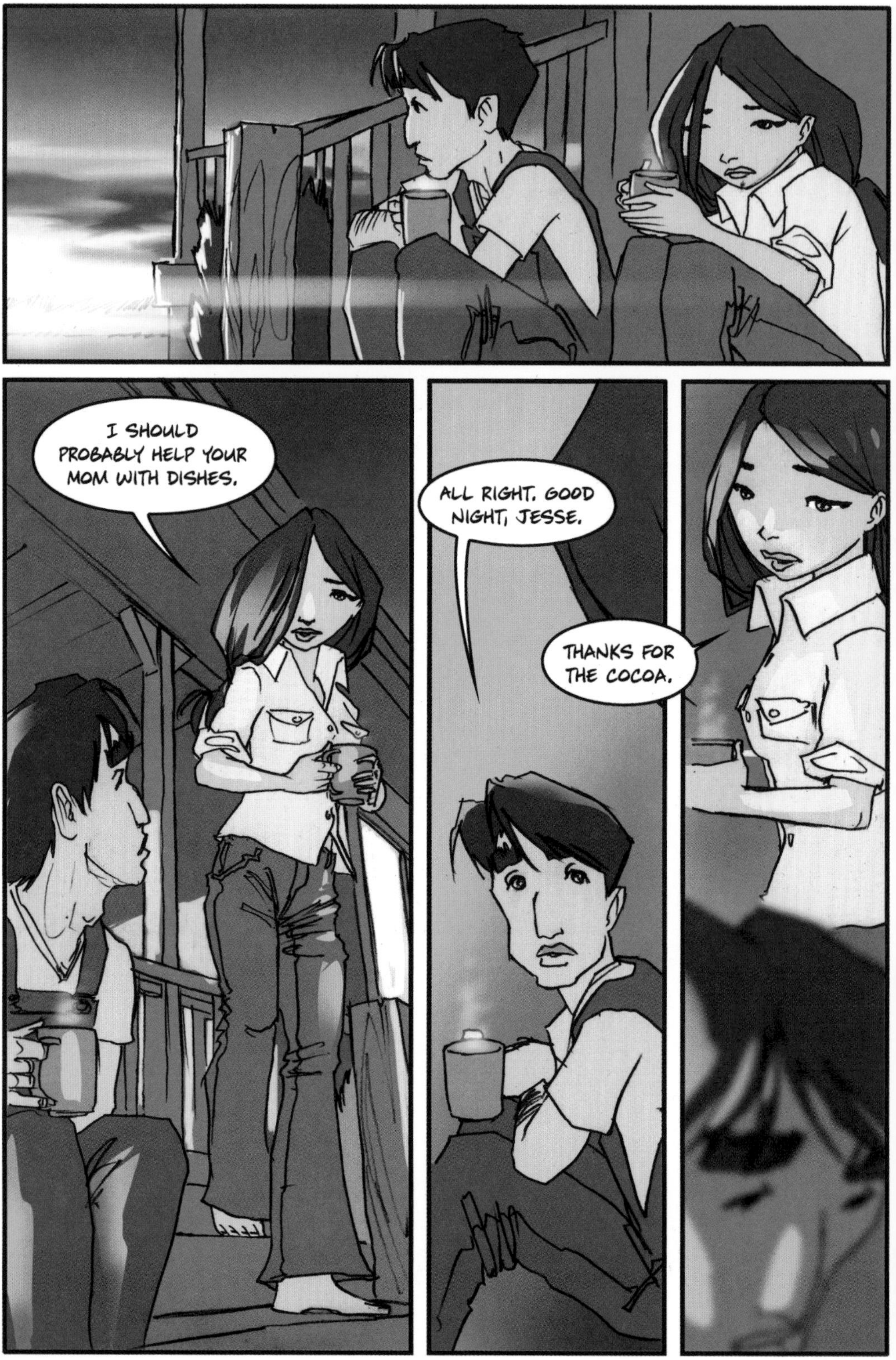
I SHOULD PROBABLY HELP YOUR MOM WITH DISHES.
ALL RIGHT. GOOD NIGHT, JESSE.
THANKS FOR THE COCOA.

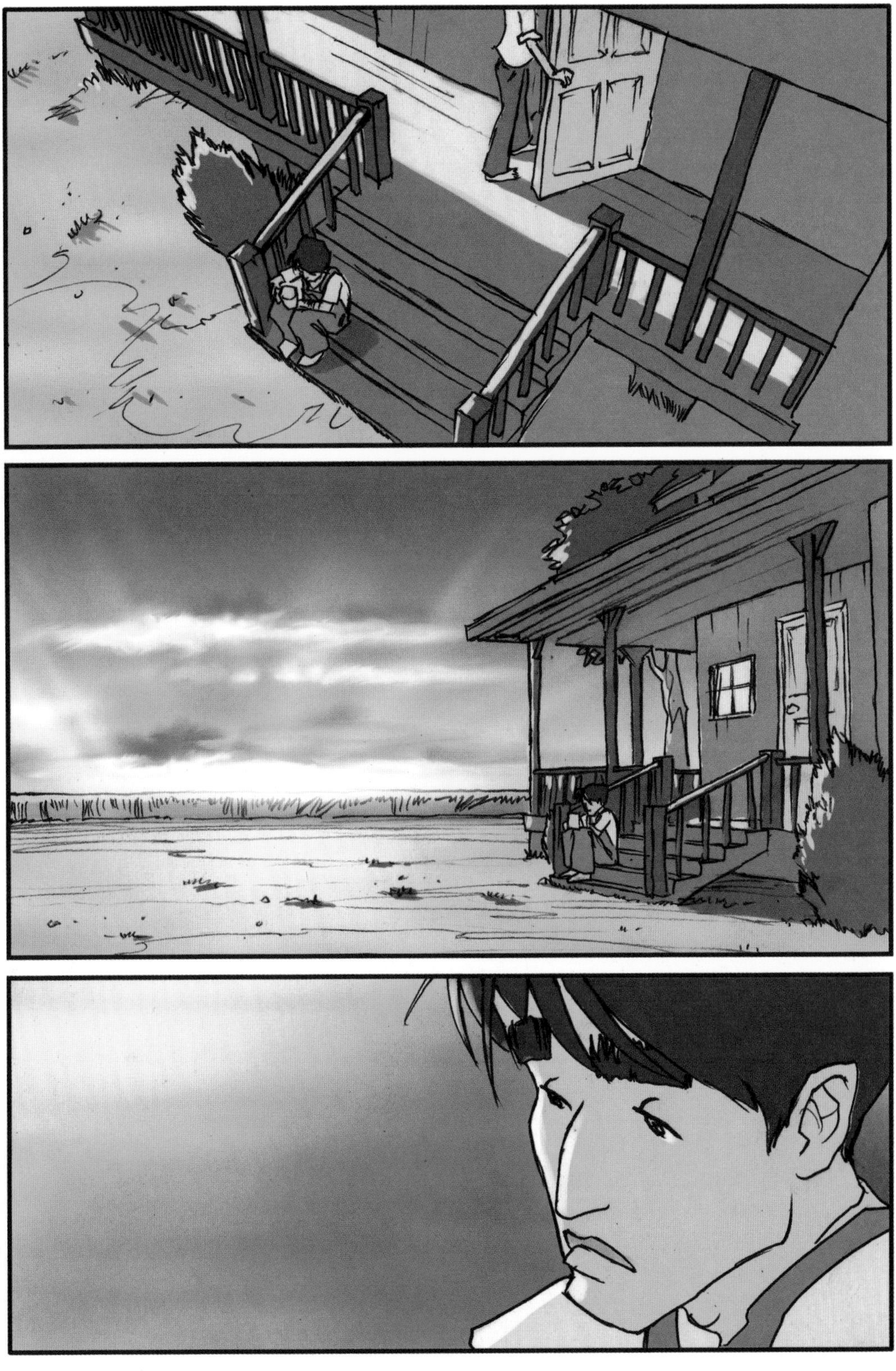

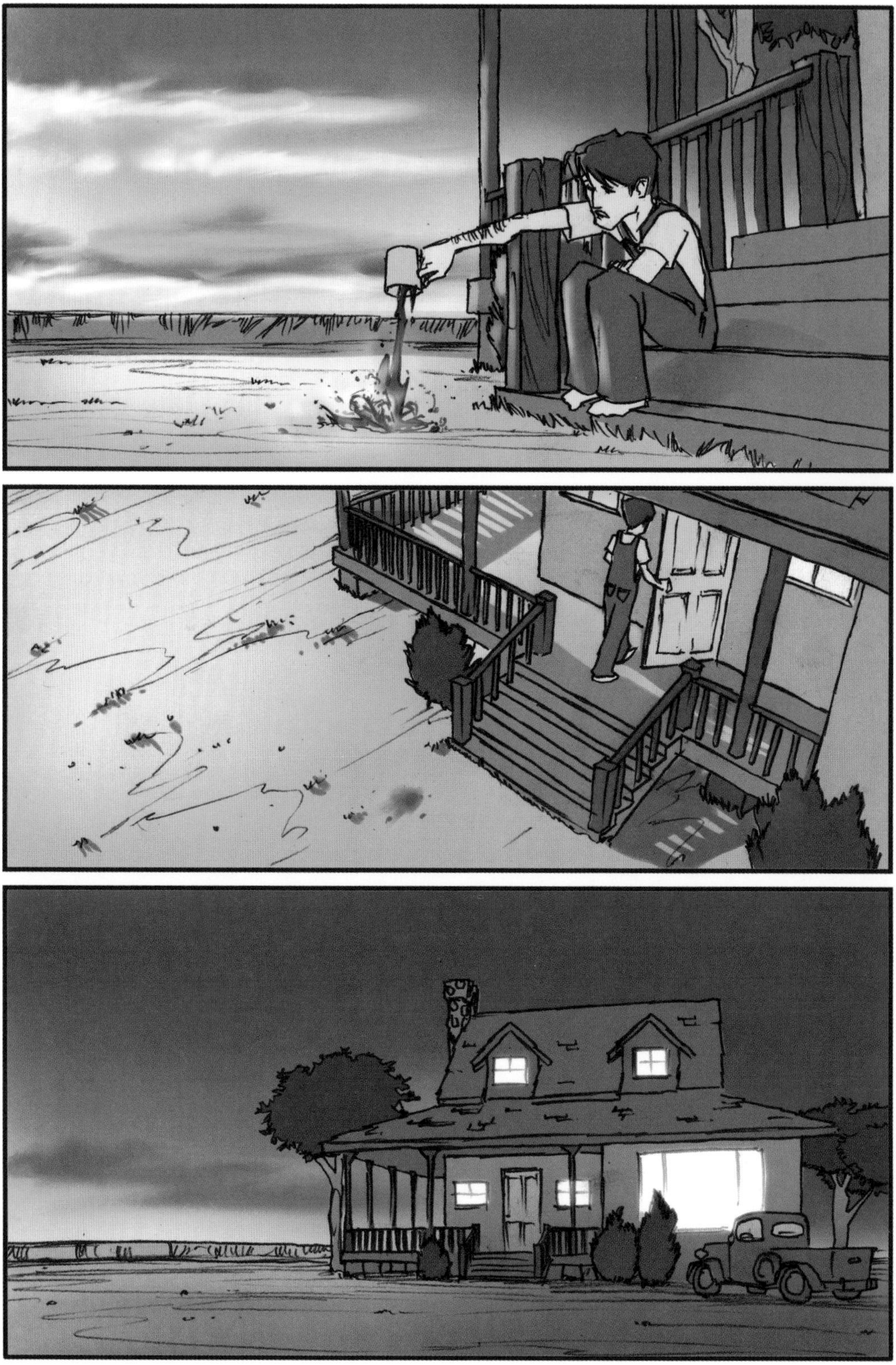

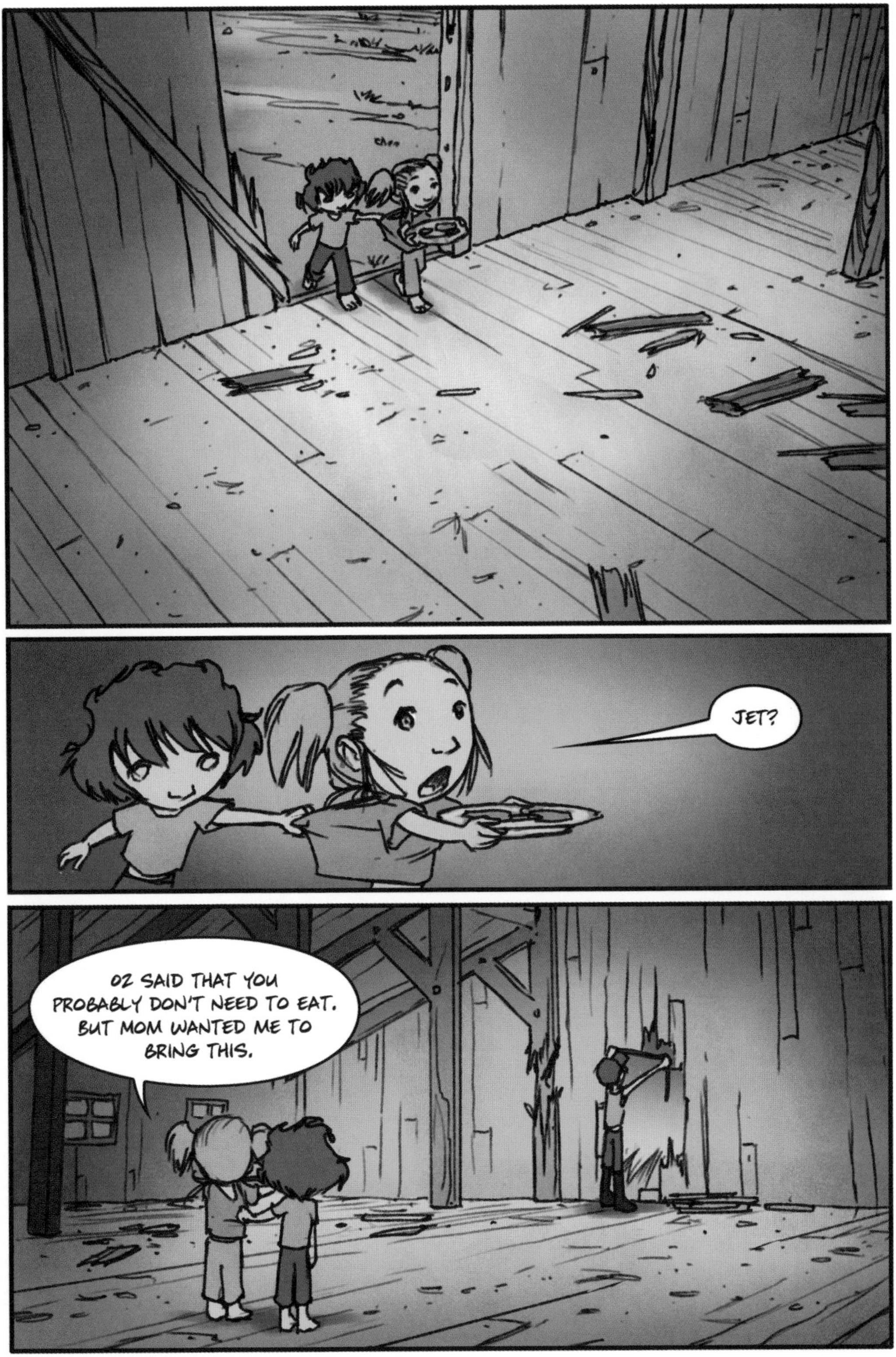
JET?
OZ SAID THAT YOU PROBABLY DON'T NEED TO EAT. BUT MOM WANTED ME TO BRING THIS.

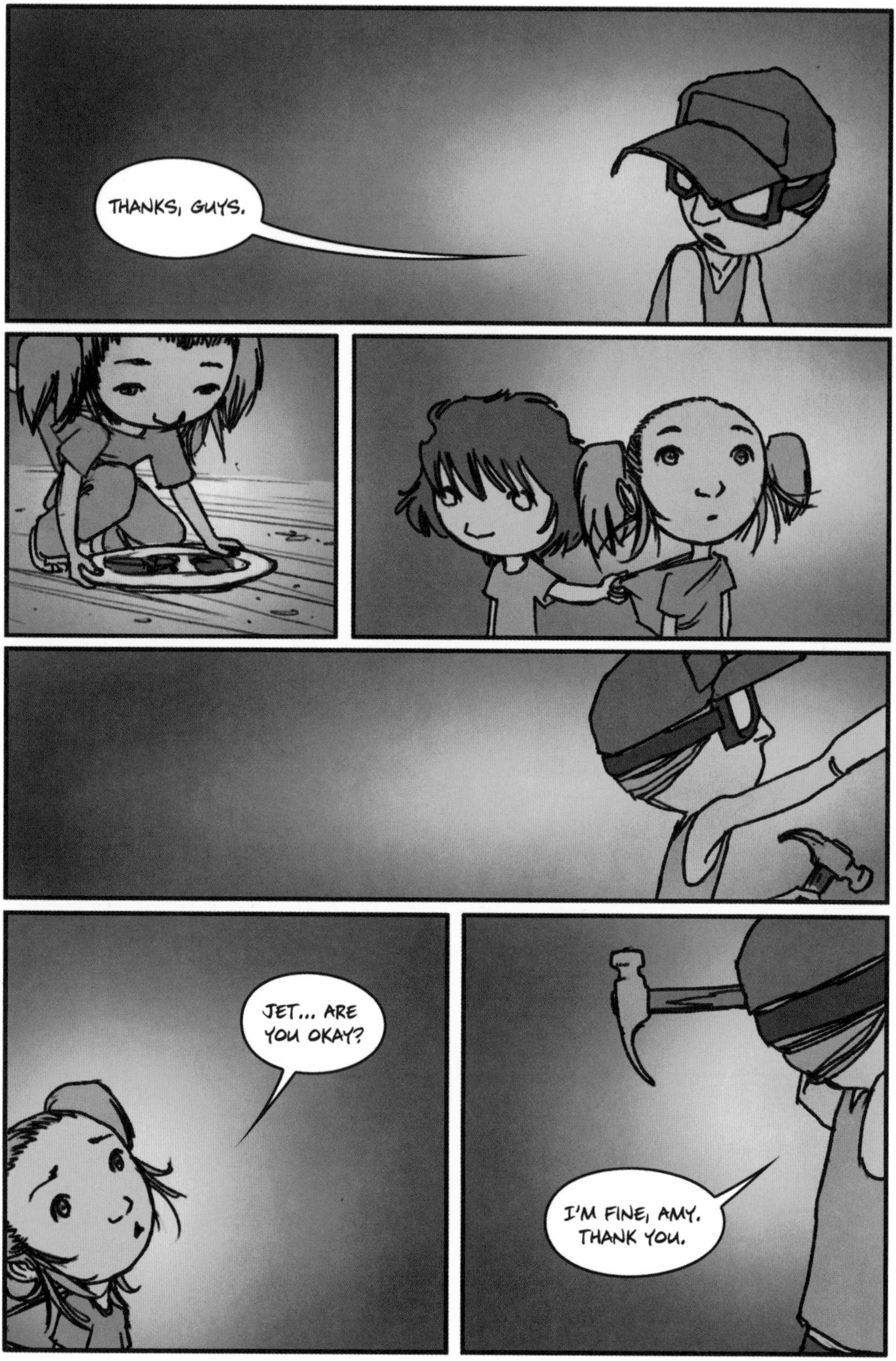
THANKS, GUYS.
JET... ARE YOU OKAY?
I'M FINE, AMY. THANK YOU.

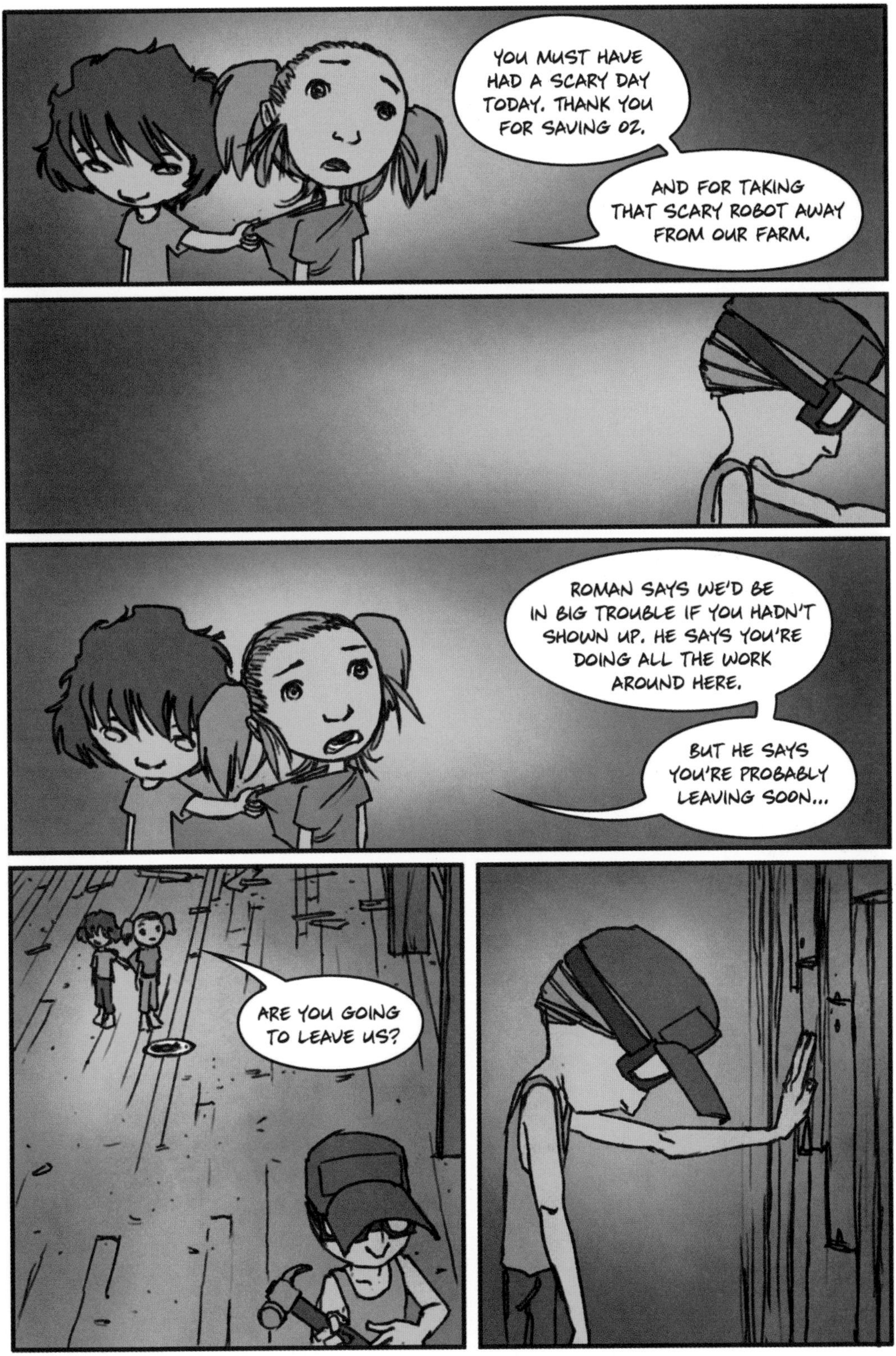
YOU MUST HAVE HAD A SCARY DAY TODAY. THANK YOU FOR SAVING OZ.
AND FOR TAKING THAT SCARY ROBOT AWAY FROM OUR FARM.
ROMAN SAYS WE'D BE IN BIG TROUBLE IF YOU HADN'T SHOWN UP. HE SAYS YOU'RE DOING ALL THE WORK AROUND HERE.
BUT HE SAYS YOU'RE PROBABLY LEAVING SOON...
ARE YOU GOING TO LEAVE US?

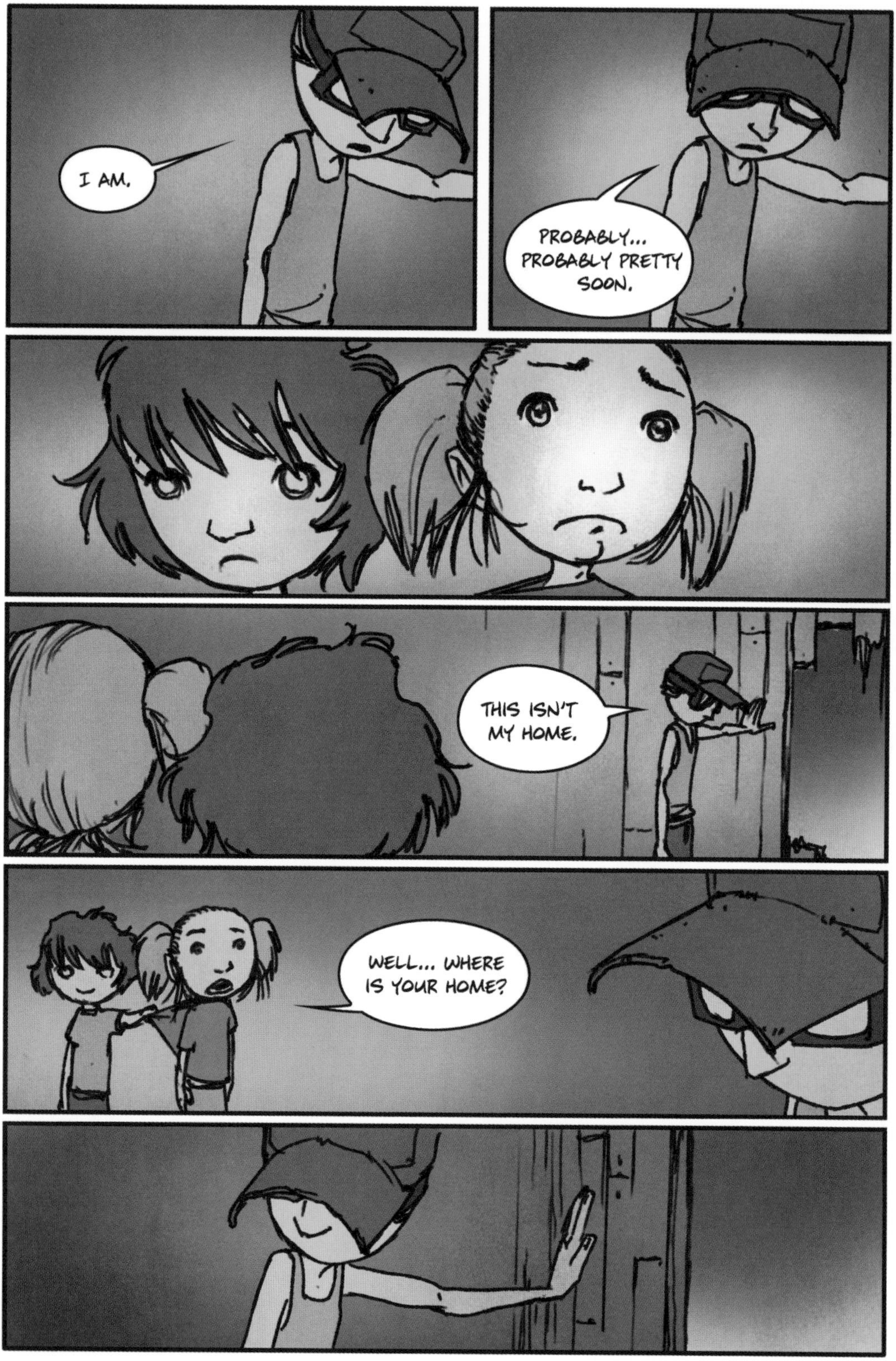
I AM.
PROBABLY... PROBABLY PRETTY SOON.
THIS ISN'T MY HOME.
WELL... WHERE IS YOUR HOME?

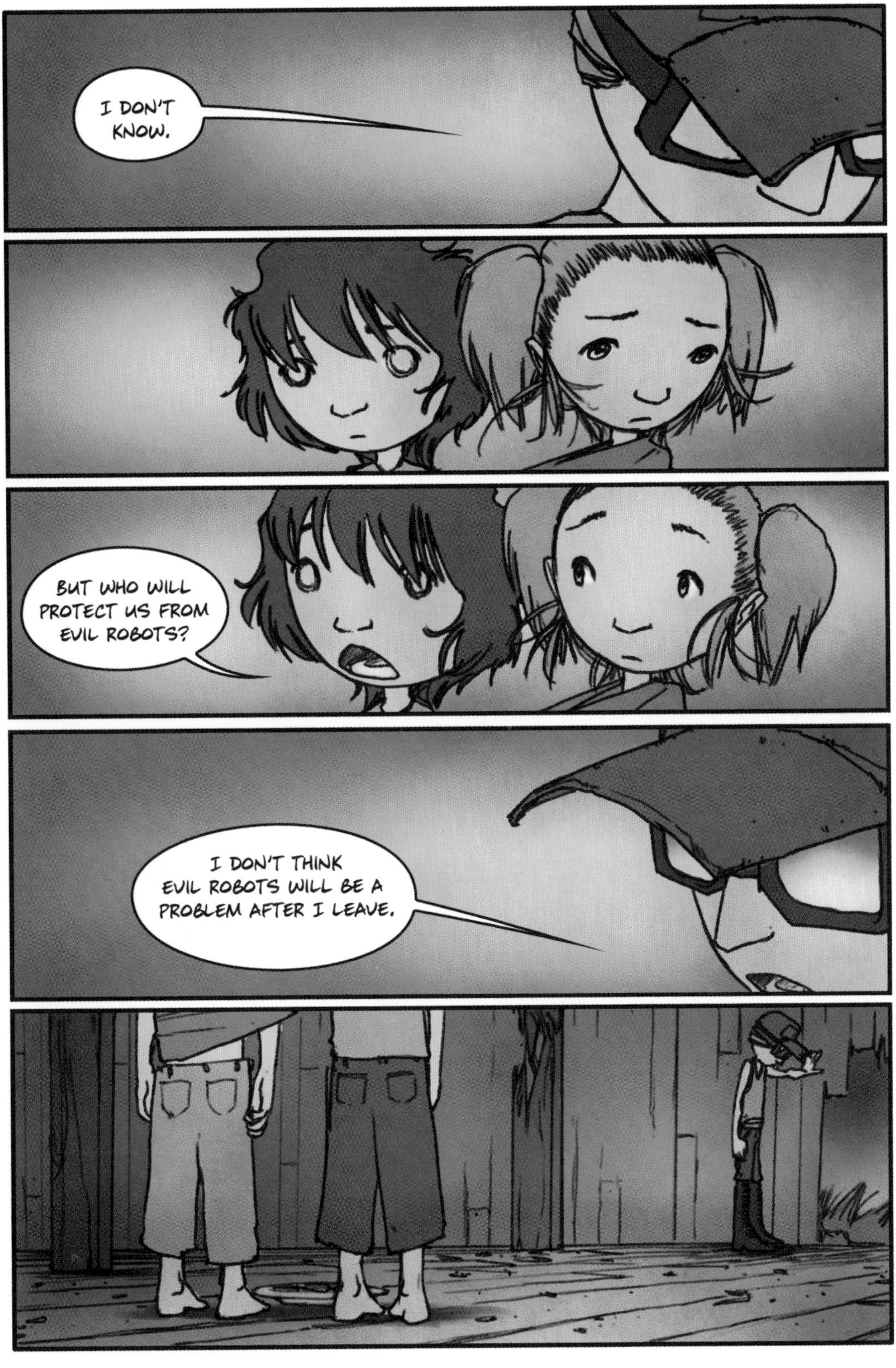
I DON'T KNOW.
BUT WHO WILL PROTECT US FROM EVIL ROBOTS?
I DON'T THINK EVIL ROBOTS WILL BE A PROBLEM AFTER I LEAVE.

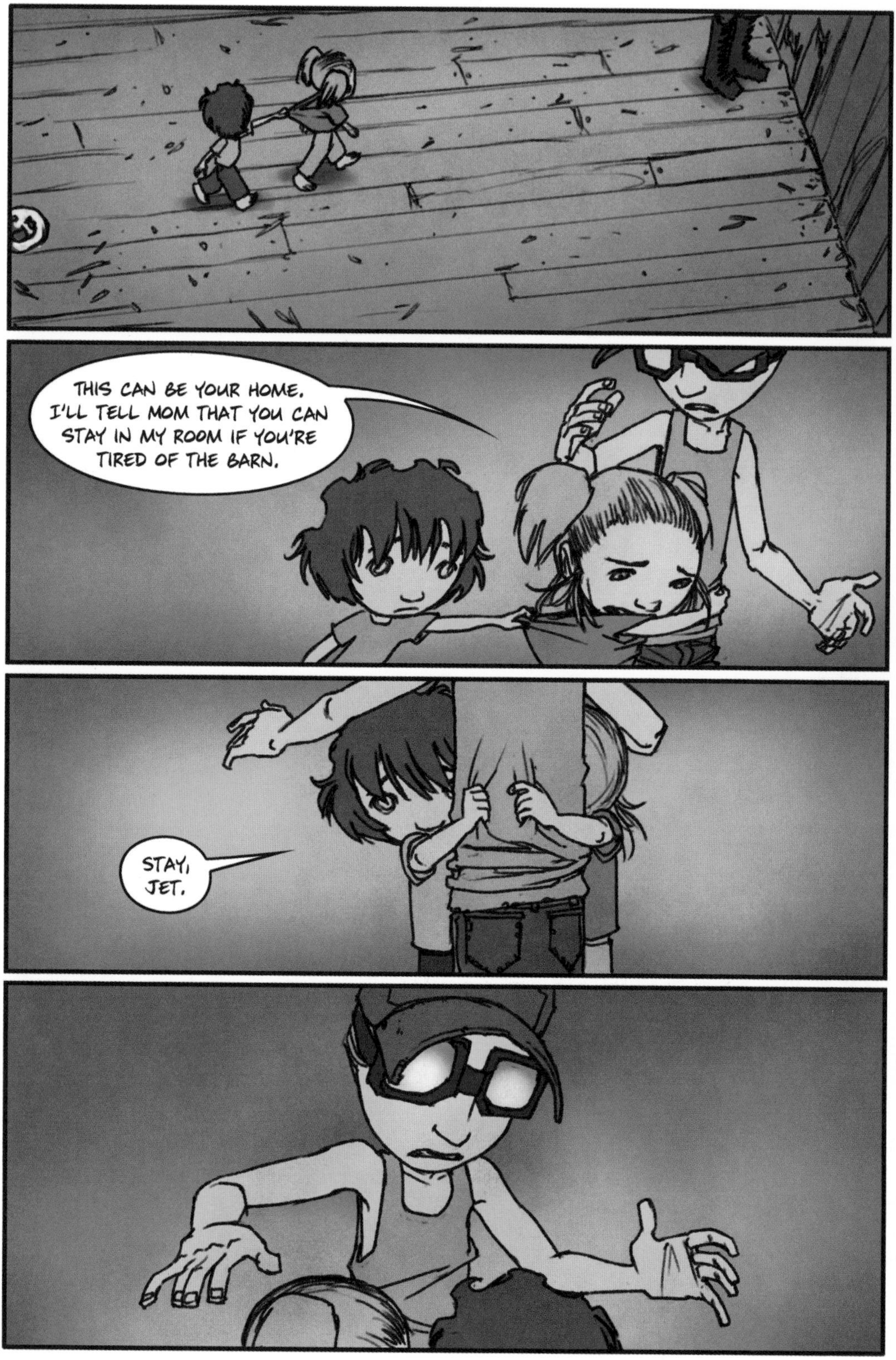
THIS CAN BE YOUR HOME. I'LL TELL MOM THAT YOU CAN STAY IN MY ROOM IF YOU'RE TIRED OF THE BARN.
STAY, JET.

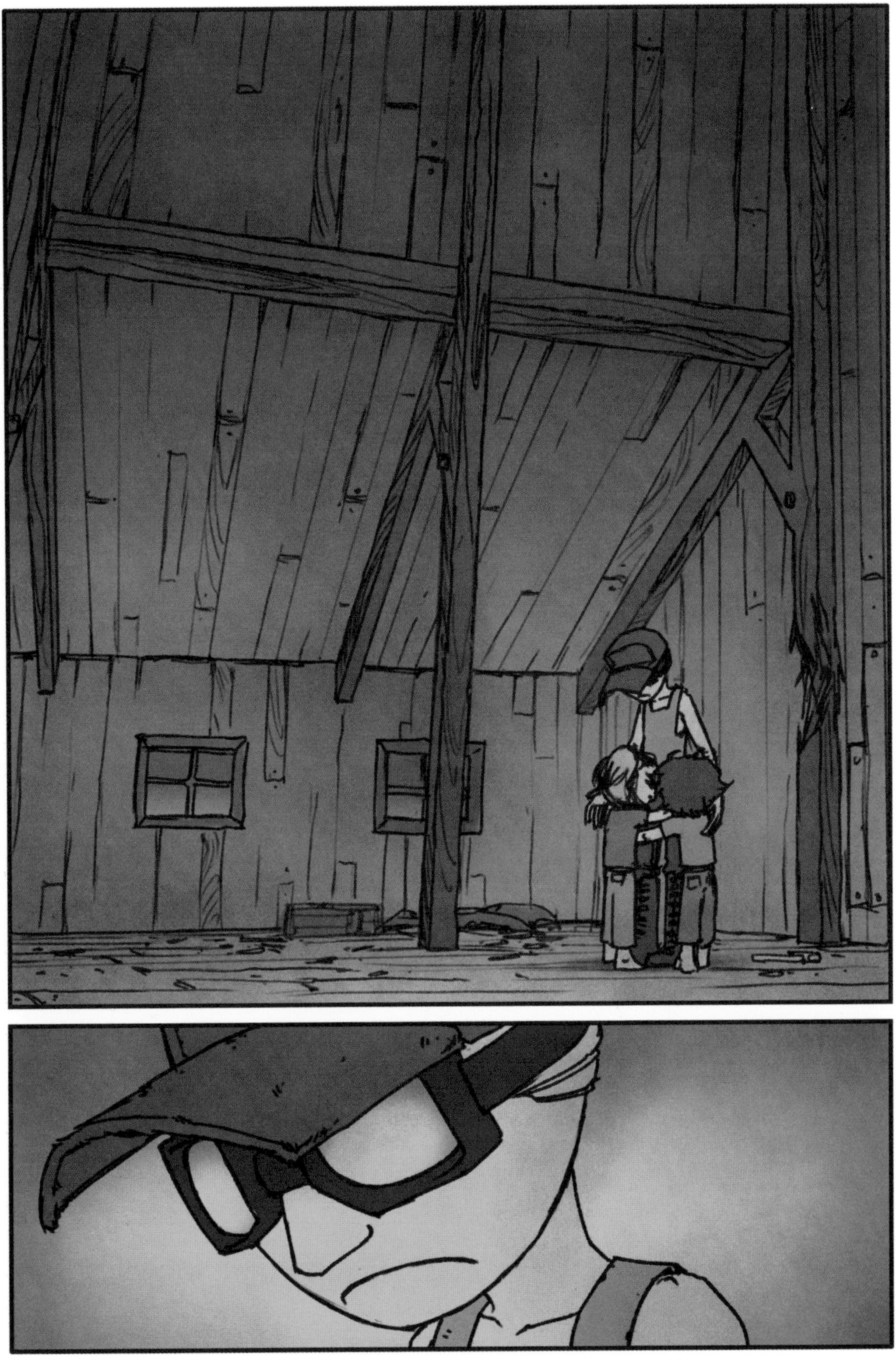

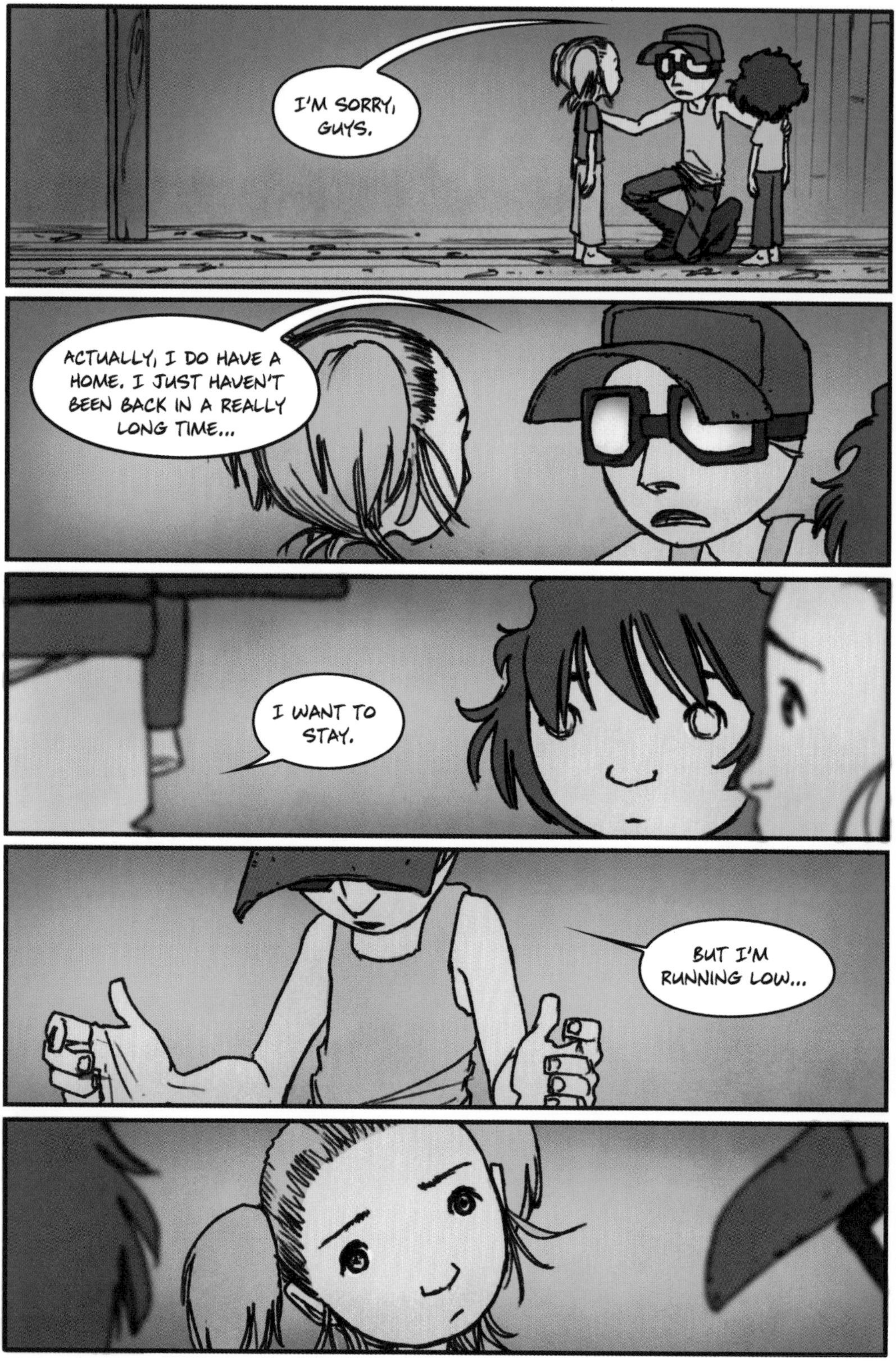
I'M SORRY, GUYS.
ACTUALLY, I DO HAVE A HOME. I JUST HAVEN'T BEEN BACK IN A REALLY LONG TIME...
I WANT TO STAY.
BUT I'M RUNNING LOW...

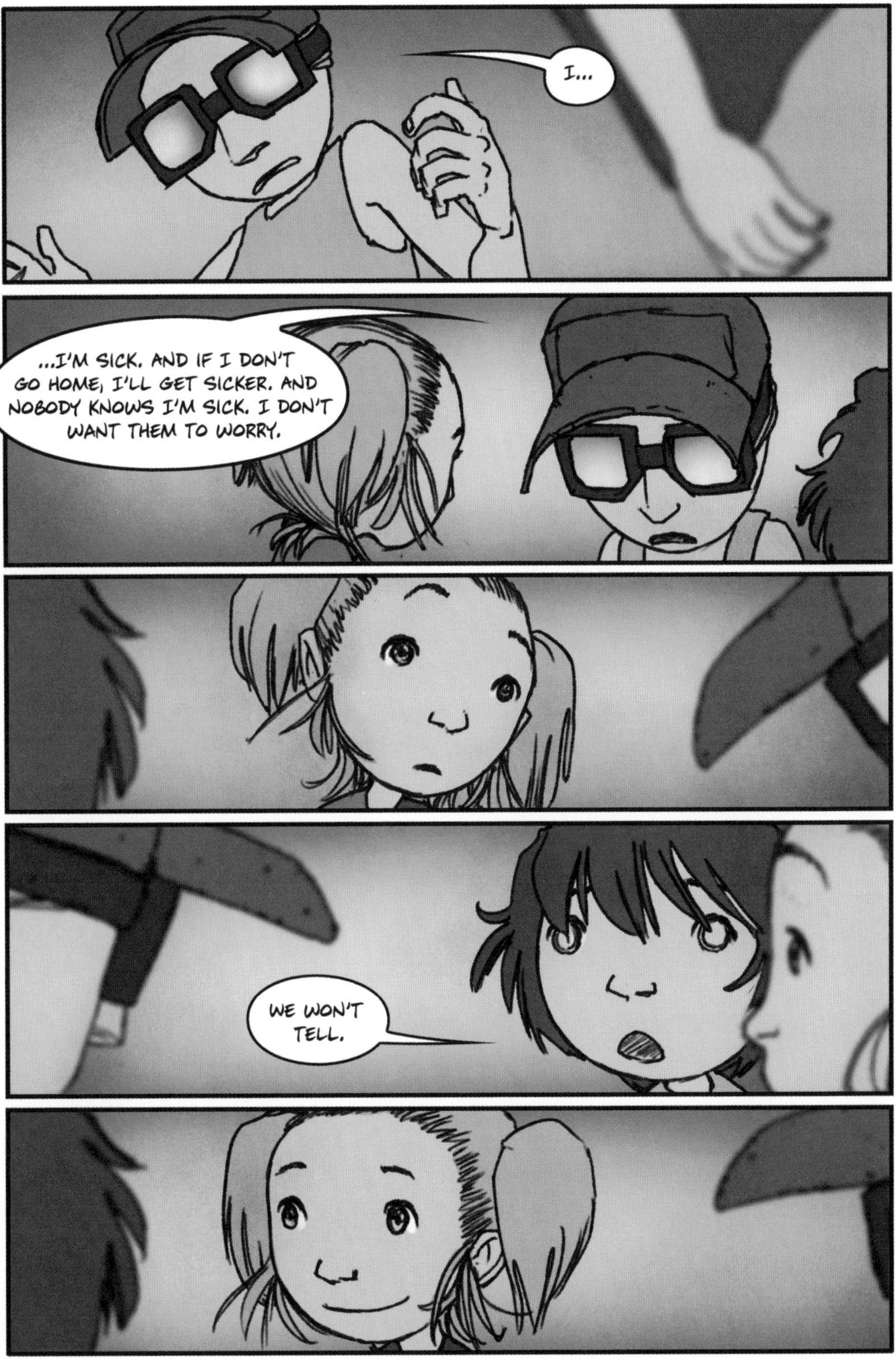
I...
...I'M SICK. AND IF I DON'T GO HOME, I'LL GET SICKER. AND NOBODY KNOWS I'M SICK. I DON'T WANT THEM TO WORRY.
WE WON'T TELL.

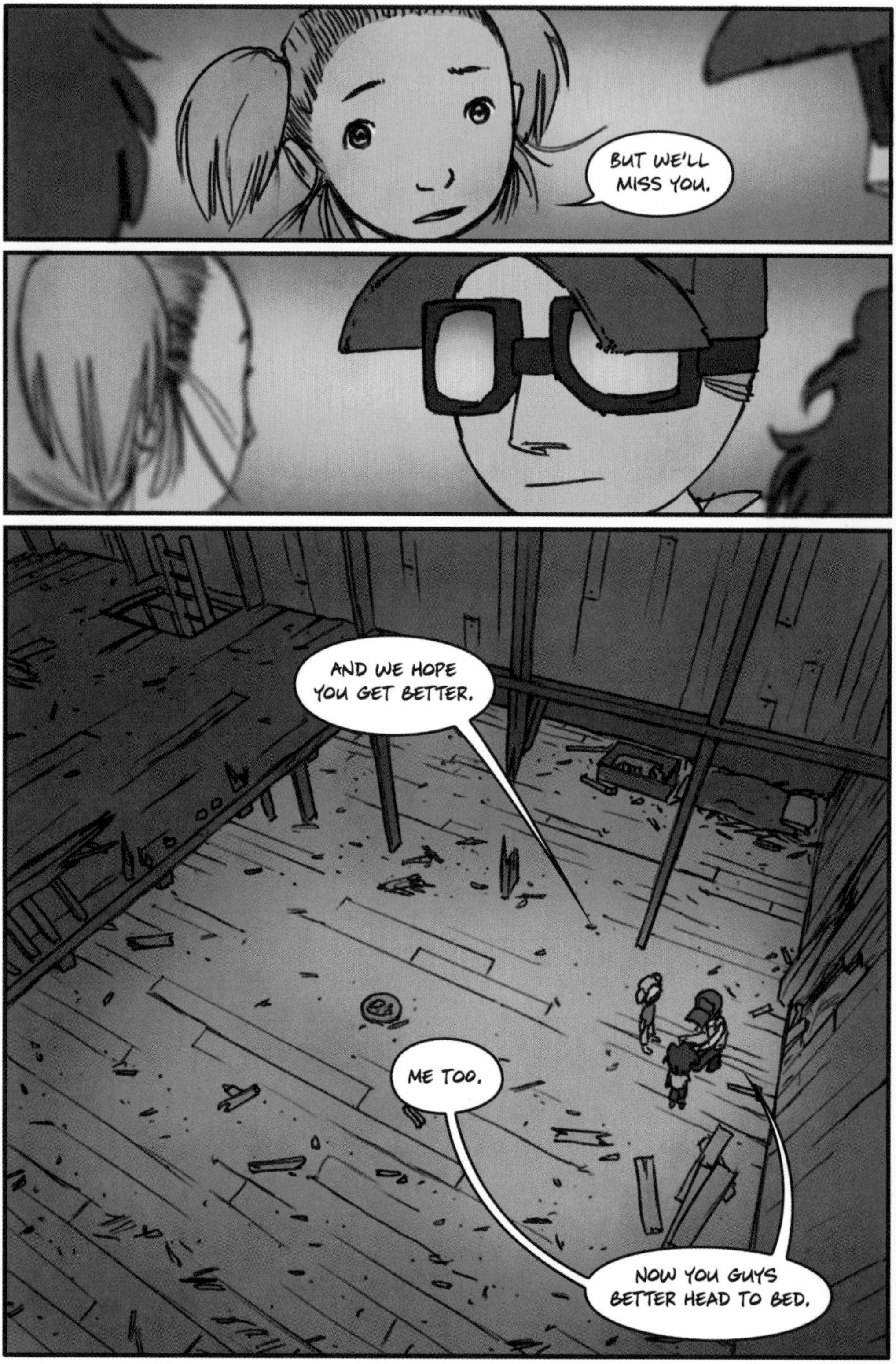
BUT WE'LL MISS YOU.
AND WE HOPE YOU GET BETTER.
ME TOO.
NOW YOU GUYS BETTER HEAD TO BED.

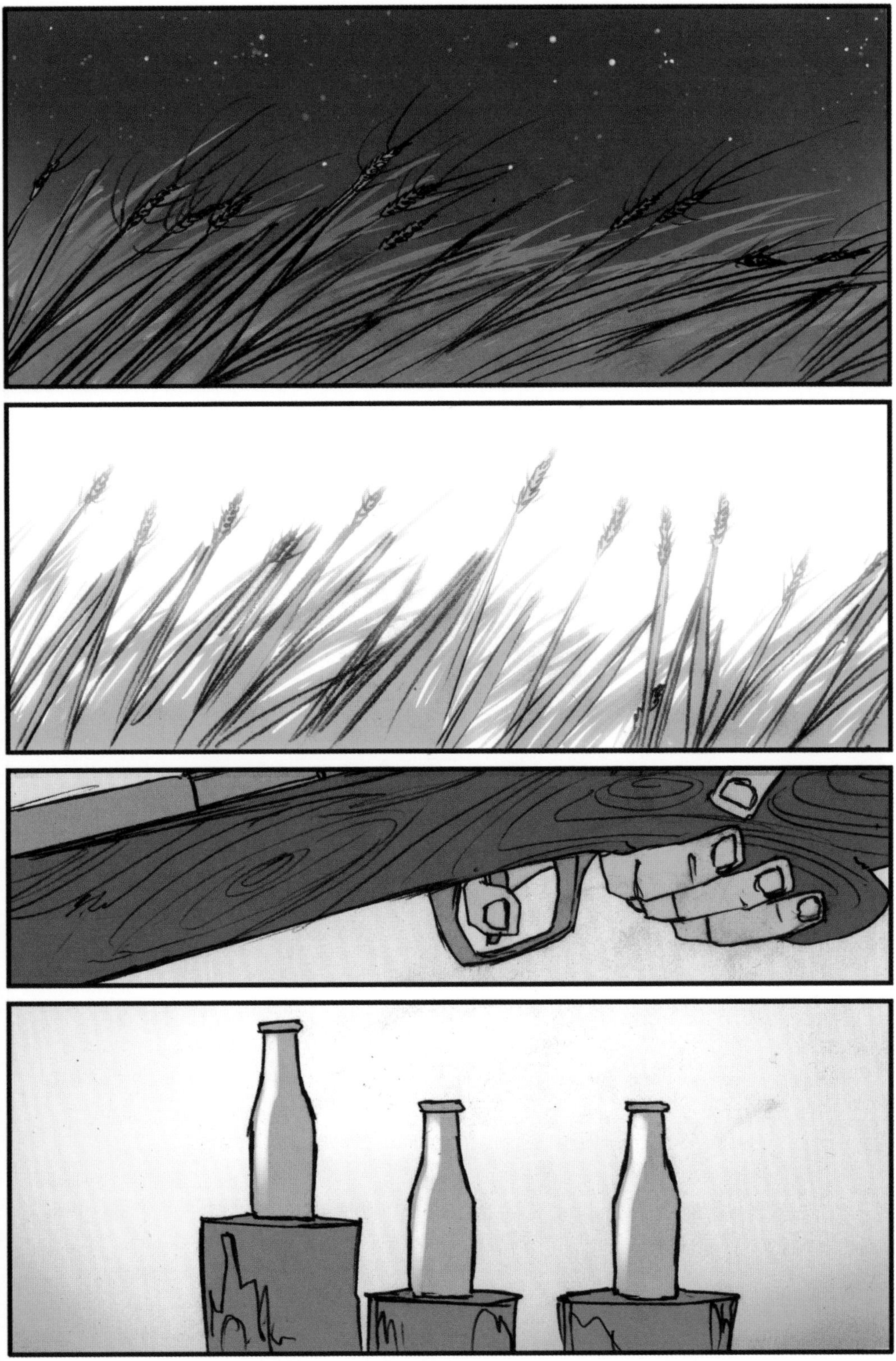

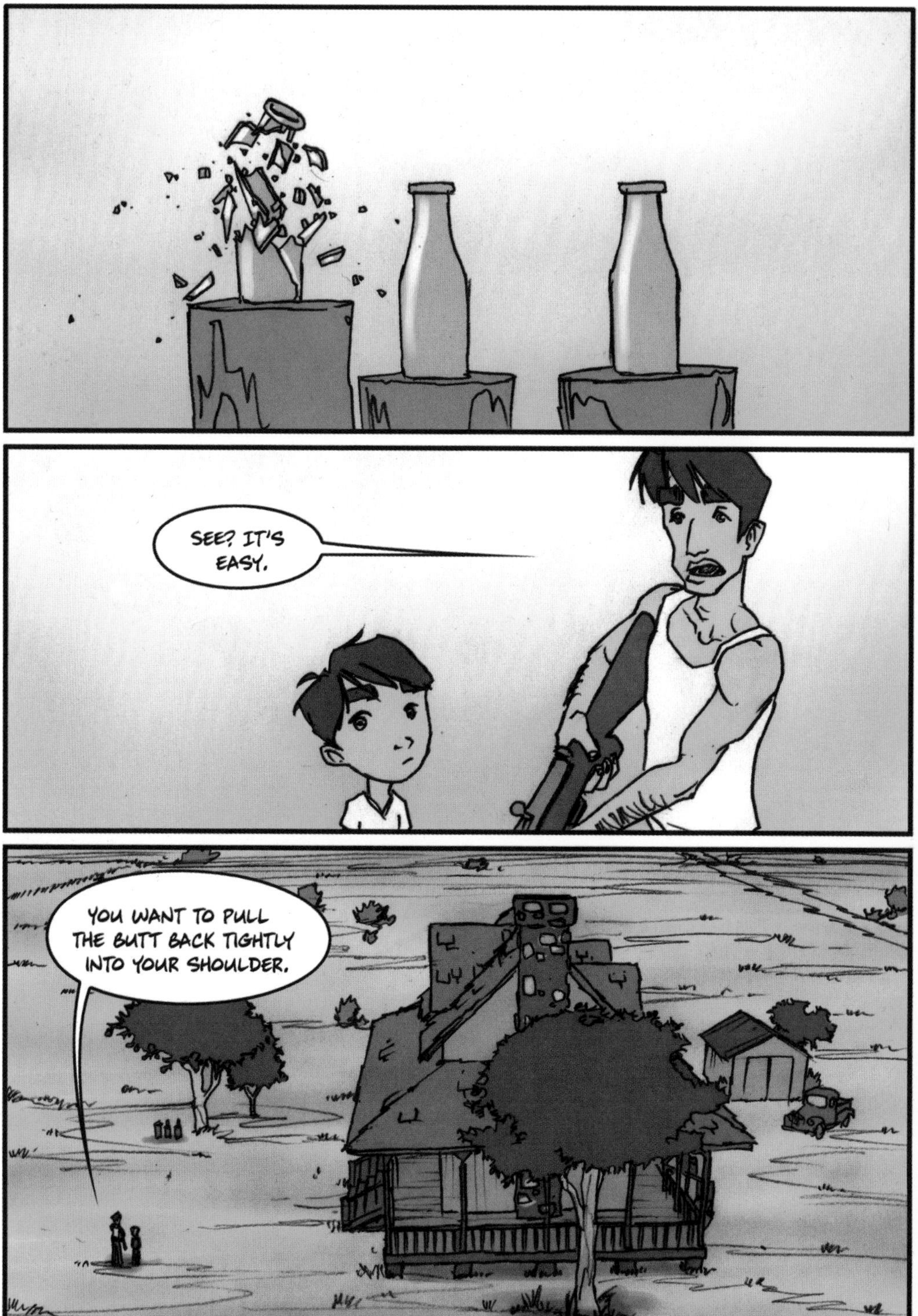
SEE? IT'S EASY.
YOU WANT TO PULL THE BUTT BACK TIGHTLY INTO YOUR SHOULDER.

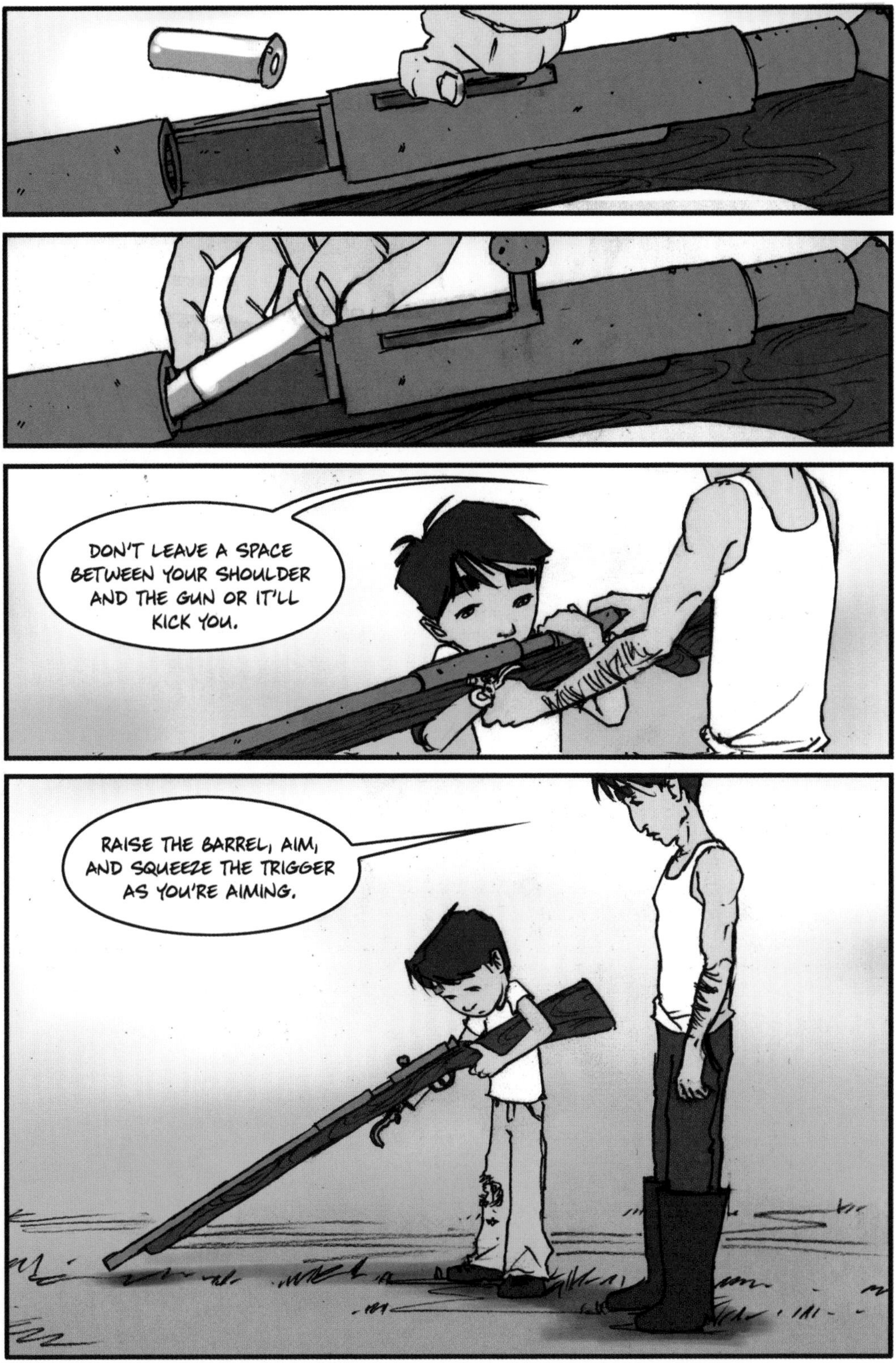
DON'T LEAVE A SPACE BETWEEN YOUR SHOULDER AND THE GUN OR IT'LL KICK YOU.
RAISE THE BARREL, AIM, AND SQUEEZE THE TRIGGER AS YOU'RE AIMING.

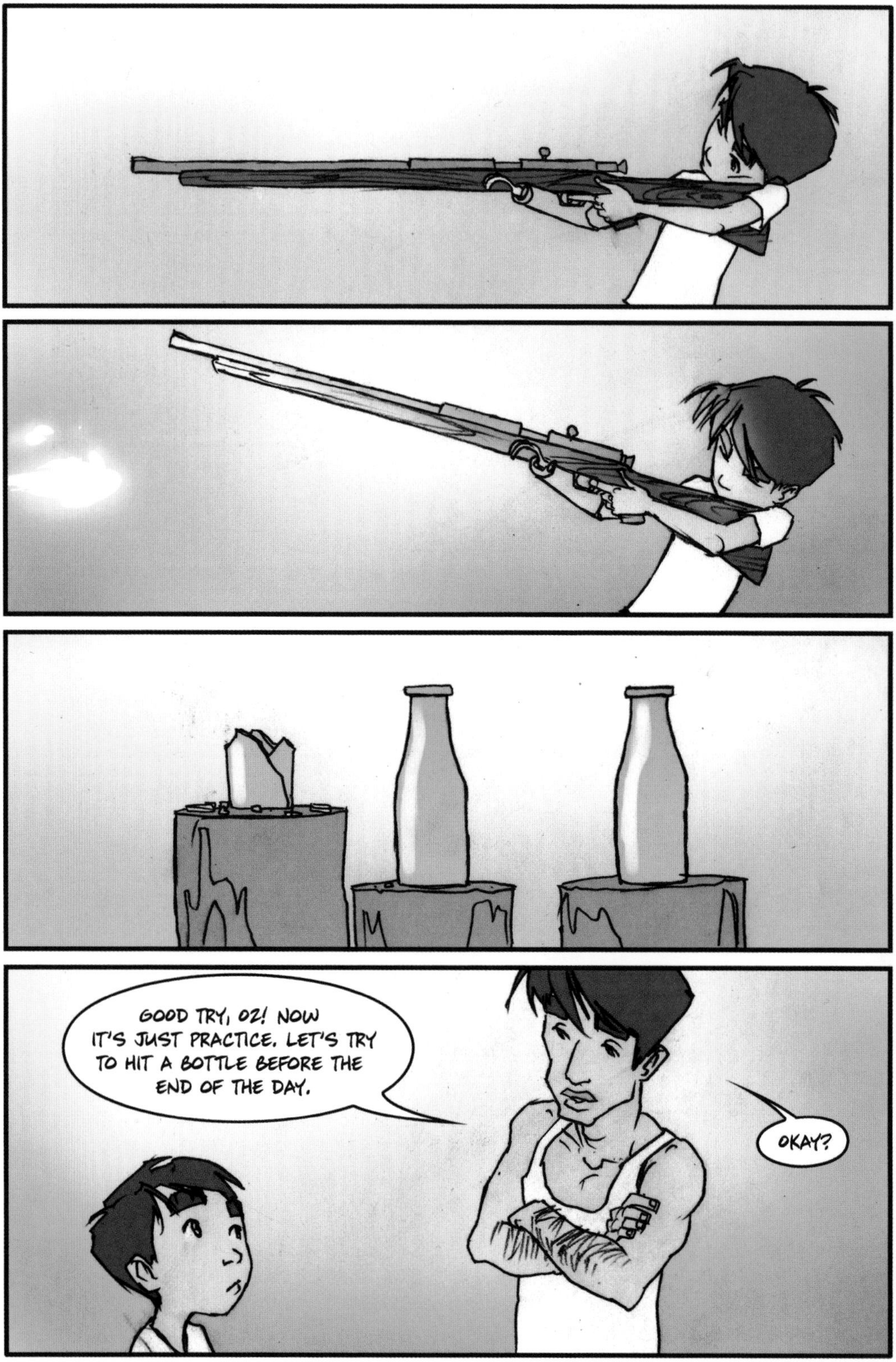
GOOD TRY, OZ! NOW IT'S JUST PRACTICE. LET'S TRY TO HIT A BOTTLE BEFORE THE END OF THE DAY.
OKAY?

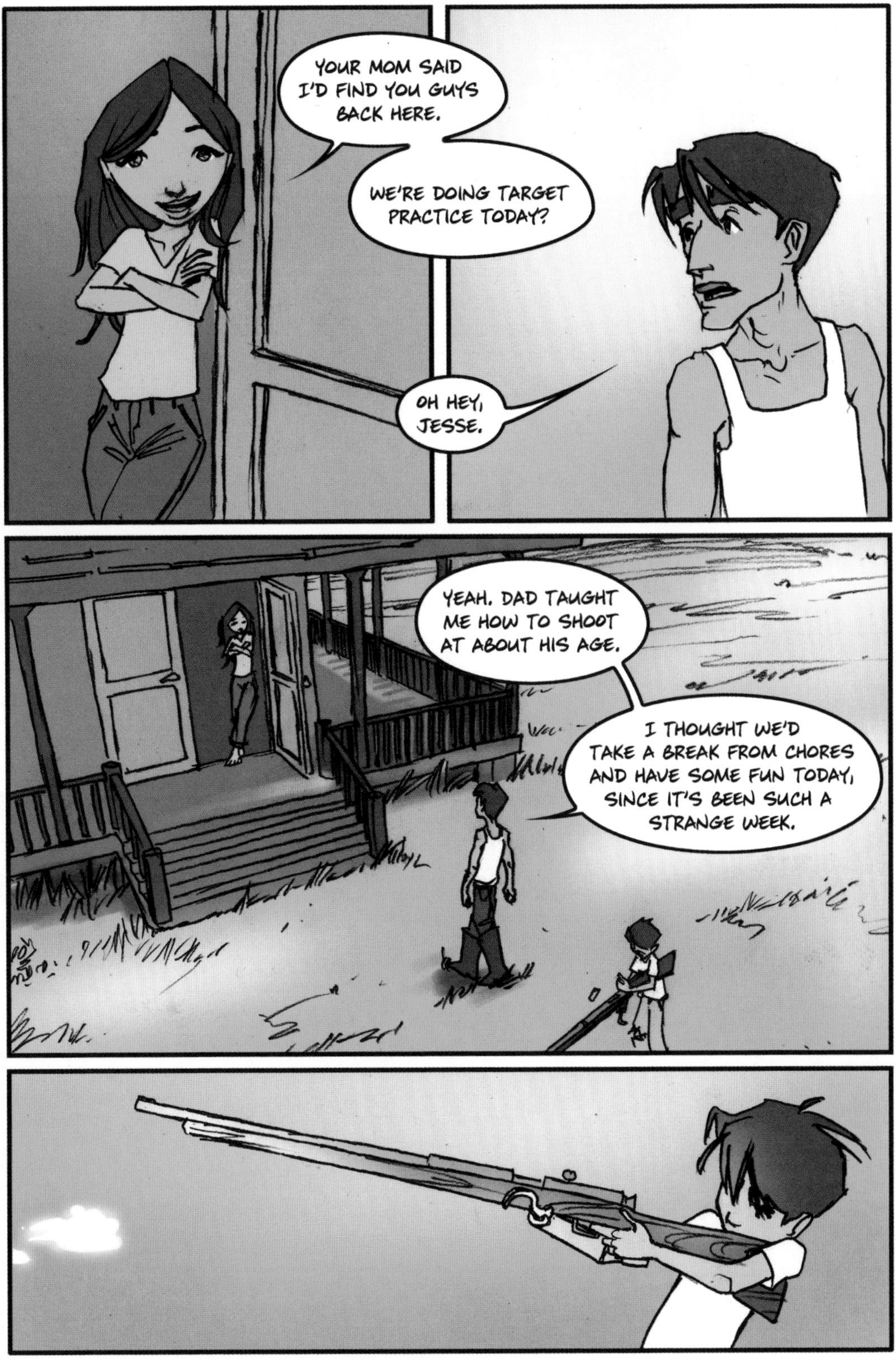
YOUR MOM SAID I'D FIND YOU GUYS BACK HERE.
WE'RE DOING TARGET PRACTICE TODAY?
OH HEY, JESSE.
YEAH. DAD TAUGHT ME HOW TO SHOOT AT ABOUT HIS AGE.
I THOUGHT WE'D TAKE A BREAK FROM CHORES AND HAVE SOME FUN TODAY, SINCE IT'S BEEN SUCH A STRANGE WEEK.

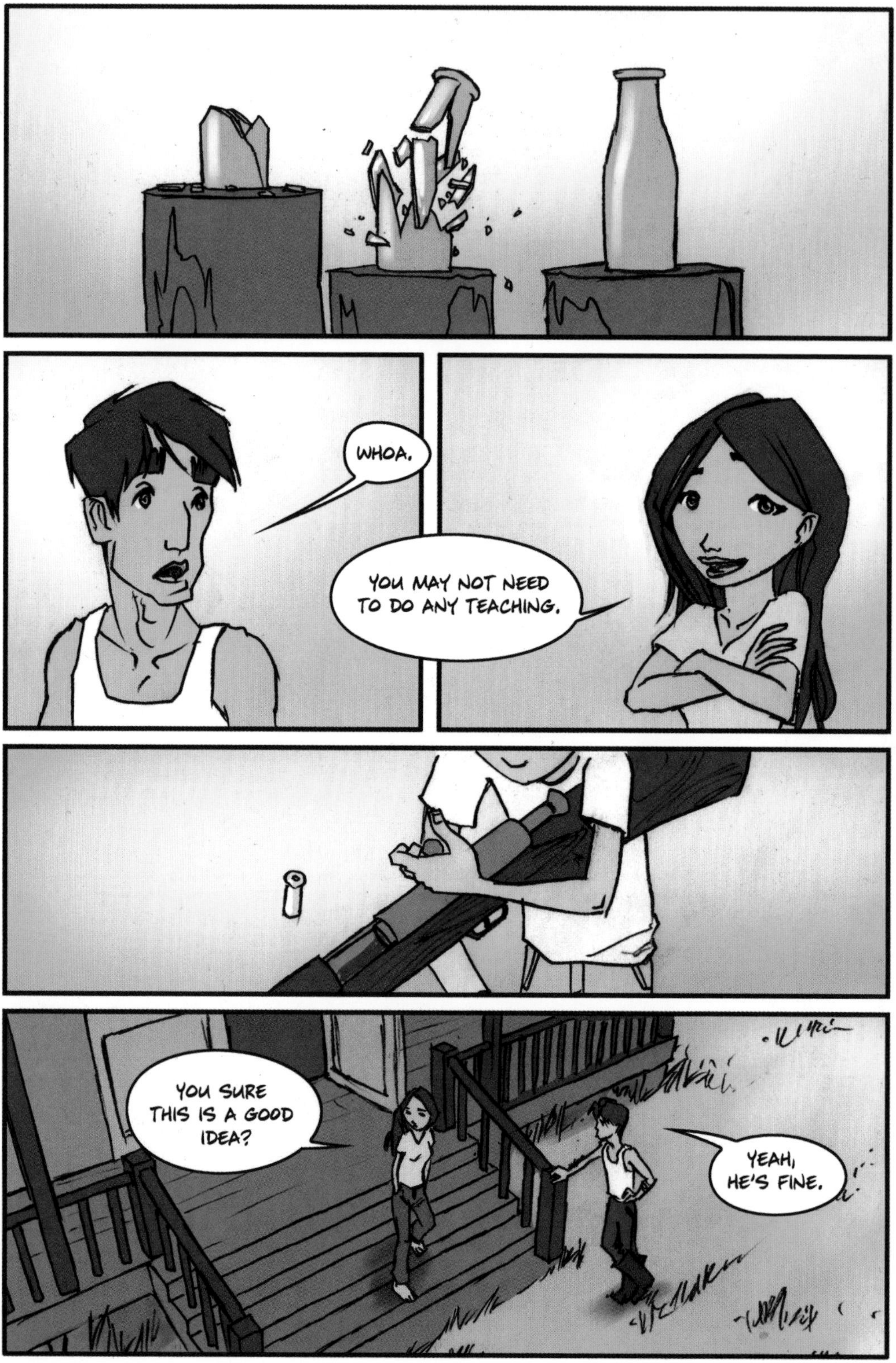
WHOA.
YOU MAY NOT NEED TO DO ANY TEACHING.
YOU SURE THIS IS A GOOD IDEA?
YEAH, HE'S FINE.

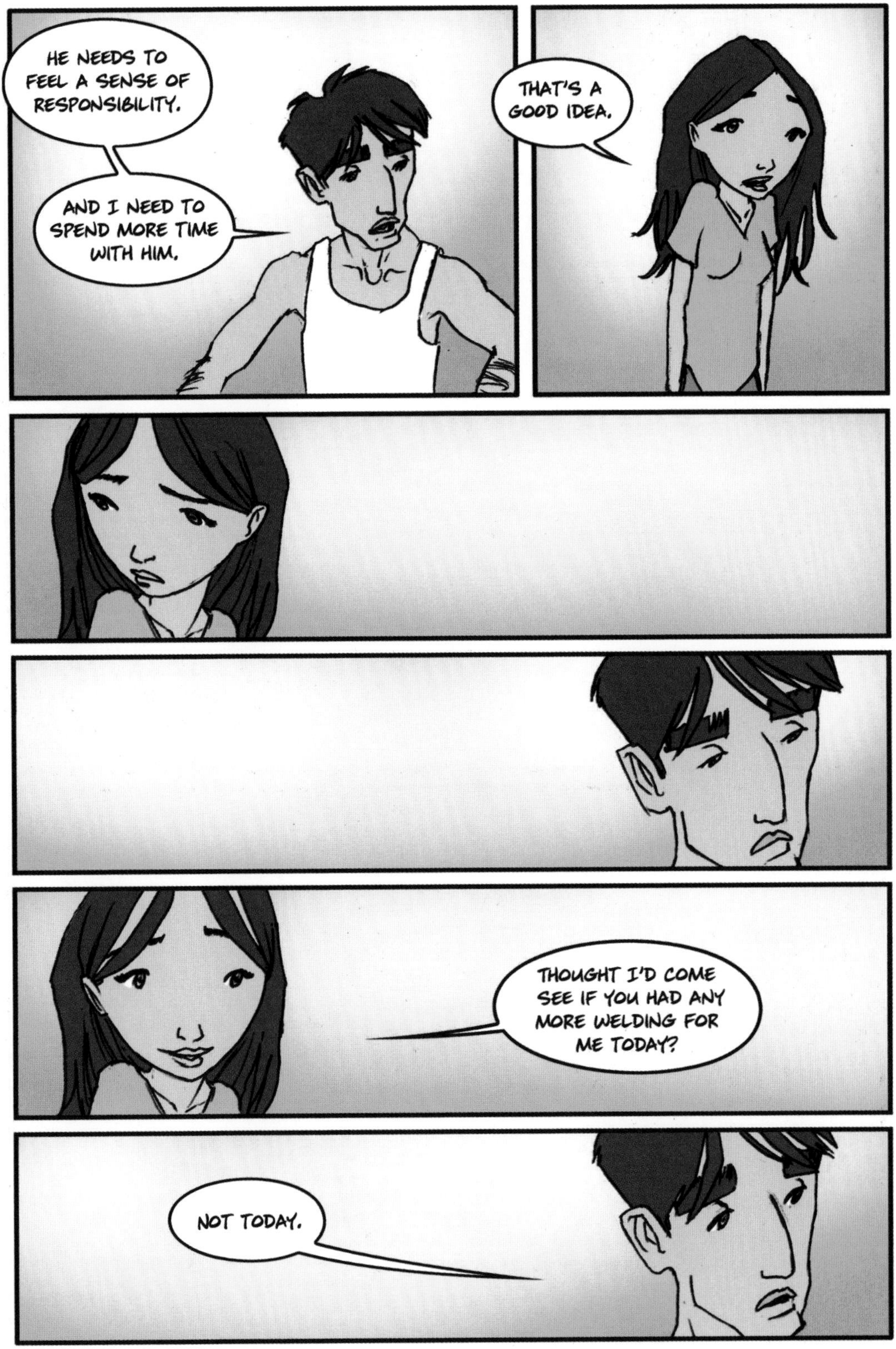
HE NEEDS TO FEEL A SENSE OF RESPONSIBILITY.
AND I NEED TO SPEND MORE TIME WITH HIM.
THAT'S A GOOD IDEA.
THOUGHT I'D COME SEE IF YOU HAD ANY MORE WELDING FOR ME TODAY?
NOT TODAY.

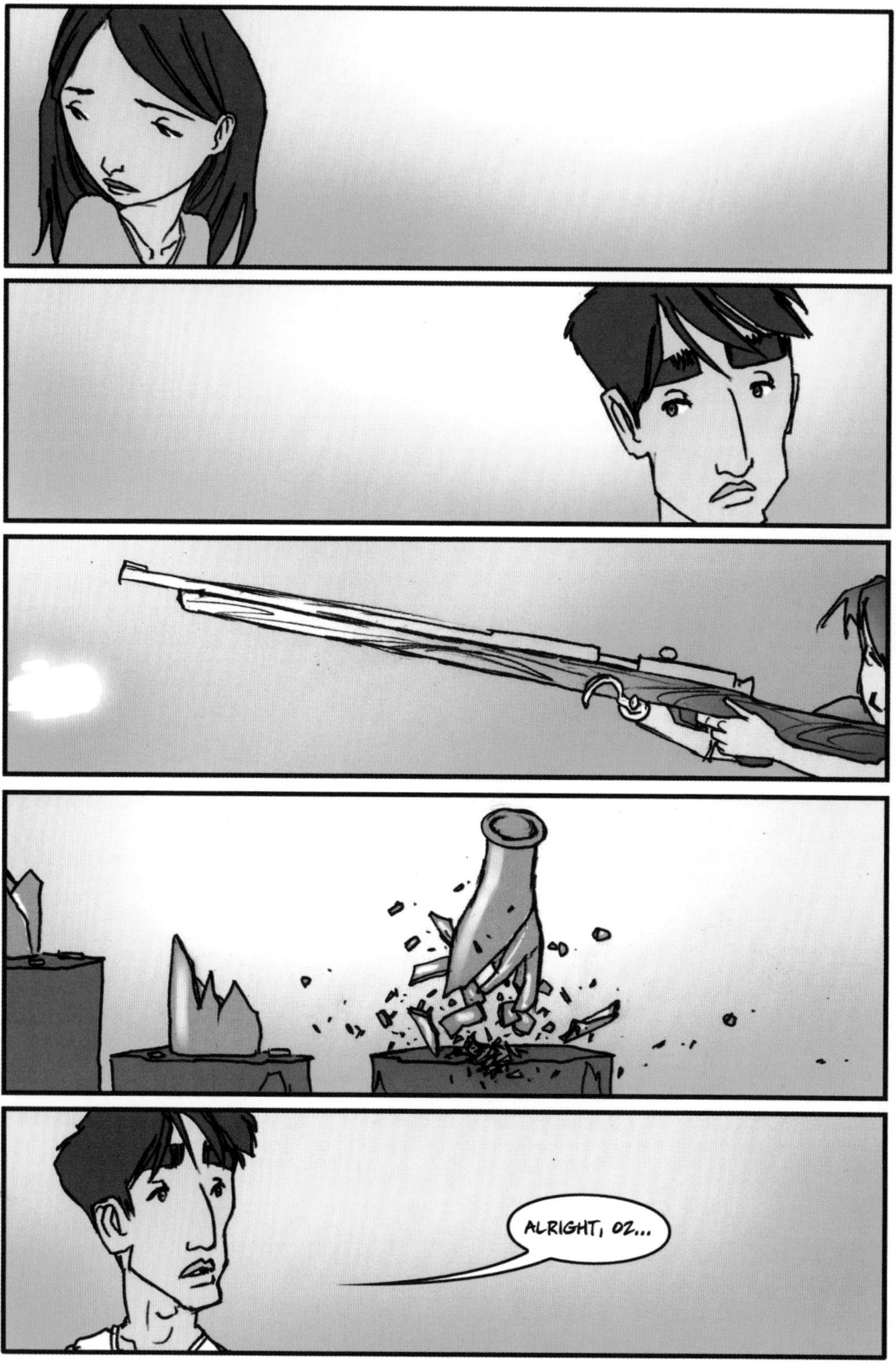
ALRIGHT, OZ...

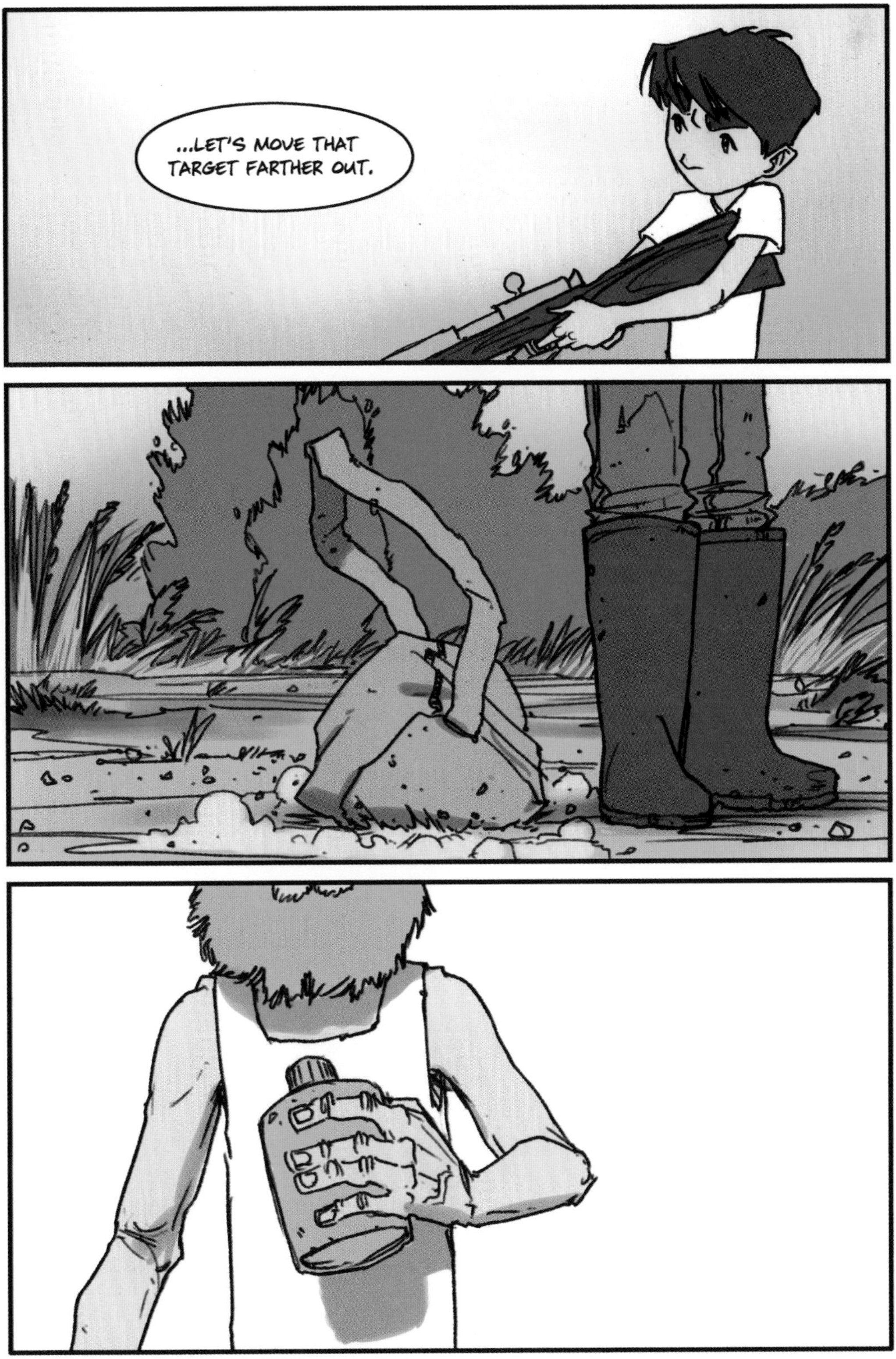
...LET'S MOVE THAT TARGET FARTHER OUT.

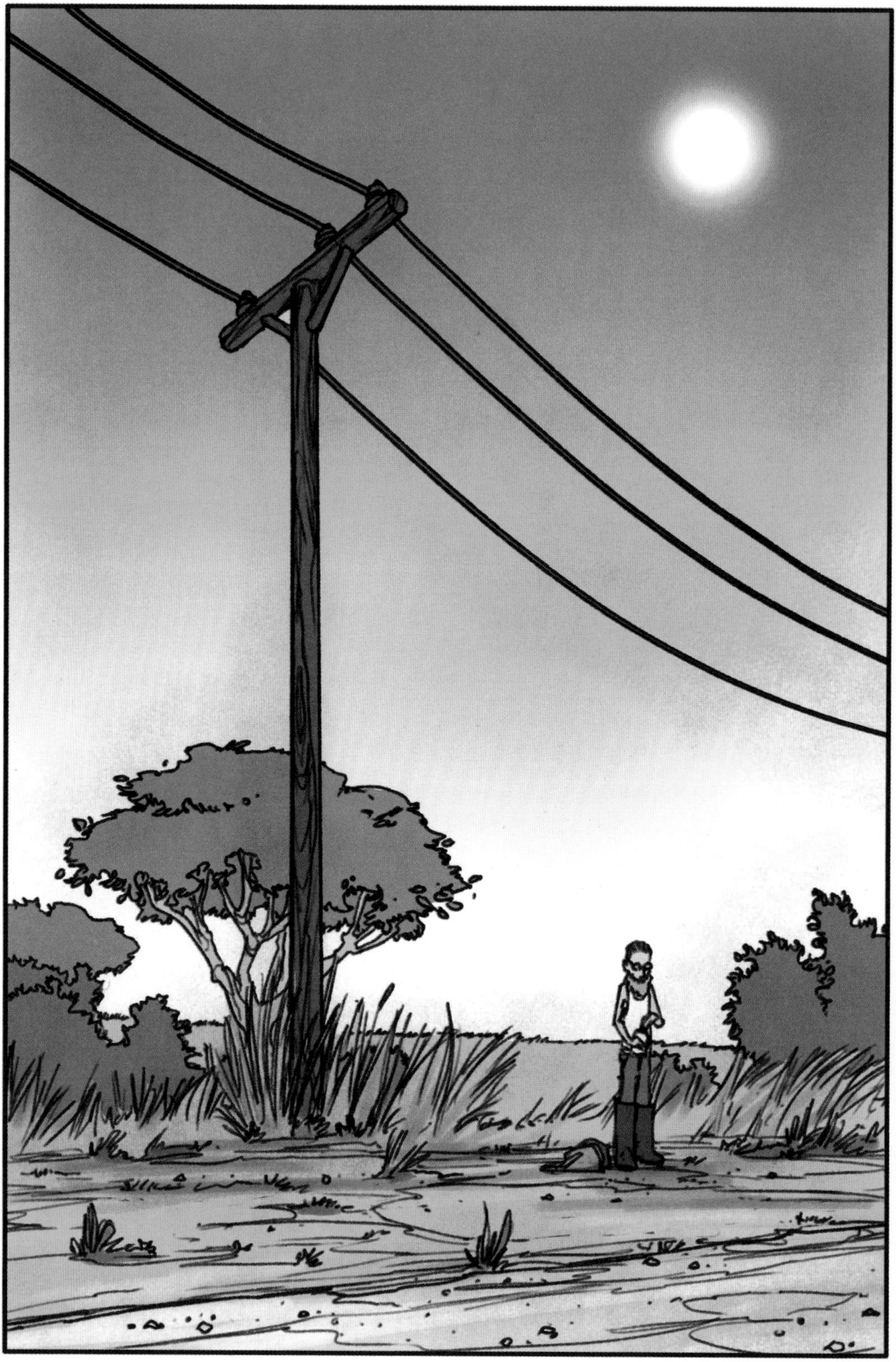

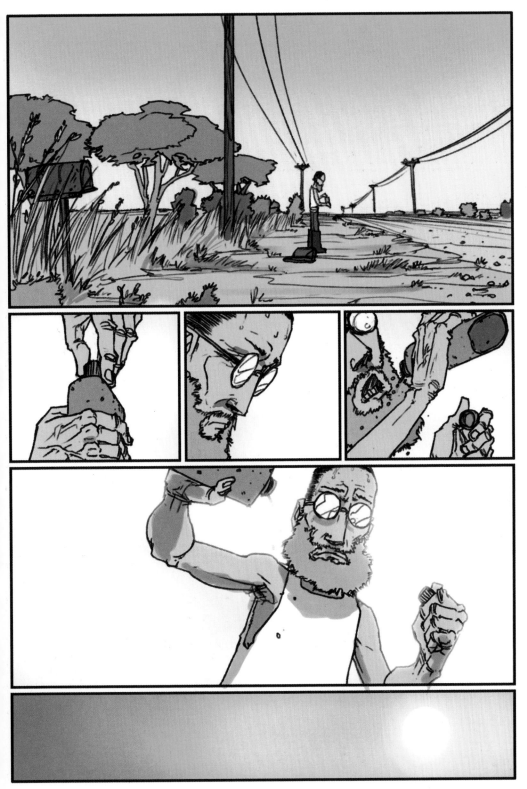

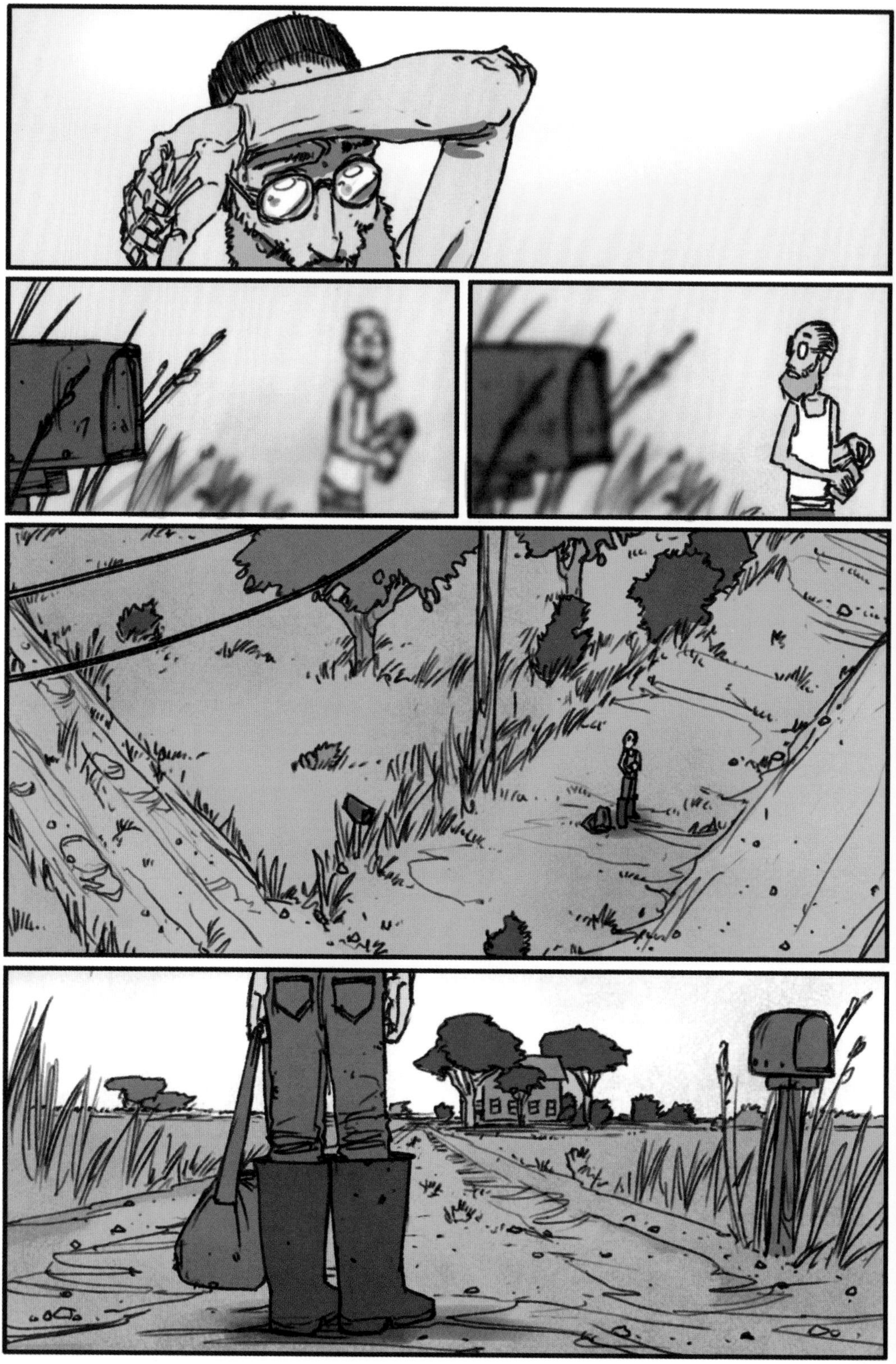

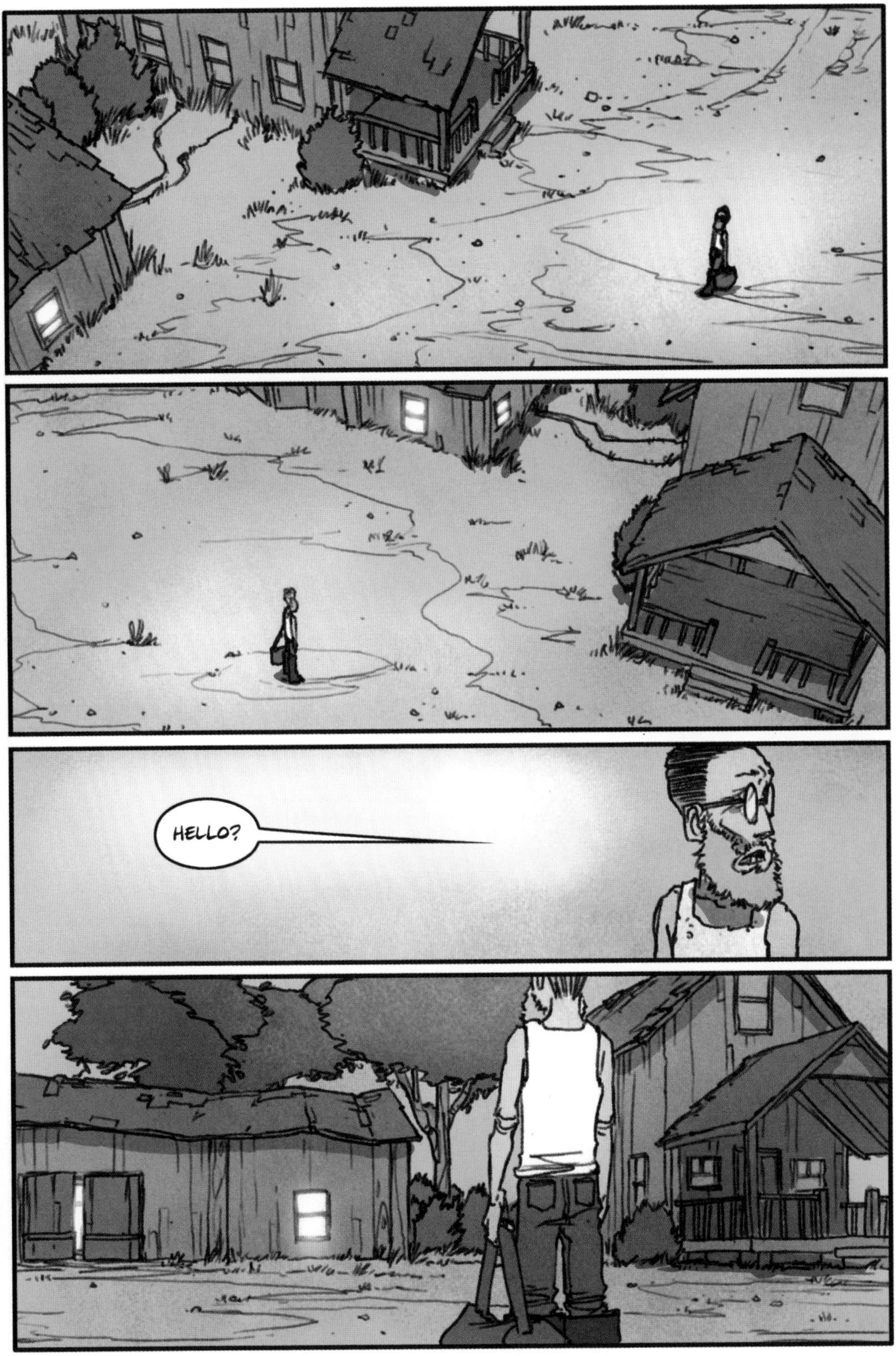
HELLO?

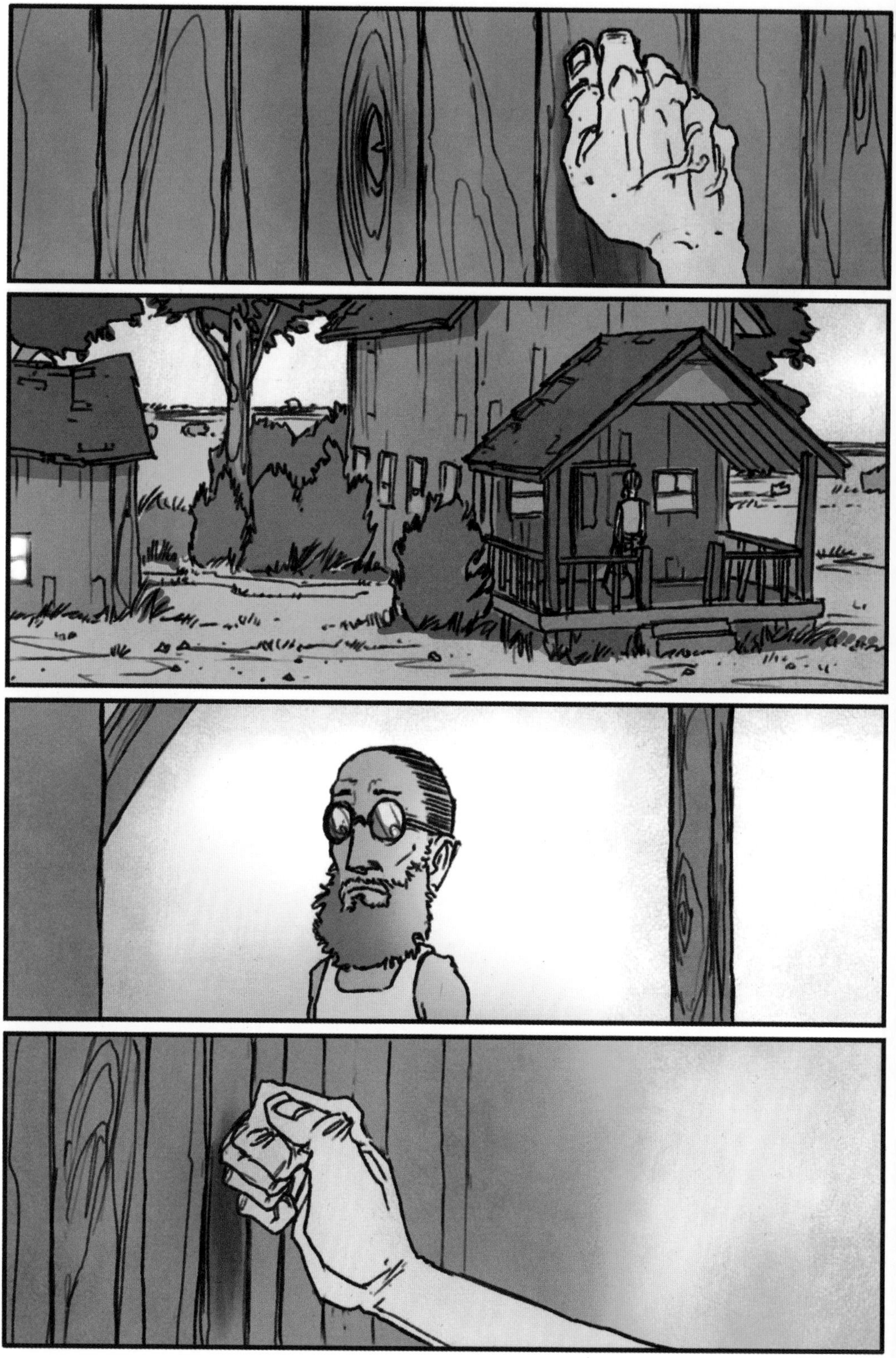

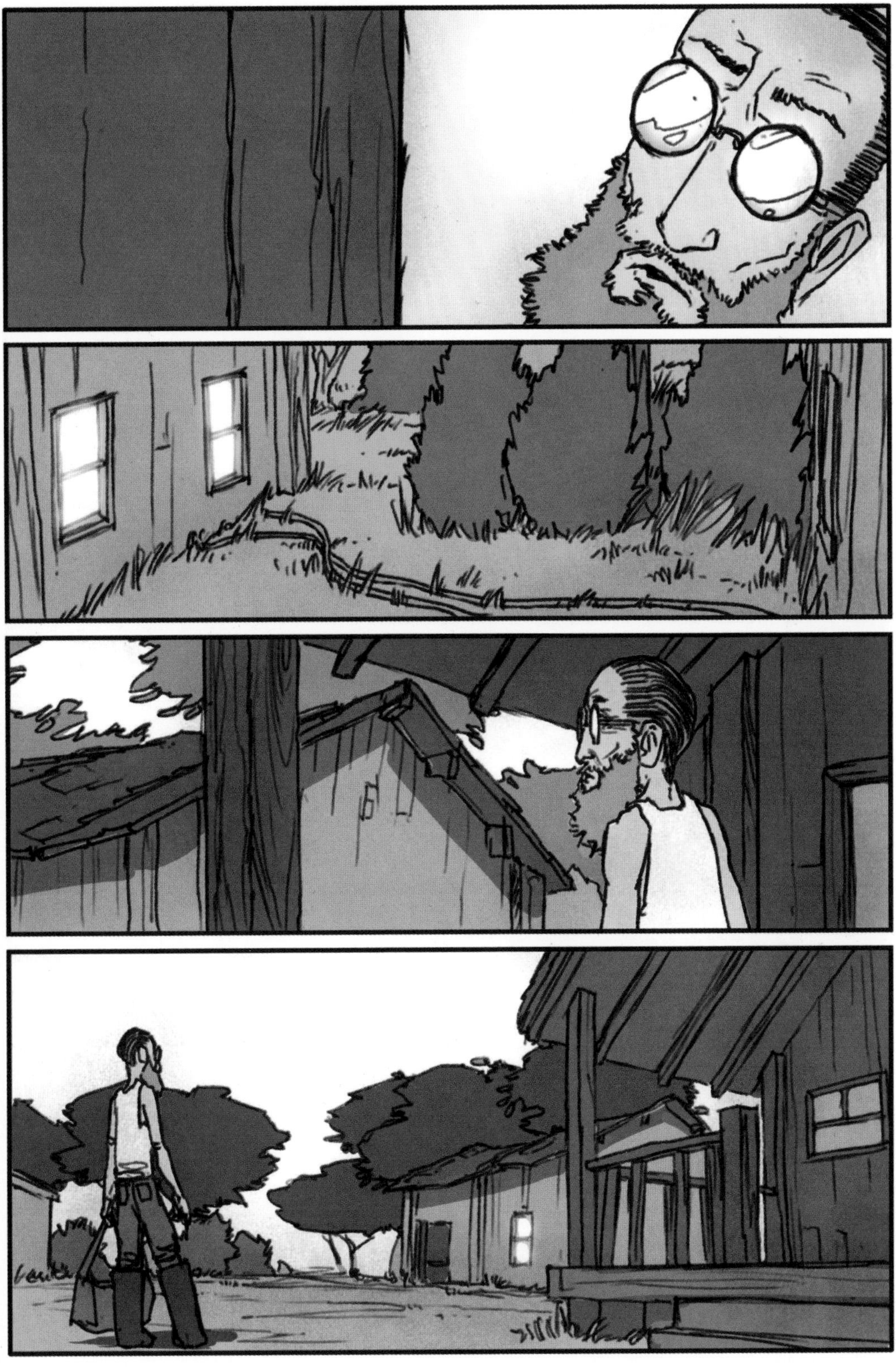

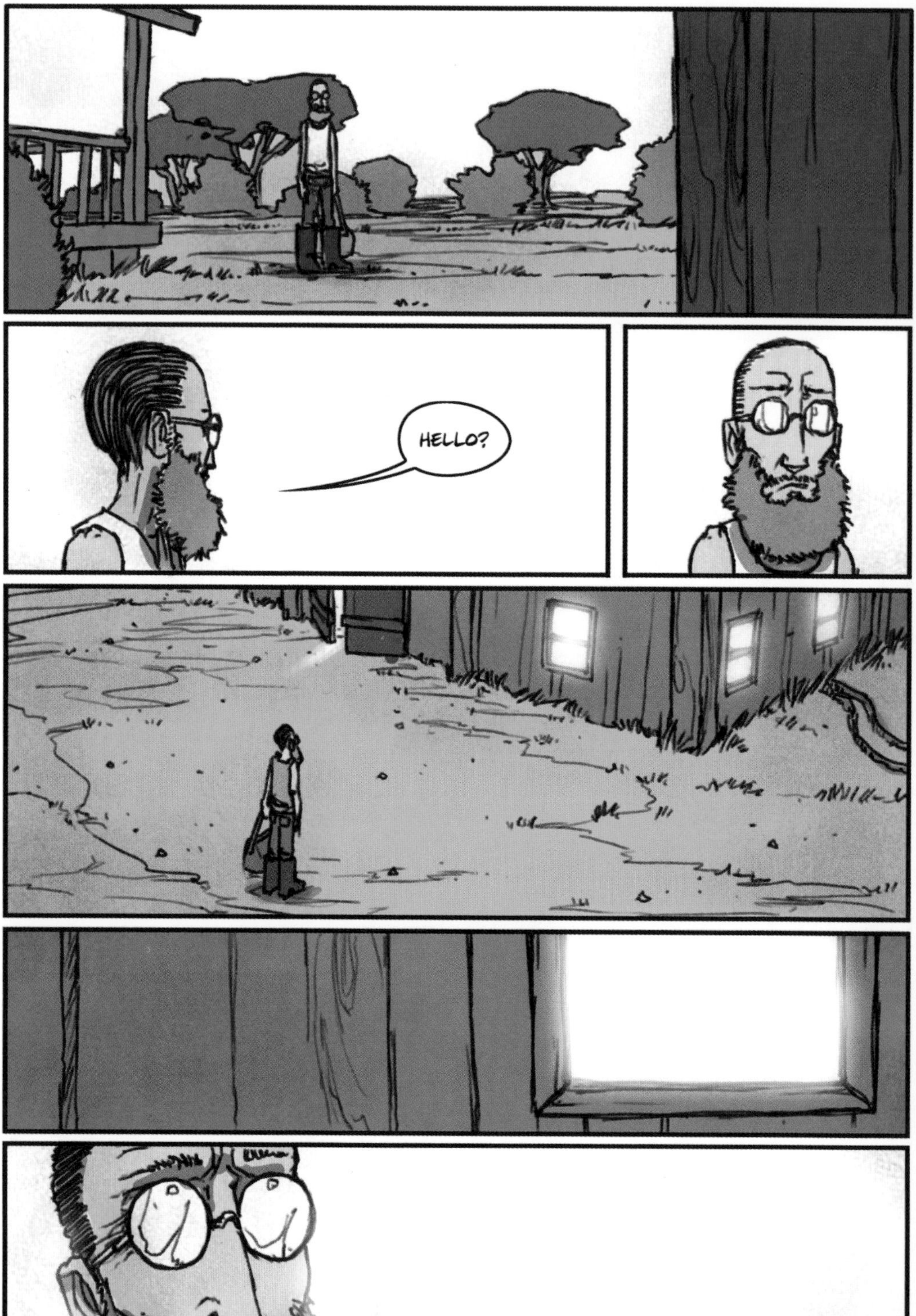
HELLO?

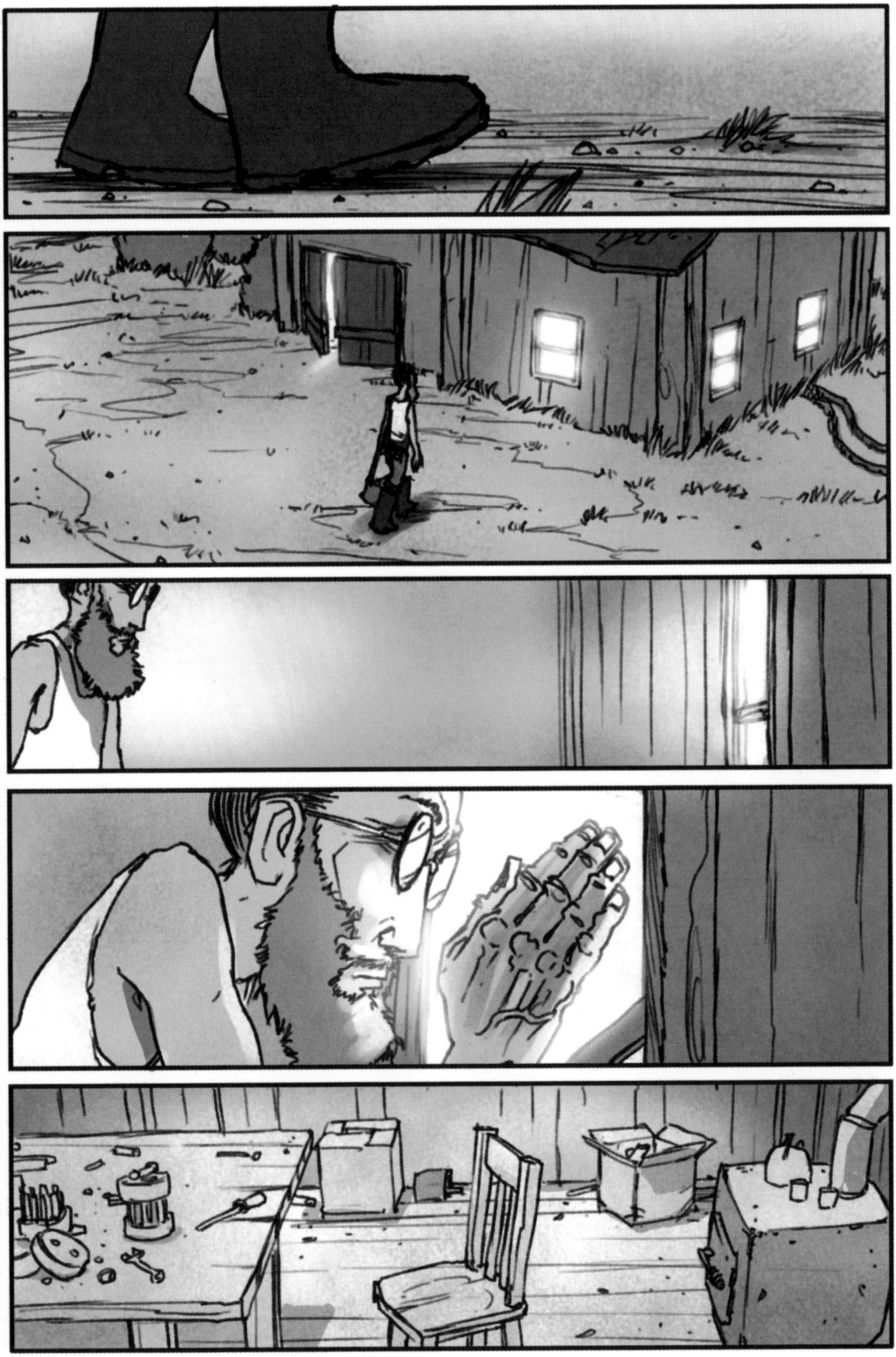

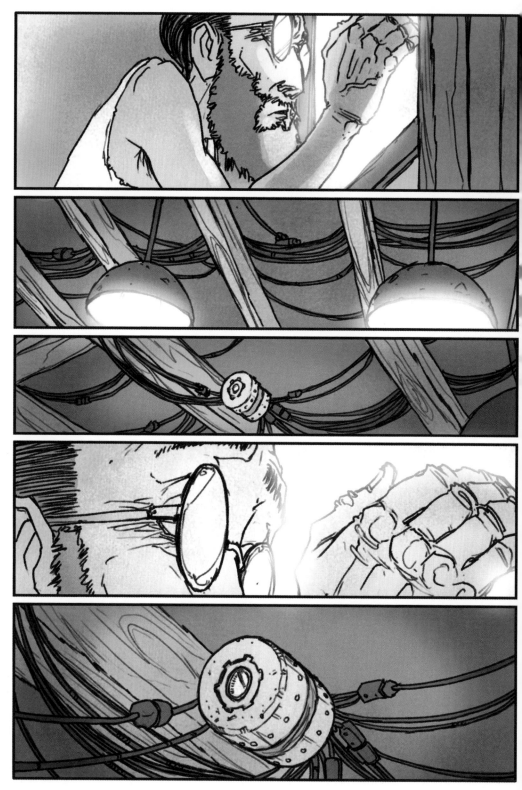

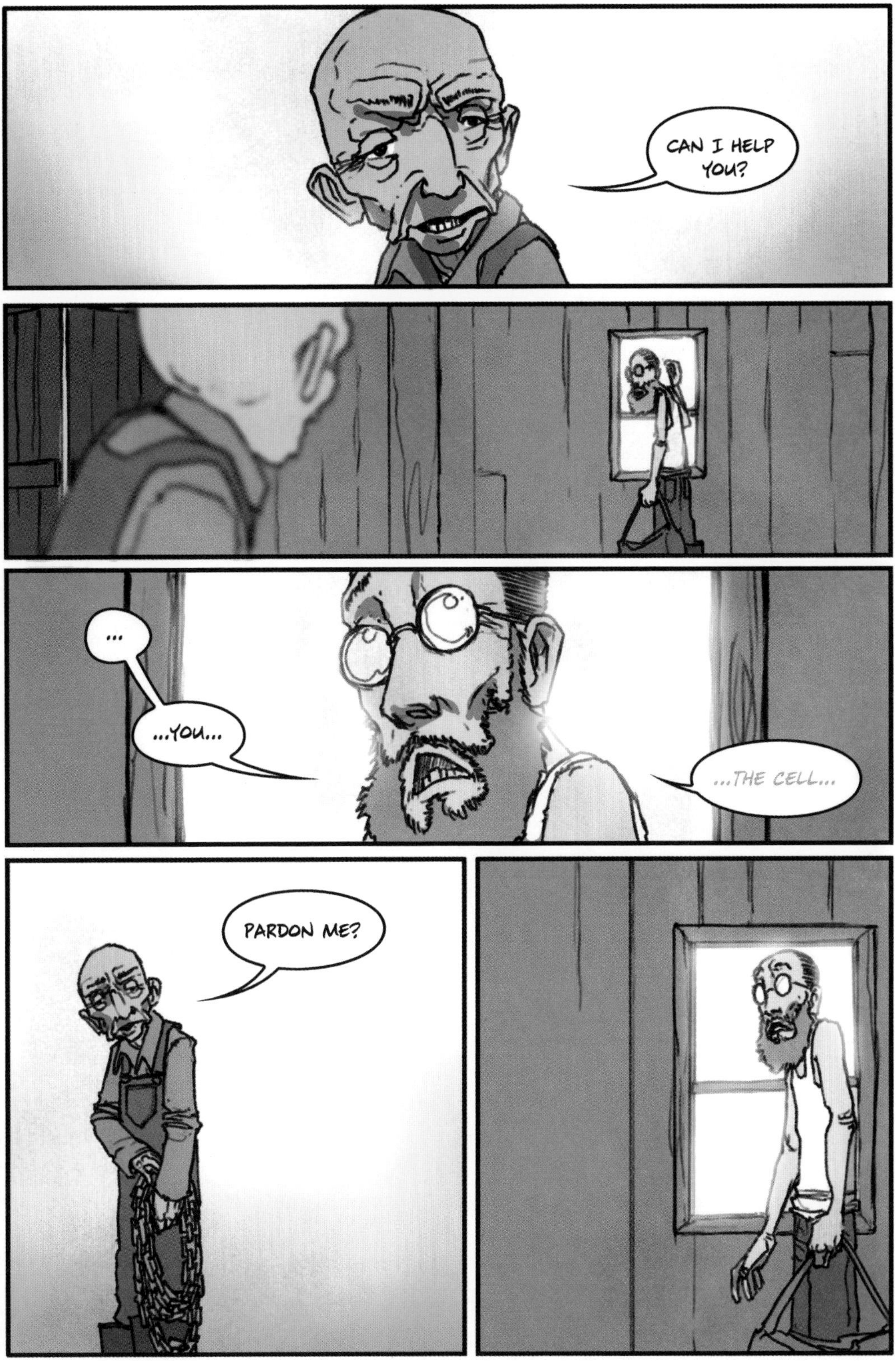
CAN I HELP YOU?
...
...YOU...
...THE CELL...
PARDON ME?

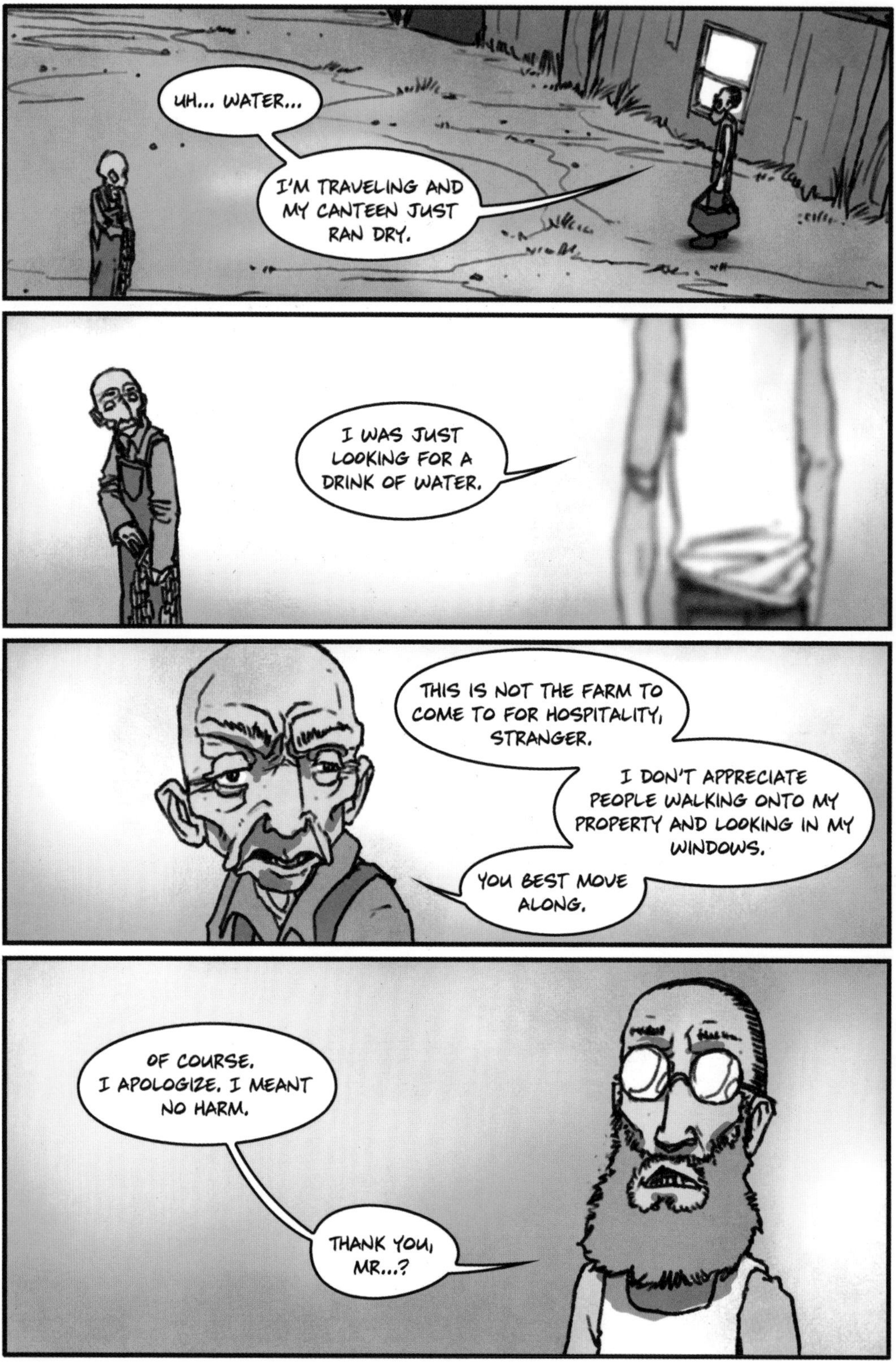
UH... WATER...
I'M TRAVELING AND MY CANTEEN JUST RAN DRY.
I WAS JUST LOOKING FOR A DRINK OF WATER.
THIS IS NOT THE FARM TO COME TO FOR HOSPITALITY, STRANGER.
I DON'T APPRECIATE PEOPLE WALKING ONTO MY PROPERTY AND LOOKING IN MY WINDOWS.
YOU BEST MOVE ALONG.
OF COURSE. I APOLOGIZE. I MEANT NO HARM.
THANK YOU, MR...?

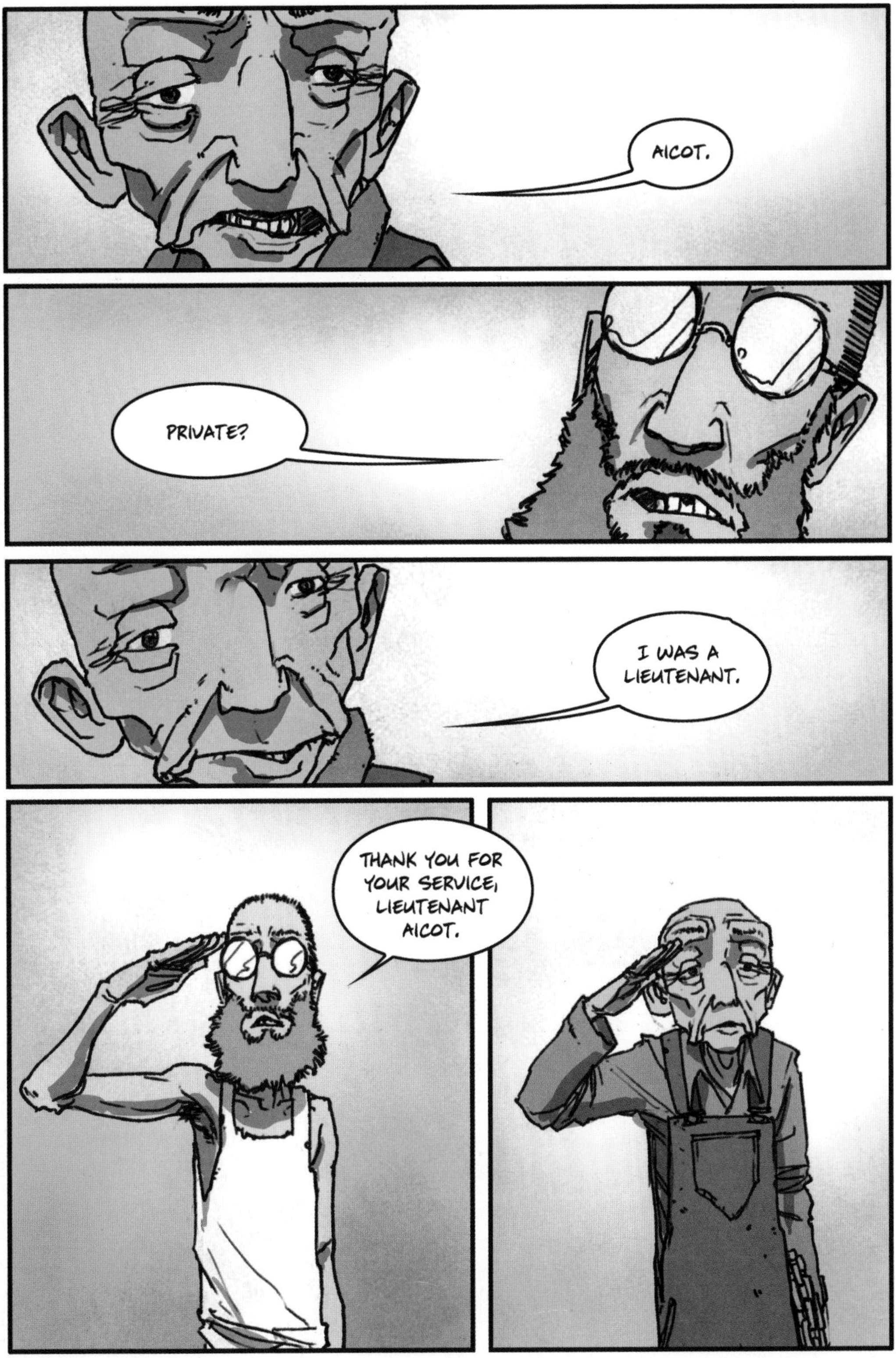
AICOT.
PRIVATE?
I WAS A LIEUTENANT.
THANK YOU FOR YOUR SERVICE, LIEUTENANT AICOT.

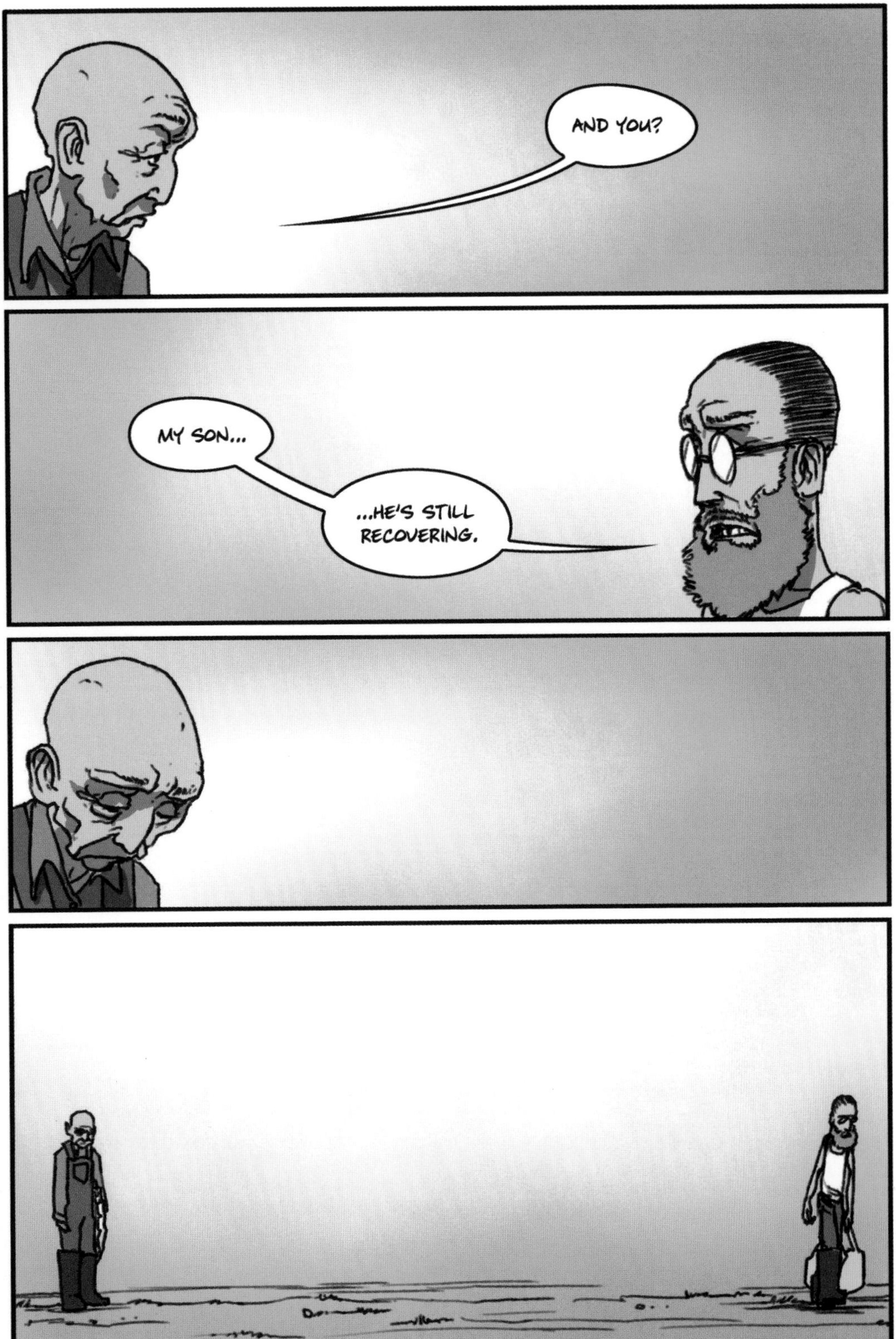
AND YOU?
MY SON...
...HE'S STILL RECOVERING.

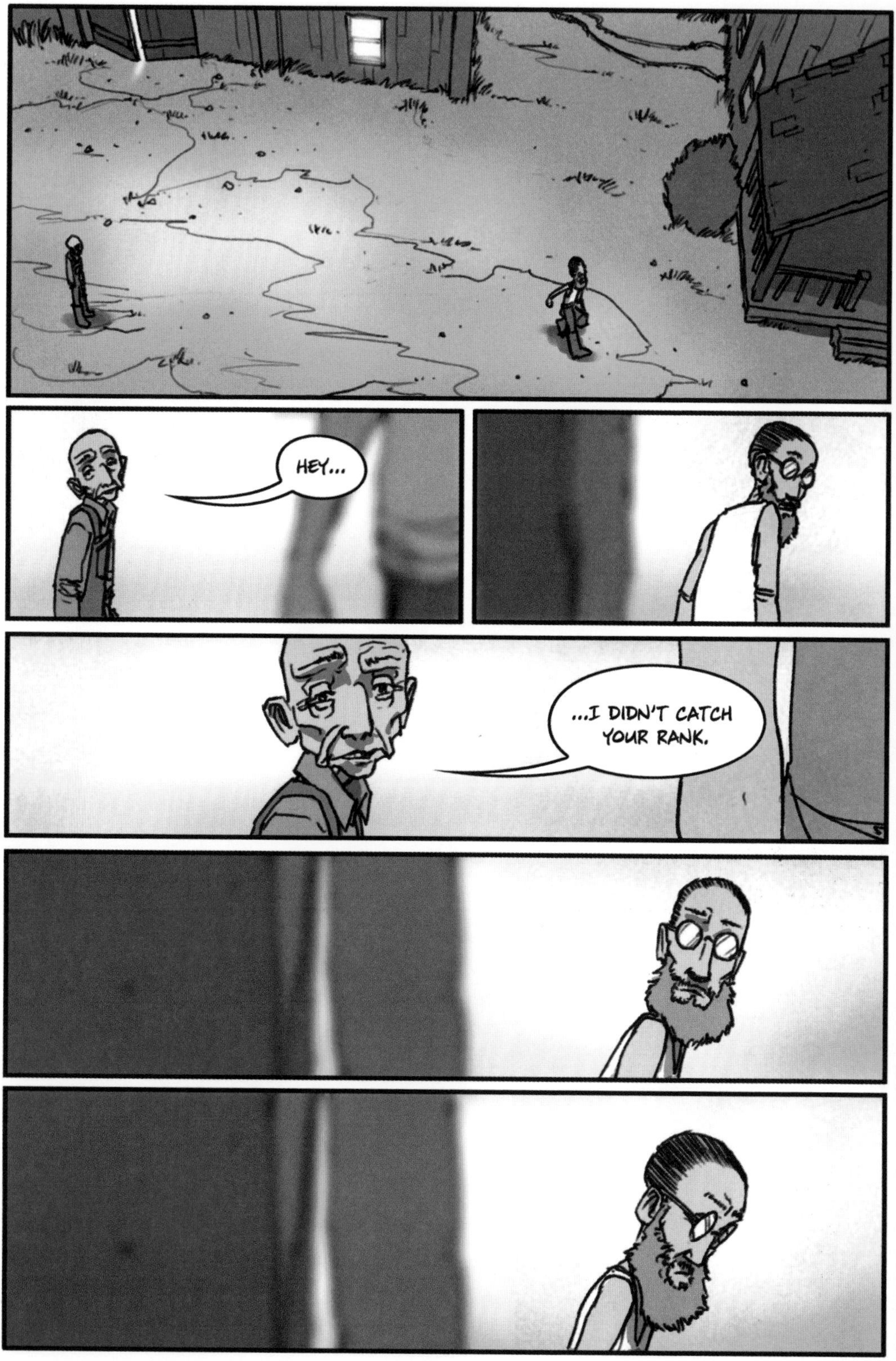
HEY...
...I DIDN'T CATCH YOUR RANK.

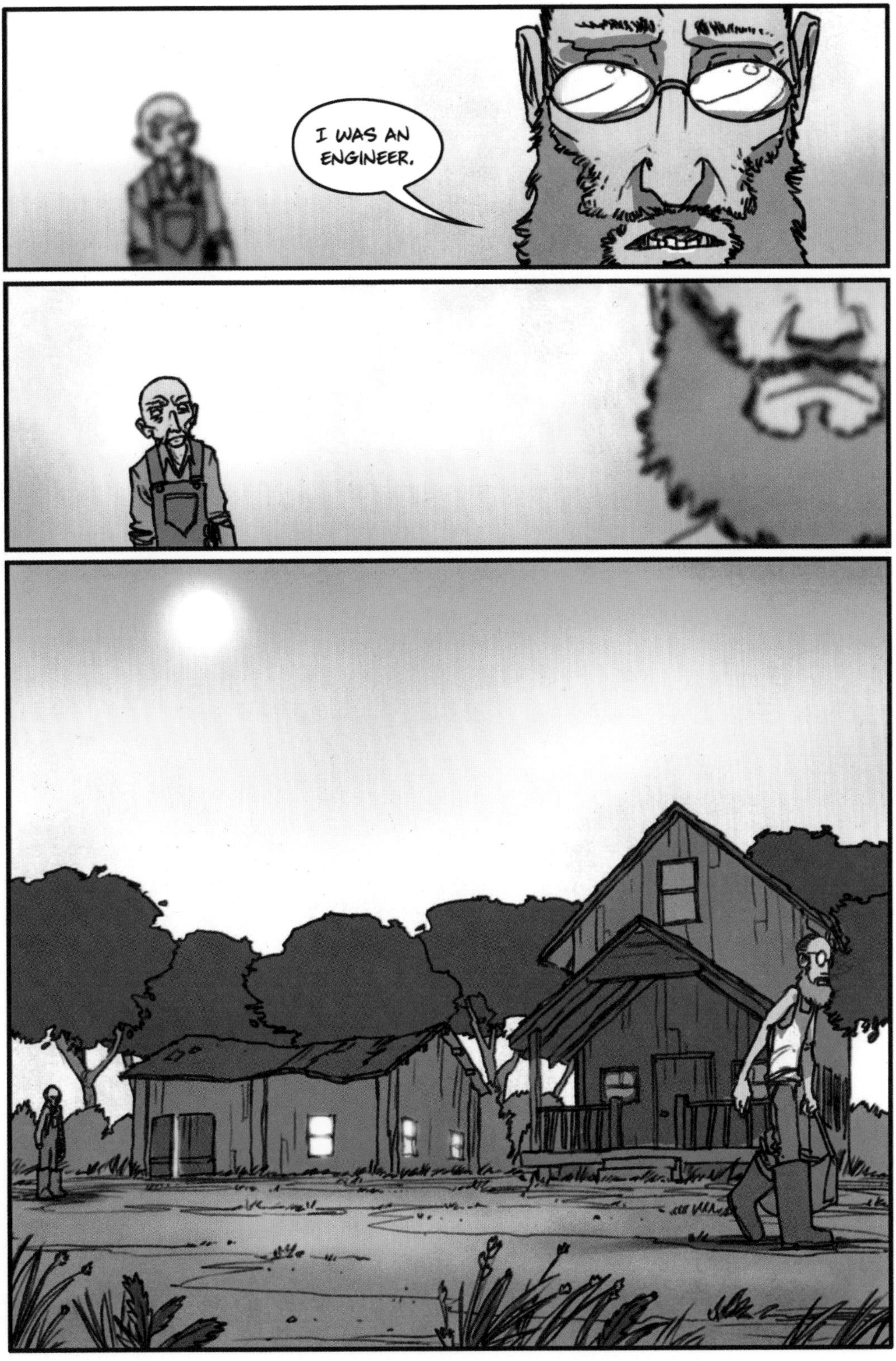
I WAS AN ENGINEER.

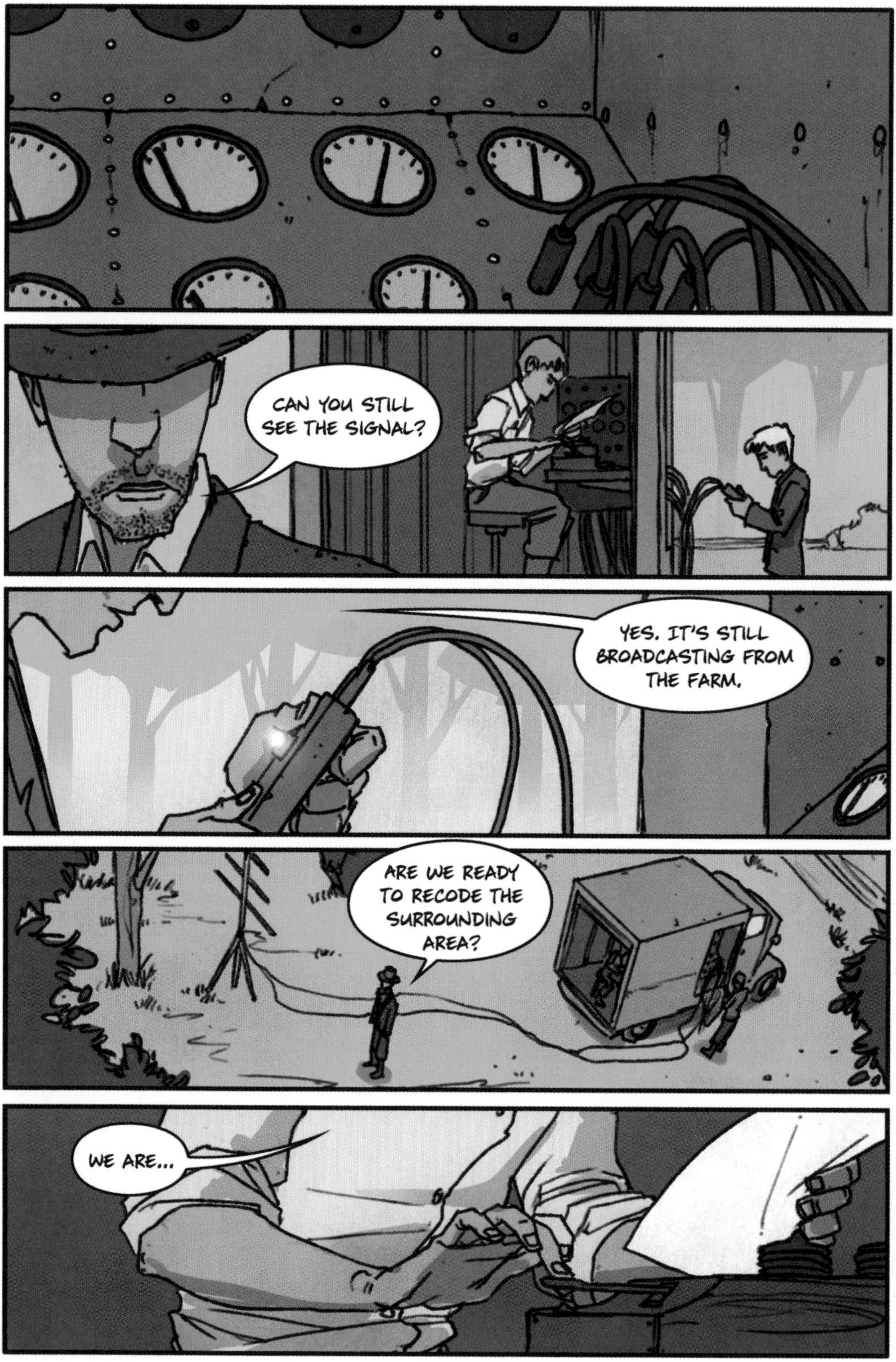
CAN YOU STILL SEE THE SIGNAL?
YES. IT'S STILL BROADCASTING FROM THE FARM.
ARE WE READY TO RECODE THE SURROUNDING AREA?
WE ARE...

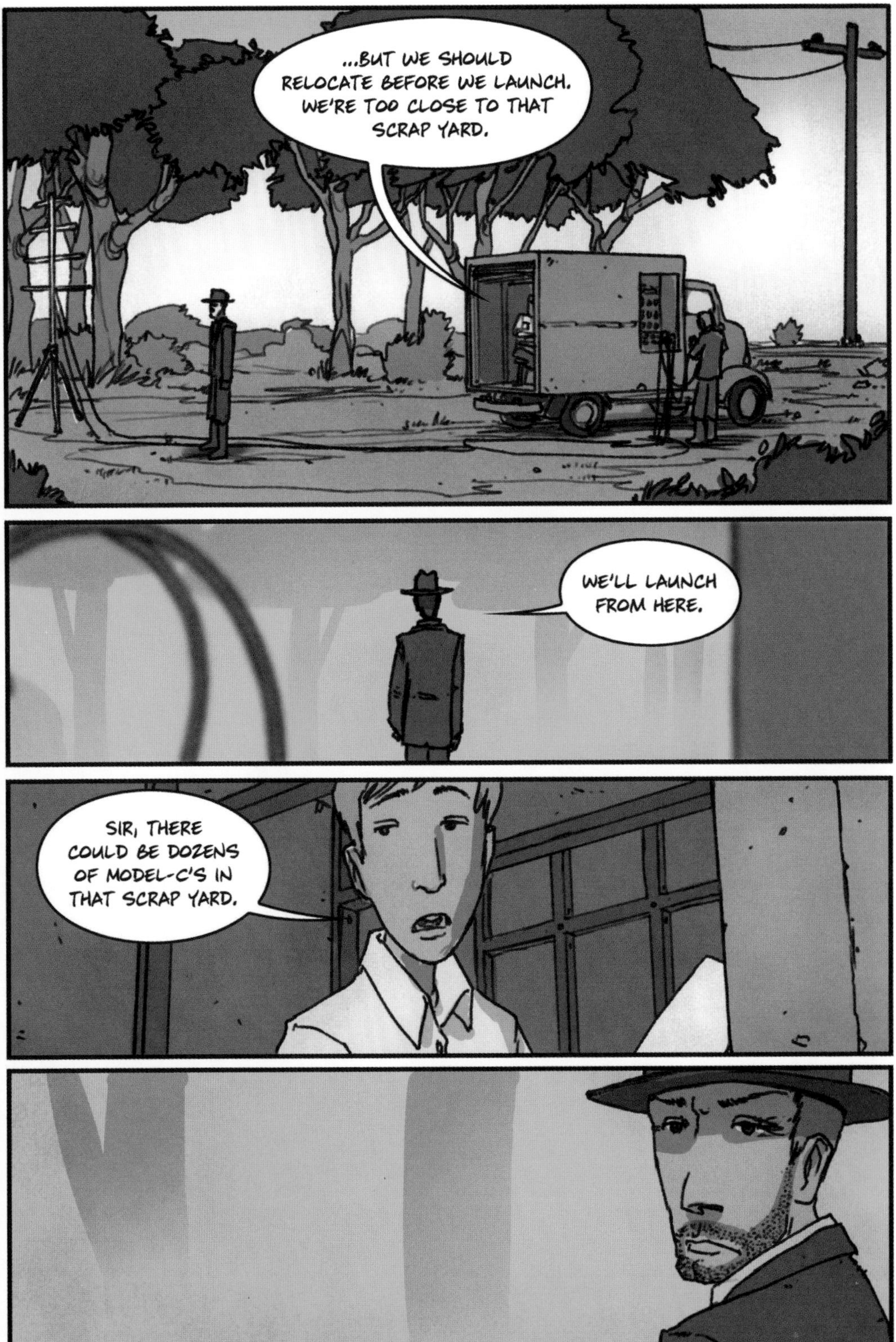
...BUT WE SHOULD RELOCATE BEFORE WE LAUNCH. WE'RE TOO CLOSE TO THAT SCRAP YARD.
WE'LL LAUNCH FROM HERE.
SIR, THERE COULD BE DOZENS OF MODEL-C'S IN THAT SCRAP YARD.

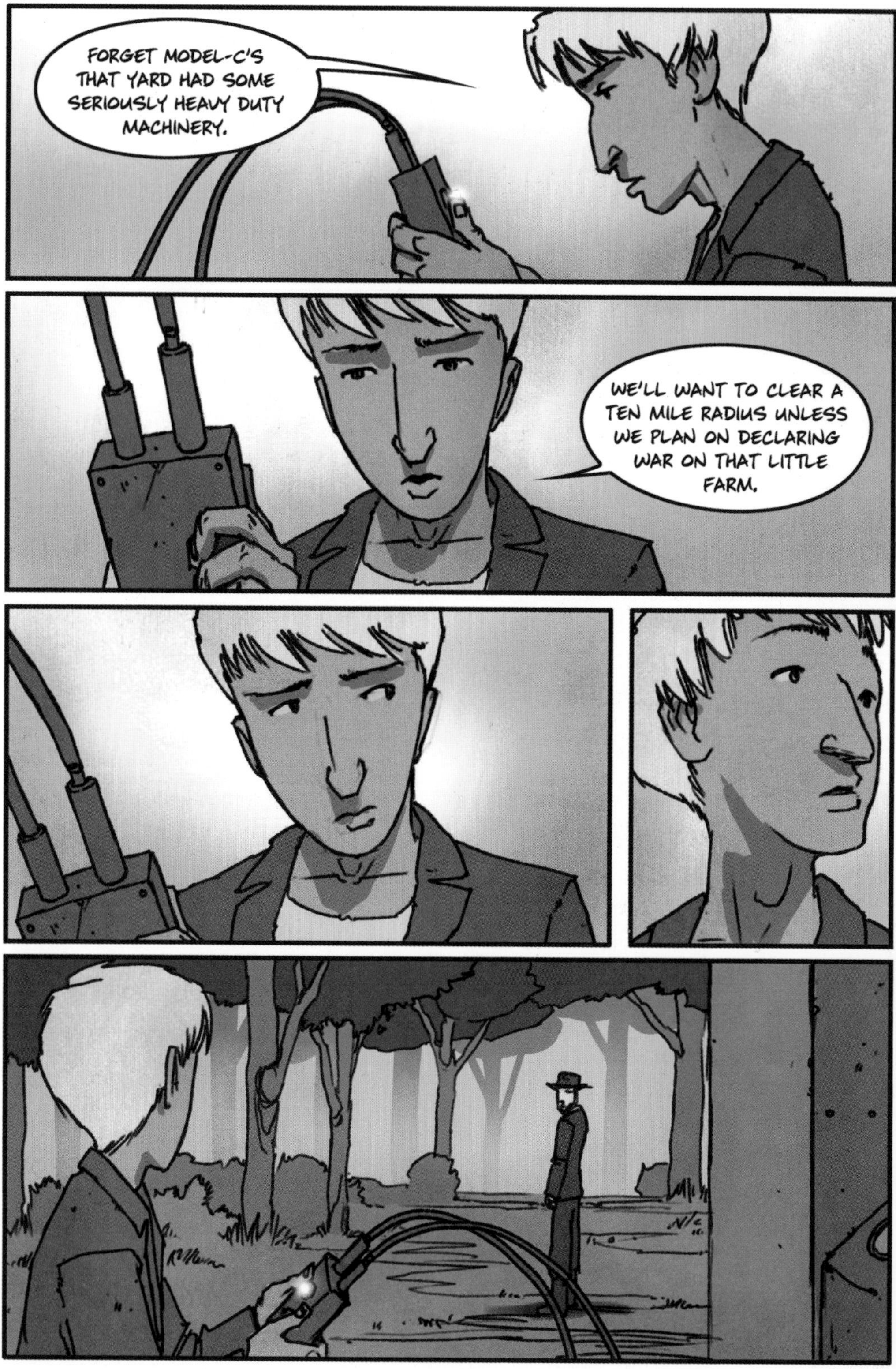
FORGET MODEL-C'S THAT YARD HAD SOME SERIOUSLY HEAVY DUTY MACHINERY.
WE'LL WANT TO CLEAR A TEN MILE RADIUS UNLESS WE PLAN ON DECLARING WAR ON THAT LITTLE FARM.

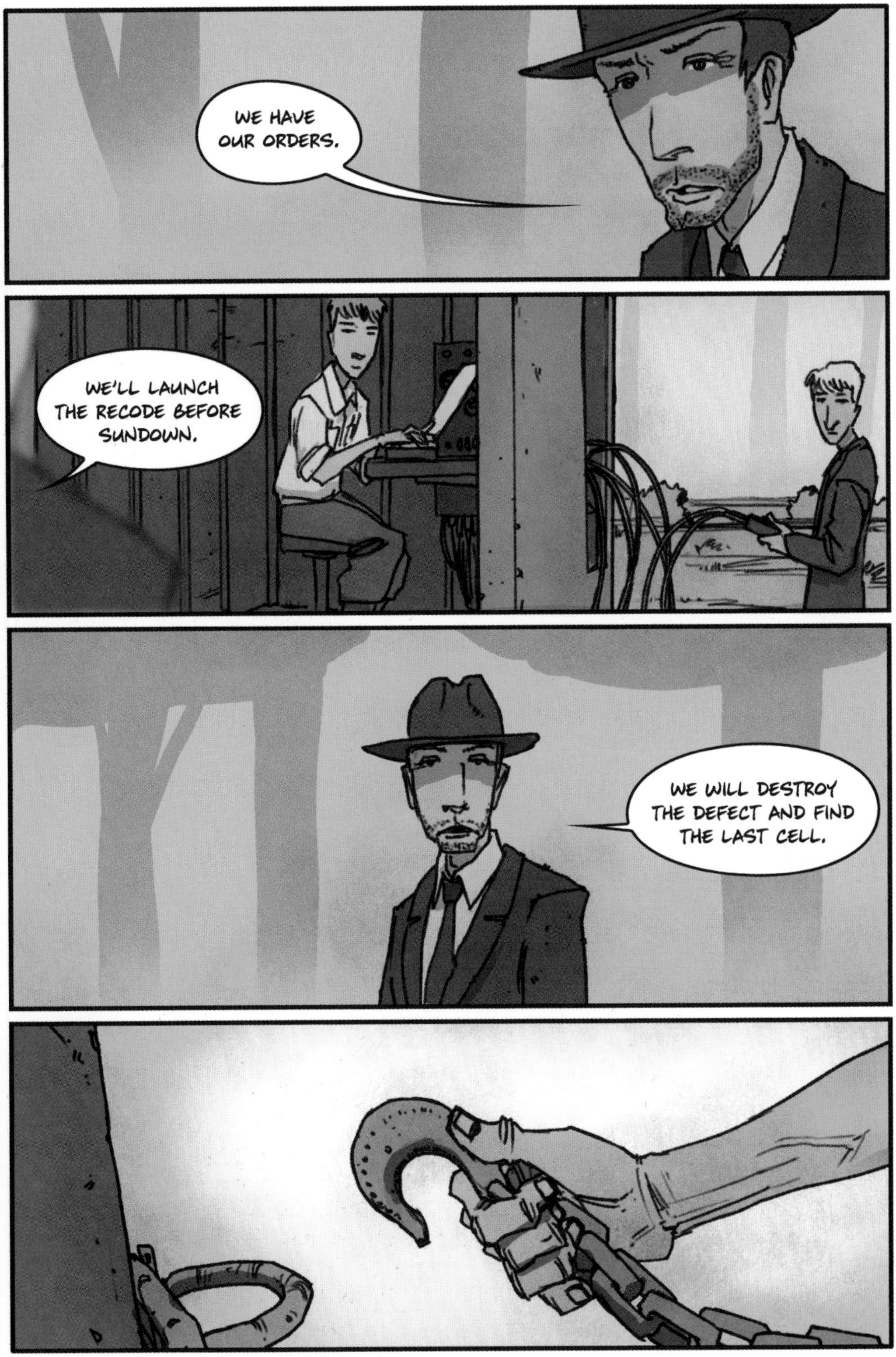
WE HAVE OUR ORDERS.
WE'LL LAUNCH THE RECODE BEFORE SUNDOWN.
WE WILL DESTROY THE DEFECT AND FIND THE LAST CELL.

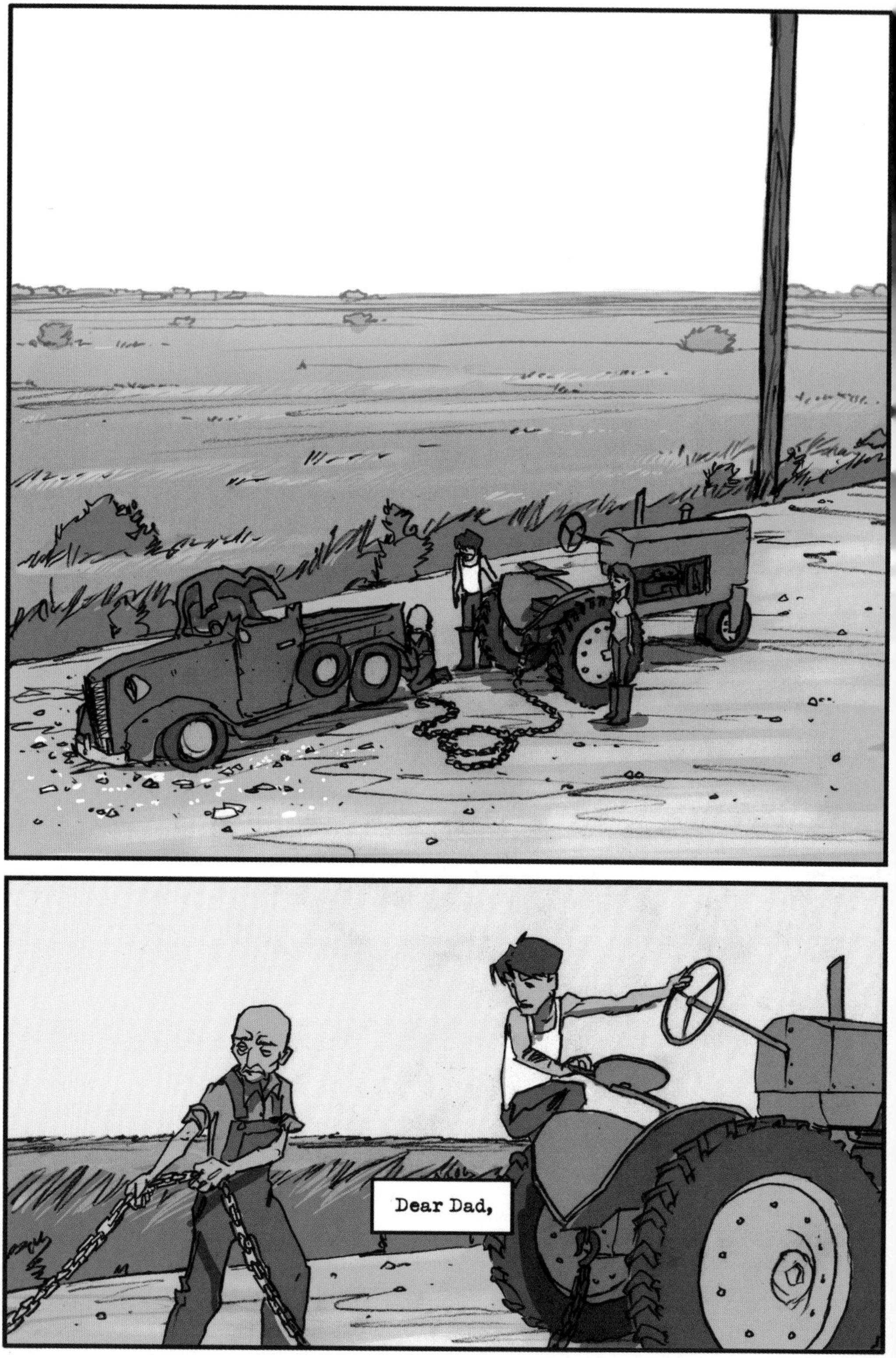
Dear Dad,

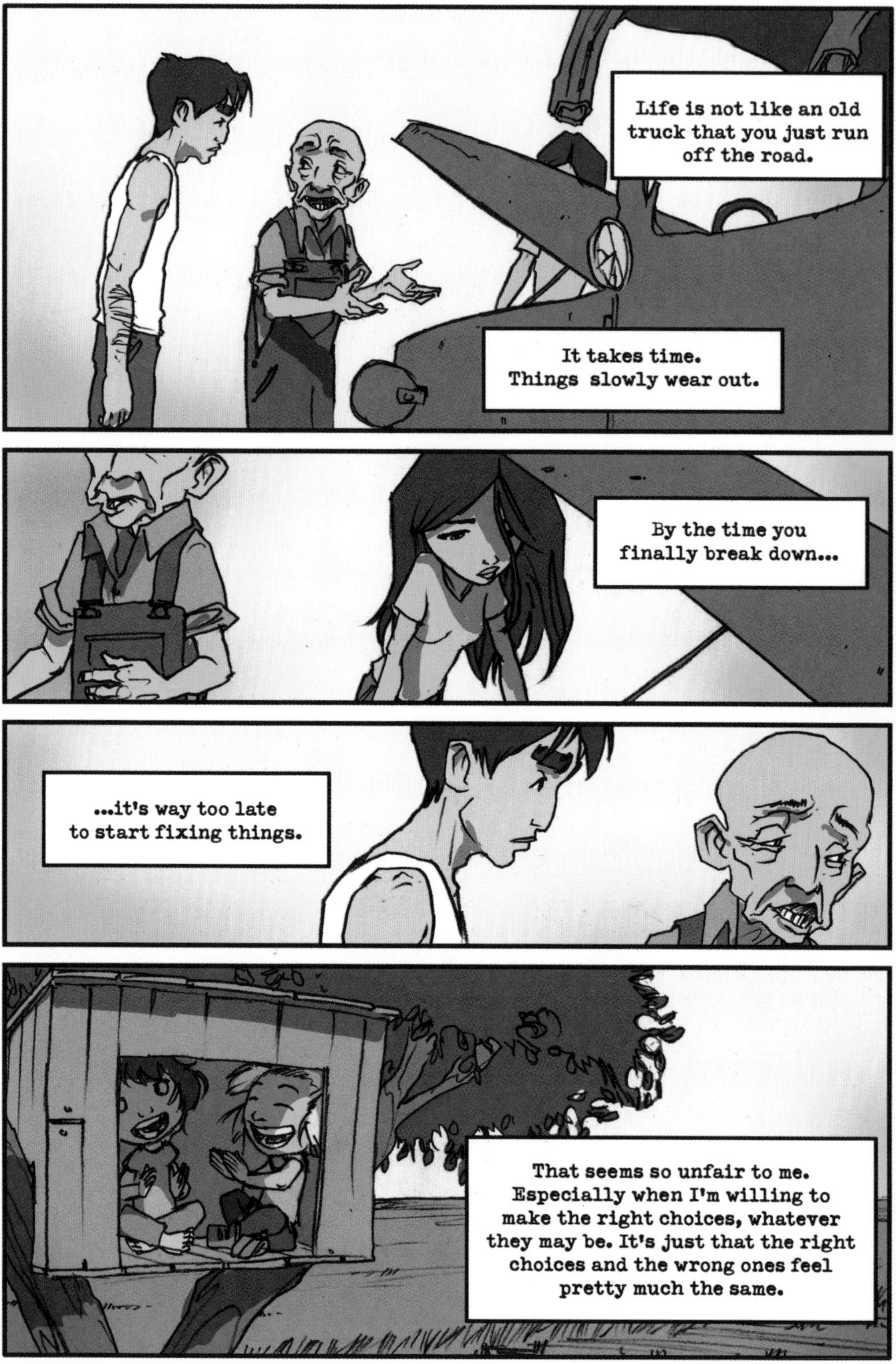
Life is not like an old truck that you just run off the road.
It takes time. Things slowly wear out.
By the time you finally break down...
...it's way too late to start fixing things.
That seems so unfair to me. Especially when I'm willing to make the right choices, whatever they may be. It's just that the right choices and the wrong ones feel pretty much the same.

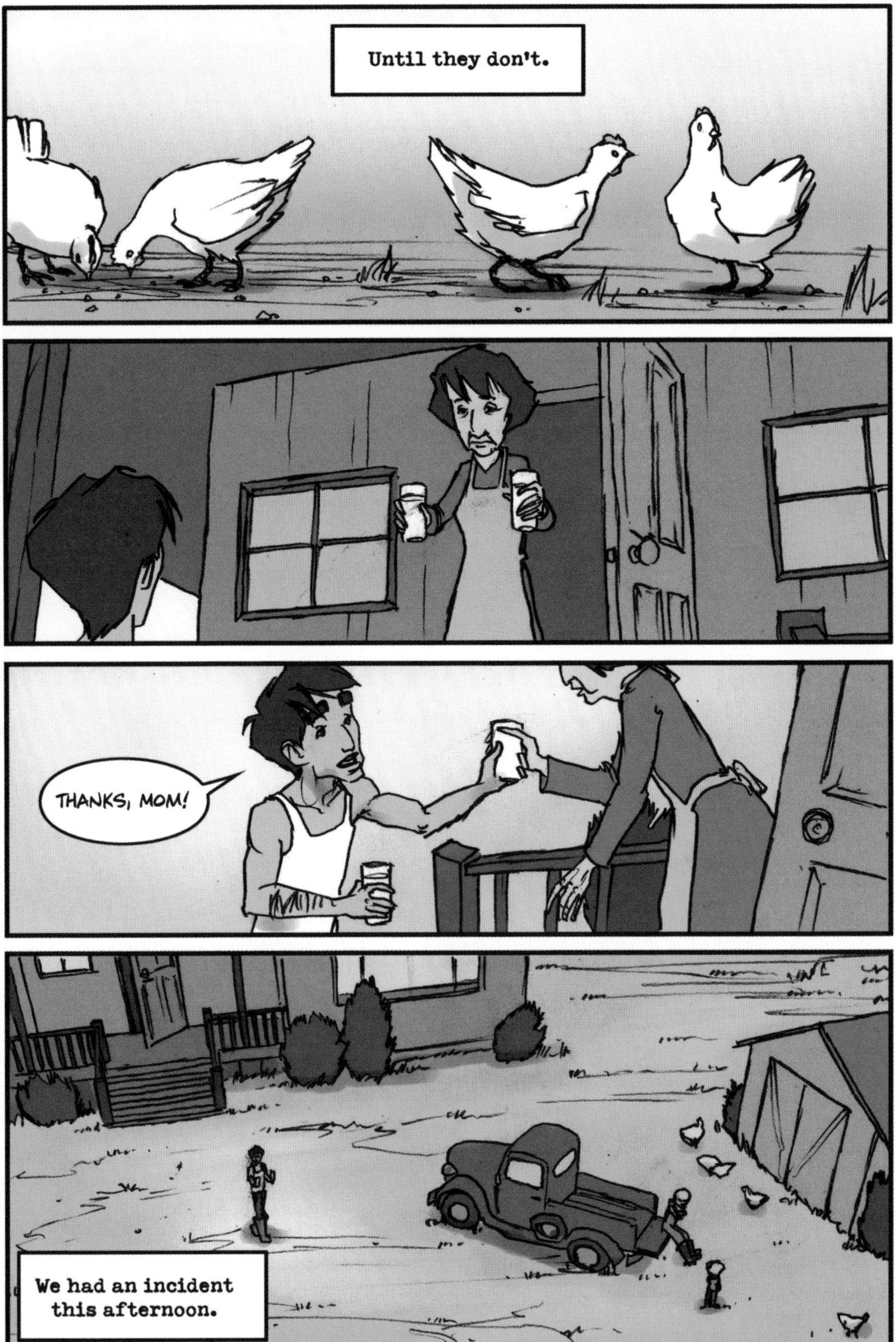
Until they don't.
THANKS, MOM!
We had an incident this afternoon.

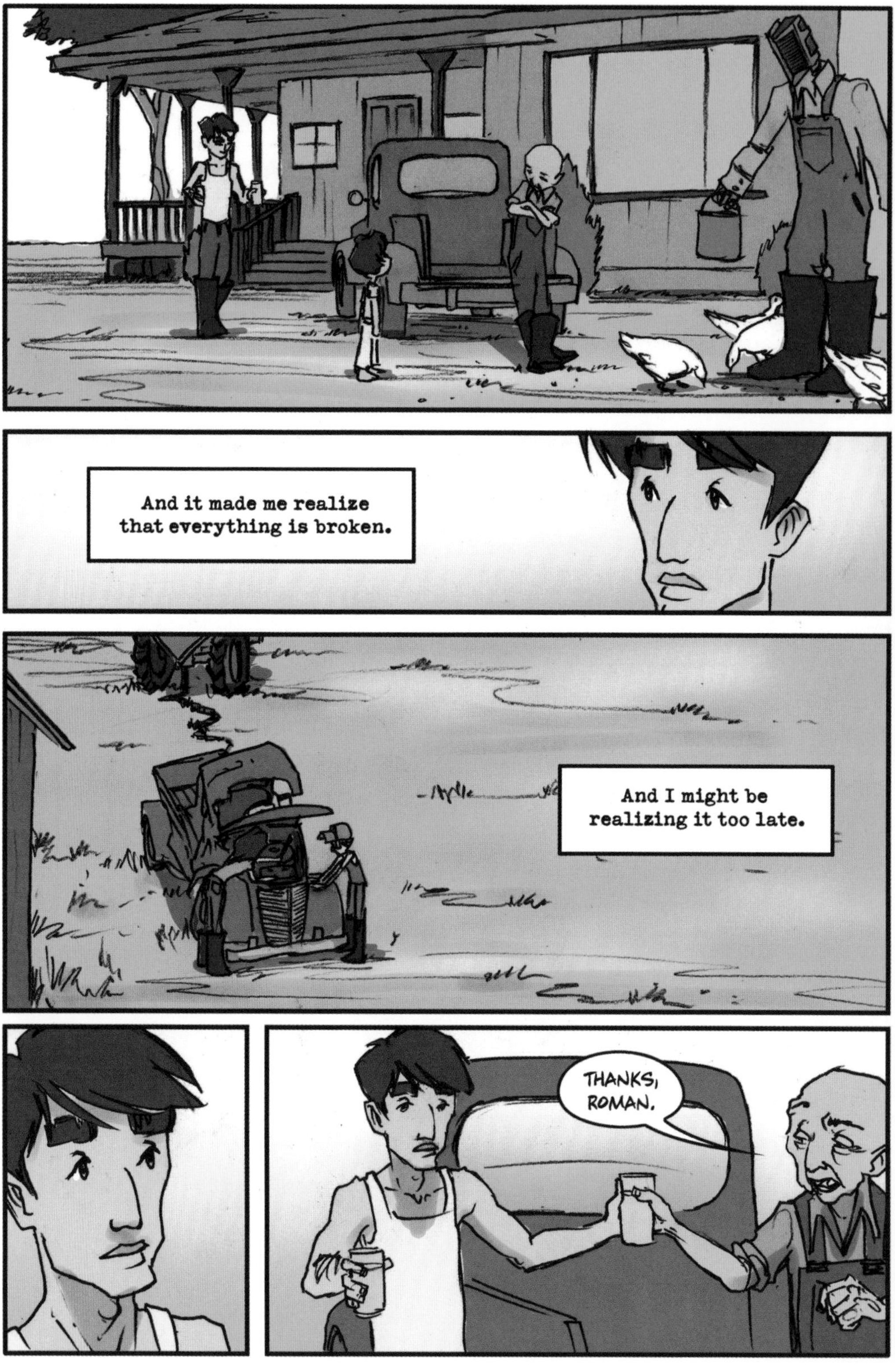
And it made me realize that everything is broken.
And I might be realizing it too late.
THANKS, ROMAN.

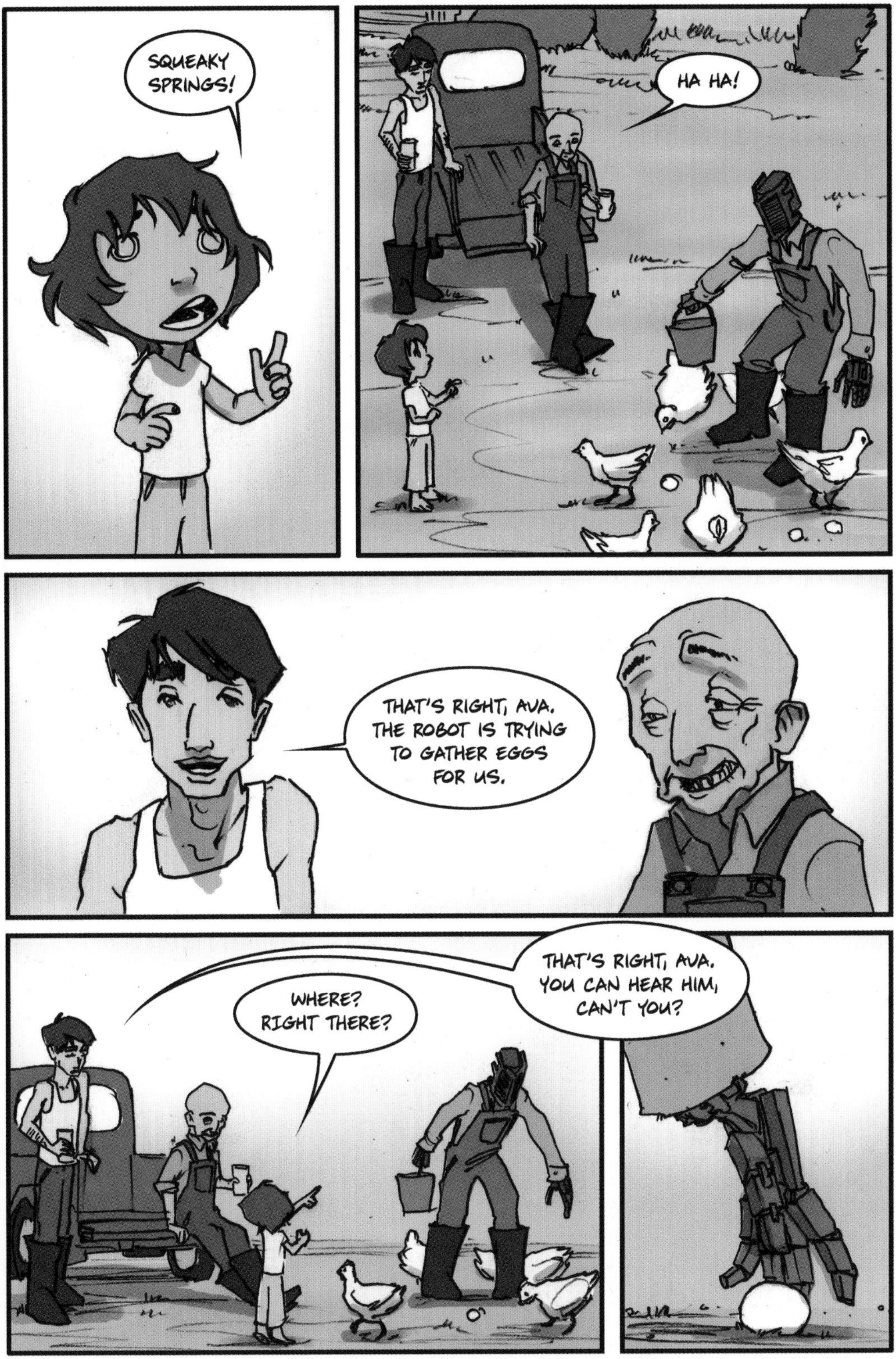
SQUEAKY SPRINGS!
HA HA!
THAT'S RIGHT, AVA. THE ROBOT IS TRYING TO GATHER EGGS FOR US.
WHERE? RIGHT THERE?
THAT'S RIGHT, AVA. YOU CAN HEAR HIM, CAN'T YOU?

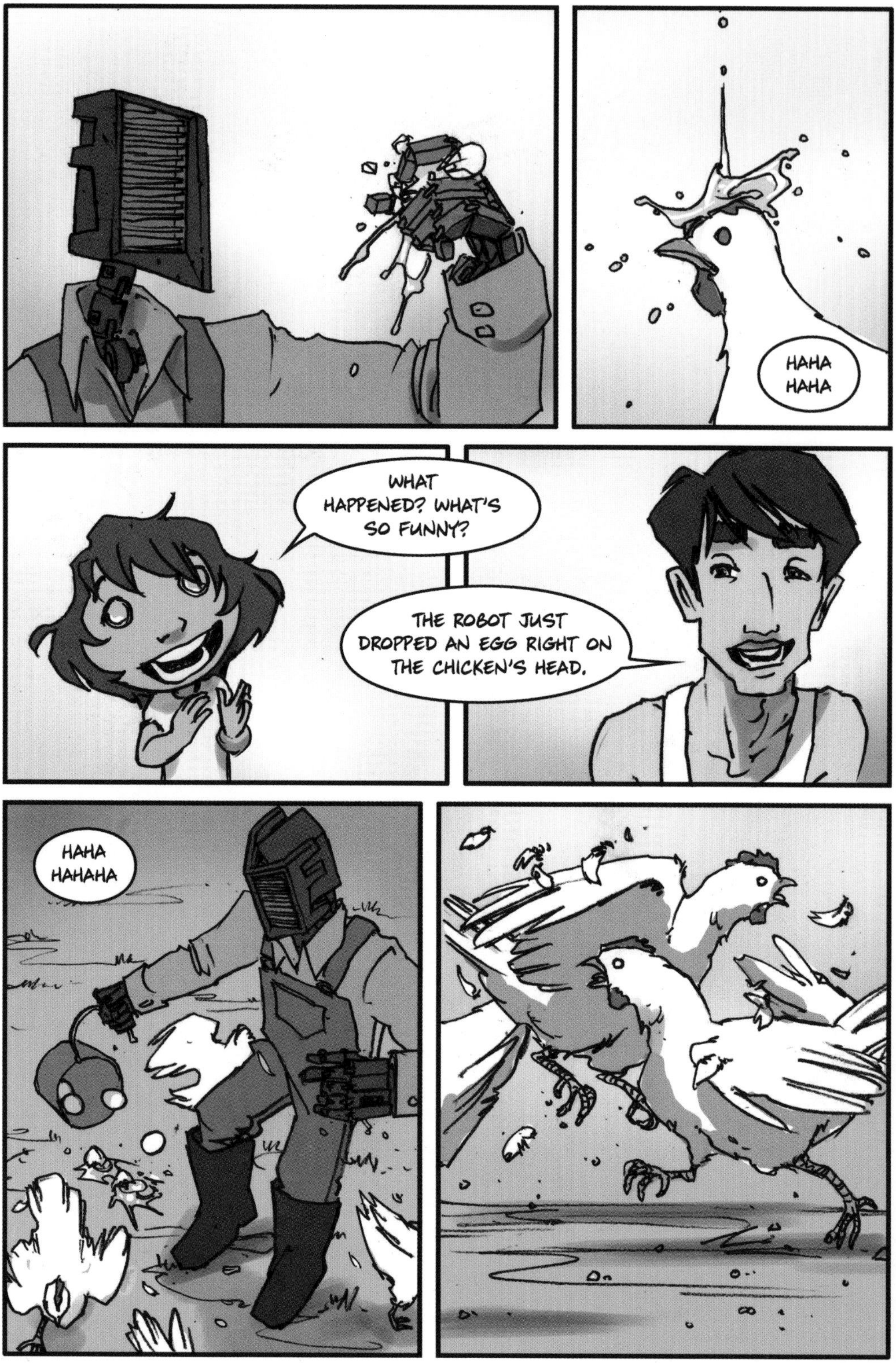
HAHA HAHA
WHAT HAPPENED? WHAT'S SO FUNNY?
THE ROBOT JUST DROPPED AN EGG RIGHT ON THE CHICKEN'S HEAD.
HAHA HAHAHA

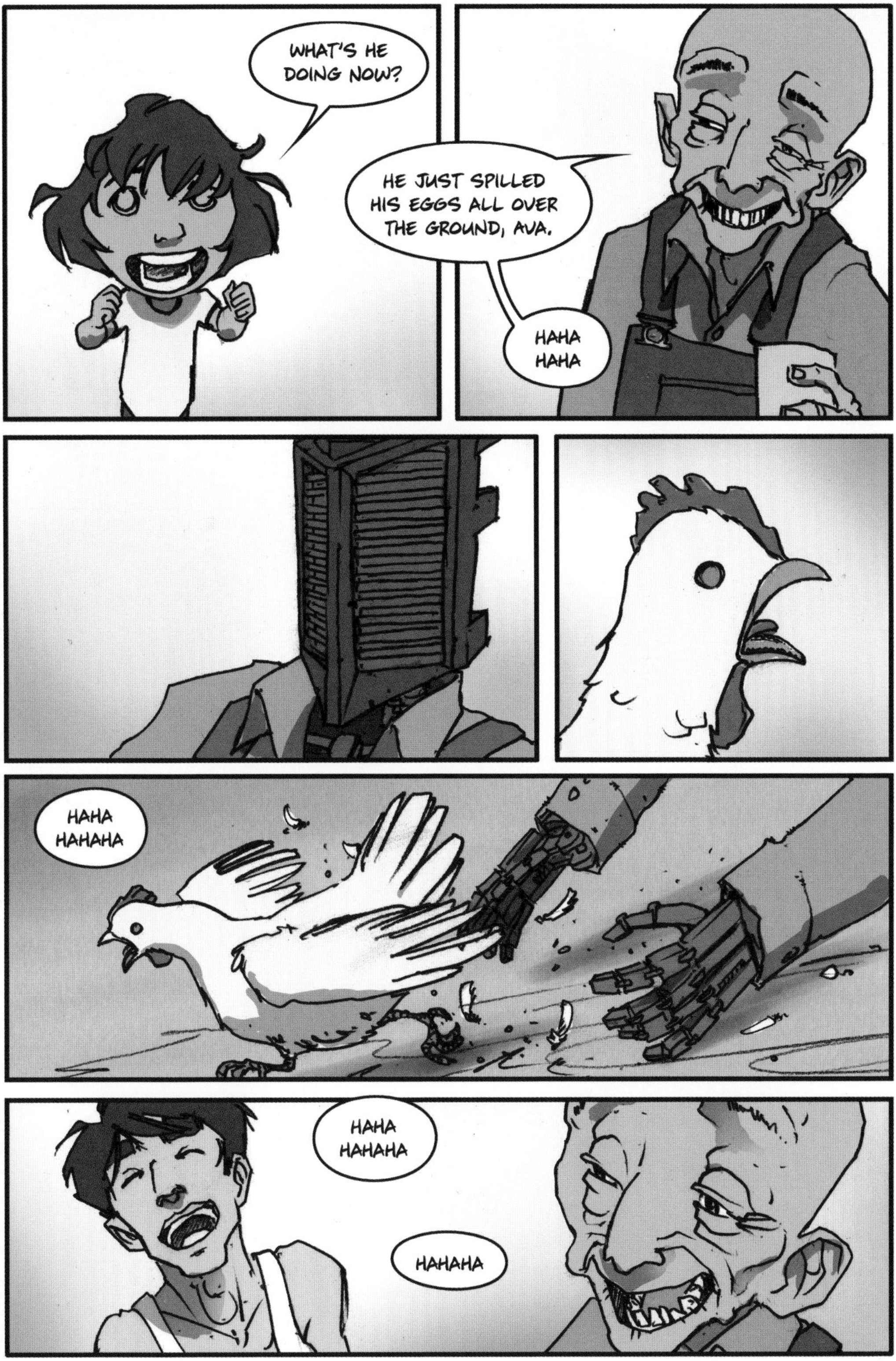
WHAT'S HE DOING NOW?
HE JUST SPILLED HIS EGGS ALL OVER THE GROUND, AVA.
HAHA HAHA
HAHA HAHAHA
HAHA HAHAHA
HAHAHA

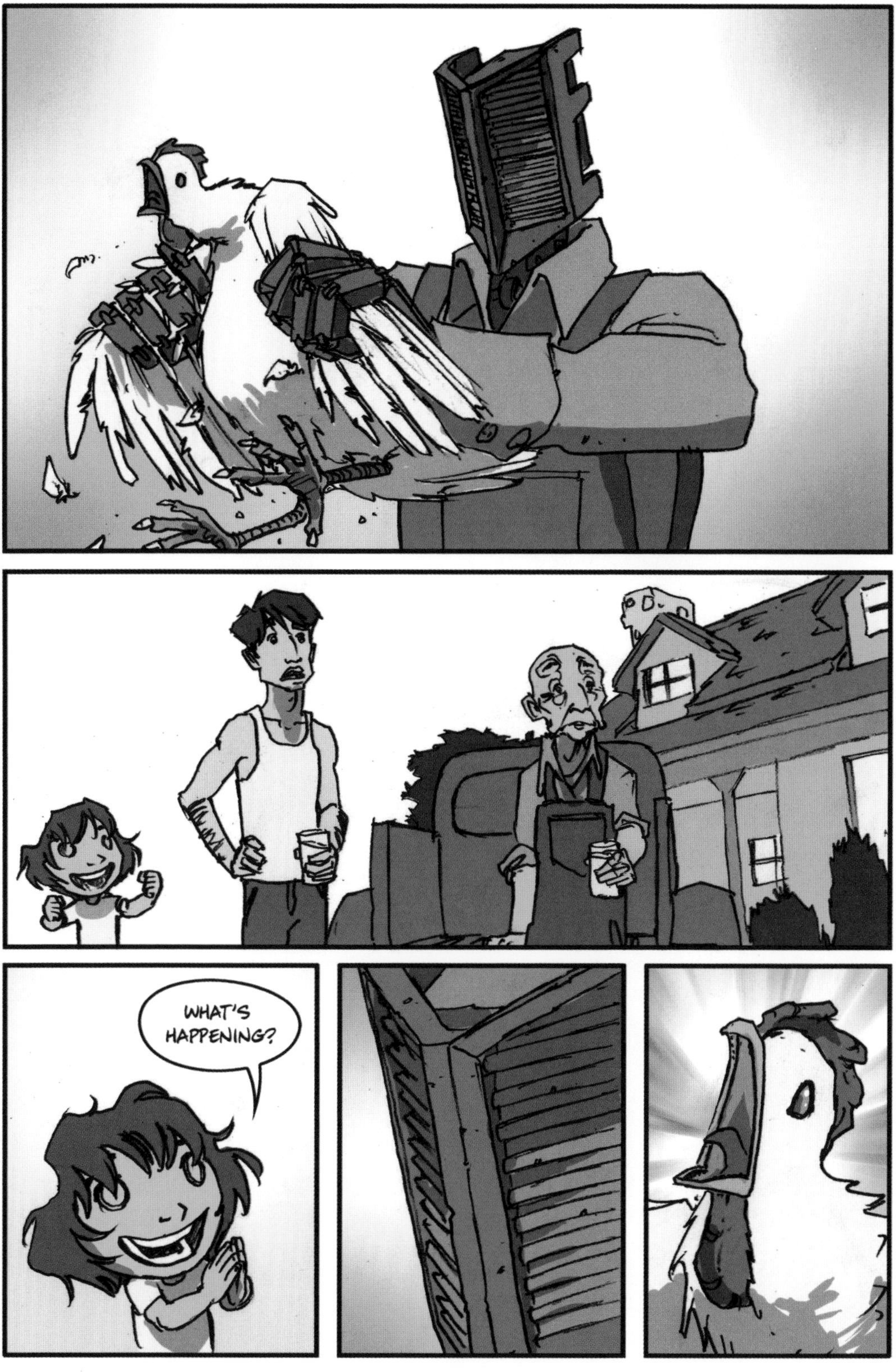
WHAT'S HAPPENING?

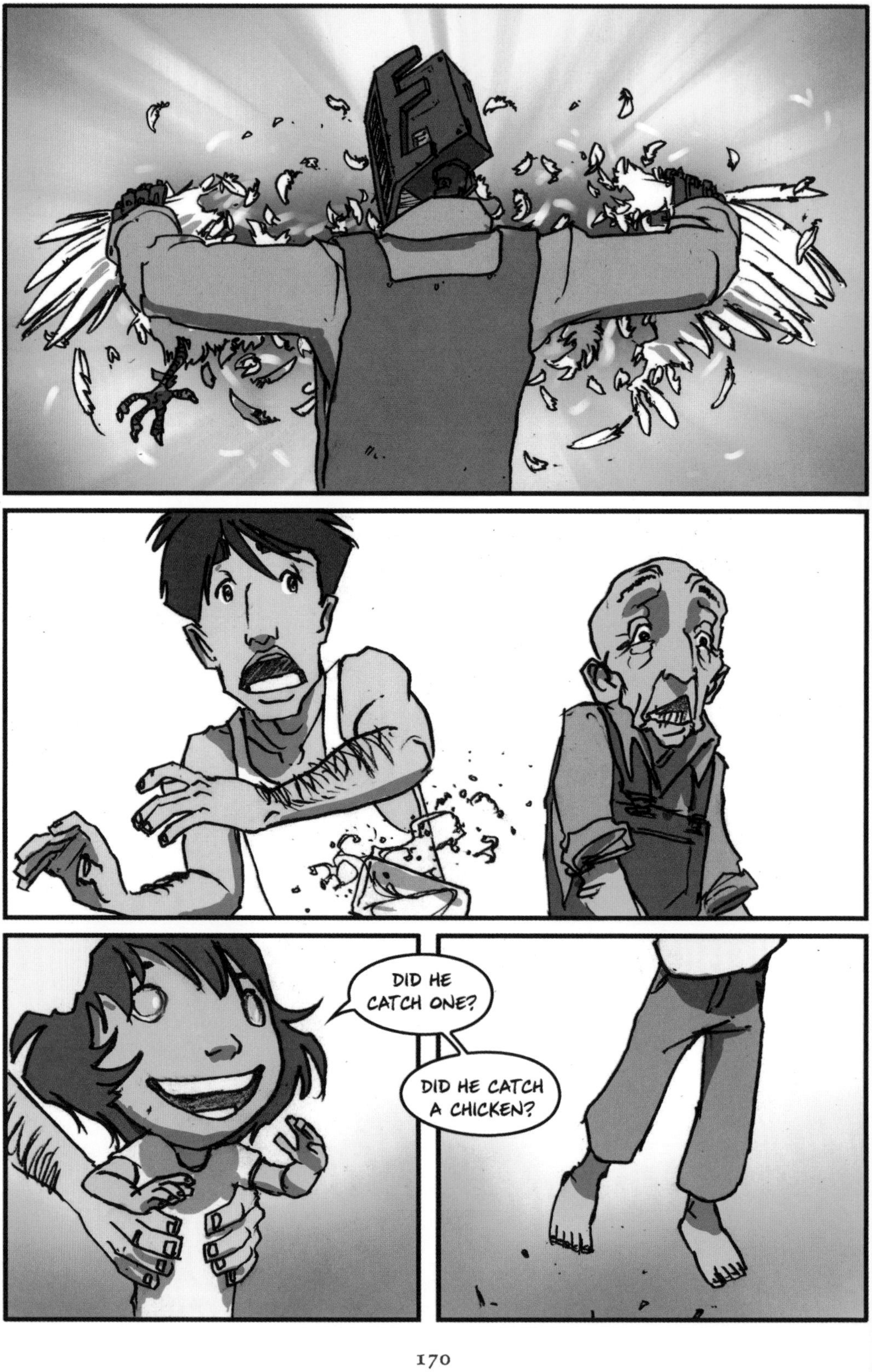
DID HE CATCH ONE?
DID HE CATCH A CHICKEN?

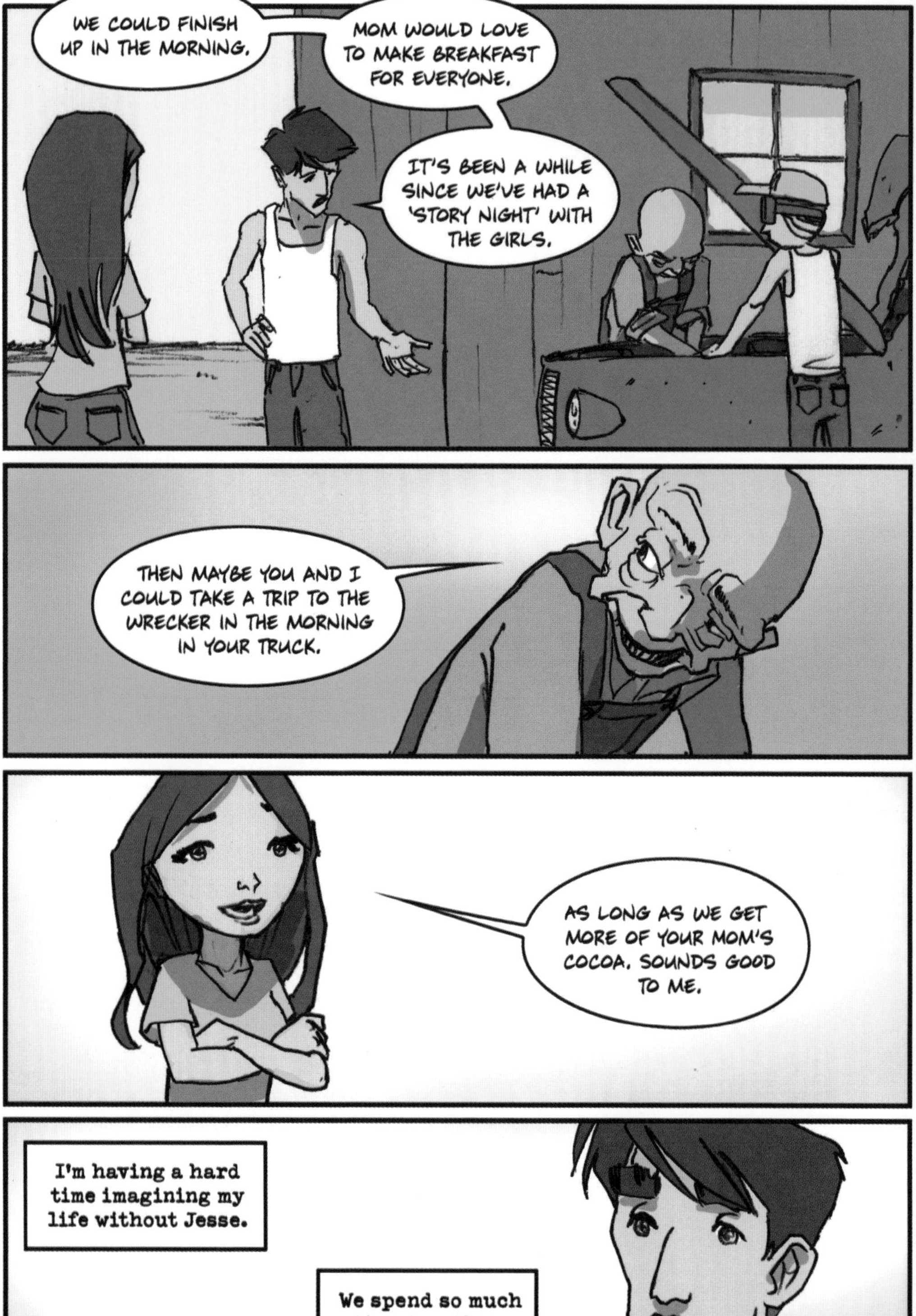
WE COULD FINISH UP IN THE MORNING.
MOM WOULD LOVE TO MAKE BREAKFAST FOR EVERYONE.
IT'S BEEN A WHILE SINCE WE'VE HAD A 'STORY NIGHT' WITH THE GIRLS.
THEN MAYBE YOU AND I COULD TAKE A TRIP TO THE WRECKER IN THE MORNING IN YOUR TRUCK.
AS LONG AS WE GET MORE OF YOUR MOM'S COCOA. SOUNDS GOOD TO ME.
I'm having a hard time imagining my life without Jesse.
We spend so much time together.

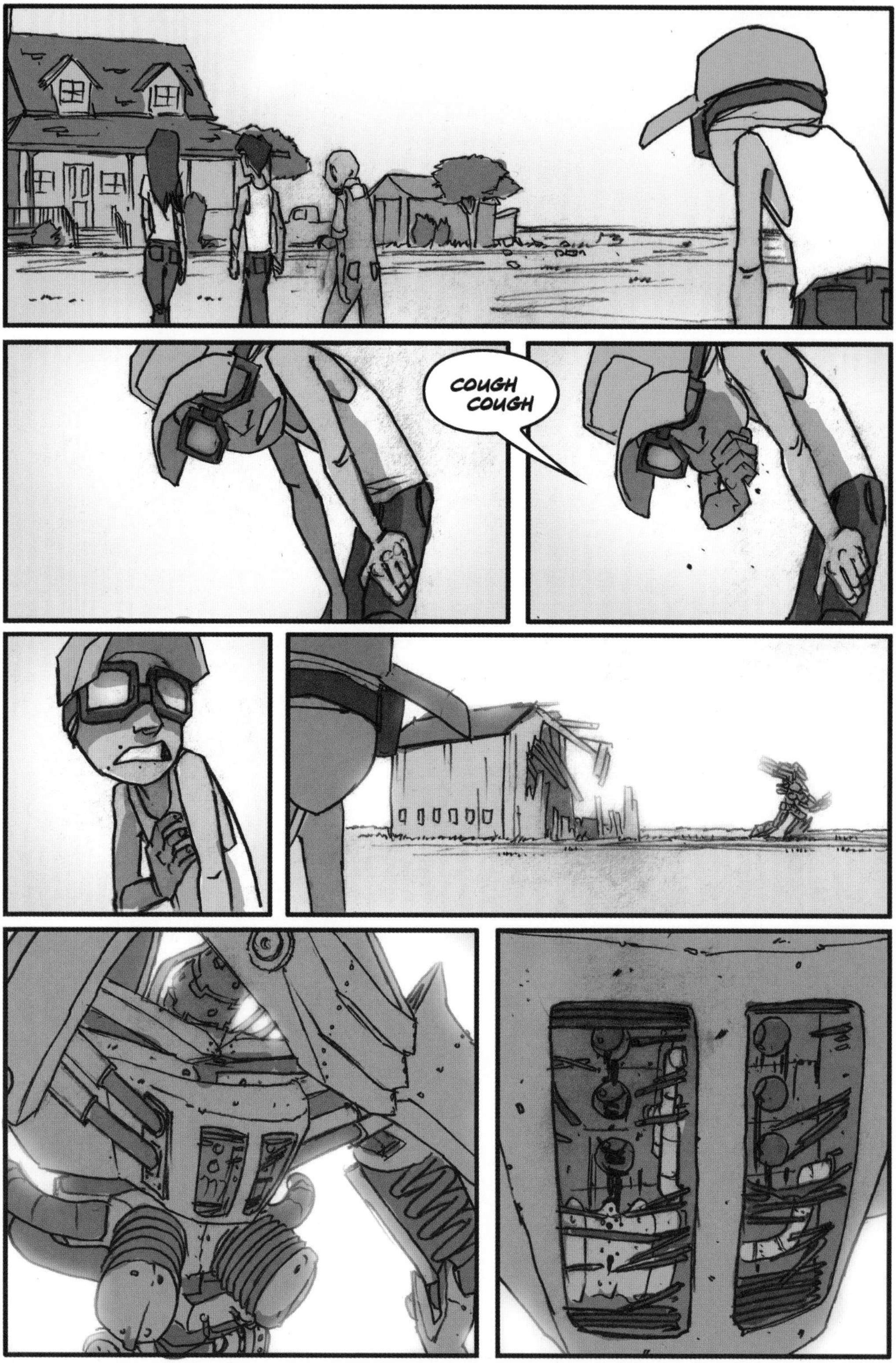
COUGH
COUGH

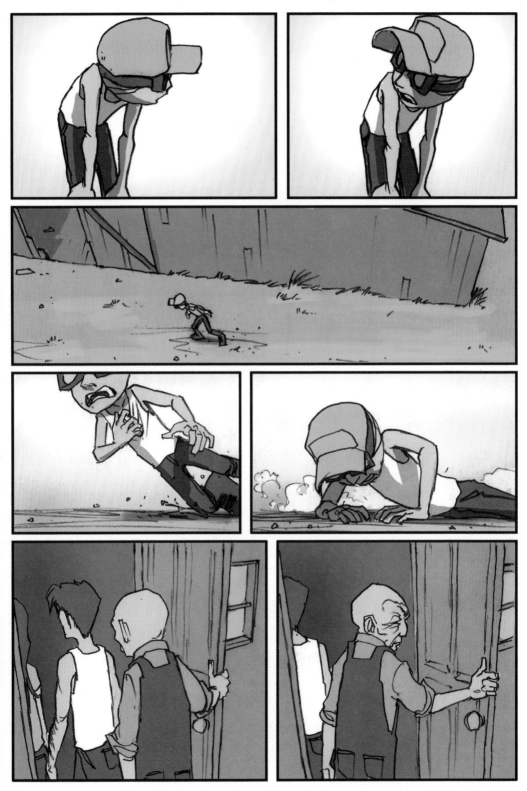

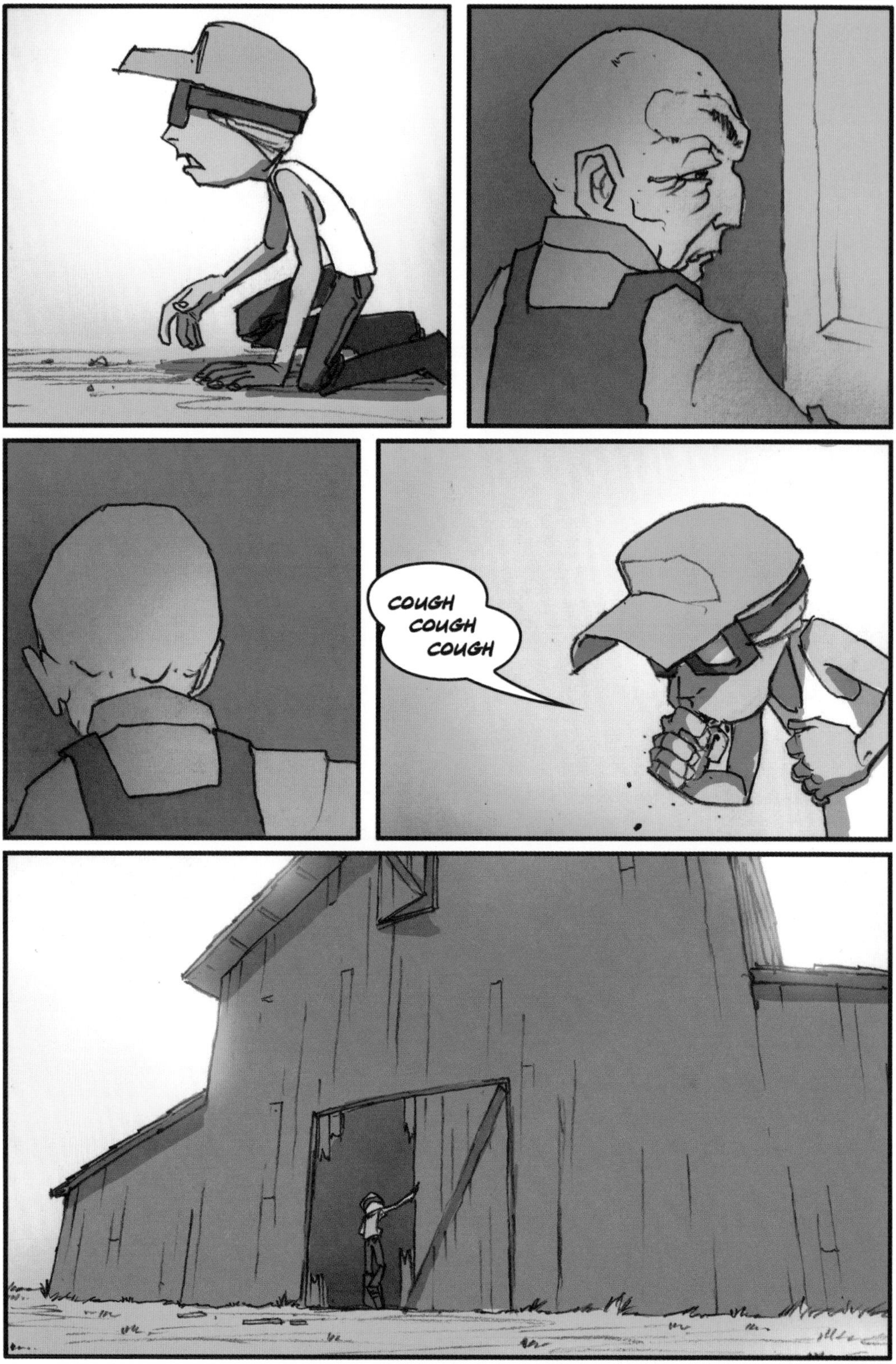
COUGH
COUGH
COUGH

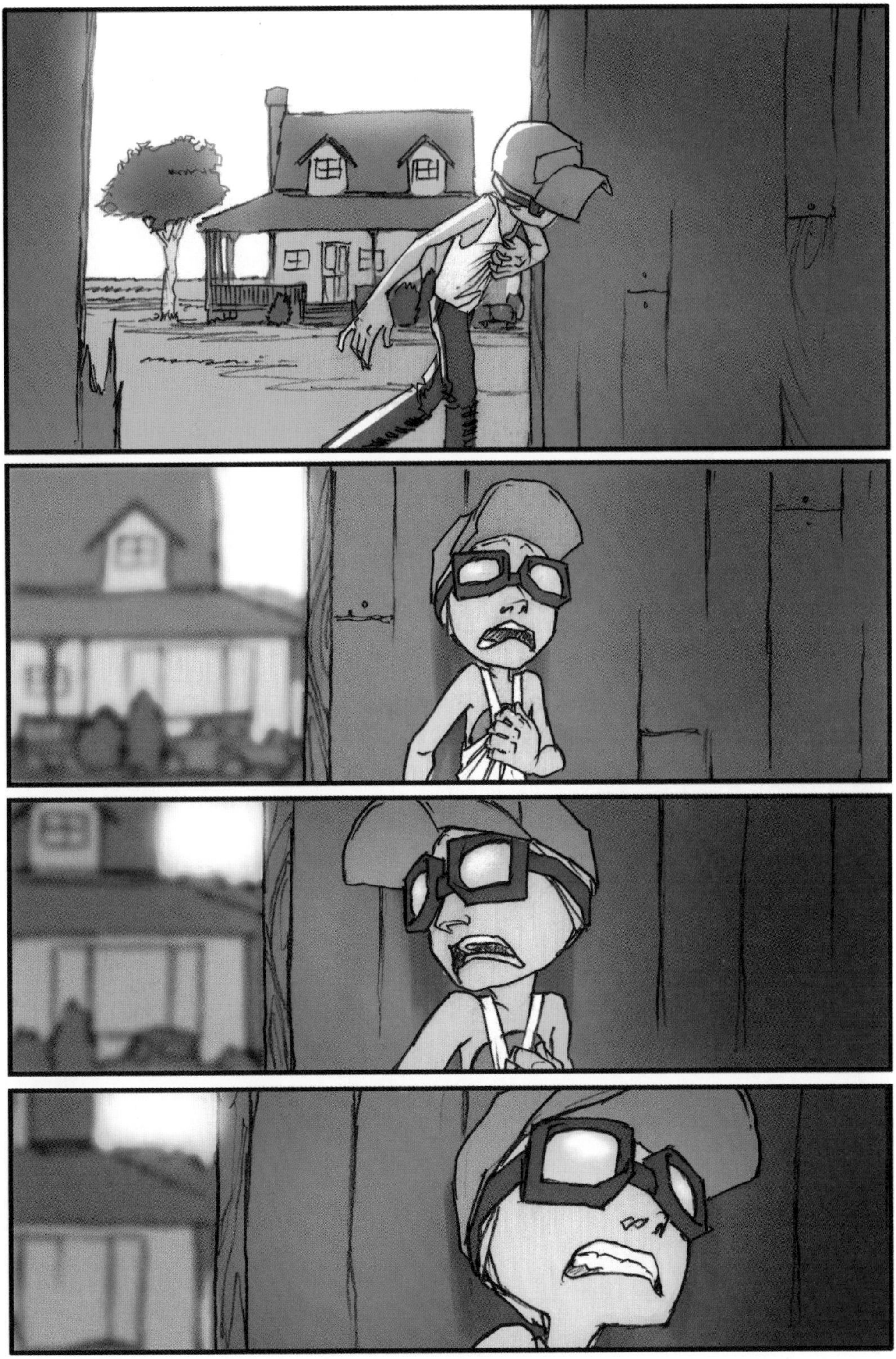

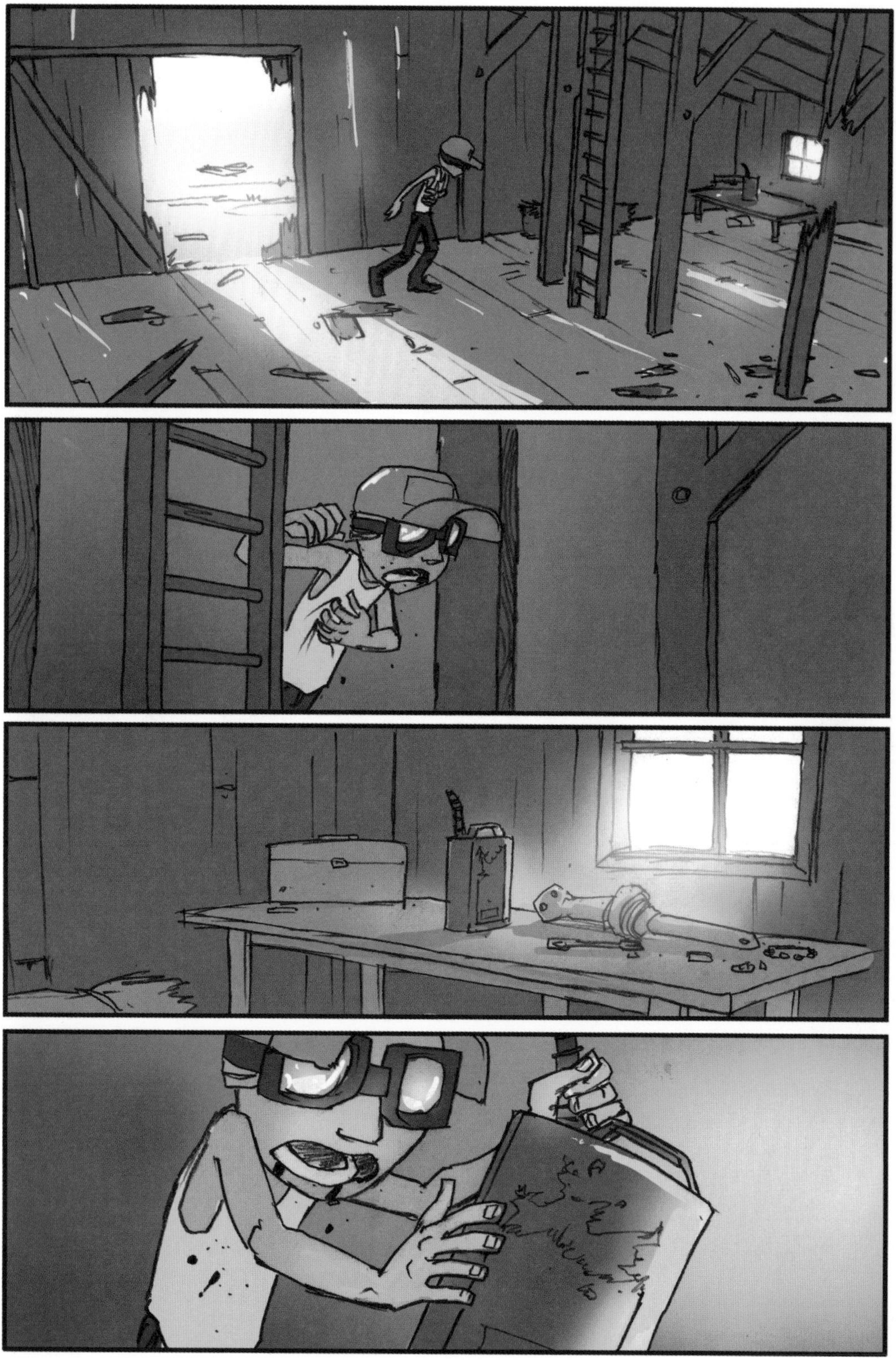

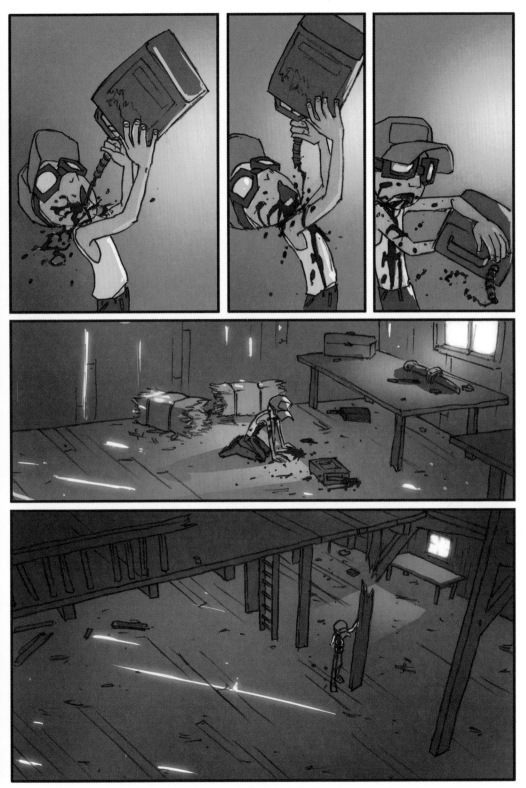

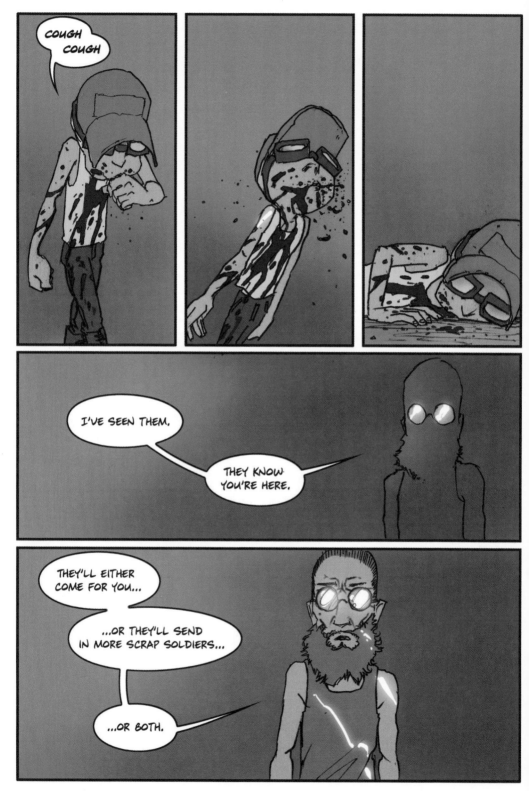

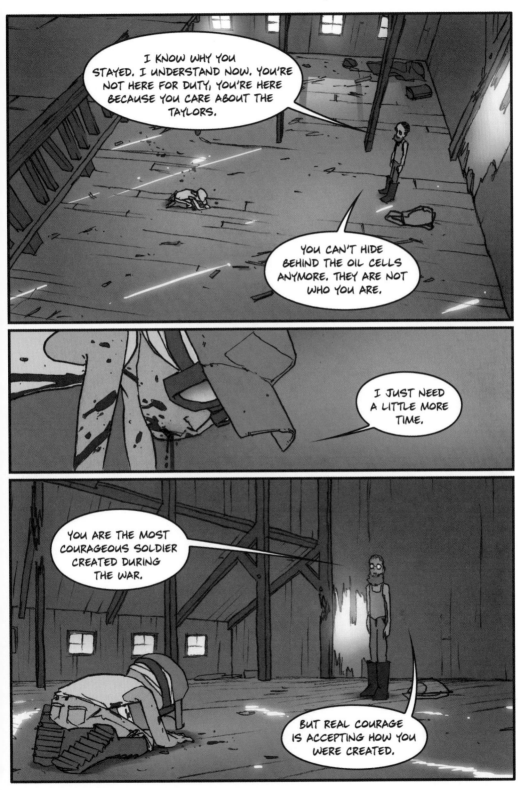

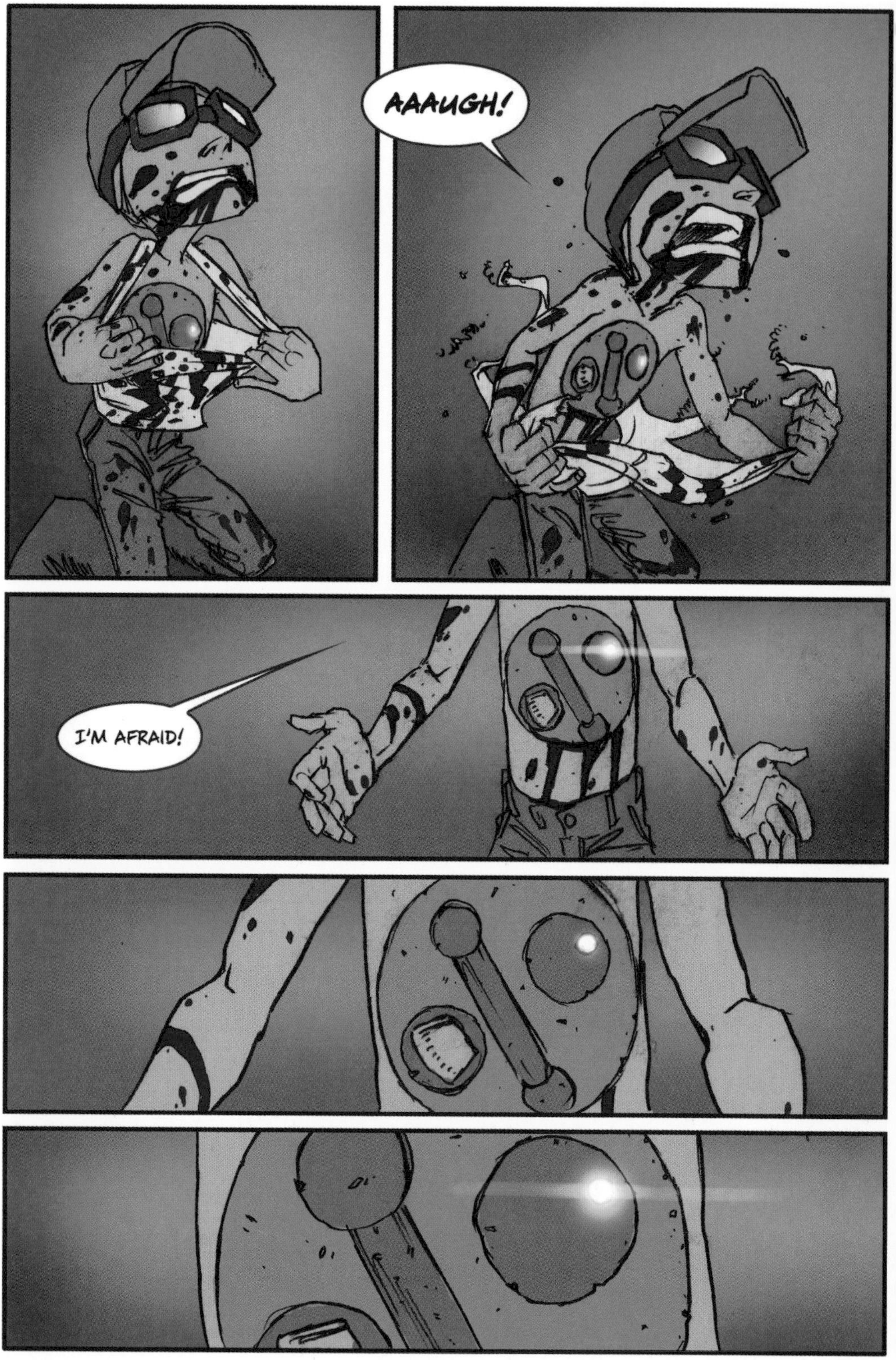
AAAUGH!
I'M AFRAID!

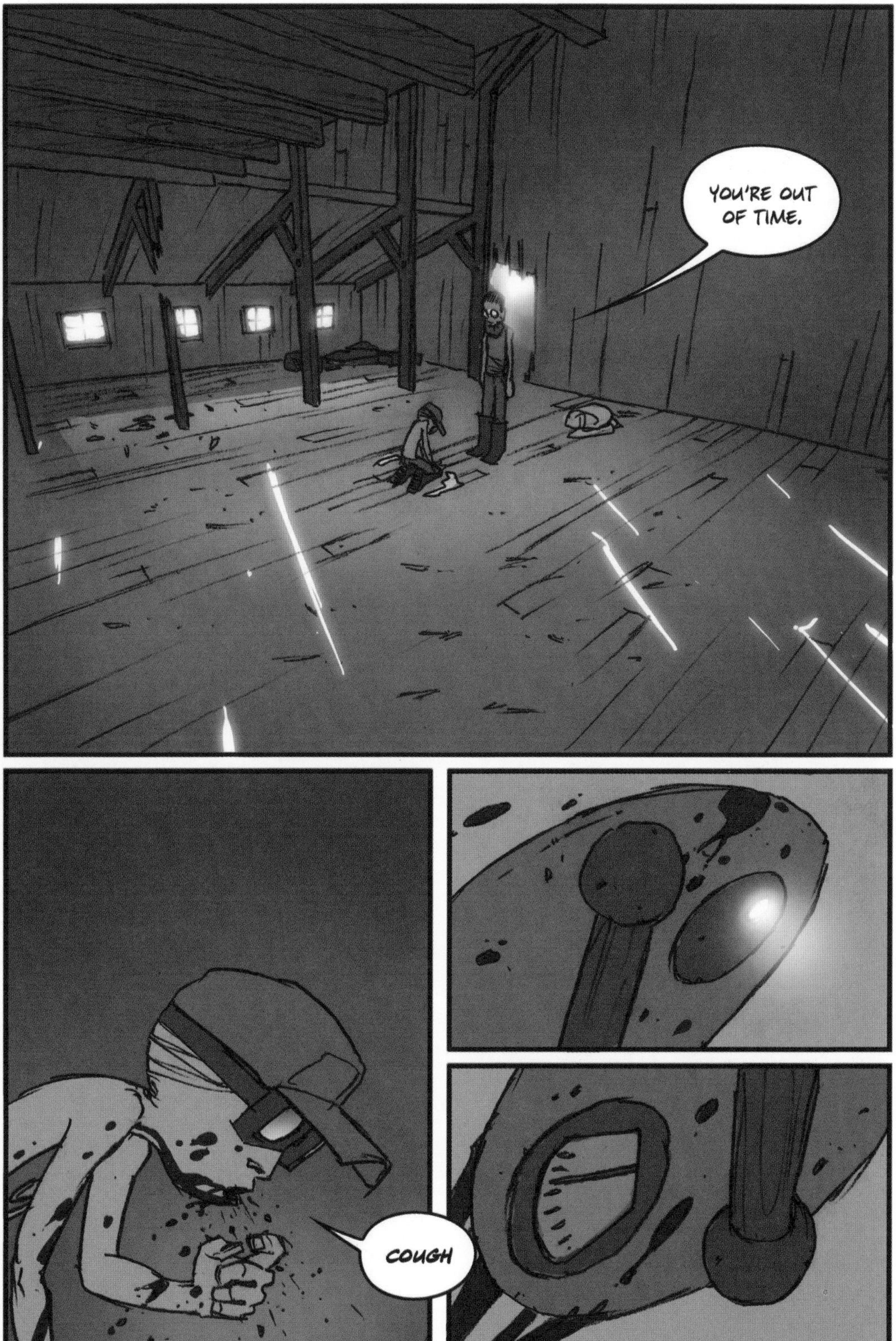
YOU'RE OUT OF TIME.
COUGH

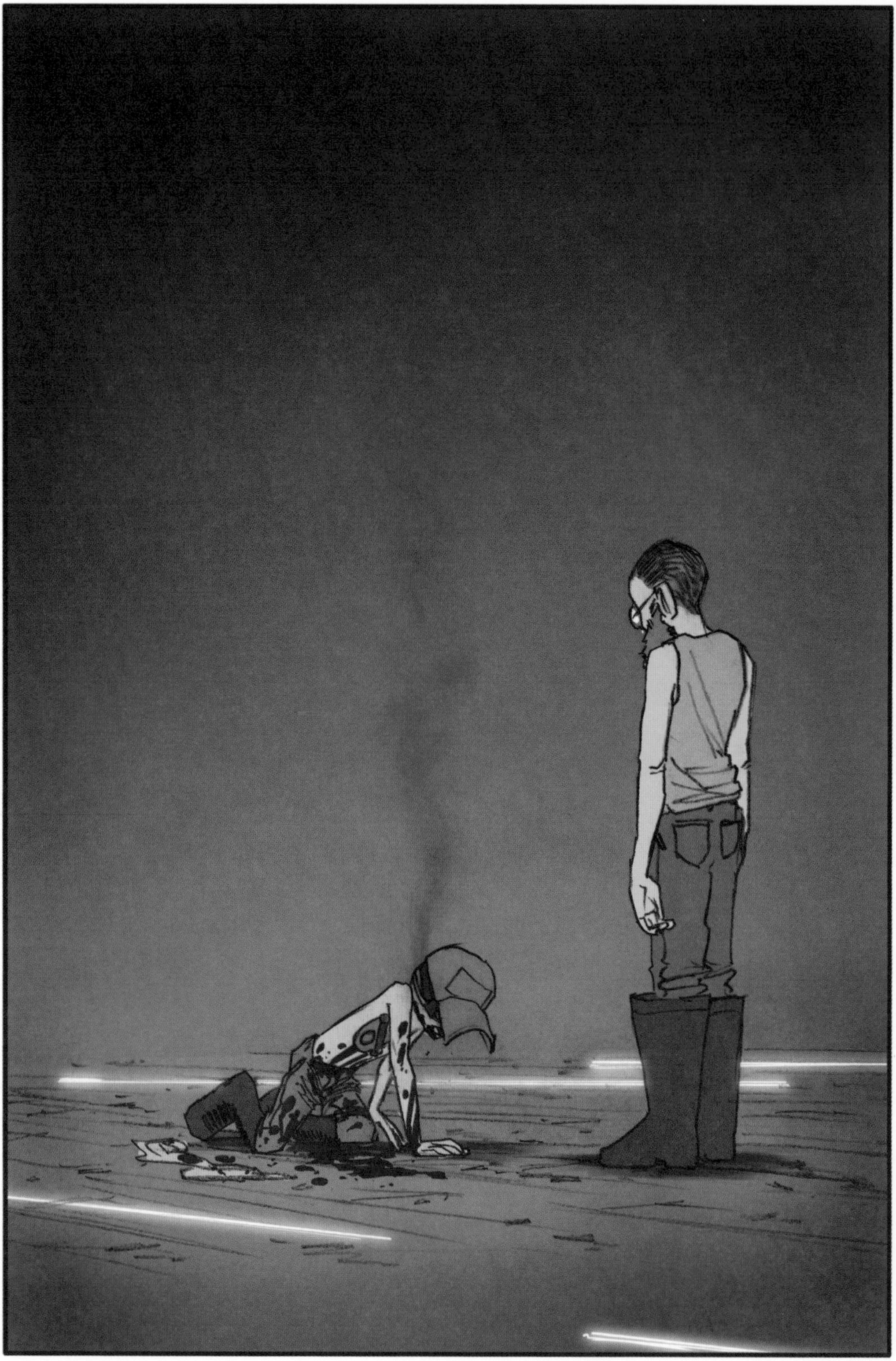

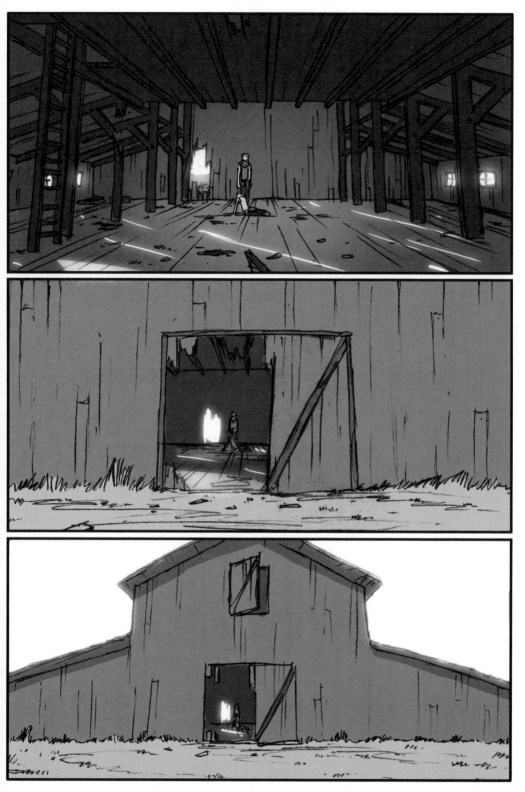

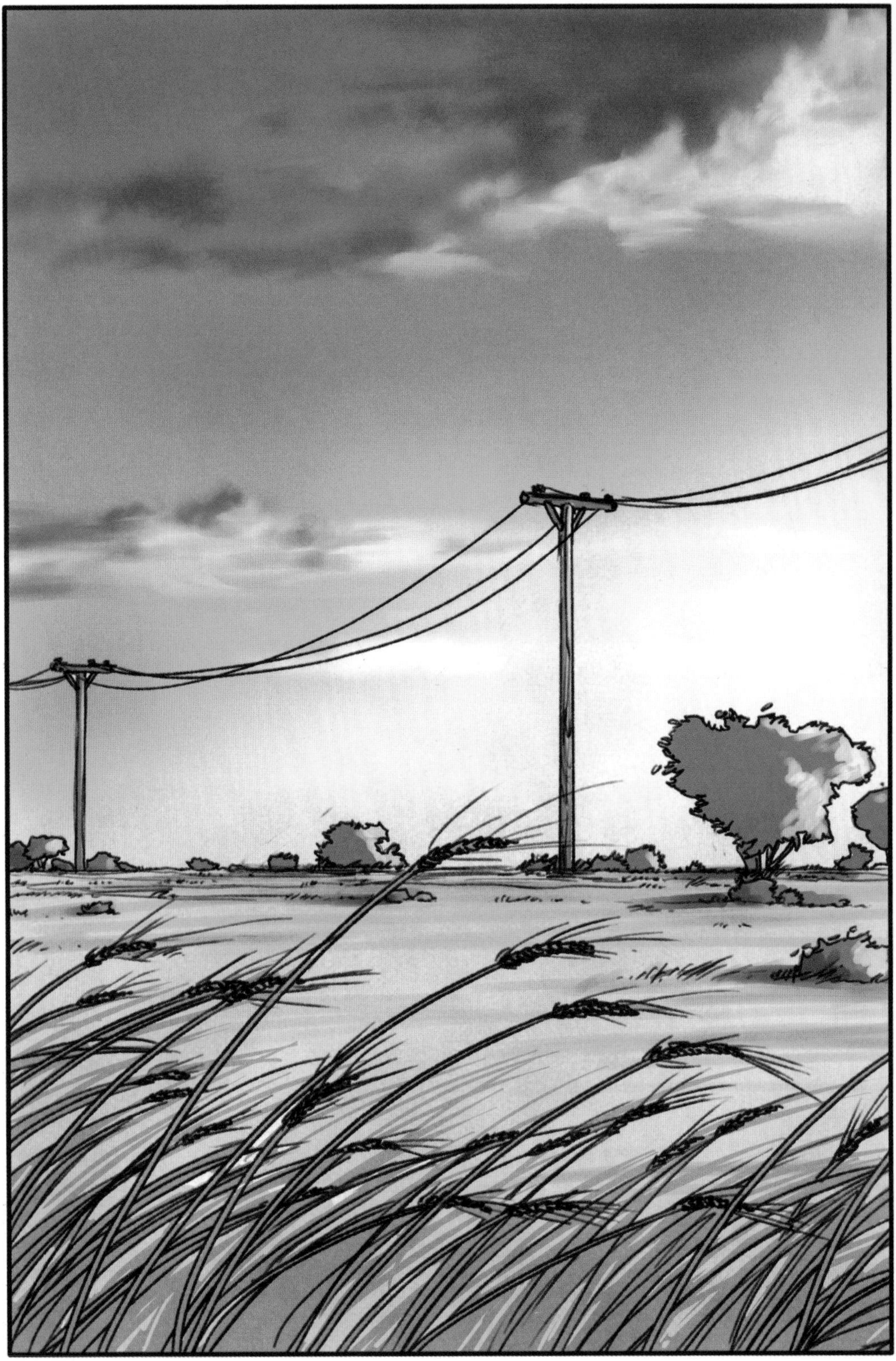

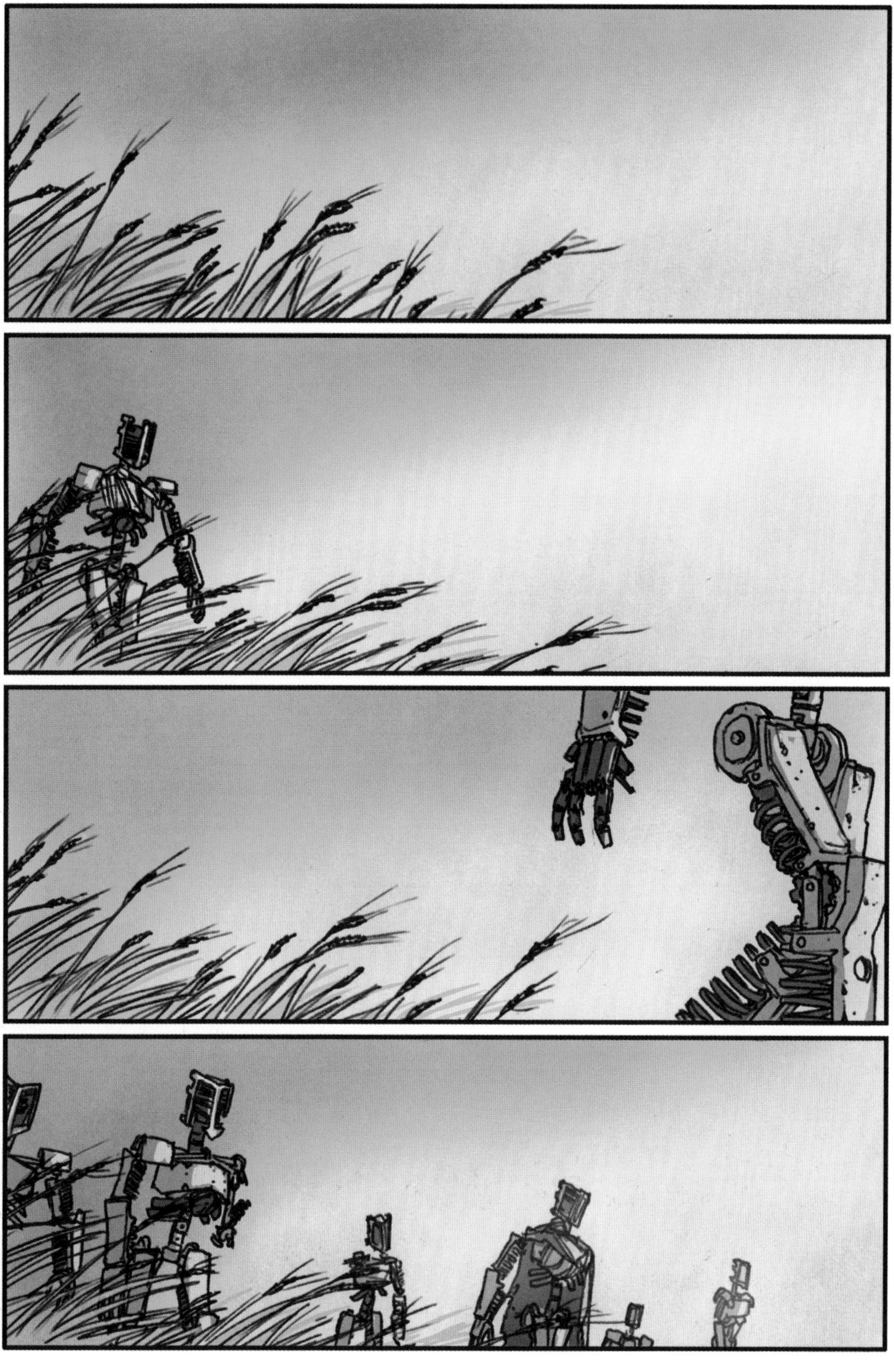

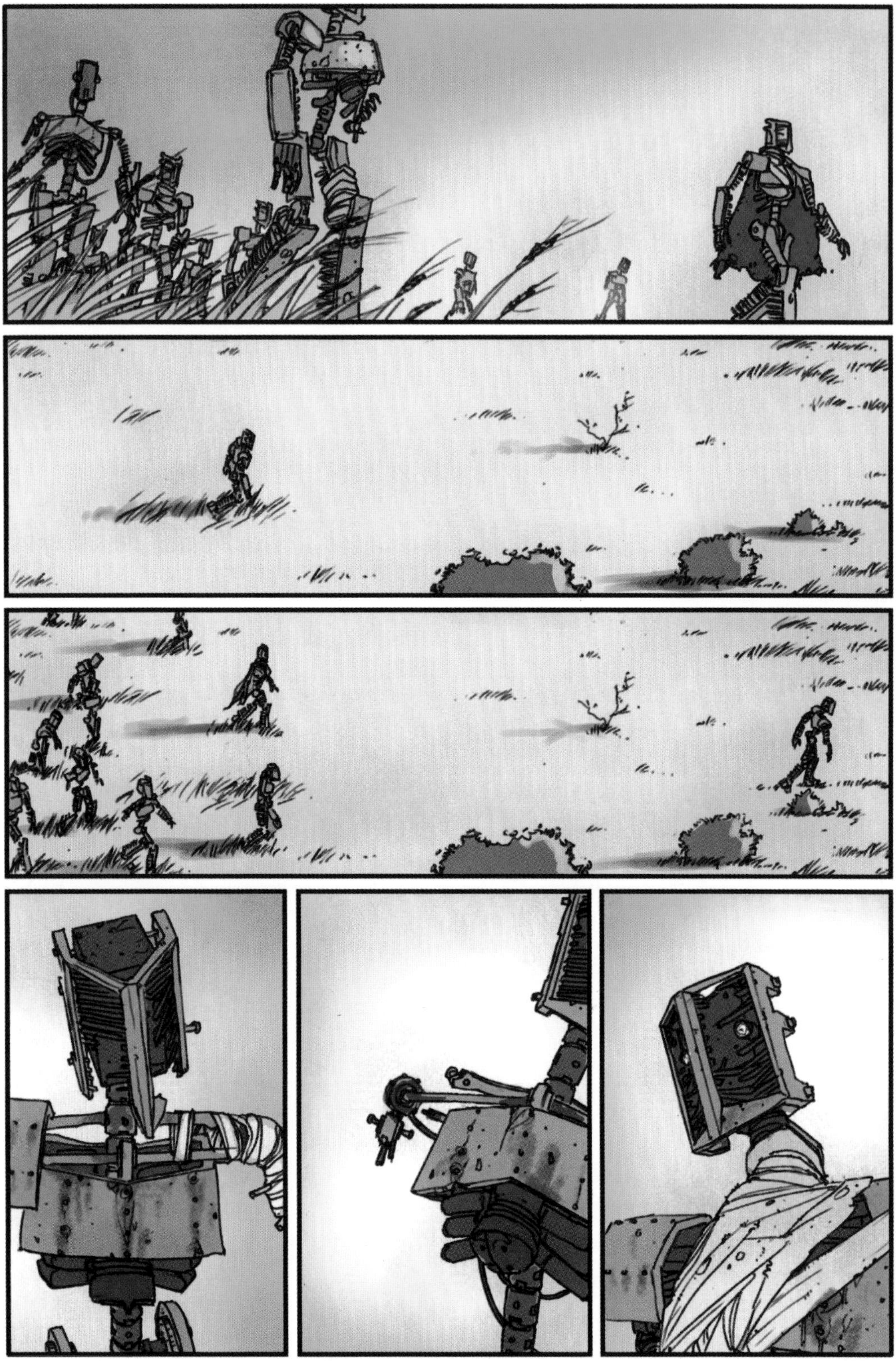

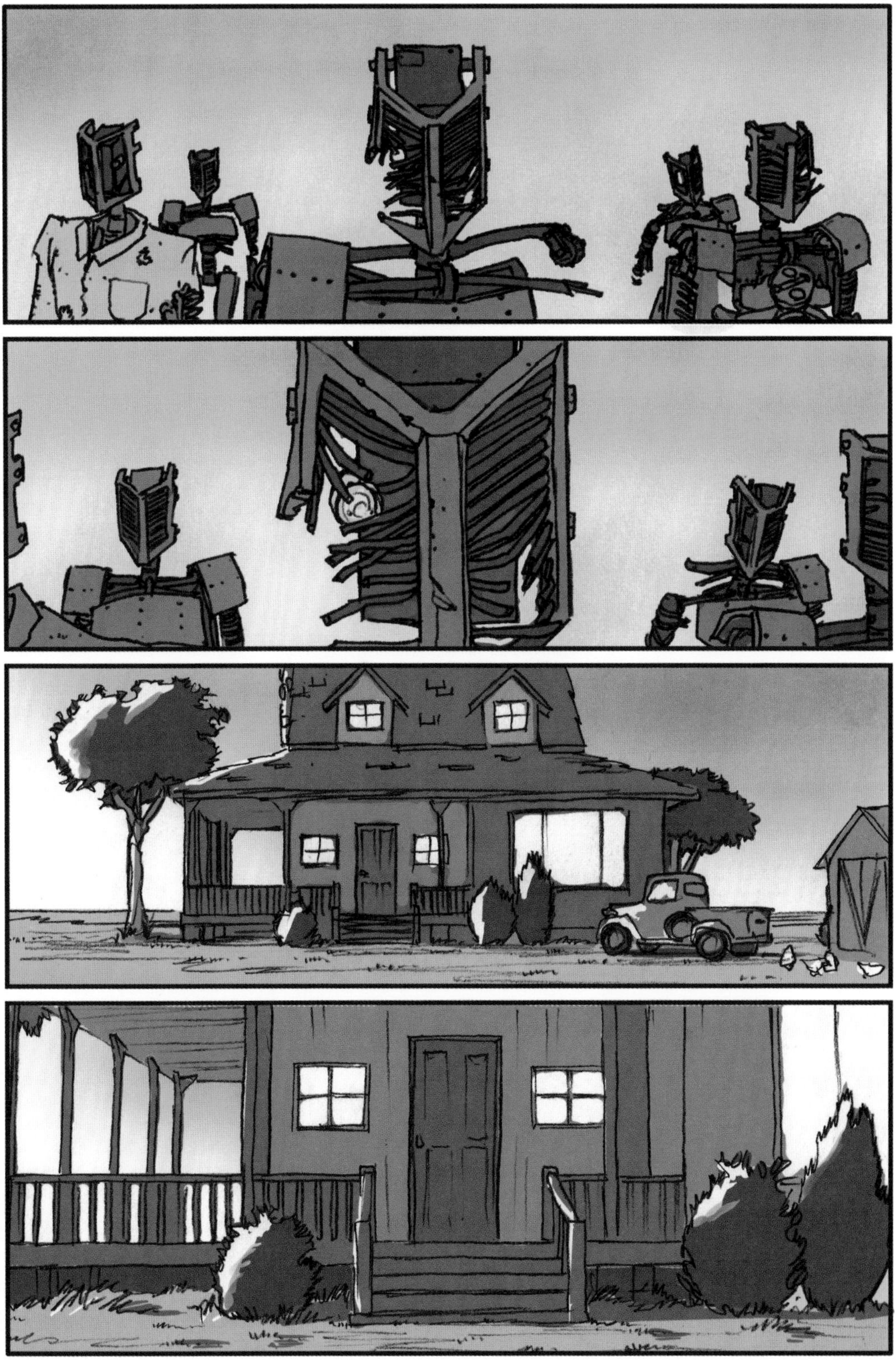

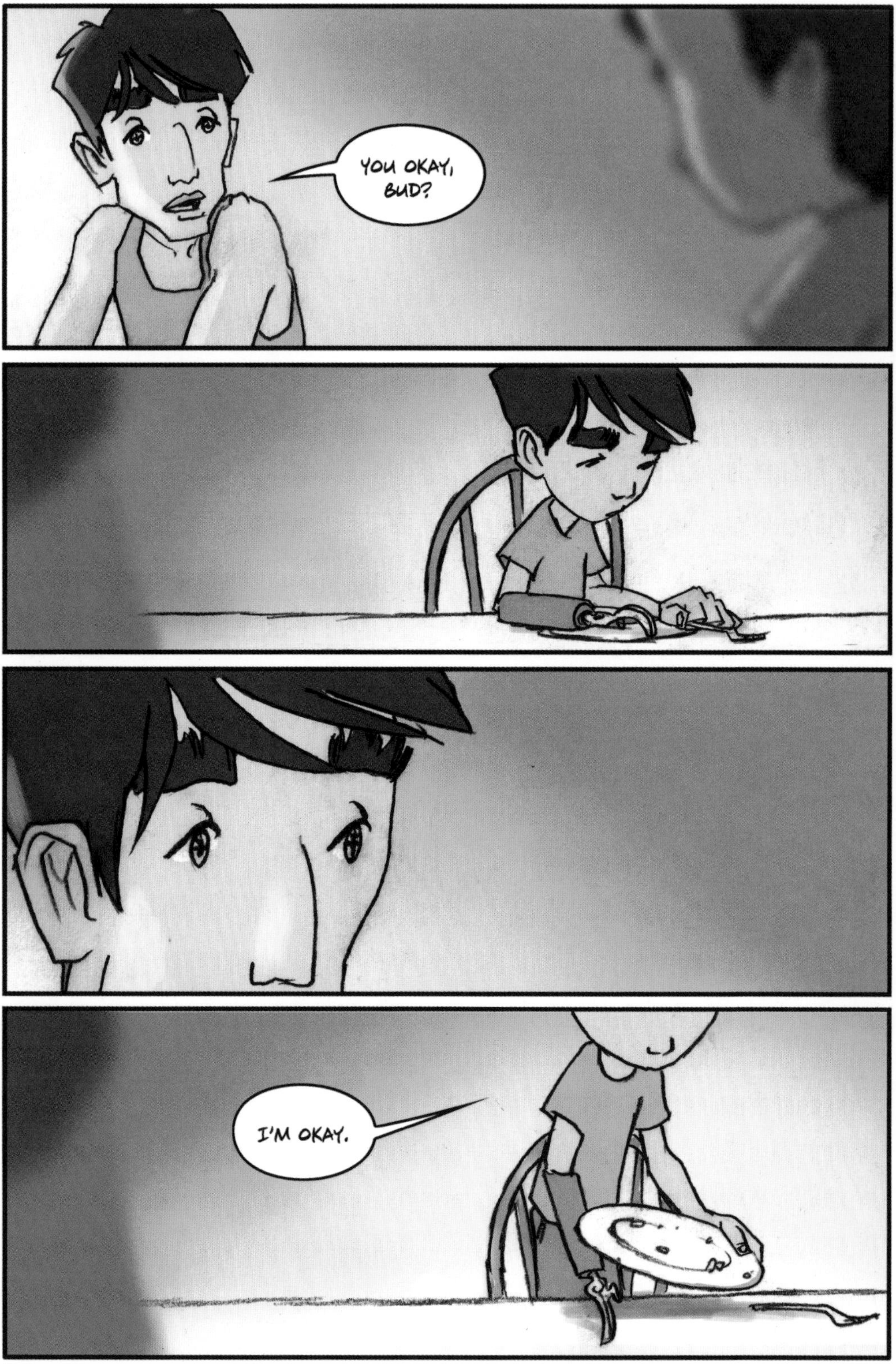
YOU OKAY, BUD?
I'M OKAY.

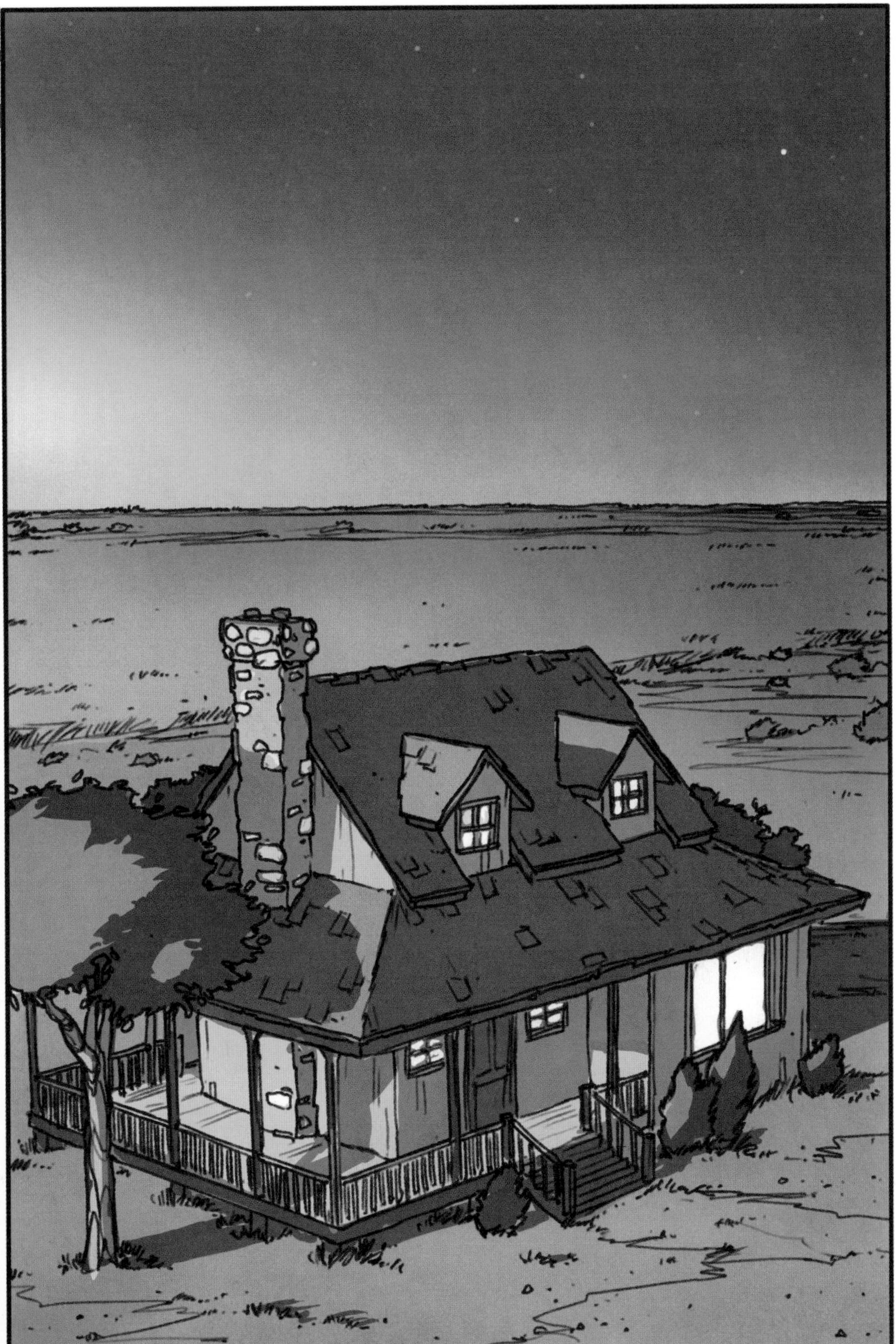

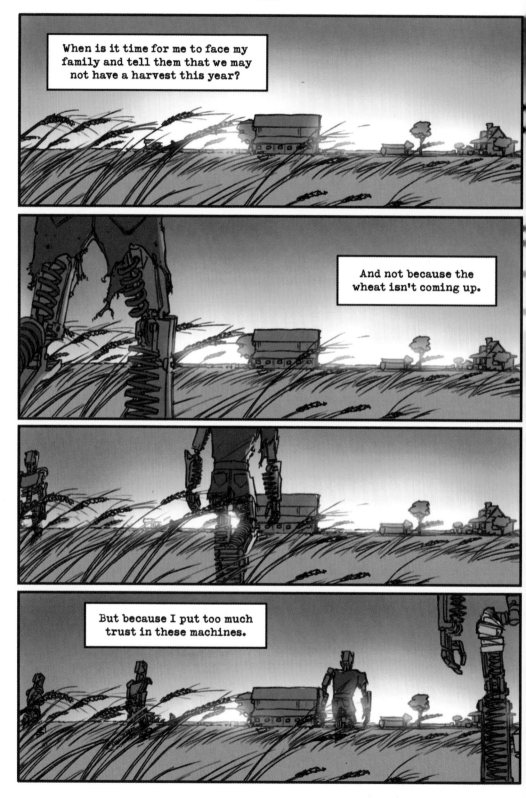

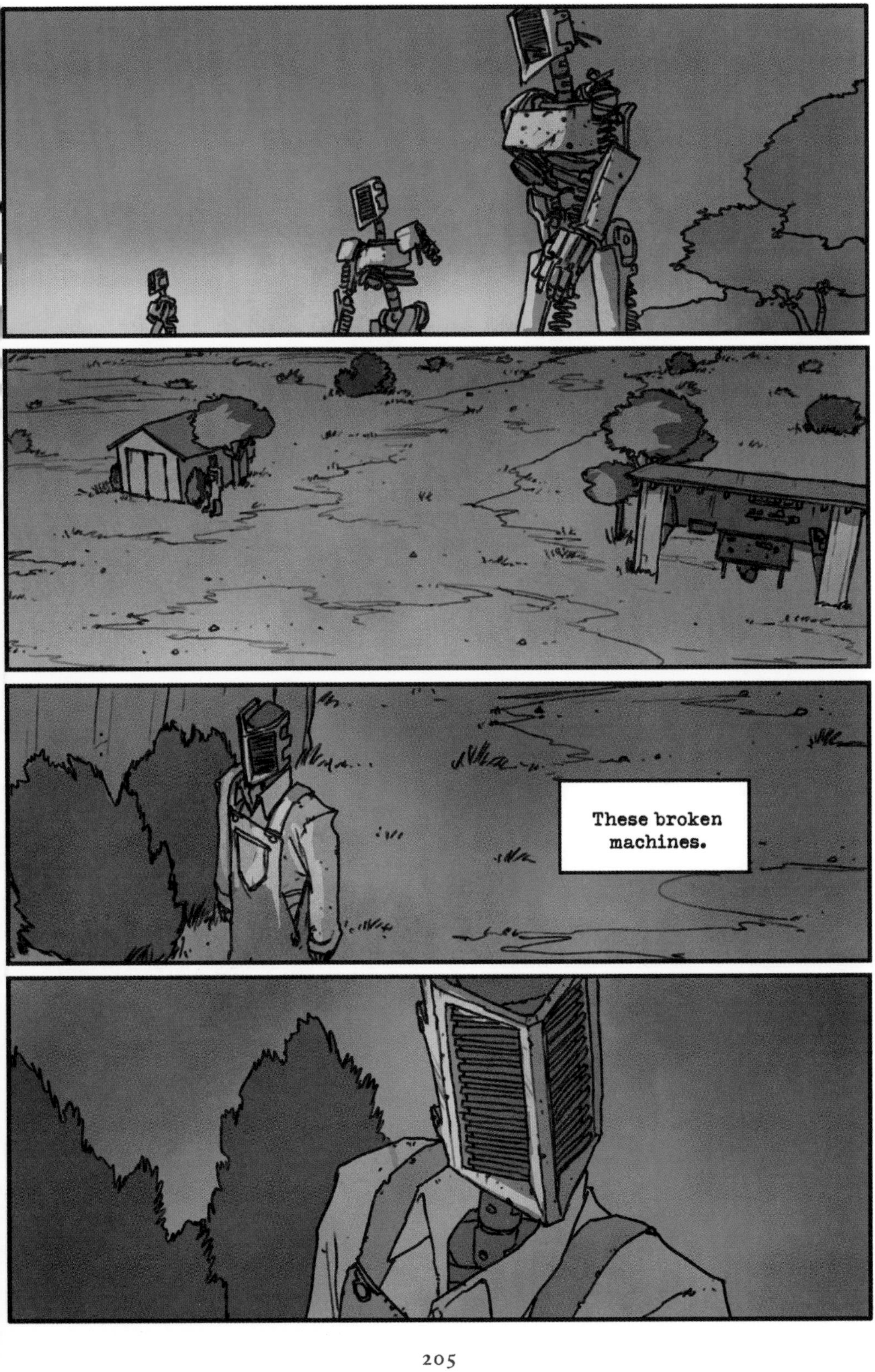
These broken
machines.

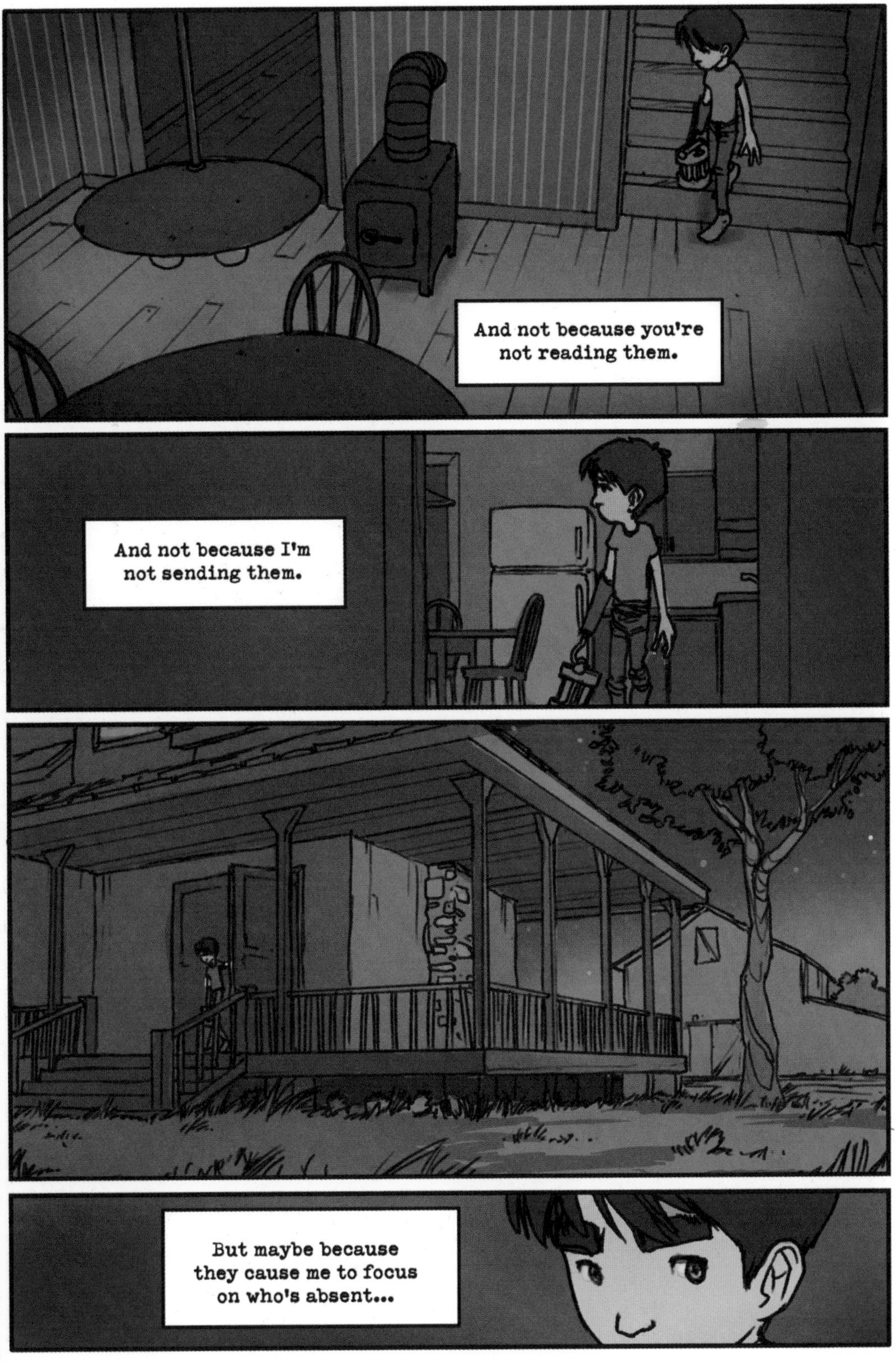
And not because you're not reading them.
And not because I'm not sending them.
But maybe because they cause me to focus on who's absent...

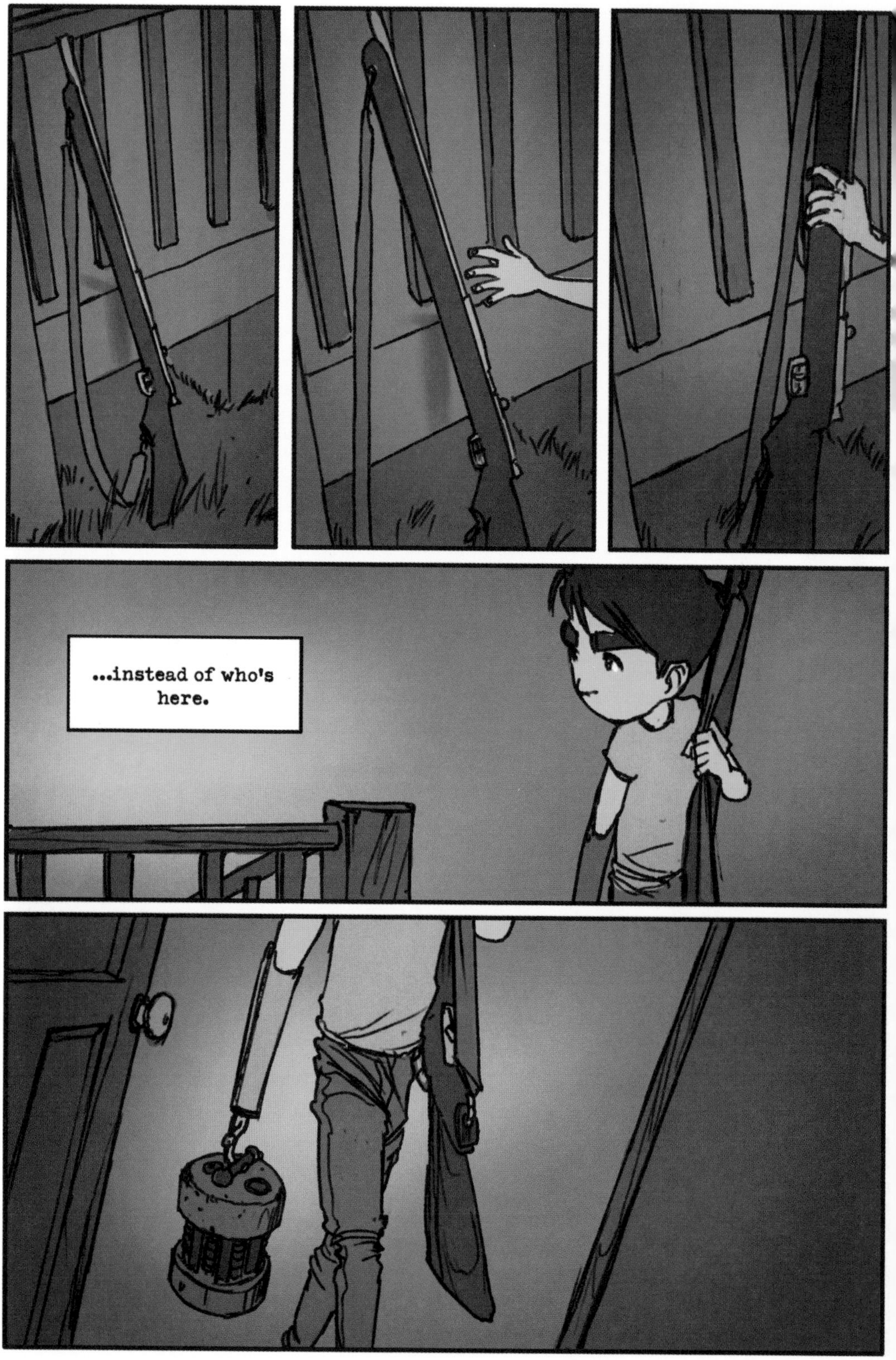
...instead of who's here.

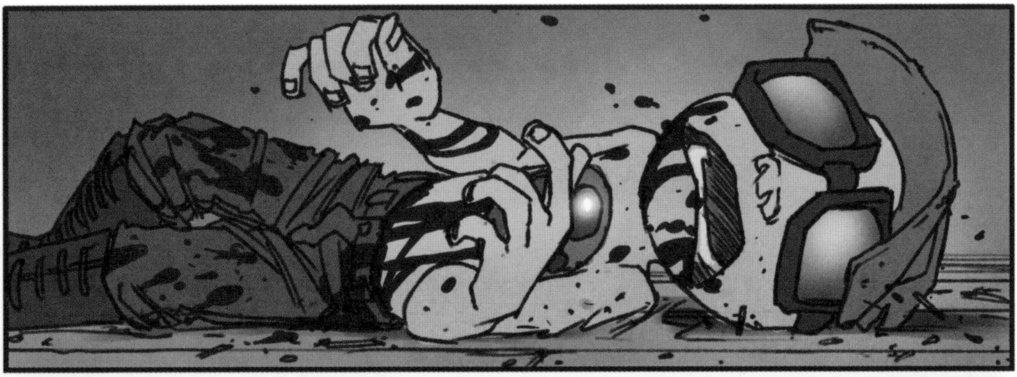

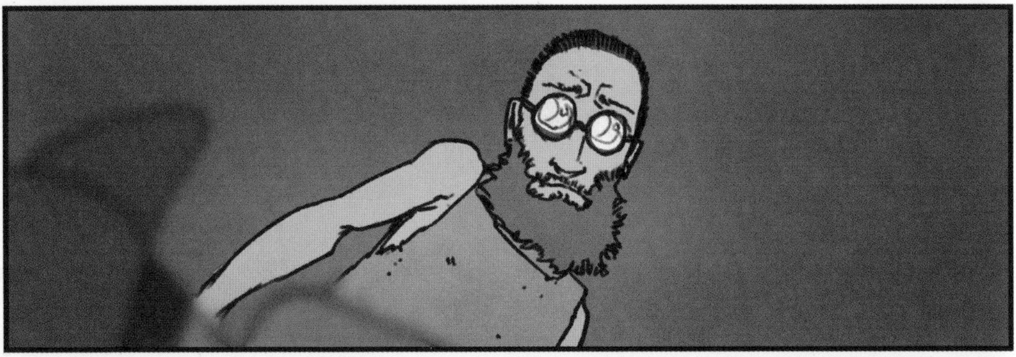

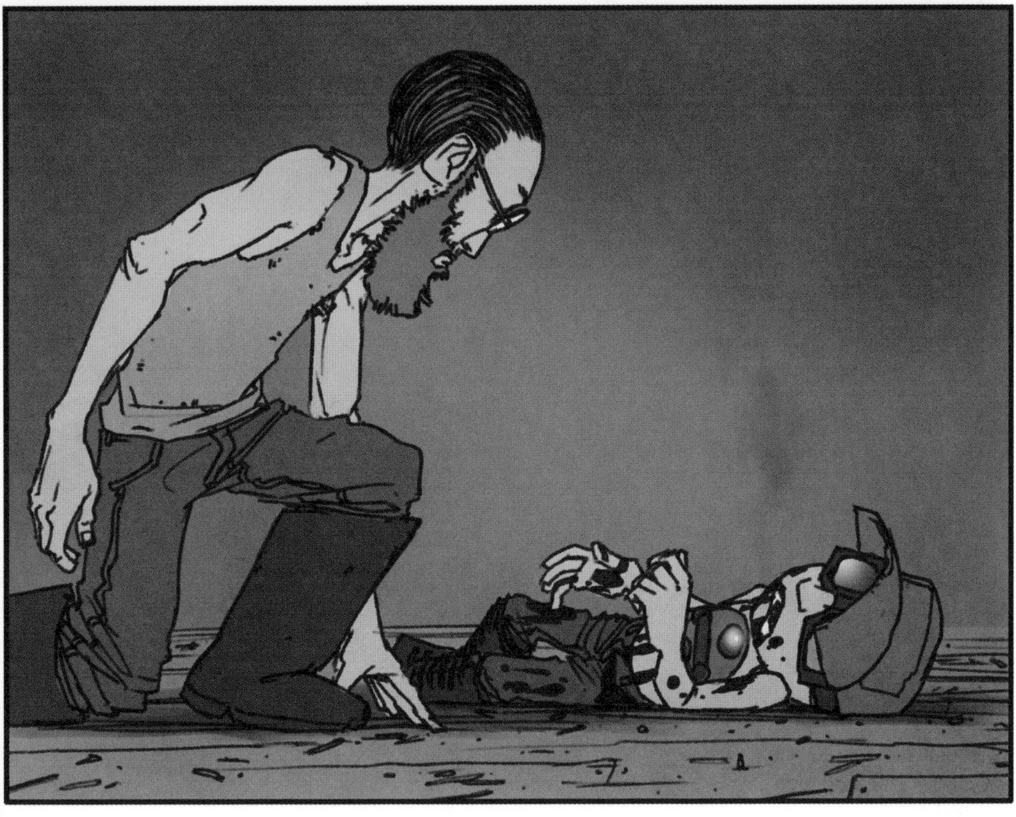

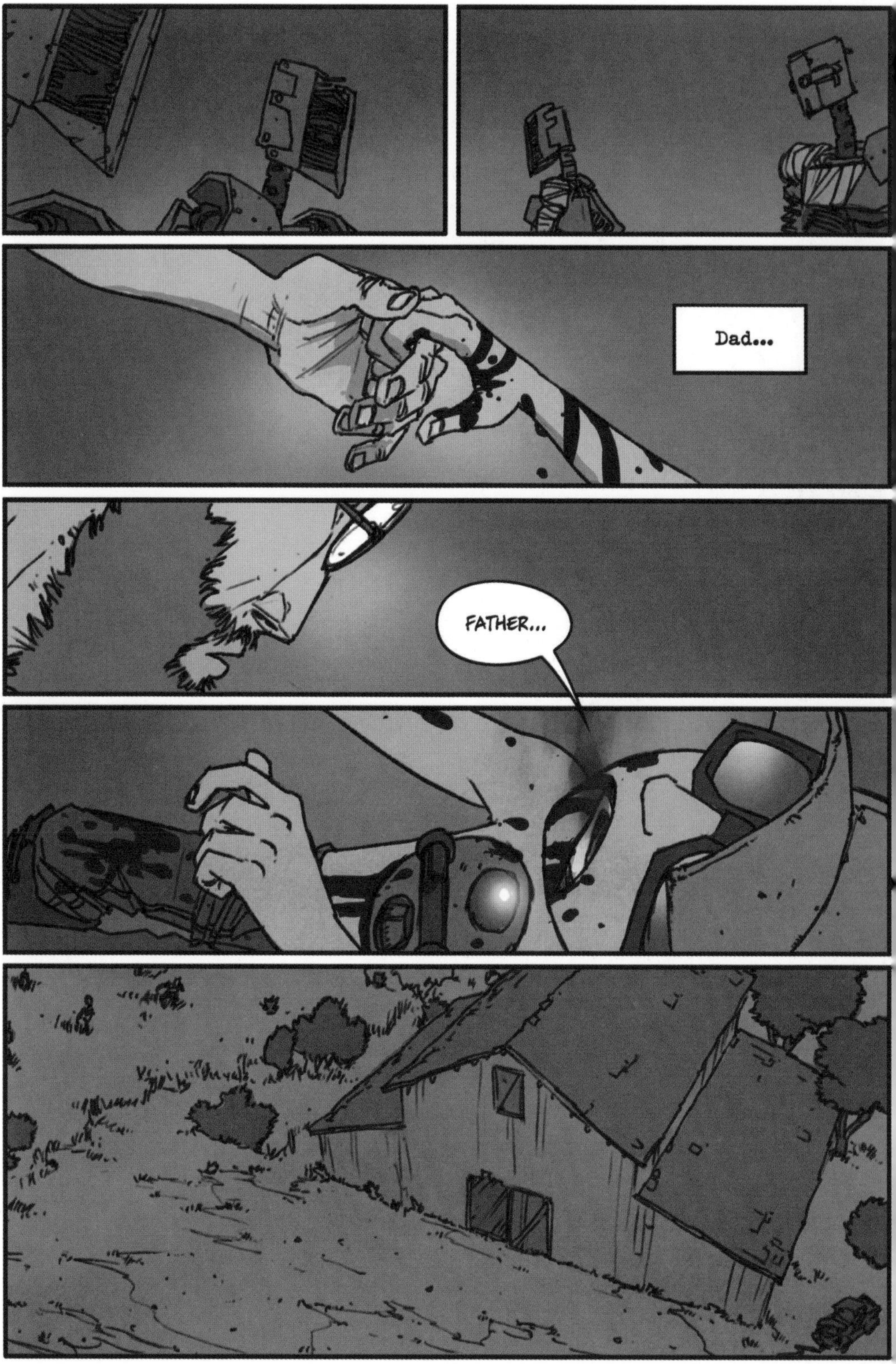
Dad...
FATHER...

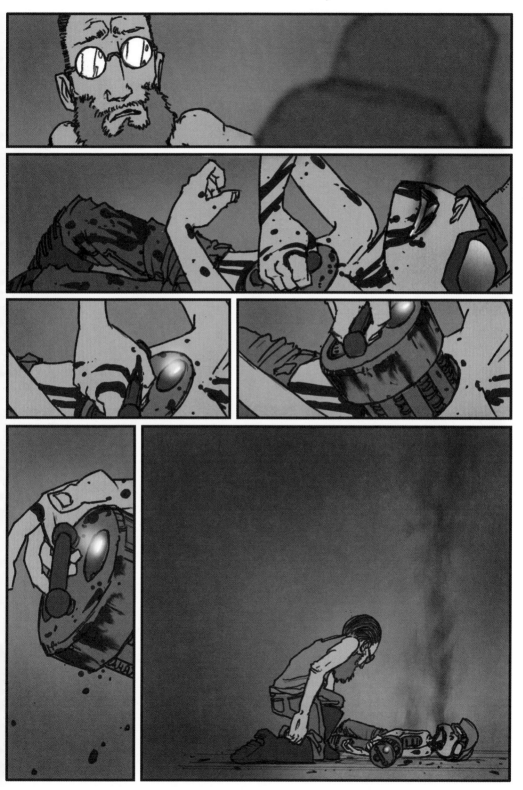

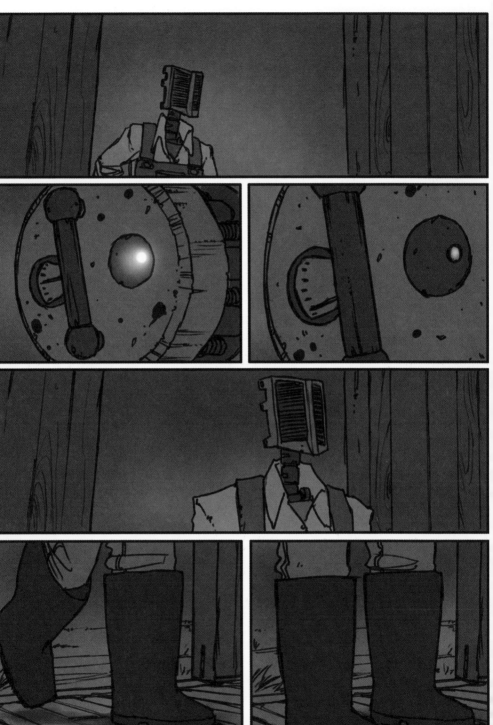

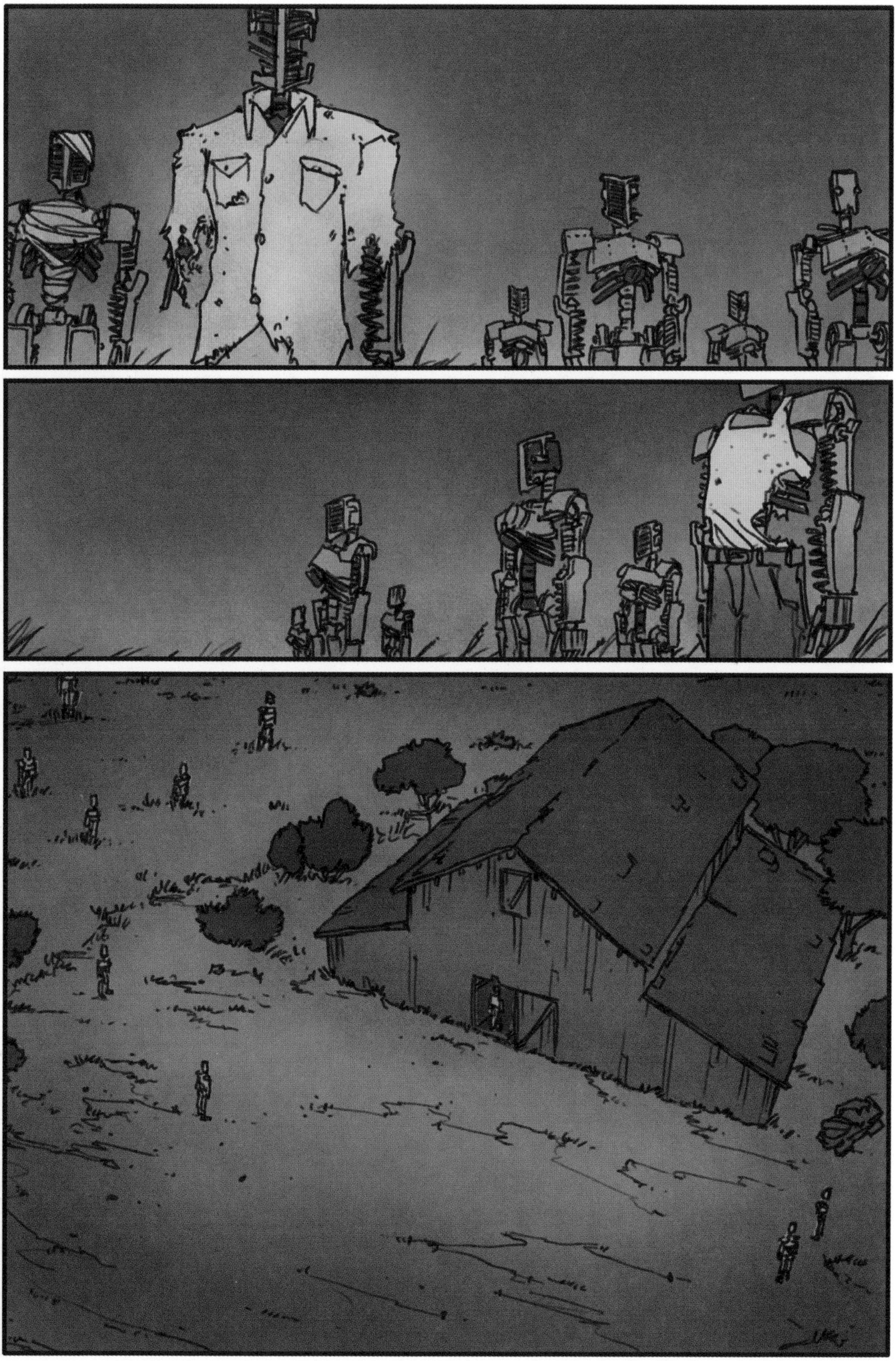

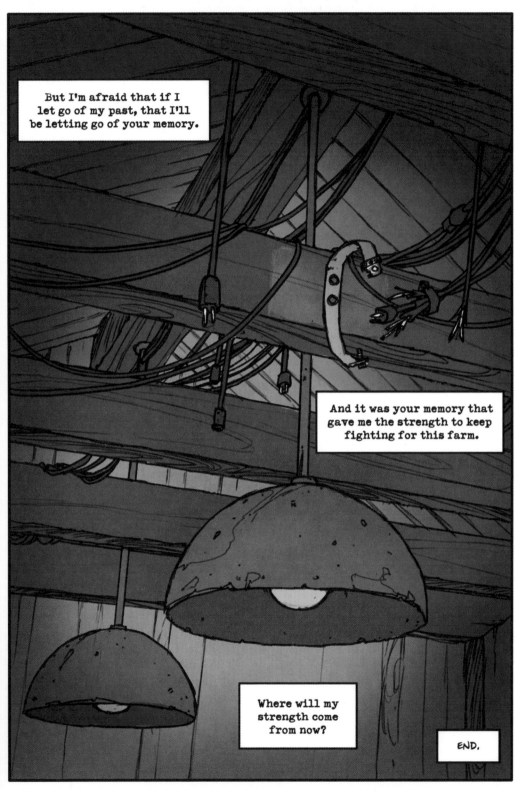

Exclusive Reprint of
Free Comic Book Day Short Story

THE CHORES

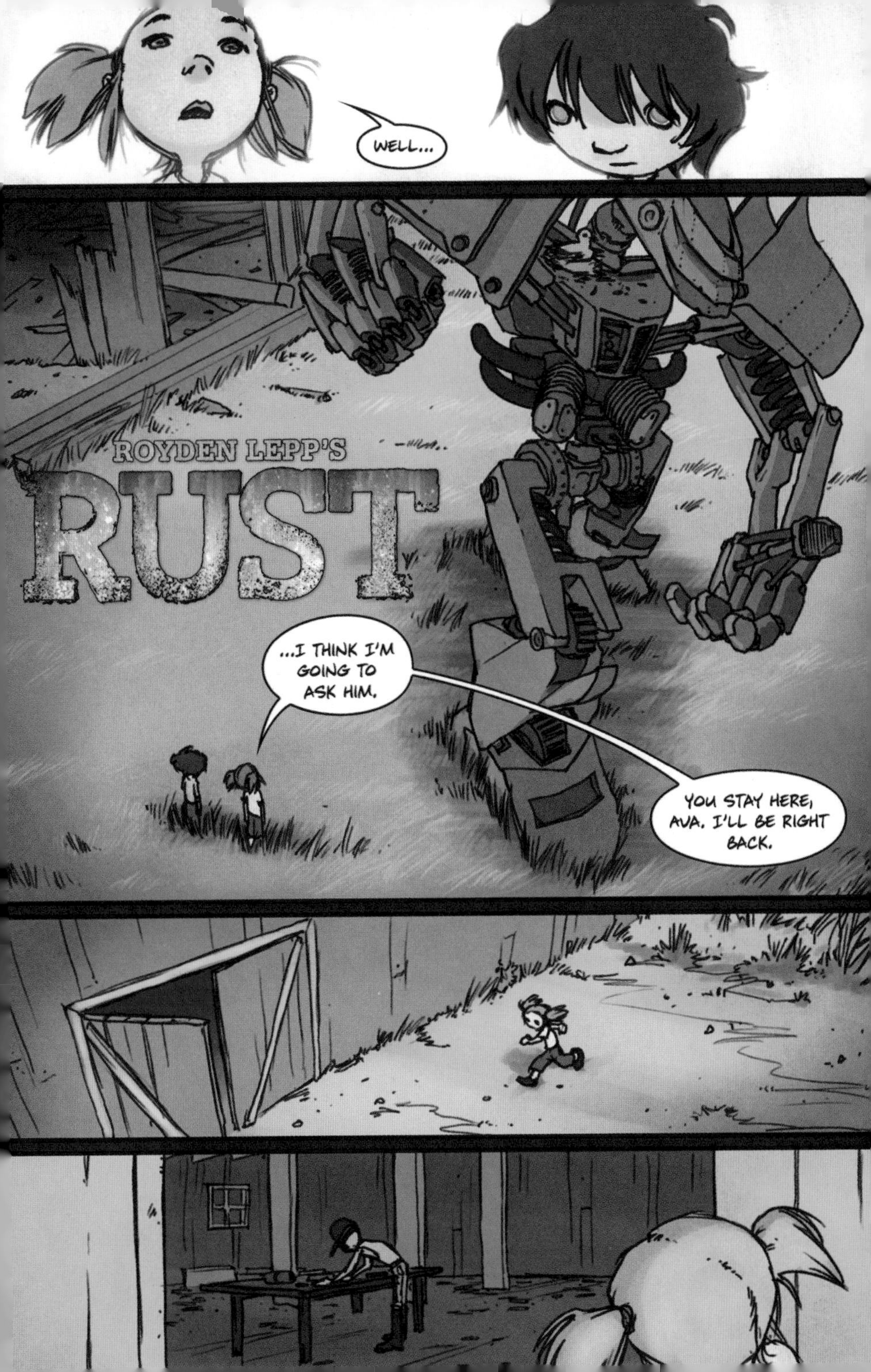
WELL...
ROYDEN LEPP'S
RUST
...I THINK I'M GOING TO ASK HIM.
YOU STAY HERE, AVA. I'LL BE RIGHT BACK.

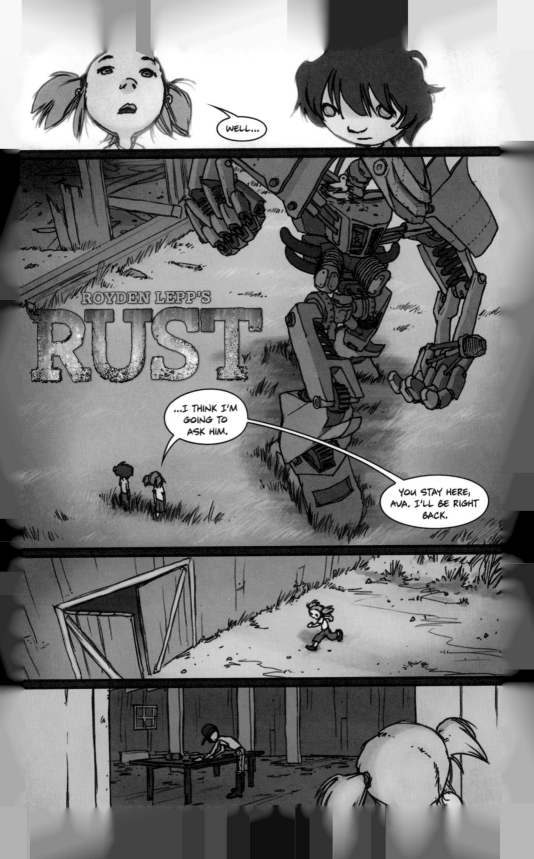

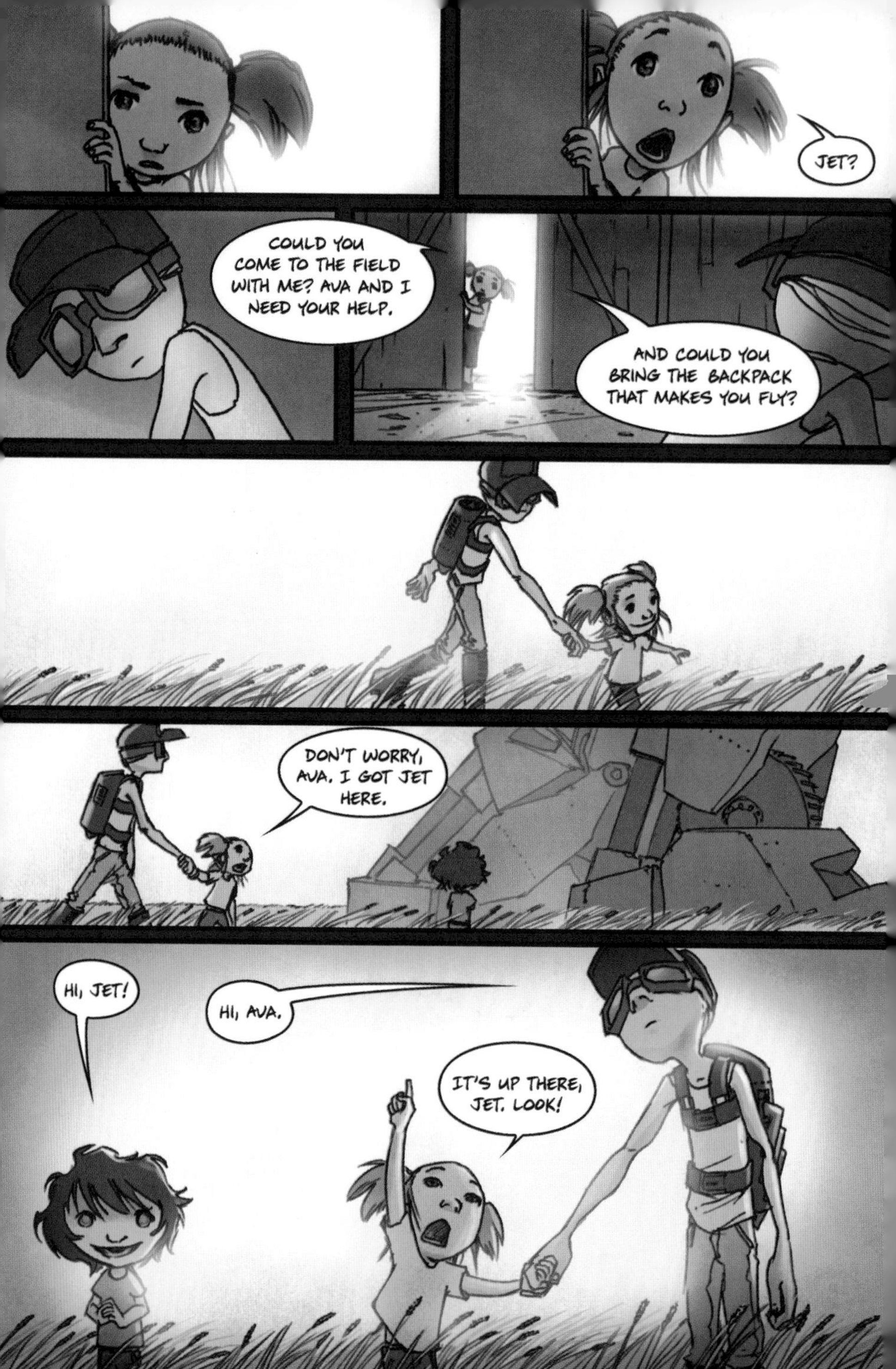
JET?
COULD YOU COME TO THE FIELD WITH ME? AVA AND I NEED YOUR HELP.
AND COULD YOU BRING THE BACKPACK THAT MAKES YOU FLY?
DON'T WORRY, AVA. I GOT JET HERE.
HI, JET!
HI, AVA.
IT'S UP THERE, JET. LOOK!

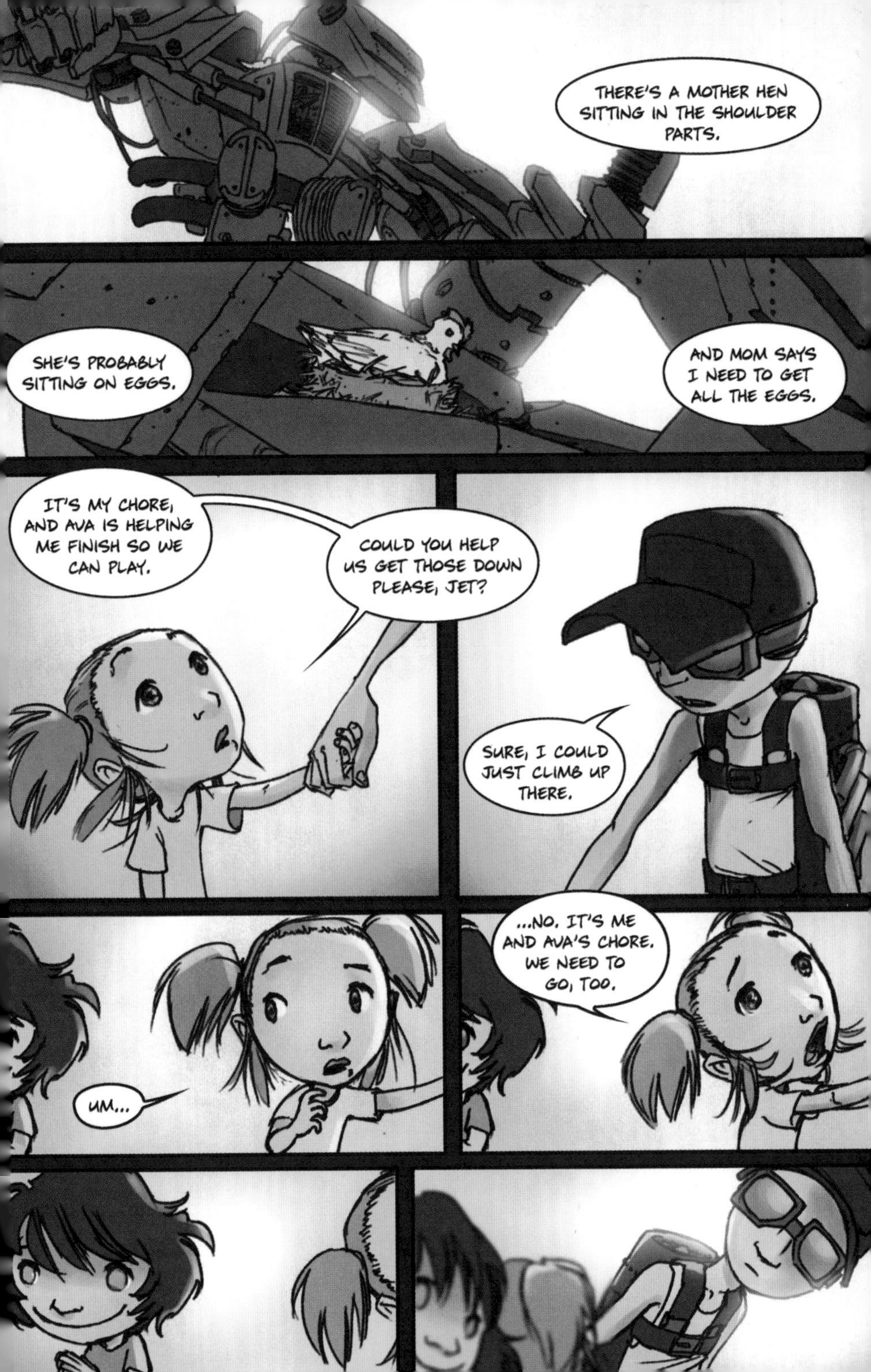
THERE'S A MOTHER HEN SITTING IN THE SHOULDER PARTS.
SHE'S PROBABLY SITTING ON EGGS.
AND MOM SAYS I NEED TO GET ALL THE EGGS.
IT'S MY CHORE, AND AVA IS HELPING ME FINISH SO WE CAN PLAY.
COULD YOU HELP US GET THOSE DOWN PLEASE, JET?
SURE, I COULD JUST CLIMB UP THERE.
UM...
...NO. IT'S ME AND AVA'S CHORE. WE NEED TO GO, TOO.

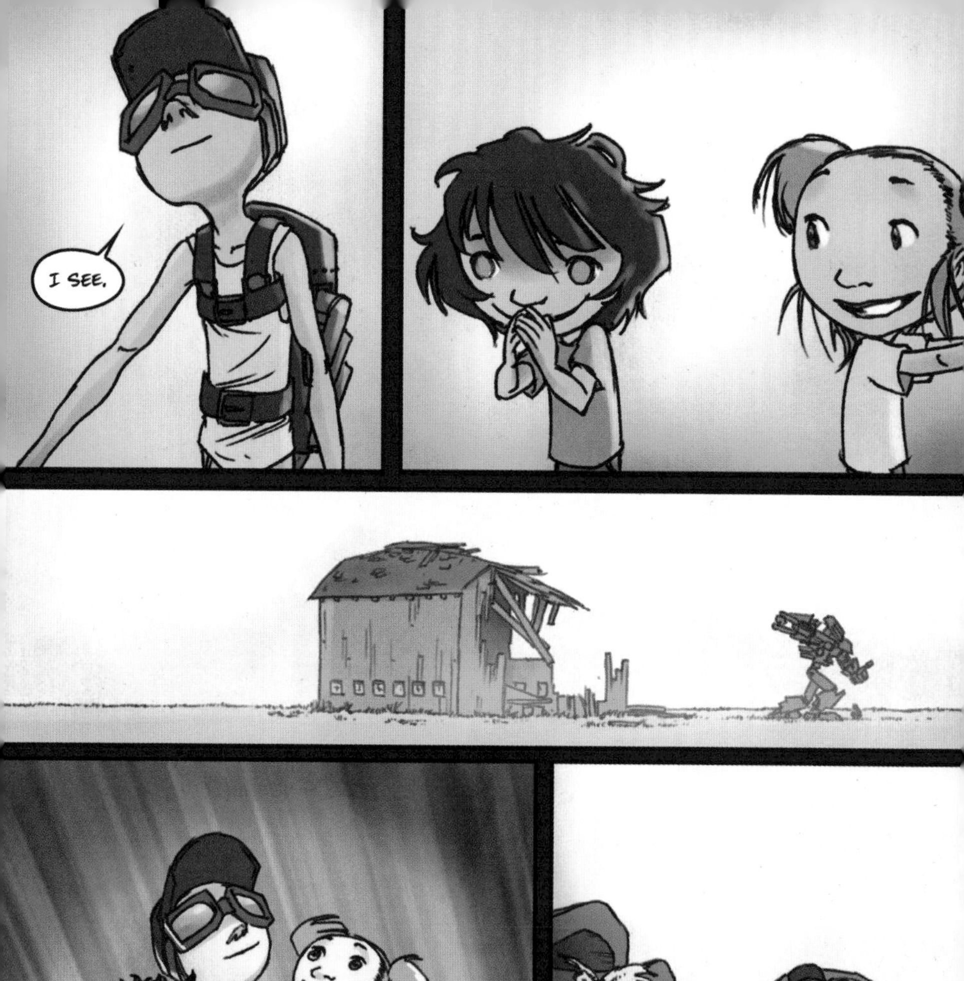
I SEE.

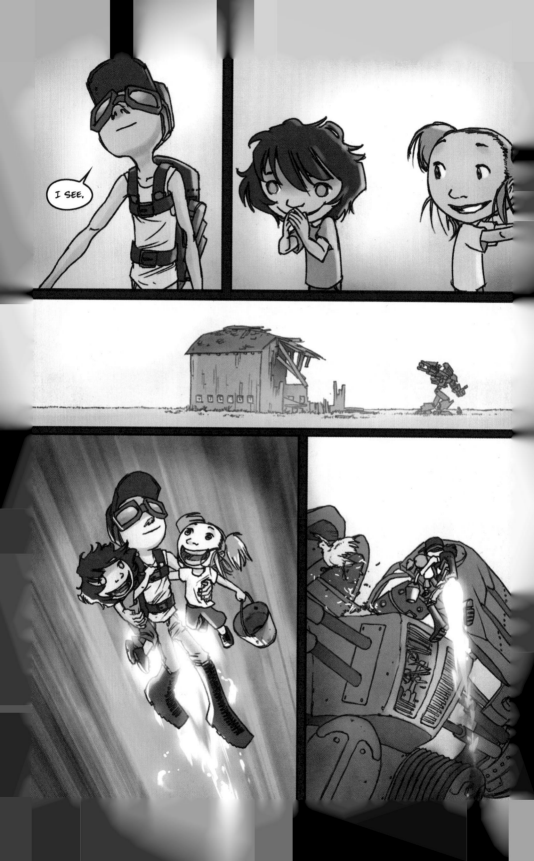

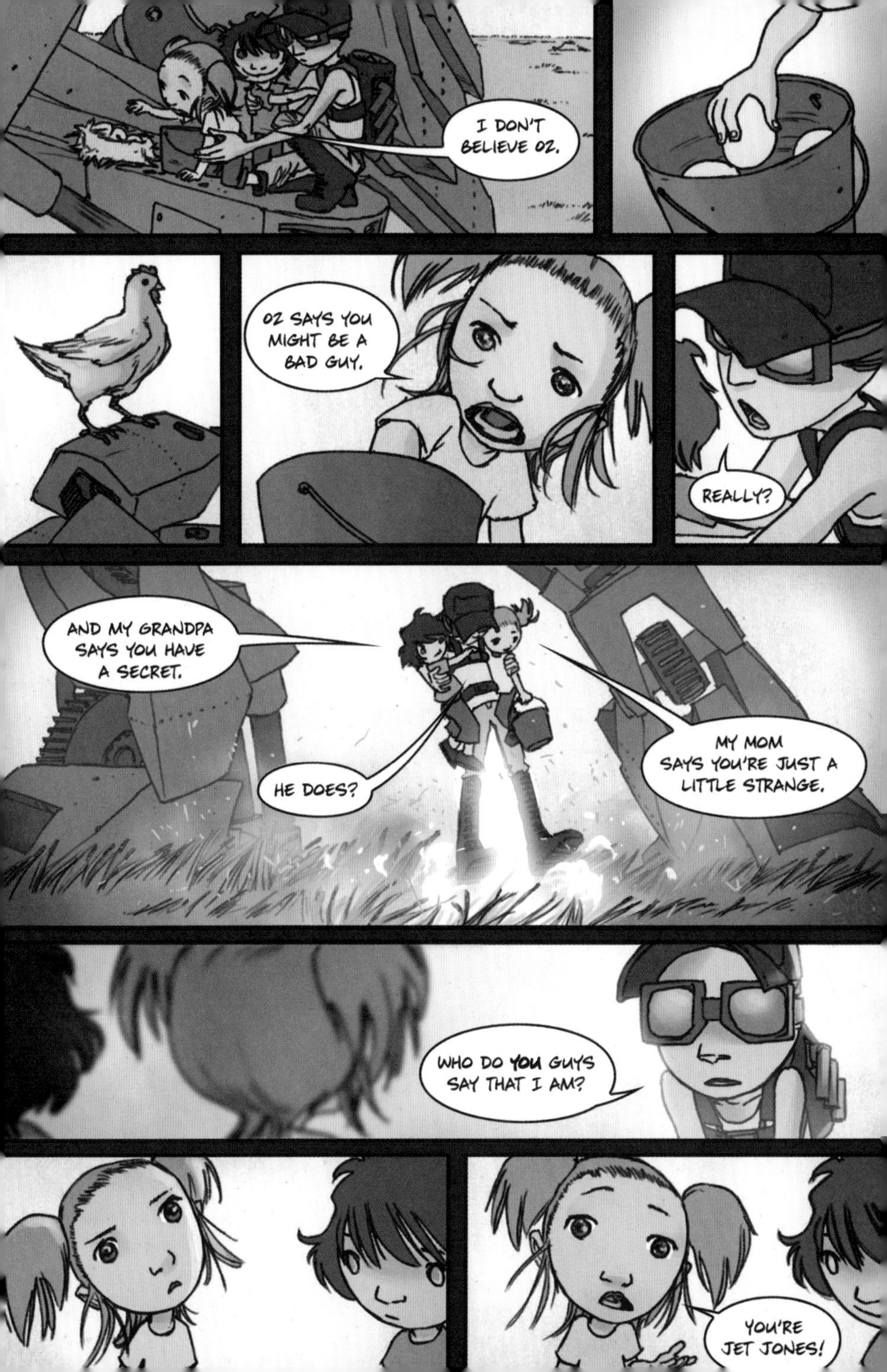
I DON'T BELIEVE OZ.
OZ SAYS YOU MIGHT BE A BAD GUY.
REALLY?
AND MY GRANDPA SAYS YOU HAVE A SECRET.
MY MOM SAYS YOU'RE JUST A LITTLE STRANGE.
HE DOES?
WHO DO **YOU** GUYS SAY THAT I AM?
YOU'RE JET JONES!

ROSS RICHIE CEO & Founder • **JACK CUMMINS** COO & President • **MARK SMYLIE** Chief Creative Officer
MATT GAGNON Editor-in-Chief **FILIP SABLIK** VP of Publishing & Marketing • **STEPHEN CHRISTY** VP of Development
LANCE KREITER VP of Licensing & Merchandising • **PHIL BARBARO** VP of Finance • **BRYCE CARLSON** Managing Editor
MEL CAYLO Marketing Manager • **SCOTT NEWMAN** Production Design Manager • **IRENE BRADISH** Operations Manager
DAFNA PLEBAN Editor • **SHANNON WATTERS** Editor • **ERIC HARBURN** Editor • **REBECCA TAYLOR** Editor
IAN BRILL Editor • **CHRIS ROSA** Assistant Editor • **ALEX GALER** Assistant Editor • **WHITNEY LEOPARD** Assistant Editor
JASMINE AMIRI Assistant Editor • **CAMERON CHITTOCK** Assistant Editor • **HANNAH NANCE PARTLOW** Production Designer
DEVIN FUNCHES E-Commerce & Inventory Coordinator • **ANDY LIEGL** Event Coordinator • **BRIANNA HART** Executive Assistant
AARON FERRARA Operations Assistant • **JOSÉ MEZA** Sales Assistant • **ELIZABETH LOUGHRIDGE** Accounting Assistant

RUST: DEATH OF THE ROCKET BOY, May 2014. Published by Archaia, a division of Boom Entertainment, Inc.

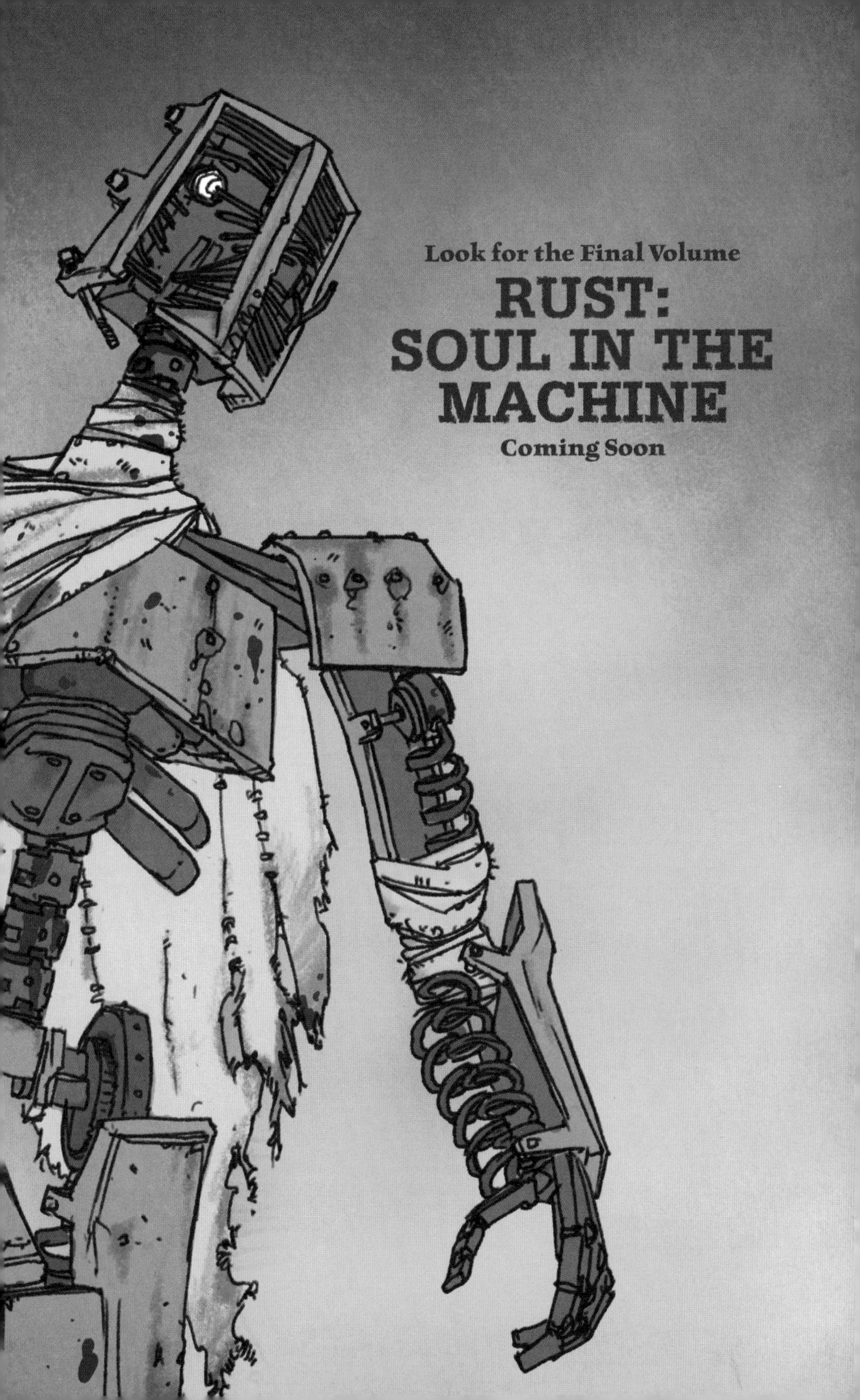
Look for the Final Volume
RUST:
SOUL IN THE MACHINE
Coming Soon

ABOUT THE AUTHOR

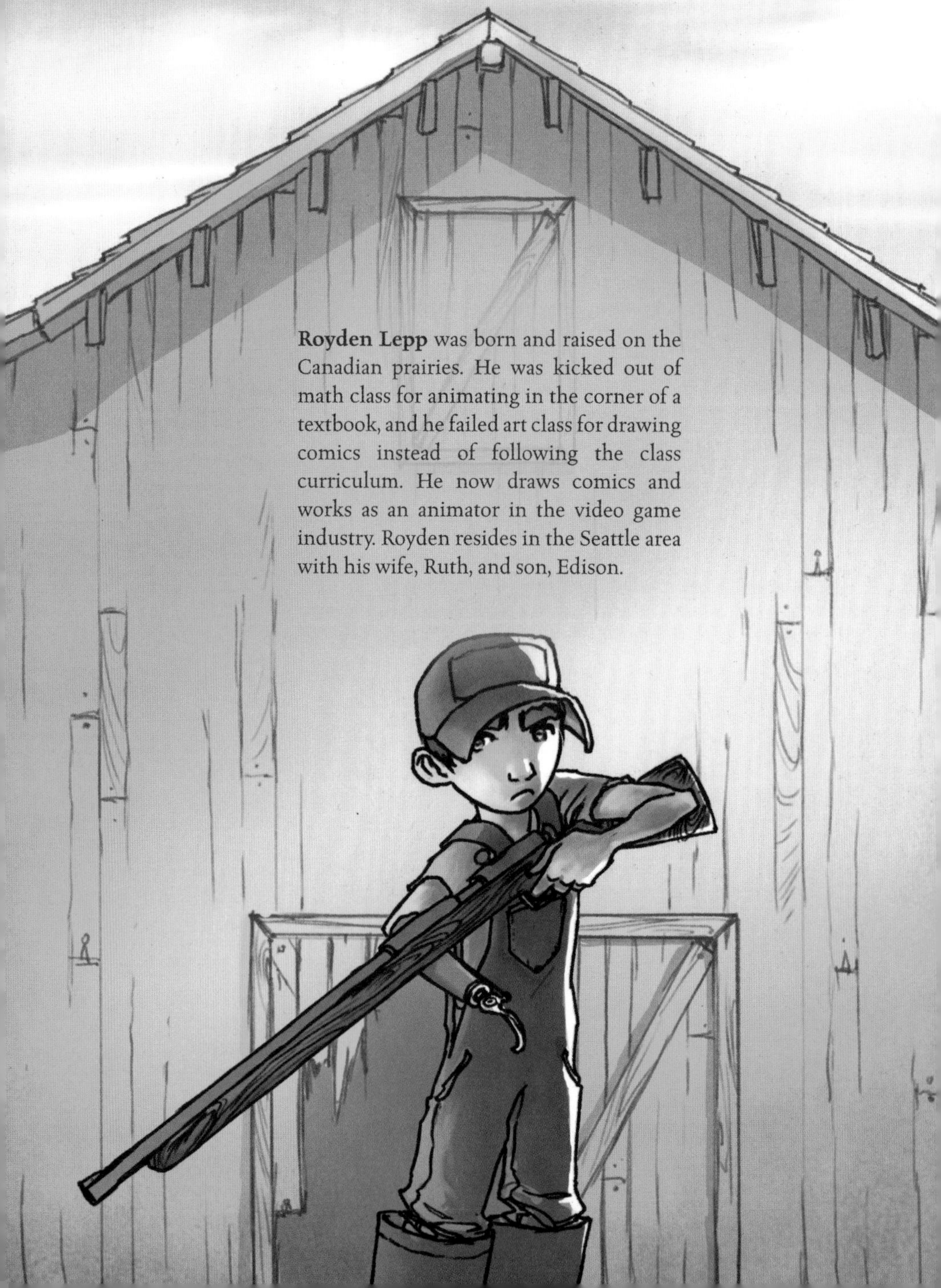

Royden Lepp was born and raised on the Canadian prairies. He was kicked out of math class for animating in the corner of a textbook, and he failed art class for drawing comics instead of following the class curriculum. He now draws comics and works as an animator in the video game industry. Royden resides in the Seattle area with his wife, Ruth, and son, Edison.

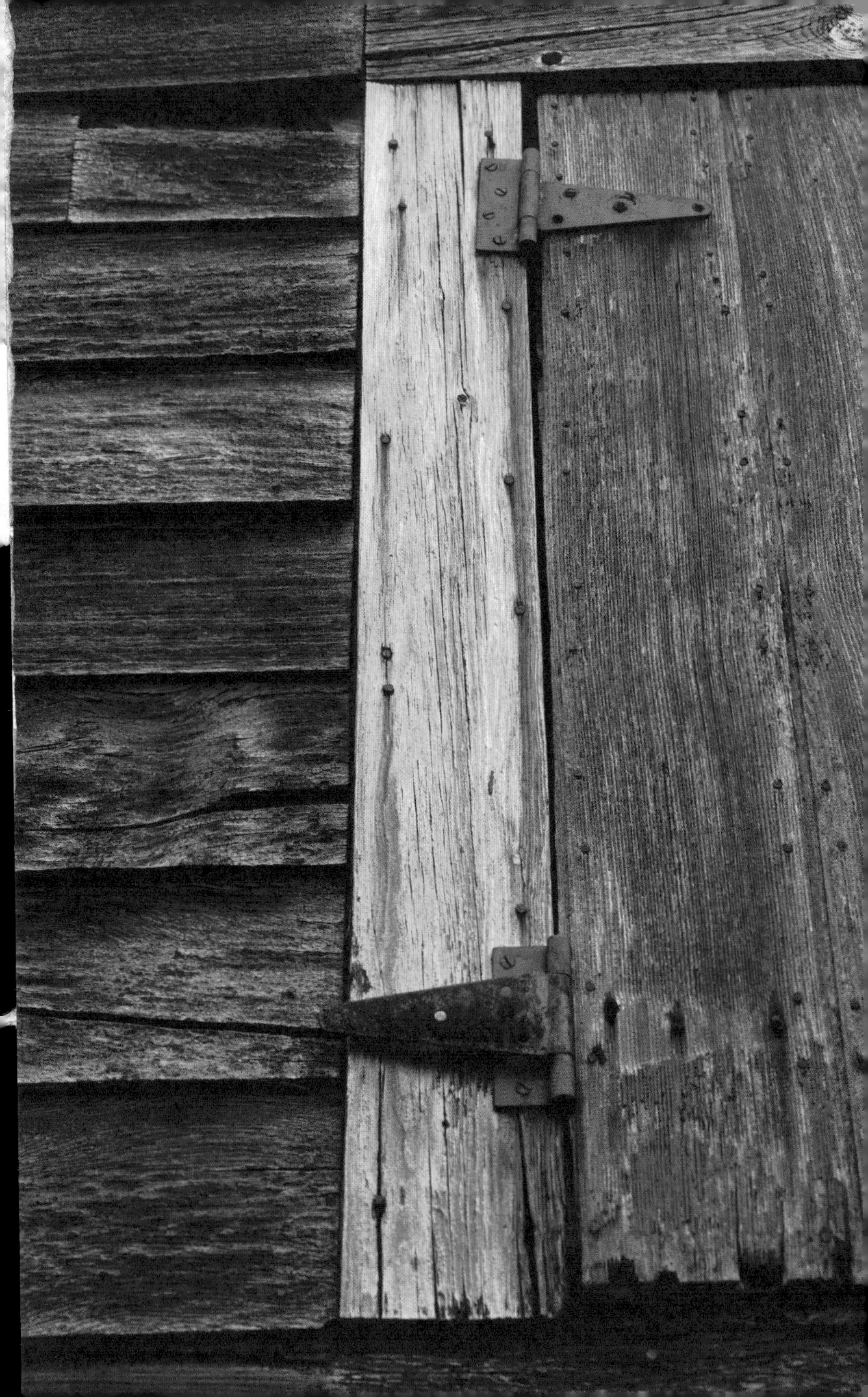

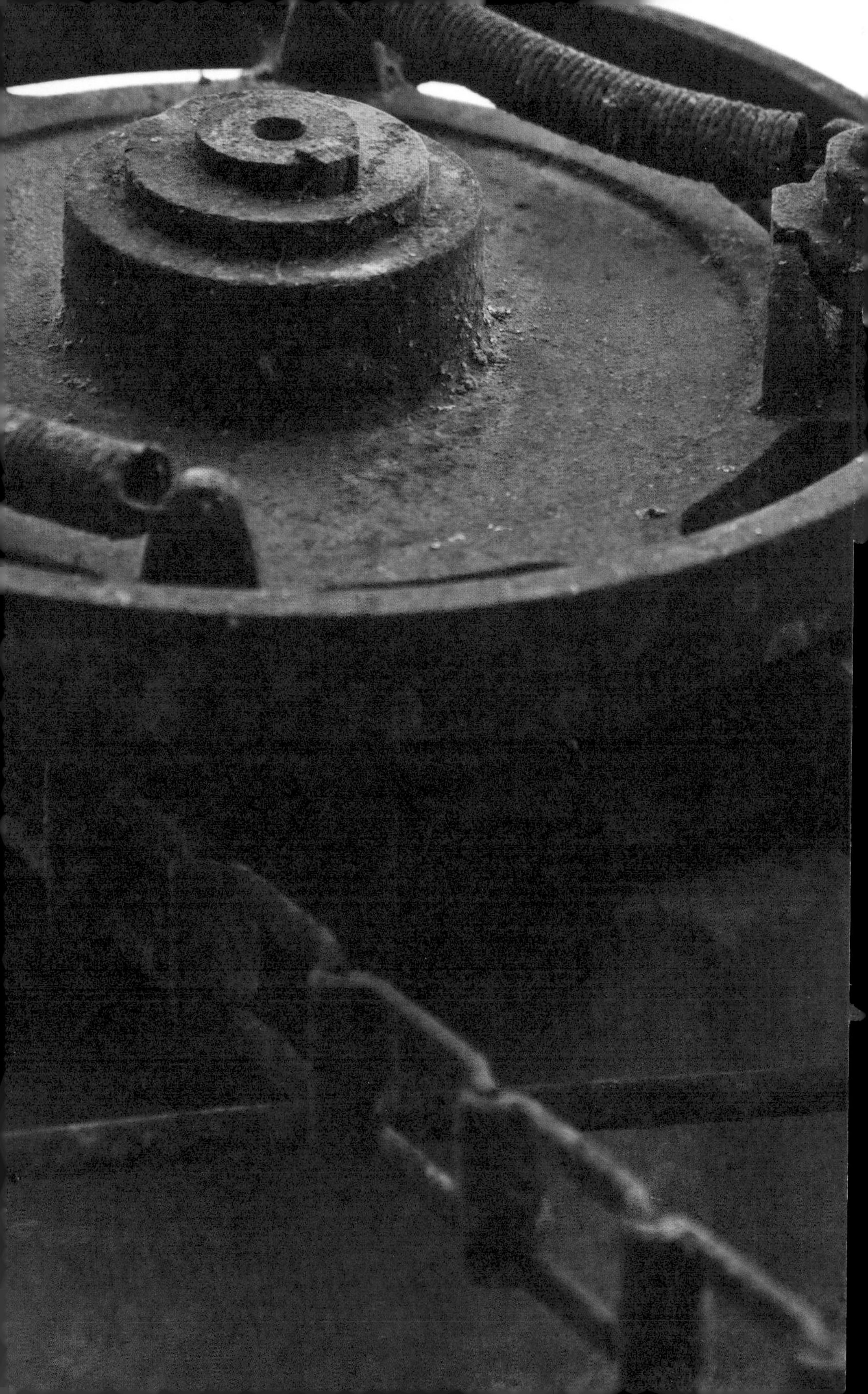